CONRAD EDISON

AND

THE ANCHORED WORLD

OVERWORLD ARCANUM
BOOK TWO

JOHN CORWIN

ISBN- 978-1-942453-06-2

Printed in the U.S.A.

To my wonderful support group:
Alana Rock
Karen Stansbury

My amazing editors:
Annetta Ribken
Jennifer Wingard

My awesome cover artist:
Regina Wamba

Thanks so much for all your help and input!

Books by John Corwin:

The Overworld Chronicles:
Sweet Blood of Mine
Dark Light of Mine
Fallen Angel of Mine
Dread Nemesis of Mine
Twisted Sister of Mine
Dearest Mother of Mine
Infernal Father of Mine
Sinister Seraphim of Mine
Wicked War of Mine
Dire Destiny of Ours
Aetherial Annihilation
Baleful Betrayal

Overworld Underground:
Possessed By You
Demonicus

Overworld Arcanum:
Conrad Edison and the Living Curse
Conrad Edison and the Anchored World

Stand Alone Novels:
No Darker Fate
The Next Thing I Knew
Outsourced
Seventh

For the latest on new releases, free ebooks, and more, join John Corwin's Newsletter at www.johncorwin.net!

ENTER THE GLIMMER QUEEN

When Conrad meets a strange girl while practicing for the Arcane University entrance exam, she takes him through a crack in the world and into a mysterious realm called the Glimmer. Conrad's parents are seeking help from the Glimmer Queen so they can once again rule the Overworld.

The Glimmer holds secrets so ancient, they predate even the First Seraphim War, and a great power that could grant Conrad's parents immortality.

If Conrad can't find a way to convince the Glimmer Queen from helping his parents, evil will once again rule the Overworld.

Chapter 1

Trudging down the street with my head down, I didn't see the hooded man until it was too late.

"What's a young lad like you doing on these dangerous streets so late at night?" he asked, a leering grin on his face.

I sidestepped to go around him. "Excuse me, sir. I'm meeting friends for dinner."

"Well, ain't that lovely." He gripped my shirt and jerked me into the mouth of an alley. A blade flashed and he leaned close, rancid breath washing over my face. "Your parents send their love."

Ice gripped my chest. I struggled weakly, like a mouse caught in a cat's claw. "My parents?"

He bared his teeth. "They want the rest of their souls back, boy." My assailant gripped my throat, pinning me against the brick wall. The knife stabbed toward my chest.

With a startled yelp, the man flew backward and smacked into the opposite wall. A spatter of red appeared where his head hit it. Desmond, my vampire housemate appeared, a concerned look on his face.

He looked me up and down. "Are you okay, Conrad?"

I ran a hand along my chest to feel for puncture wounds. "Yes, thank you."

His sister Sonia appeared, face twisted in annoyance. "Desmond, what in the—" She looked at the unconscious man and back to me. "What's going on here?"

"That man was apparently trying to kill Conrad." He tilted his head slightly and gazed at me with glowing red eyes. "Why would someone want to do that?"

1

"Um, apparently my parents sent him." They'd only risen from the dead a month ago and seemed quite eager to finish what they'd failed to do.

"Your parents?" Sonia licked her lips and looked at the man. "You must be quite the disappointment." Fangs flashed beneath her plump lips. "Perhaps no one will miss a murderer." She knelt next to the man, her short sparkly dress rising up her thighs, but reeled back with a hiss before she sank fangs into his neck. "He stinks like a demon."

"I noticed," Desmond replied in a matter-of-fact tone. The silent arch of an eyebrow raised an unasked question.

Only my closest friends, Ambria and Max knew the full extent of what my parents had done to me and I was hesitant to tell the vampires the truth. They might not like me much if they knew.

"Why are we wasting time here?" Sonia said. "I don't even know why you bothered saving the puny boy." She stalked closer to me. "I've heard the blood of the young is tasty."

Desmond sighed. "Well, it's a lucky thing we left the house right after you, Conrad." He stepped out of the alley and beckoned me to follow. "Where were you headed?"

"To the Copper Goose to meet Ambria and Max for dinner," I said. I looked at the unconscious man and trembled. "I don't suppose you're heading that way too?"

He chuckled. "We're headed to a club nearby. You're welcome to walk with us."

"He's so slow," Sonia complained. She jabbed a finger at the unconscious man. "If it'll make you feel any better, I can break his neck. Then you won't have to be a frightened little boy."

I shook my head. "No, please don't kill him. The man isn't evil— it's the demon controlling him."

Sonia huffed. "You're so stupid. Demons can't possess people unless they allow it. That means the owner of the body is a real git."

I certainly hadn't allowed my parents to let a demon inside me, or given them permission to stow their souls in my body while they played dead, but that hadn't stopped them.

"Sonia, let the boy alone." Desmond gripped her arm and pulled her away from the man. "Let's go."

We resumed walking down the street, Sonia whining and giving me dirty looks.

"It's bad enough having children living in our house," she said. "Now we have to babysit them as well."

Desmond gave me a friendly smile. "What are you hiding, Conrad?"

I looked away. "I'd rather not say."

"Why you don't want to tell me?" he asked.

I shrugged. "I don't think you'd like me much if you knew."

"We already don't like you," Sonia said.

"Not true," her brother said. "I think Conrad's a good housemate."

"Because we don't have to see him and his little girlfriend all day," she shot back.

My face warmed. "Ambria isn't my girlfriend."

Sonia burst into laughter. "Aw, how cute." She traced a fingernail down my arm, sending chills up my spine. "How old are you? Ten?"

"Twelve," I said weakly and stepped out of her reach.

"Goodness," she said in a mocking voice. "And you don't even have a girlfriend."

Desmond blew out a breath. "Sonia, please."

She sniffed and stuck her nose in the air. "Why do you always ruin my fun?"

A massive copper goose came into view as we rounded the corner and entered a square. *Finally, we're here.* "Thank you for saving me, Desmond."

"No problem." He put a hand on my shoulder. "Be more careful from now on, okay?"

I nodded. "Definitely."

Sonia gripped her brother's arm and dragged him away. "Let's go, let's go! I'm starving."

A shudder ran through my shoulders at the thought of what she wanted to eat. I walked inside the restaurant and spotted my friends at a table near the back.

"Where have you been?" Ambria Rax stood up and planted her fists on her hips. "You should have been here ages ago."

"I was about to eat without you," Max said.

Ambria rolled her eyes. "Max thinks more about food than anything else."

3

I took a seat and shrugged. "Sorry, I decided to walk."

Ambria sniffed. "How silly. Your broom would've been much faster."

"Well, I wouldn't have been so long if a man hadn't tried to kill me."

That drew startled glances from the pair.

"What?" Ambria's voice rose to a squeak.

Max leaned forward. "Are you joking?"

I shook my head and told them what happened.

"Goodness, Conrad, you really have to be more careful." Ambria patted my hand.

Max groaned. "Just great. Now we have to watch for assassins all the time."

"Sorry," I said. "It's just, without the curse, I feel so much better now. I like walking and running. Before, it was hard just to walk short distances."

"I understand," Ambria said. "But from now on, we should take our brooms whenever possible."

"Agreed," I said.

"Agreed," Max said. He rubbed his belly. "Can we order now? I'm starving."

We ordered and our food arrived a short time later. I consumed my brisket in short order despite my attempts to savor every bite. Since Dr. Rufus Cumberbatch had lifted the living curse from me and released my parents' souls back to their bodies, life had been so much better. But remnants of my parents' souls still remained attached to my own. If Ambria and Max hadn't rescued me that day, my own mother would have slit my throat to release those remnants.

Ambria patted the corners of her mouth. "That was wonderful, don't you think?"

Max grunted and continued to eat.

"You know you can't ask Max that until he's had his third helping," I said with a grin.

She laughed, but it quickly died away.

"Something wrong?" I asked.

"Besides your parents trying to murder you?" Ambria twisted her teacup nervously on the table. "Actually, I can't stop thinking about the entrance exam."

4

Max grunted and said something unintelligible with his full mouth.

I'd given the entrance exam quite a bit of thought, but for some reason, I wasn't nervous about it. "Do you feel we've studied enough?"

She nodded. "I think so, but I just want to get it over with."

Max swallowed. "It's just anxiety, Ambria. You'll get over it." He eyed his clean plate. "I wonder what they have for dessert."

Ambria sniffed. "Perhaps you should give up magic and become a chef."

He considered it for a moment. "Probably not a good idea." He patted his stomach. "I've got to watch my weight if I'm going to become a world-class broom racer."

"Max Tiberius, you're absolutely hopeless." Ambria touched my hand. "Please don't tell me you want to be a broom racer too."

Her touch sent a tingle up my fingers, not unlike when Sonia had touched my arm.

"Conrad, why are you looking at me so strangely?" Ambria said.

I pulled back my hand and grabbed my teacup. "Oh, I was just thinking about the, um, exam."

She threw up her hands. "Oh, this awful exam is going to drive us mental!" She clenched her fists. "Let's have a study session first thing tomorrow morning, okay?"

Max sighed. "You realize it's unhealthy to study too much, don't you?"

Ambria narrowed her eyes at him. "Don't you dare make up excuses, Maxwell Tiberius." She waggled her index finger at him. "First thing tomorrow, okay?"

"I'm so sick of studying, though."

Her eyes widened. "I can't believe you'd say that. Do you know how many normal people would give anything to trade places with us and learn magic?"

Max looked confused. "You mean noms?"

She nodded. "Yes, Max, noms. They'd do anything to leave their boring magicless lives to come study magic."

"I agree," I said. "Complaining that you have to study too much to learn magic is like complaining that your life is too amazing."

5

Max squinted, as if trying to see what we were talking about. "Well, I suppose I've never lived like a nom, but I guess it would be pretty awful not to have magic." He put some silver tinsel money on the table and stood up. "But I'll never give up my divine right to complain about whatever I want."

Ambria grunted and pushed back her chair. "In that case, I'll never give up my right to tell you how foolish you are."

I chuckled and paid for mine and Ambria's meals.

Outside, Max and Ambria took their brooms from the broom rack on the cobblestone sidewalk.

"I suppose we'll have to walk home," Ambria said.

"Even without assassins roaming Queens Gate, you've got plenty of ruthless vampires prowling the streets, Conrad." Max tutted and shook his head.

"Very foolish, Conrad." Ambria squared her shoulders and looked down the dimly lit street. "Well, I suppose we should go. We'll see you tomorrow, Max."

Max climbed on his broom and hesitated. "Maybe I should walk with you guys just in case."

Ambria arched an eyebrow. "Perhaps you are capable of thinking of something besides your stomach." She smiled.

Max shrugged. "Sometimes I surprise even myself."

We crossed the street when we reached the alley where the man had tried to kill me.

"It looks empty," Ambria whispered.

"It's dark as pitch in there," Max said. "How could you know?"

"Let's just go," I said.

"Do you think that demon knows where you live?" Ambria said.

I thought back to the flash of recognition when I'd looked up at the attacker. "No. I think he was walking around looking for me."

Max groaned. "Well, he certainly wasn't far from the house."

When we turned to go, a dog loped around the corner and raced toward us, a limp evident in its step.

"It's hurt," Ambria said.

Four pale teenagers smartly dressed in jeans and neatly pressed oxfords appeared behind the dog. Laughing and pointing, they flashed toward us.

Max jerked to a stop. "Vampires!"

Ambria knelt and inspected the hurt dog. "They want to hurt him. We can't let that happen."

Max groaned and pulled out his wand. "We don't have the power to stop one vampire, much less four of them."

Her eyes flashed. "I don't care. I won't abandon this poor animal." She produced her wand and looked at me.

I showed her my wand at the ready.

"What a succulent meal we've discovered." A tall vampire with fabulously styled brown hair and fair, delicate skin stepped forward. "Looks like we don't have to use those filthy club feeders tonight, boys."

The shortest vampire punched a fist into his palm and grinned. "Yeah, Edward."

Ambria stuck out her chin. "Why are you chasing a poor dog?"

"Ooh," another vampire said. "We've got a brave one here."

"Look at her cute little wand," jeered the fourth.

"Yeah, we've all got cute little wands and we know how to use them," Max said, holding his at the ready.

Edward bared his teeth in a grin and looked at me. "I found the frightened one."

The image of a screaming vampire flashed through my mind and I instantly knew it wasn't one of my own memories. It was something one of my parents had witnessed.

"Take care of the brave ones, and let's have fun with the scared boy," Edward said.

Two vampires blurred forward and grabbed Ambria and Max. The dog growled and slammed against the third vampire, knocking him to the ground. Edward stalked toward me, a leer on his face.

I should have been frightened out of my mind. I barely knew any spells and I certainly wasn't strong enough to fight a night stalker. My arm extended of its own accord, my wand flicked, and in a strained voice I said, "*Torsious!*"

Edward twisted through the air and crashed against a building hard enough to crack the bricks. I turned to the other assailants and aimed my wand at the short one's arm. "*Torsious!*" His arm twisted violently and broke with a loud crack. Once again my arm flicked out and once again a vampire's body bent in unnatural ways, sending him to the ground. The fourth vampire screamed and tried to run, but my spell caught his leg and yanked it from the socket.

Filthy creatures, my mother's voice said in my mind. It wasn't really Delectra speaking, but the soul fragment still stuck inside me. I'd taken to calling it Della, and named Victus's fragment Vic.

I realized Ambria and Max were staring wide-eyed at me.

"How did you do that?" Max asked.

I motioned forward. "Don't just stand around. Run!"

Having been chased by all sorts of supernatural horrors, we excelled at running. We made it back to the brownstone at the corner of Dowling and Bucket Streets, the dog close on our heels despite its awful limp.

Panting, Max stopped outside the house and dropped his broom on the ground. "Can't we enjoy a nice quiet evening for once?"

Ambria sat on the steps and leaned against the balustrade. "Conrad, never, ever, ever, leave home without your broom again."

The dog curled up on the steps next to Ambria and looked up at her with big blue eyes.

Max jerked upright. "Hang on, that's not a dog."

"Looks like a Husky," I said.

"It's a wolf." He shook his head. "Okay, who are you?"

The dog stared at him imploringly for a long moment then went behind a shrub. A moment later, a young girl rose, her head peeking around the foliage. "Hello."

"Amazing!" Ambria said.

"Why did she go behind the bush?" I asked.

"Because lycans don't usually wear clothes in wolf form," Max said.

Ambria put her hands to her cheeks. "Oh, how embarrassing."

"I'd be grateful if you could spare something," the girl said.

"What's your name?" I asked.

"I'm Blue," she replied.

Max wrinkled his forehead. "That's a color, not a name."

"It's a lovely name," Ambria said. "Wait right there, I'll be back with clothes."

Blue looked wonderingly at me. "You must be an awfully strong Arcane to beat an entire group of vampires like that."

"What were you doing wandering the streets alone at night?" Max asked before I could say anything.

She looked down. "I'm looking for a pack."

Max looked confused. "A lycan pack? What about your family?"

Ambria appeared with a bundle in her hand. "Leave her alone, Max." She went behind the bush and a moment later, the two girls stepped into view.

Blue stood a head taller than Ambria and had long wavy hair. "Thank you for saving me."

"Any time," Ambria replied. "I'm Ambria. The blond boy who eats too much is Max, and this is Conrad."

"Nice to meet you," I said.

"Do you have any place to stay?" Ambria asked her.

Blue looked down and shook her head. "Not right now."

"Aren't lycans born into packs?" Max said.

"I didn't like my pack so I ran away." Blue turned her gaze on him. "You can't choose family, and I don't like mine. I know it's hard to understand."

Max burst into laughter. "Actually, we all completely understand that feeling, don't we, Conrad?"

I managed a smile. "Yes, I suppose so."

"Well, it's official then," Ambria said. "Blue is our newest housemate."

Chapter 2

Someone stomping up the stairs jerked me awake so early the next morning, the sun wasn't up yet.

"Who brought a dog in this house?" Sonia shouted loudly enough to wake the dead.

I walked into the upstairs hallway and jumped back as the furious vampire stormed my way.

"Where is it?" Sonia said in a low hiss.

Ambria stepped into the hallway and leveled a glare at the woman. "If you really must know, I invited a werewolf to stay with us."

Sonia's eyes flared angrily. "You invited a lycan to stay in my house?"

Blue appeared behind Ambria, eyes wide.

The vampire jabbed a finger toward her. "You"—she pointed a thumb over her shoulder—"out!"

Ambria shook her head. "Absolutely not. We saved her from vampires last night and we're not about to put her back in the streets."

"She has nowhere to go," I said.

"Vampires? Hah!" Sonia looked from me to Ambria. "You couldn't rescue her from mice."

"Conrad broke their arms and threw them around like rag dolls," Blue said. "He's the strongest Arcane I've ever seen."

Sonia's eyebrows rose. "That puny boy whipped a gang of vampires?"

Desmond appeared behind Sonia and put a hand on her shoulder. "Let's go to sleep and sort this out in the evening."

Sonia's lips peeled back. "I refuse to live in the same house as a dog."

Ambria shook her head sadly. "Do you really hate dogs so much?"

"I'm not a dog," Blue said. "I'm a lycan."

"You're a mongrel," Sonia shot back.

"Well, you're a mean vampire!" Ambria shouted. "Why are you so angry all the time?"

Desmond gripped his sister's arm. "That's enough, Sonia. We're going to bed."

Sonia tried to jerk her arm free, but Desmond was too strong. She stabbed a finger at Ambria. "This isn't over, you little brat."

"I'm sorry," Desmond said. "Your friend can stay as long as she likes."

His sister hissed and turned away, finally freeing her arm, then stomped downstairs without another word.

Ambria wiped her forehead and breathed a sigh of relief. "Thank you, Desmond."

He nodded. "We still need to discuss this. Having too many people coming and going from this house might alert the neighbors." He glanced downstairs. "Just remember, we're squatters. If someone alerted the authorities, they could kick us out."

"I don't know who they'd tell," Ambria said. "I certainly haven't seen any police patrolling the streets."

Desmond chuckled. "You may be right." He turned and walked downstairs.

"Why would nom police be in Queens Gate?" Blue asked.

"Well, I meant Templars, or whoever they use in the Overworld." Ambria slumped against the wall and put a hand to her chest. "Sonia frightens me."

I nodded. "Me too."

I returned to my room and tried to go back to sleep, but only tossed and turned for the next hour. I finally got up at eight, showered, and ate breakfast. The rubbish bag in the kitchen looked dangerously close to bursting, so I decided to take it outside.

After dropping the bag at the curb, I retrieved my *Elementary Magic* textbook from upstairs and sat on the front porch to study in the fresh, cool morning air.

The boy next door came outside, a large dartboard under one arm. He and his family had just moved in a week ago, but this was the first time I'd seen any of them since that day.

He looked at me and I waved back. Deciding it might be nice to meet him, I set down the book and walked over to the stone wall separating our yard from his.

"Hello," I said in the cheeriest voice I could manage.

He set down the dartboard and walked over, a serious look on his face. "I can't be your friend."

Considering that this was the first time I'd spoken with him, his statement came as something of a surprise. I took a step back. "Excuse me?"

He leaned on the low wall. "Nothing personal, but I won't have time for new friends." He puffed out his chest. "I have to train to defeat a terrible evil."

"Impressive." I didn't know how playing darts would prepare him, unless he planned to prick the enemy to death.

He held out a hand. I hesitantly shook it and wondered if I should be offended that he didn't want to be my friend.

"I'm Harris Ashmore," he said. "Perhaps you've heard of me."

I had, in fact, never heard of such a person. "My name is Conrad Ed—Edwards."

"I'm something of a big deal," Harris assured me. "There's a foreseeance about me and everything."

Della filled in the blank. *Foreseeance—prophecy*, she said. I fell back upon the word I'd used earlier with a slight and insincere embellishment. "Very impressive."

"I suppose you could call it fate." Harris hopped into a sitting position atop the wall. "I was orphaned at a young age. My parents were brutally murdered so I live with my aunt and uncle."

It sounded as though he'd rehearsed this story. "I'm sorry to hear that." I wondered what he would think if I told him how my parents had killed themselves and used a demon to bind their souls to mine so they could be resurrected by a demonologist years later.

"Most people are sheep." Harris pointed toward a distant green pasture dotted with the white wooly animals. "They keep their heads down and follow the flock wherever it goes."

I'd once had a man mind-control a flock of sheep and a brood of chickens in an attempt to kill me. "I suppose a lot of people just want to live their lives in peace."

He snorted. "No, they're just stupid." Harris thumped an ant off the wall. "My parents fought the status quo. They didn't let powerful people push them around. They were brave."

At this point, I simply wanted to go back to my textbook, but didn't want to be rude. "You must be proud."

"That was why they were murdered by a cowardly monster." He bared his teeth. "One day I'll also fight a great evil, but in my case, Foreseeance Five Triple Zero says that I'll win."

I was a bit confused by the name. "Is Five Triple Zero the same thing as five thousand?"

He didn't seem to hear my question, instead looking to the sky and proclaiming, "Once again shall the evil rise. The son of the fallen is the only hope for victory." His eyes turned back toward me. "So you see, I have the weight of the world on my shoulders. It would be hard for us to be friends."

Self-aggrandizing little twerp, Vic said.

I decided to go. Just as I opened my mouth to excuse myself, he said something that froze my heart to ice.

"The Overlord killed my parents." His teeth clenched. "No one can understand that pain."

"I-I'm sorry," I stammered and backed away. "I have to get back to studying."

"But I'm just getting to the good parts," Harris said.

I turned around and headed for the house just as Max landed his broom in the front yard. His eyes locked onto the other boy. "Is that Harris Ashmore?"

"Yes." I walked around him, grabbed my book, and went inside.

Max came inside and closed the door. "Really? He's kind of a big deal."

"Yes, I got to hear all about it."

"Oh, then I suppose he mentioned, um..." He went silent for a moment. "Anyway, I'll bet it was kind of awkward when he found out who you are."

"I told him my last name is Edwards." I sank into a chair, weighed down by guilt. "My father killed his parents. I can't let anyone know my real last name, Max."

"Maybe we should talk to Galfandor about that." He shrugged. "I wish I could change my last name. Nobody ever wants to be my friend when they hear I'm a Tiberius."

"Perhaps because you smell funny," said a girlish voice from behind us. Ambria stepped into the den. "Why are you two moping in here when we need to study for the entrance exam?"

"Harris Ashmore." Max poked a thumb toward the window.

"Who?" Ambria looked outside. Harris had started playing with his rocket darts. "Is he a new friend?" Her tone sounded hopeful.

"No." I stood. "He explained to me why we couldn't be friends and then I realized why he was right."

"Conrad's dad killed his parents." Max's eyes brightened. "Isn't that unbelievable?"

Ambria grimaced. "Oh, it's awful, Conrad." She hugged me. "I'm sorry your parents were evil masterminds."

"Me too." I patted her on the back, glad that I had at least two true friends.

"Conrad and I were just talking about how nice it would be to change our last names so people wouldn't hate us." Max watched Harris spear a rocket dart into the bull's-eye painted on a tree. "I wish I could be Harris's friend."

Ambria huffed. "We're all the friends you need, Max." She grabbed me by the hand and took Max by the wrist. "Now, let's get back to studying."

Max sighed as she dragged us toward the stairs. "Next up is spell casting. We can't exactly practice that in the house and all the gauntlet rooms at the university are full."

"Then we'll go outside." Ambria opened the door to the closet beneath the staircase and picked up our wands off the cot inside.

"I wonder why the family who used to live here left all this stuff behind." Max ducked inside the small space and grabbed an *Elementary Enchantments* textbook from a tall stack including *Elementary Potions* and *Elementary Magic*. He dropped onto the cot and looked inside the front cover. It read: *Property of the Underlord*.

"Looks like their child had big ambitions," Ambria said.

14

"You don't suppose he wanted to be like the Overlord, do you?" Max said, casting a curious glance at me.

My stomach knotted. *Why would any child want to be like my father?* I took the textbook from Max and dropped it on the floor. "Let's go practice."

"Touchy subject?" He stooped beneath the low sill and shut the door behind him.

I couldn't help that every time I thought of my mother, I flashed back to her holding a gleaming knife at my throat while my father watched with a smirk. A deep burn grew a little hotter every time I flashed back to that recent memory. I feared my parents so much it made me weak in the knees and made me hate them all the more.

I force my jaw to unclench. "I'd rather not think about them."

"I completely understand." Ambria squeezed my hand and glared at Max. "Bringing up Conrad's parents is terribly mean, Max. You should be ashamed."

"But the name Underlord was in that book," he protested. "Isn't it kind of strange?"

"Can we just practice?" I groaned. I wasn't in the mood for another one of their arguments.

Ambria huffed. "Shall we go outside and practice?"

I jabbed a finger straight up. "I think we should go up the cliff and practice in Colossus Stadium."

Ambria frowned. "Why can't we practice in the yard?"

"Because the boy whose parents were murdered by Delectra and Victus is out there." I shook my head. "I want to get out of here."

"Oh." She frowned and retrieved our flying brooms from the foyer. "Let's go."

Blue stepped up to the railing at the top of the stairs and looked down at us. "What's going on?"

"We're going to practice for the university entrance exam," Ambria said. "Want to come watch?"

Blue shook her head. "I'm going back to sleep." She vanished from view and a door clicked shut.

"What a sleepyhead," Max said. He grabbed his broom and we went into the back yard. Max's gaze wandered toward Harris's house, but the other boy was no longer playing darts. Now he sat on the back deck with a red-headed boy and a girl with curly brown hair.

The ginger looked up and saw us. A grin split his face and he nudged his companions. "Hey look," he shouted. "It's Cryberius Tiberius."

Max turned away and walked quickly to the street corner.

"Where you going, Cryberius?" the boy called.

Ambria growled and opened her mouth. I grabbed her arm and led her away before she engaged in a shouting match.

"Why'd you do that?" she said. "That boy needs to watch his mouth."

"Yes, but if you'll remember, we don't want to draw attention to us," I said. "We don't own the house we live in, and I don't want them knowing my last name."

She pursed her lips as if she wanted to argue, but sighed instead.

Max was already on his broom, a smile plastered on his face. "Ready?"

"Are you okay, Max?" Ambria patted his arm.

"I'm fine, geez." His broom rose higher. "Let's go."

We hopped on our brooms and levitated next to him.

Simply hovering on a broom made me feel immediately better. It made me feel free. "Race you to the top," I said to Max.

"Oh, no you don't!" Max called after.

I looked back and saw him gaining on me. Ambria, the least experienced of us, lagged far behind, an angry frown on her face. I had my mother—or at least her soul fragment—to thank for my piloting skills. My mother had once been a champion boom racer before she became a villain.

I crested the cliff's edge and continued to climb until I hovered above the trees. The crystal dome of the library sparkled in the distance, reflecting sunlight on the towering spires of Arcane University on the other side.

"First one to the stadium wins!" Max shouted as he sped past.

"Wait up!" Ambria called from below.

I zipped after Max. We dodged between trees and flashed over the Unicorn Garden. The walls of Colossus Stadium loomed a few hundred yards away. I lowered my head and hugged the broomstick for better aerodynamics. Slowly but surely, my broom gained on Max.

Our brooms were identical and we flew at top speed. I didn't think it was possible to catch him before we reached the stadium. My

16

mother's experience took control and steered me directly behind Max. Suddenly, I began to overtake him rather quickly. Just before we reached the stadium, I flicked the broom handle to the right and pulled even with him. It would have been a tie, but my feet tapped the stirrups in an alternating pattern, causing my broom to waggle.

Max shouted in surprise as he lost ground and I crossed the finish line first.

I spun to a stop. A grin should have been on my lips. Instead, I felt somewhat disturbed.

"What was that move?" Max said.

"I don't know." I bit my lip. "It was something Della knows how to do. I don't know how it slowed you."

"Della?" he asked.

I tapped a finger to my temple. "That's what I call her soul fragment."

"Weird." He waved it away. "I think I know what happened." Despite his loss, Max looked happy. "You shifted your slipstream into mine and caused more air to drag on my broom." He put a hand on his chin. "It's brilliant. If I can learn how to do that, I could become an amazing broom racer."

"I wish I could explain it," I said. "For some reason, getting right behind you made me go faster." The answer flashed into my head. *Aerodynamic slipstream reduces friction.* The thought must have come from my father's soul fragment, because it sounded more scientific than magical.

Ambria coasted to a stop, an angry scowl clouding her face. "Why do you idiots always want to race?" She huffed. "You know I can't keep up. I nearly hit the trees at the top of the cliff."

"You should have seen what Conrad did." Max didn't seem the least bit fazed by Ambria's frustration. "I should've won, but he pulled off a brilliant move at the end."

"Do I look like I care?" Ambria's glare could have burned a tree to ash.

Max looked away from her and toward the stadium. "Uh, let's go inside and practice."

We flew over the walls and into the derelict structure. Colossus Stadium had once been a grand venue where giant golems built by students from Arcane University fought equally proportioned robots from Science Academy. It had been severely damaged during the Second Seraphim War about six years ago and never repaired.

Broken rocks littered the muddy field. Black scars marred the stands, and broken flag poles hung from their holders far above. Some parts of the fallen goliath golems were still recognizable. A giant head with a single crystal eye lay near the center of the field. A massive hand rested against a wall. A towering pair of roughly hewn feet stood upright, as if ripped off the goliath during battle.

We landed in a clearing near the giant head. Ambria took off a satchel and set up a stool with a candle. She paced off ten feet and dug her heel into the mud to mark the spot. She unrolled a scroll and read it aloud. "Using magic, light a candle from a distance of ten paces. Snuff the candle with magic afterward. Consider which spells are sufficient for the task."

"That's easy," Max scoffed. "*Ignitus* and *ventus*."

"Why do all spells end with 'us'," I asked. "Did someone make them up?"

"Supposedly, the words don't matter." Max withdrew his wand from a pocket. "After the war, they decided to standardize all the spells and used Ezzek Moore's original spell book to do it."

"Well, they all sound a bit ridiculous." Ambria regarded the candle. "Though, commanding a candle to simply burn sounds a bit boring." She took a deep breath, flicked the wand toward the candle, and said in a commanding voice, "*Ignitus!*"

The wick burst into flame.

Ambria hopped up and down, clapping her hands. "I did it!"

Max snorted. "I should hope so. I know you've been secretly practicing."

She gave him a stern look. "I know you've been practicing too."

"Yeah, because I didn't want to look bad." Max's admission was honest, if not a little smug.

I hadn't practiced at all.

"Well, can you put it out?" Max put his hands on his hips and looked at the burning candle.

"Of course." She turned, drew in a breath and flicked her wand at the candle. "*Ventus*," she whispered. The flame flickered fitfully and puffed away. Ambria flourished a hand toward the spot where she stood. "Your turn, Max."

18

Max cracked his knuckles, stretched his arms over his head and took the position.

Movement near golem head drew my attention. I saw a face with inhumanly large eyes vanish behind cover. *Who was that?* I heard Max loudly grunting as if he intended to lift one of the nearby boulders rather than light a candle. I knew it would be polite to watch him, but decided instead to investigate the person.

"Well, are you going to do something?" Ambria said.

Max groaned. "Be quiet for a minute. I'm mentally preparing myself."

I walked toward the golem head and peered around it. A foot disappeared around the boulder behind it. Jogging now, I jumped around the corner and saw a young girl's startled face. With long green hair and silvery skin, she didn't look like any kind of girl I'd seen before.

"Who are you?" I asked.

She danced back, huge eyes growing round. A glimmering dress floated around her body like sunlight sparkling on mist. She didn't answer, backing up, the fear on her face morphing to caution. Pointed ears poked through her long straight hair and I found myself staring rudely.

I pointed to my chest. "I'm Conrad."

Head tilted, she leaned forward. "Conrad." Her voice was delicate and musical. "Conrad," she said again, her strange accent rolling the "r".

I nodded encouragingly. "Yes, Conrad." I dared a step forward. "What's your name?"

She spoke haltingly, as if speaking a foreign language. "What's your name?"

"I already told you my name." I pointed to myself again. "My name is Conrad."

"Where did he go?" Ambria said just before bumping into my back.

The girl's eyes flared and she jumped back. She pointed at me and shouted, "Conrad!"

"Who and what in the world is that?" Ambria asked.

"What's going on over here?" Max barged onto the scene.

With that, the girl giggled, turned, and ran.

19

I chased after her.

"Who was that?" Max said.

Round the boulders we ran, dodging this way and that until we entered the clearing near the stadium's main gates. The girl ran with a prancing gait, almost like a deer and nearly as fast. She reached the gate and ducked through a large hole in the base.

"What is she?" Max asked, huffing and puffing somewhere behind me. "I've never seen green hair and silver skin."

"That's what I want to find out." I crawled through the hole and saw the girl running to my right. Taking a deep breath, I went after her.

She looked back, a sly smile on her face, and seemed to slow, though not enough to let me stop and catch my breath.

"Wait for me!" Ambria called.

I glanced back and saw my friends several paces behind.

We ran along the curving walls of the stadium and all the way back to the iron fence surrounding the Fairy Garden. Max had warned us about entering this place, but I threw caution to the wind and followed the girl through a black iron gate.

"Don't go in there!" Max cried out, but it was too late—I was through.

Chapter 3

Max had once given us an aerial tour of the university, and even though I'd only glimpsed this place for a moment, it had obviously changed for the worse. A crumbling yellow brick road passed by what had once been a clear blue pond but was now murky and choked with what looked like oil. The vibrant carpet of green grass had faded to patches of brown and sickly yellow, and rows of tree stumps rose like headstones to commemorate where a thick forest once stood. Only the blackened ruins of the mansion beyond the tree stumps seemed unchanged.

I spotted the girl standing at the edge of the pond, a sad look on her face.

"Whoa, all the trees are gone," Max said.

Ambria stepped to my side. "It looks awful. I expected the Fairy Garden to be much prettier than this."

"It was." Max shook his head. "I don't understand what happened."

"All the trees are gone," I said. "Why would someone chop them down?"

"I'll bet she knows what happened," Ambria said, pointing to our quarry.

I nodded. "Let's ask her."

The girl tilted her head as we approached.

"What happened here?" Max asked, saying each word slowly and loudly.

The girl danced backward.

"Oh no, not again," Ambria groaned. "Please don't run."

Max wiped sweat from his forehead. "I should've grabbed a broom."

21

I touched his arm to stop him from walking forward. "Are you certain you've never seen a supernatural being like her before?"

He looked at me and shook his head. "I've never seen or heard of anyone with skin or hair like hers, though I suppose she could be some sort of shape shifter."

"Maybe fairies are real," Ambria said. "Why else would she come to the Fairy Garden?"

"She could be an elf," I suggested.

Max sighed. "I suppose there could be some beings similar to what we think of as fairies or elves, but I've never heard of them."

The object of our musings danced on the tips of her feet, mud squirming between her toes, and watched us with a curious expression.

"Stay here," I told the others, and stepped cautiously forward.

The girl stopped dancing and tilted her head, a cat-like expression on her face. "Conrad," she said.

I nodded and pointed to myself. "Conrad." I pointed to her. "What's your name?"

She went still, took a deep breath, and unleashed a high pitched squeal.

I plugged my ears and grimaced. Max groaned and Ambria shrieked.

The girl giggled and said in heavily accented English, "I am Evadora."

"Well, why didn't you say so in the first place?" Max said.

Evadora skipped in a circle, splatting mud with her feet. "Evadora, Evadora, Evadora!"

Ambria watched the girl dance, her forehead wrinkled. "I think Evadora is a bit odd."

"She's completely mental," Max said.

Evadora waved her hand. "Come." She pranced away toward the ruined forest.

"Doesn't she ever get tired?" Ambria muttered darkly as we trotted after the girl.

Curiosity outweighed my desire to rest and I picked up the pace, eager to narrow the distance. Though Evadora dashed through the graveyard of trees, dodging and leaping stumps, I opted for the muddy brick path through the center of the devastation.

"I'm not an expert on trees or anything," Max panted, "but some of the dried sap looks odd."

A quick glance at a stump confirmed what he said. The sap looked dark crimson.

"It looks like dried blood," Ambria said.

Evadora leapt atop a particularly wide stump and drew a long rusty knife from somewhere beneath her dress. She plunged the knife into the wood. A terrible ghostly keen seemed to rise from the dead tree itself. The girl withdrew the knife and licked bright red blood from the blade. She giggled. "Not dead yet!"

Ambria screamed.

Max leapt back. "Are those trees alive?"

But Evadora transfixed on Ambria and the question glided past unheard. She leapt from the stump and ran toward my friend, the dagger still in her hand.

I took out my wand and stepped in the girl's way. "Not another step closer," I warned the silver-skinned girl.

Evadora flicked her hand and the blade vanished, replaced by a small crystal bottle. She pointed to Ambria. "Please."

I looked at Ambria's tear-stained face and then back to Evadora. "Please what?"

"What do you want from me, you awful little creature?" Ambria said. "What are those tree things?"

"May I have?" Evadora took another tentative step forward, large eyes pleading.

Max leapt in front of Ambria and shielded her with his arms. "What is it you want?"

Evadora's lips peeled into a smile. "Tears."

"You want my tears?" Ambria said in a shocked voice.

The other girl nodded rapidly. "Please, please, please."

"And you won't harm me?"

Evadora shook her head so quickly, it appeared she was having a seizure. "Just tears."

Ambria took a deep breath and touched mine and Max's arms. "Fine. But then you have to tell us everything we ask you, agreed?"

"Everything." Evadora drew out the word slowly as if to encompass the entire world.

"If I'd known she wanted tears, I would have just kicked Conrad in the knee," Max said as he stepped aside.

I held onto my wand and tried to remember how to cast the *torsious* spell. Some knowledge gained from my parents' soul shards was only temporary, especially if I didn't pay close attention when using it.

Evadora held the crystal bottle to Ambria's cheek and two tears spilled inside it. By now, Ambria's eyes were drying since the episode with the tree stump had merely frightened her.

The bottle glowed darkly. "Ooh," Evadora breathed. "Fear."

"Well, I certainly wasn't crying from sadness," Ambria said.

Max peered at the bottle. "Are you a nutter?"

Evadora nodded. "I like nuts."

He groaned. "No, I mean are you mental?"

"I am physical," she said.

"What sort of being are you?" Ambria asked.

Evadora looked down at her hands and feet, then looked at Ambria. "I am a being like you."

Max threw up his hands. "Just great. We can ask her anything, but her answers are rubbish."

I tried to think of a good question and finally came up with something. "Evadora, where are you from?"

She tucked away the bottle and pointed toward the ruins of the mansion. "The crack in the world."

My gaze followed her finger, but I didn't see a crack. Behind the mansion were a few trees and the stone face of a cliff that climbed into the clouds. "Show us," I said.

She nodded and bounded along the path. We ran after, following her around the burnt remains of the mansion and to the back. We stepped through a grove of trees and over a mound of gravel. Evadora stopped and pointed at a crack in the base of the cliff.

"That's just a cave," Max said.

"Yes, a cave," Evadora said. "A crack in the world is a cave. A cave in the world is a crack." She giggled and ran a hand along the stone. "The world is thin here."

Ambria got down on her knees and peered inside. "Where does it go?"

"The rift and the other world," Evadora whispered. She made a strange squealing noise not unlike the one earlier. "I do not know what you call it."

"How do you speak our language?" Max said.

She tilted her head. "With words."

His fists clenched. "How did you learn our language?"

"I hear words, I learn words," she said. "I listen to the people at your place talk."

Ambria tentatively touched the girl's strange skin. "Are you a fairy?"

"What is fairy?" Evadora asked.

"Well, they have wands, or at least some do," Ambria said. "Some have wings and are tiny." She held her hands apart about a foot. "Some are normal size and look like humans, and they can talk to animals."

Evadora tilted her head. "Talk to animals?"

Ambria nodded.

Evadora pursed her lips and warbled.

I was so startled I jumped back.

A bird fluttered in and landed on Max's shoulder. It looked at Evadora and warbled back.

Max's eyes went wide. "Can you believe it? There's a bird sitting on my shoulder."

"You must be a fairy," I told him.

He flattened his lips.

"So you can talk to animals," Ambria said in amazement.

"It is how this bird calls for other birds." Evadora shrugged. "I hear it, I learn it."

The bird made an agitated noise and flew off. Ambria burst into laughter and pointed at Max's shoulder where the departing bird had left a moist gift.

"It pooped on my shoulder!" Max said.

Evadora giggled. "Pooped, pooped, pooped!" She grabbed Max's hands and bounced up and down. "I like this word."

Ambria laughed so hard, she had to hold her stomach. Max chortled until he cried.

Evadora went absolutely still and watched a tear trickle down Max's face. "Please have?"

25

He almost wiped the tear, but Evadora's face contorted with horror.

She grabbed his hand. "Please, no." Eye large and pleading, she looked into his. "Can I have?"

Max nodded. "Yes, but you have to give us better answers when we ask questions."

She nodded eagerly and the crystal bottle reappeared in her hand. She carefully nudged the tear with the lip of the bottle and it dribbled inside. A warm yellow glow lit the bottle for a moment and faded. Evadora corked the bottle and smiled. "Happy."

I looked at the bottle. "What do you do with the tears you collect?"

"To help with the nothing," she said. "It is easy to forget."

Ambria's eyebrows pinched. "Forget how to cry?"

"To laugh, to cry, to be mad." Evadora sighed. "I want to help, to bring these to the queen."

"Ooh, a queen." Ambria bounced on her toes. "I want to meet a queen!"

I didn't know what to believe, but Evadora's claim about this crack leading to another world had piqued my interest. I took out my wand and waved it. "*Illumus*." The tip glowed brightly and I poked it into the supposed crack in the world. The tunnel looked large enough for a person to crawl through, but I couldn't see more than twenty feet or so inside. "When was the first time you came here?" I asked our strange guest.

She held up one finger. "Two."

Ambria held up the correct number of fingers. "This is two."

Evadora nodded. "Yes."

Max shook his head like a wet dog. "Two what?"

"Two of the many days," she said.

"Weeks or months?" I asked.

"Weeks," she replied. "The man came through the crack."

My mouth fell open. "What man?"

"Who?" Max said.

She pointed to me. "The man like you."

I exchanged confused looks with the others. "What man like me?"

"He looks like you," Evadora replied.

26

"Oh no." Ambria's lip trembled. "I think she means your father."

My stomach knotted. "Evadora, can you describe him?"

She nodded. "His hair like yours. Face like yours. He came with the pretty woman with long black hair."

Max blew out a breath. "That sounds like Victus and Delectra all right."

Evadora shrugged. "He came through the crack. I followed him back."

"What happened to the trees in the Fairy Garden?" I asked. "Did the man do that?"

She nodded. "It was the price."

I didn't like the sound of that. "The price for what?"

"The help of the queen." Evadora got down on her knees and peered into the dark tunnel. She pointed forward. "I show you."

Max waved his hands in front of his chest. "No way am I following that mental girl into a dark narrow tunnel."

"She made a bird poo on your shoulder, Max," Ambria said with a grin. "How evil could she be?"

I held up my glowing wand. "I'll go with her. The rest of you stay here."

"Now hold on," Max said. "I'm not letting you go in there alone."

"And I'm not waiting out here." Ambria looked around and shivered. "This place feels haunted."

"Yes, many spirits," Evadora said, pointing in the direction of the ruined forest. "The guardians all gone." She slashed a finger across her throat and smiled. "Dead or mostly dead."

Max shuddered. "You're not supposed to smile when you talk about murder, you wicked little thing."

Evadora's forehead pinched. "No? If I not supposed to smile, then what?"

"Murder is awful," Ambria said. "It makes me frown and cry." She grimaced.

Evadora produced her bottle, eyes eager. "More tears?"

Ambria shook her head. "No, I'm just explaining emotions."

"You know what happiness is, right?" I asked the silver girl.

She nodded. "Yellow."

"That's a color, not an emotion." I tapped a finger to my chin. "When the bird pooped on Max, that was happiness."

27

Evadora nodded. "Yes, that was happy. But murder is not happy?"

I shook my head. "Murder is death. It's the blackest of the black."

She seemed to absorb that. "I never saw death before coming here. It is a bad thing?"

"It means that what was living goes away forever and turns to dust." Ambria picked up a handful of dirt and let it spill from her fingers.

Evadora's eyes went wide and she fell back against the cliff face. Her skin turned grayer until it nearly matched the stone. "Gone," she whispered. "Death is gone. It is bad."

Is she like a chameleon? I put a comforting hand on her shoulder. Her skin felt cold to the touch and I nearly jerked away. "We can teach you about us if you can teach us about your people."

She looked up at me and her skin began to warm. "That is nice, Conrad." Evadora knelt again and crawled into the tunnel. "Come with me," she called back.

"Is it just me or has her speaking improved since we met her?" Max said.

Ambria nodded. "It seems the more she hears us talk, the better she speaks our language."

"Let's go," I said, and crawled into the tunnel after the girl. The tunnel ceiling rose until we could stand up. We went perhaps twenty feet more when the tunnel opened into a sea of stars. I yelped and stopped. Max bumped into me, but I gripped the side of the wall and held on. Beyond the tunnel's end was nothing but the void of outer space. Balls of pulsating white energy floated through the void, casting a bright glow around them.

Evadora stepped into the empty black space. I expected her to fall, but her feet padded as though they were on solid ground.

"What is this place?" I asked.

"The rift." She pointed to the glowing balls. "Rift guardians."

Max peeked around me and gasped. "Are we in outer space?"

Evadora shook her head. "The space between worlds." She pointed to a black starless area about fifty yards away. As one of the glowing light balls drifted past, I realized it was the opening to a stone tunnel slightly larger than this one.

28

Ambria poked her head between Max and me. "How are we supposed to get over there? Fly?"

Evadora shook her head. "No, you run very fast." She pointed at the light balls. "Dodge the attacks."

Max warily observed one of the pulsating spheres. "Dodge what attacks?"

"Zap!" Evadora said. "The rift guardians kill intruders." She stepped forward. "Follow me." She stepped a few feet out and stood in the void. "Once you walk past here, the guardians kill."

I stepped out, but stayed a foot or two back from the limit. Max and Ambria crowded me on both sides.

A ghostly keening sent chills down my spine and I realized it was one of the guardians. Another one responded with a higher pitch, and drifted toward the other side of the rift, trailing a ball of white plasma behind.

Ambria shivered violently. "C-c-creepy."

"Can we go now?" Max backed away a step. "This place scares me."

My skin crawled and it took everything not to dash back through the tunnel. We were in a rift between worlds, and it was haunted by ghosts.

Chapter 4

"How do we get past the guardians?" I asked Evadora.

"Just follow me fast," she said.

Max shook his head. "I'm not going another step. If you want to follow that mental girl, you go right ahead."

"Me either," Ambria added.

Evadora pointed to the tunnel on the other side. "Come."

I spotted more of the ghostly guardians drifting our way. "No." I pointed back to the tunnel. "We're going back."

Evadora sighed. "Bye."

"You're not coming?" I asked.

"I go home," she replied. She looked at the nearby guardians and suddenly bounded forward as if walking on an invisible bridge in outer space.

The keening of the guardians turned to a wail and they streaked toward her. Jagged bolts of electricity exploded from the nearest one, raking the space behind Evadora. Just as one of them swooped in to cut off the other tunnel, she made a wailing sound to match the guardians. The balls of light stopped in place as if confused—just long enough for Evadora to enter the other tunnel.

"This place is a nightmare," Max said. "Let's go." He dashed back through the tunnel.

I stared at the place Evadora had entered for a moment before following my friends back through the tunnel. We emerged in the grove behind the ruined mansion a few minutes later, my knees sore, pants worn thin from crawling on rock.

I stood up and pushed through the branches of the trees concealing the crack and we made my way to the rear of the mansion.

"There is no way I will ever go in there again," Max said. "If you want to see where the other tunnel goes, Conrad, be my guest."

"Perhaps if we brought our brooms we could make it," Ambria said.

"Did you see how fast those guardians moved?" Max said. "Unless you can trick them like Evadora, you're dead."

I brushed off my pants. "I've got to find out what's over there."

"Probably a cave filled with ghosts," Max said. "Or demons. You're crazy if you go back."

Ambria's lips peeled back in disgust. "Max, where's your sense of adventure?"

Max snorted. "You ran out of there just as quickly as I did."

Just as she opened her mouth to reply, I heard voices in the distance and put a finger to my lips. "Someone's coming," I whispered.

"Quick, in here," Max hissed, and darted to the back door of the mansion. He tugged on it, but it wouldn't open.

Ambria grabbed my sleeve and pointed toward a large tree. We ducked behind the trunk and peered around. A man and woman walked around a pile of rubble and headed for the grove of trees. My heart seemed to stop in my chest when I saw their faces.

The man stood tall with thick black hair and a handsome face with a square jaw. The woman's fair skin looked smooth beyond perfection, and her lustrous black hair hung down to her waist. My parents looked far healthier now than they had when first resurrected by their demonologist minion, Rufus Cumberbatch.

Ambria's hand tightened painfully on my wrist and she turned a terrified gaze on me. I should have been every bit as frightened. Instead, I trembled with anger. I wanted to leap from behind the tree and cast deadly spells at the pair. Unfortunately, nothing suitable came to mind, perhaps because my parents' soul fragments didn't want me to harm them.

"Do you think she will believe us, Victus?" my mother, Delectra, said.

"I see no reason why not," my father replied. "If we succeed, we will have all the time in the world."

Delectra shuddered. "We will pave the way to our eternal rule."

31

"Please slow down." A short blonde woman appeared around the corner.

Max's breath caught in his throat. "Aunt Serena?" he whispered.

My parents stopped and turned toward the newcomer.

"If you'd like I could engineer longer legs for you," Victus said. "Perhaps frog legs so you could leap through the air."

Serena slashed a hand through the air. "Shush, Victus." She smoothed her white dress and nodded toward the grove. "How did you break through?"

"An earth elemental," Victus said. "The original passage was well hidden, but a little detective work revealed the ancient fissure."

"Clever." She tapped a finger to her chin. "How did you make it past the rift guardians?"

"It took a great deal of experimentation," Delectra said, "but I finally crafted a shield they cannot penetrate."

Serena smiled. "I knew you had it in you, dear."

Delectra scoffed. "You know nothing of my magic."

"I know enough." The short woman didn't seem the least bit offended by my mother's condescension. "What I don't understand is if you're so wonderful with magic, why do you need me for this venture?"

"When it comes to magical research, you are second to none," Victus said. "Delectra and I have other matters to attend. Once we introduce you to the queen, everything will be up to you."

"Everything about these folk is buried in folklore and superstition." Serena rubbed her hands together eagerly. "If the legends are true, I think we can get more from this bargain than you think."

Victus yawned. "Yes, perhaps, but I want you to concentrate on the goal at hand, Serena." He stepped closer and gripped her shoulders. Eyes hard, forehead pinched, he glared at her for a moment. "We will take this patiently, one step at a time. Do you understand?"

Serena inspected her nails, as if my father's commanding glare wasn't inches from her nose. "Victus, I was Daelissa's top Arcane because I produce results." Her calm eyes met his. "I do not lose sight of goals. I attain them no matter how unreachable they seem."

32

Victus released her and straightened, his face a picture of perfect calm. "That is all I needed to hear."

"Hmm, well that's good." Serena walked into the grove.

Delectra rolled her eyes and Victus smiled back at her, caressed her cheek. "All will be good, my love," he said.

She pressed her head against his chest. "I know."

"Are we supposed to crawl through here?" Serena called out. "How undignified."

Victus shook his head. "It was difficult enough just to break through." He led his wife into the grove.

I tried to imagine my evil parents crawling on all fours through the tunnel and had to stifle a laugh. We waited several minutes then crept from our hiding place. I walked to the trees concealing the crack and peered through.

"What are you doing, Conrad?" Ambria asked. "We need to go now!"

"Wish I could put a boulder here," I said.

"Do you really think that would stop your parents from getting out?" Max gripped my arm. "If your mum can block those guardians with a spell, a boulder wouldn't be anything for her. Let's go."

I shook my head. "I want to see what's on the other side of the rift. Maybe I can sneak past the guardians."

"You must have a death wish today." Max stepped in front of me. "We can see what's in there another time."

"There's only one way in and out," Ambria said. "If your parents caught you in the tunnel, you'd never get away."

My heart filled with jumbled emotions. I hated my parents for what they did to me. I wished they loved me. I wanted to kill them and make sure they stayed dead.

Cora covers the bruises on her face with makeup.

"How can you see what you're doing without a mirror?" I ask.

Mum flinches we she realizes I'm watching her. "Conrad, you shouldn't see me like this."

"Is Bill evil?" I ask her.

She leans on the sink as tears spill from her eyes. "He wasn't like this before. Something happened to him—something awful." She looks at the blank spot on the wall where a mirror should be.

"He hits you a lot," I reply. "He must be evil."

Cora kneels next to me. "But I love him, Conrad. How can I love someone evil?"

I shake my head. "I don't know."

"Conrad?" Max shook me by the shoulders.

I flinched back to reality. *Cora was my real mum, not the evil, twisted Delectra.* Cora was the only foster parent who really loved me and I'd loved her with all my heart. But the curse my parents put on me to preserve their souls had given Cora cancer. They'd killed her and death had returned my wicked parents.

"Let's go," I said in a broken voice. *I'll never have the love of my real parents.*

We ran back around the mansion, through the field of stumps, and past the pond.

Ambria stopped and screamed as we passed the blackened waters.

I stumbled and went down on my knees a few feet from the water and saw what frightened her so. A pale white arm lay on the muddy bank. I got up and peered into the water. A woman's face was barely visible through the murk. I touched her arm, expecting the cold clamminess of death but instead found the tiniest bit of warmth.

"Help me, Max." I gripped the arm and tugged.

Max grimaced. "Why do you want to pull a dead body out of the pond?"

"She's not dead." I glared at him. "Come help."

He leaned down and grabbed the woman's dress and together we pulled her from the water. Her eyes fluttered and opened to reveal black eyes with no whites. She gripped my shirt.

Max yelped and jumped back.

"The anchored world must not be freed," the woman said in a feeble voice. "Else all will be cast adrift in an endless ocean of stars."

"Who are you?" I asked.

Max crawled toward her. "Oh no. That's the Lady of the Pond."

"We need to get her to a healer," Ambria said.

The woman went limp. I put an ear to her lips and detected a faint breath. "Are there healers at the university?"

"Yeah," Max said. "I'll get her feet. You get her under the arms."

"I'll hold her back," Ambria said.

We lifted the woman and awkwardly carried her down the path and out of the gates. Though she wasn't heavy, we shuffled along slowly and finally reached the university.

"The healer station is near the dining hall," Max said, and led us through the curving corridor.

"How interesting," said a familiar voice from behind us.

I craned my neck and saw Galfandor, the school headmaster, exiting a stairwell. "We found her in the Fairy Garden," I explained.

"Yes, that's usually where the Lady of the Pond resides." He placed a hand on the woman's forehead. "What did you do to her?"

"We didn't do anything," Ambria protested. "Someone killed all the trees out there."

"And tried to kill the lady too," Max said.

"It's no secret who did this," I said angrily.

Galfandor raised an eyebrow. "Best not to say it aloud, young man." He stepped forward and motioned us to follow. "Come along. I'll see Mirjana receives treatment."

"Mirjana?" I said.

He nodded. "That is the lady's name."

We trudged along behind him and finally reached the healing ward. No one was in the lobby, so we took our patient into the back. Empty beds lined the walls. A tall thin man with a neatly oiled and curled moustache sat in a chair against the back wall reading a newspaper.

He dropped the paper and leapt up, excitedly rubbing his hands together. "What have we here?"

Galfandor motioned to the first bed. "This will do nicely."

The thin man hovered over the woman. "Is this my first patient of the year?"

"Yes, and a rather important one at that, Percival," Galfandor said.

"Oh?" He touched Mirjana's wrist. "She's alive, but only barely." Percival peered at us and then back at Galfandor. "Who is she?"

Galfandor smiled. "The Lady of the Pond."

The other man leapt back. "From the Fairy Garden?" His eyes narrowed on us. "What did you do to her?"

"Nothing, sir." I placed Mirjana's dangling hand on the bed. "The forest in front of the mansion has been completely cut down, and the pond looks polluted."

Galfandor hissed between his teeth. "Yes, well, we need to talk about that, children." He turned to Percival. "Let me know the moment she's awake."

The healer pressed a hand to his patient's forehead. "If I can wake her. I don't know if our magic will work on her."

"What sort of supernatural being is she?" Ambria asked.

Percival shrugged. "All I know is that she lives underwater as easily as on land."

"A mermaid!" Ambria's eyes widened. "Oh, how wonderful."

Max covered his face with a hand. "There's no such thing as mermaids, silly."

Galfandor cleared his throat. "Follow me, please, children." He left the ward and led us on a rather long hike through twisting hallways, upstairs, downstairs, and finally to doorway that had to be on the opposite end of the university, judging from the distance we'd travelled.

"Where in the world are we?" Ambria said, looking with awe at a huge gallery of portraits with serious-looking people staring back at her. Her gaze wandered to something else and her mouth dropped open. "Did you kill and stuff those poor owls?"

I saw a shelf filled with a variety of life-like owls arranged from largest to smallest. A huge brown one looked nobly down at us while the smallest, a white owl, looked as though it had been frozen into place while taking flight.

Galfandor chuckled. "Someone had the bright notion to use owls as delivery birds." He tutted. "After two teachers nearly lost their eyes and several children were viciously mauled and clawed, we decided that birds of prey simply aren't safe in this environment."

"Safe?" Ambria chirped. "You're concerned about child safety?" She laughed. "You didn't seem concerned about our safety when we rescued the orphans from the Goodleighs all by our little selves."

Galfandor didn't seem the least bit offended. "On the contrary, Miss Rax. I was concerned about your safety, but I was in no position to help."

"Did you kill all those birds?" Max asked.

36

The old man shook his head. "No, they're merely under preservation spells. I could lift the spell and they'd be free to fly away." Galfandor seemed to think the matter settled and walked down the hallway and into an office. Windows on all sides overlooked the university grounds. To the right I saw the crystalline dome of the library, and straight ahead lay the valley. Science Academy gleamed silver in the distance on the opposite mountaintop.

"Whoa what a view!" Max ran to the windows and looked around.

Galfandor sat in a red leather chair and looked at me seriously. "Now we can talk about what happened in the Fairy Garden."

I sat down on the couch across from him. Galfandor was someone I couldn't quite classify as a friend, though he'd indirectly helped us rescue other children from the Goodleighs' manor and had given us good advice on most matters. Whatever secret motives he might have, he at least seemed to want to help us and hopefully wouldn't betray us.

Besides, he was the only adult we could really ask for advice or help. In light of that, I knew telling him everything was the best course of action. Starting with Evadora, I told him about our short trip into the rift and what we'd heard from my parents and Serena.

Galfandor nodded and grunted several times, but said nothing until I finished.

"Well," he said, "it appears you've once again stumbled into trouble, children."

Max wrinkled his forehead. "What's on the other side of the rift?"

The old man put a hand to his chin. "The anchored world, she said? I don't believe I've ever heard of such a thing."

Max snapped his fingers. "I just thought of something. What if the place on the other side of the rift is where the pocket dimensions like Queens Gate are located?"

"Yes, yes, I suppose it could be. The rift must be some sort of barrier to keep curious folks out." Galfandor stroked his beard. "The mystery of the pocket dimensions would be a mystery worth solving."

"You certainly can't convince me to go back in that awful place," Ambria stated firmly. "Besides, we have the exam to study for."

The thought of school brought another pressing issue to mind. "Sir, supposing I pass the exam, is there a way to hide my last name from the school—change it, I mean?"

The headmaster raised an eyebrow. "Hmm, yes, the name Edison certainly wouldn't go over well with some."

"Ooh, I'd like to change my last name too," Ambria said.

Max sighed. "Everyone already knows my last name."

Galfandor stood and went to a large leather-bound book. He flipped it open and ran his finger down a page, then thumbed through the pages. "Ah, here it is." He shook his head. "I'm afraid school policy prohibits the use of aliases."

"But everyone will hate us," Ambria said. "If anyone learns I'm the daughter of Cyphanis Rax, they might run me out of school."

The headmaster raised a finger. "It just so happens that since you and Conrad are—or in Conrad's case, were—orphans, your last names are not a matter of public record. While it does not explicitly state what name is to be used, I believe it allows you some wiggle room on the registration forms."

Galfandor pulled on a rope and a bell rang. "Since you're already here, it might be easiest to fill out the paperwork now."

"But we haven't taken the exam yet," Ambria said.

"You need to register before you can take the exam." He looked at the wall. "Ah, hello Shushiel."

A whispering sound like the rustle of cloth drew our attention to the wall behind us. Ambria was the first to shriek at the top of her lungs. I stumbled backwards over a lamp table, sending its contents crashing to the floor in my mad dash to escape a massive red spider on the wall.

Chapter 5

Max didn't seem the least bit frightened of the massive arachnid. "Wow, you've got a ruby spider?"

Shiny red fur coated the spider from the tips of its eight long legs to the top of its eight-eyed head. Black bands striped the fur on the legs, and formed a crooked E on top of the abdomen.

The headmaster walked over to the huge spider where it clung to the wall. The creature extended a strand of web with several scrolls attached to it. The front legs on its head rubbed together, making the whispering noise I'd heard earlier.

Galfandor chuckled. "Why, no, Shushiel, you look perfectly fine to me. I think our friends have never met anyone so lovely and were quite overwhelmed." He turned his gaze on Ambria and me. "Correct, children?"

Ambria clutched me like driftwood in a storm-tossed sea, but still managed to nod. "V-v-very lovely, sir."

"Yes," I croaked. "Beautiful." I felt a stirring in that part of me where Vic and Della resided and felt a sense of awe and resentment.

Shushiel leapt to the floor, eliciting another shriek from Ambria, and performed an eight-legged curtsey. She stood as tall as my knee and each of her furry red legs looked nearly as long as mine.

"She is pleased to meet you," Galfandor said.

Max leaned toward the spider. "How do you understand her?"

Galfandor smiled. "You simply have to listen carefully to her susurrations." He looked fondly at the huge spider. "The Overlord— Victus Edison—created a mutant gene in cobalt spiders in his early attempts to create allies. The gene turned them from blue to red and branded them with his initial."

I stared at the E on Shushiel's back. "My father is responsible for her?"

"For her entire species," Galfandor said. "The mutant gene caused not only unusual growth in size, but also increased the intellectual capacity of the affected spiders."

Shushiel rubbed her forelegs together in an excited whispery monologue for several moments while Galfandor listened thoughtfully. He finally translated. "Her parents were of the original thirty spiders Victus mutated. Once they realized what he intended for them to do, they escaped his menagerie of mutant monsters and made a home in the Dark Forest."

"So, she won't eat me?" Ambria said hopefully.

Galfandor shook his head. "She prefers rodents or spider bats."

The spider walked over to Ambria and susurrated.

"Shushiel says you are less horrendous looking than most bipeds," Galfandor said.

Ambria frowned. "Tell her she is a lovely shade of red."

"She can understand what we say," the headmaster replied.

Shushiel made a sound not unlike a laugh and extended a leg toward my friend. Ambria shivered and held out a trembling hand. They touched.

"Ooh, she's soft," Ambria said. She stroked a hand across the fur. "She's so fluffy!"

"Can I touch?" Max asked.

Shushiel extended another leg toward him and he eagerly ran a hand across the spider's fur.

"Well, now, isn't this nice?" Galfandor said. "Come, Conrad. Say hello to Shushiel."

I'd never been particularly afraid of spiders, primarily because I'd been too dull-witted thanks to the living curse my parents bestowed on me. Now that I was a little smarter, it was hard to approach such a large, venomous arachnid without my chest tightening. I held out my arm. Shushiel's leg reached out and touched my hand. Her fur felt velvety soft, and not the least bit bristly like it looked.

"Hello, Shushiel," I said.

She made a whispering noise with her mandibles. The words were so soft I could barely hear them, but I made out two of them.

"Hello, Conrad." She continued to speak, but so quickly I couldn't discern the words.

Galfandor chuckled. "Shushiel says since your father created her kind, she and you must be cousins."

The apprehension melted away and I nodded. "Yes, we're cousins, Shushiel."

She wiggled up and down.

"That makes her happy," the headmaster said.

Victum lividum, alpha species. A complete failure, said Vic. I flinched, though I should have been accustomed to his random musings.

Galfandor handed each of us one of the scrolls Shushiel had brought. "Please fill these out and bring them to the exam tomorrow." He looked at me and Ambria. "You two may choose your own last names, but I suggest you make them easy to remember."

"Edwards," I said immediately.

Ambria pressed her lips together. "Goodness, what name should I choose?"

"I think Bossy or Bigmouth would be excellent last names," Max said.

She swatted him with her scroll. "Bigmouth would suit you wonderfully, Max."

I unrolled the scroll and looked at the information. "Why do you still use paper when you could use an arctablet?" I asked Galfandor.

"The university frowns on using technology," he replied. "Now, children, I must attend to other matters. I wish you the best of luck on the exam tomorrow."

We said goodbye to Shushiel and left the office. Moments later, we became hopelessly lost in the tangle of corridors and stairways of Arcane University.

"This place is ridiculous." Ambria stared at the three hallways ahead of us and shook her head. "How is anyone supposed to find their way around here?"

I looked all around the room. "There aren't even any signs."

Max pointed to my pocket. "Do you have your arcphone?"

I slid it out of my pants pocket and handed it to Max. The magic phone was one of my prized possessions even though it had belonged to someone I murdered. I justified keeping it by rationalizing that the other person had been trying to kill me first, and I hadn't intentionally killed them. What made me most uncomfortable about it was that the victim had been Ambria's older brother. Even though she'd never known him and didn't hate me for the accident, I couldn't help feeling a bit guilty keeping the phone.

Max downloaded an app and activated it. *Where do you want to go?* it asked on the screen.

"We want to leave this building and go to Colossus Stadium," Max said.

The phone projected an arrow pointing behind us. Following its directions, we turned and backtracked to a room with eight exits, took a right where we'd originally taken a left, and within a few minutes, ended up near the healer's office and the exit.

"Hold on," Ambria said, and zoomed in the map. "It says Galfandor's office is almost directly above us."

"Give us directions to Galfandor's office," Max said.

A blue line on the map wended its way from one end of the building to the other, making what should have been a short walk, a rather long one.

"I can't believe that's the only route to his office," I said. "It's as if he doesn't want anyone to visit."

"Who can blame him?" Max said. "I'm sure he puts up with all sort of nutters."

"Let's go back to the stadium and retrieve our brooms," Ambria said. "We still have a lot of studying to do."

My nerves pinched at the thought of the exam tomorrow. "Yes, I guess we should."

"It's past lunchtime," Max complained. "Can't we eat first?"

In all the excitement of the morning, I'd overlooked my rumbling stomach. "Is the dining hall open?"

"One way to find out," he said.

Thankfully, it was a straight march to the cafeteria. Though the room was nearly empty except for a few professors, a wooden golem dressed in a white uniform with a black apron hung about its waist promptly exited from a swinging door and put covered dishes in front of us. A delicious odor wafted from beneath the silver cover. I lifted the lid and discovered seared ham, an over-easy egg, and several slices of bread.

I looked uneasily at the food. "Do we have to pay for this?"

Max shook his head. "I don't think so. Besides, I'm too hungry to ask."

We devoured everything on our plates. Even Ambria looked nearly as delighted as Max while she ate.

"Forget magic," Max said. "I want to go here for the food."

Ambria licked her lips. "It was wonderful."

As if on cue, two golems appeared. One cleaned away the dishes, and the other dropped off small plates with dessert, and platters with cups of dark tea.

"It's bread pudding!" Max shouted with glee.

After reveling in our gluttony, we returned to the stadium and resumed our magic practice.

"Are you certain we're safe here?" Max said. "What if Conrad's parents come through here on their way back from the crack in the world?"

"I doubt they'd bother coming in here." Ambria waved a hand around at the towering remains of the fallen goliaths. "Besides, we have plenty of places to hide."

I agreed. "They probably have a secret way of coming and going. I doubt they'll want anyone to see them until they're ready with their devious plans."

Max shrugged. "Well, if you say so. Just don't blame me if they show up and kill us."

Ambria rolled her eyes. "Enough dilly-dallying. Let's practice."

After we'd successfully completed the exercises listed in the study guide, Max flopped spread-eagled onto the ground. "Finally!" he said. "I'm so tired of studying."

"Yes, well rolling in the dirt certainly won't help," Ambria noted dryly.

I hopped on my broom and climbed into the air for an overhead view of the boulders. During practice, I couldn't help but glance around for signs of Evadora, but even from this vantage I realized she hadn't come back to spy on us.

We flew back down to the house and parked our brooms in the foyer. Ambria went upstairs and returned a moment later. "Blue isn't here," she said in a worried voice. "I wonder where she went?"

Max shrugged. "Probably hunting cats."

Ambria grimaced. "That's awful! Do lycans really do that?"

Max was too busy rummaging through the pantry. He came up empty handed. "I'm starving, and you're out of groceries."

"Because you eat everything," Ambria shot back.

"Do not." He took the lone remaining slice of bread from the breadbox on the counter and took a bite. "Let's go to a restaurant."

After dinner, Max left for his Uncle Malcolm's since he didn't like staying with his parents, and Ambria and I flew our brooms back to the house. I kept a close watch on the streets below, wondering if another of my parents' demon assassins hunted me even now.

"Your parents worry me," Ambria said. "Whatever they're planning might affect our schooling."

"I'm certain it will." As we flew over our street, I glided down for a landing. "I wonder if Galfandor will help us this time, or if we're on our own."

She shook her head. "I don't understand that old man. You'd think he'd want a safer world for children."

"I'd like to know what he's thinking." I landed my broom on the front lawn.

"Hello, Conrad." Harris Ashmore waved from the other side of the stone wall separating our yards. "Who's your friend?"

Ambria's eyes widened. "What's my last name, Conrad?" she whispered. "Help me think of something, fast!"

I drew a complete blank. "Her name's Ambria," I said, hoping the conversation wouldn't drift to last names.

The red-headed boy I'd seen with Harris yesterday ran up beside him. "Where's Cryberius?"

I didn't like his tone, or the nickname they'd given Max, so I said nothing.

"Why do you hang out with Max Tiberius?" Harris asked in a curious tone.

"Because he's our friend," Ambria shot back. "Why do you hang out with a ginger who gets his jollies making fun of other people?"

"Because I'm his friend," the other boy retorted.

The curly-haired girl I'd seen them with came around the corner of the house. "Hello," she said. "I'm Lily."

Ambria's hard gaze softened. "I'm Ambria and this is Conrad."

Harris pointed to the other boy. "This is Baxter."

Lily stepped beside Harris and looked me up and down. "Are you taking the entrance exam tomorrow? Harris said he saw you studying earlier."

"Yes," I replied. "And you?"

"Of course she is, and I am too," Baxter said. "If Harris is going to save the world, we've got to be there to help him."

"I've been looking forward to university all my life," Lily said in a dreamy voice. "I earned top marks in Arcane prep school."

"Where did you go to school?" Harris asked me.

That was a gap in my life I hadn't considered, and I was at a loss for a response.

"Oh, goodness, Conrad," Ambria said. "Look at the time. I'm so tired."

"It's not even eight," Baxter said. "What sort of ninny goes to bed that early?"

"A ninny who wants to be fresh for the entrance exam," Ambria growled. She nodded at the other two children. "It was nice meeting you Lily and Harris."

"Same," Lily said. "See you tomorrow."

"Hey, what about me?" Baxter said.

"Meeting you was not nice," Ambria said. "Learn some manners for next time."

Harris and Lily laughed. Baxter's freckled face turned bright red.

I cringed and waved goodbye, then quickly went inside, Ambria huffing and puffing angrily behind me.

"The nerve of some people." Ambria tossed her broom in the corner of the foyer. "I don't like that Baxter kid one bit."

"Who's Baxter?" asked a soft voice.

Ambria and I jumped back, only to find Blue sitting cross-legged on the floor in the family room.

"Where did you go earlier?" Ambria asked the other girl.

"Looking for my new pack." Blue looked glumly at the bare floor. "But no alphas want strays like me."

I sat down on the floor next to her. "Why didn't you like your old pack?"

She shivered and whispered, "The alpha is a bad person."

Ambria scowled. "What did he do to you, Blue?"

The other girl shook her head. "Nothing. I left before he could."

45

"Do alphas have absolute control over the pack?" I asked.

Blue nodded. "When I was little there was an alpha named Colin McCloud who led all the packs. But he went with Justin Slade to fight the war in Seraphina and took most of the lycans with him." She buried her face in her hands. "Now people like Castor can get away with whatever they want."

"Castor is the old alpha?" I asked.

"Yes." She looked up, eyes glistening with tears. "He killed my father for challenging him. I tried to convince my mother to leave with me and my little brother, but she was too afraid to run."

I knew from experience that there wasn't much I could say to make Blue feel better, so I did the next best thing and gave her a hug. She leaned against my shoulder and shook with sobs.

Ambria paced back and forth. "It sounds like everything was a lot better when this Justin Slade person was around." She stopped. "Maybe we could figure out how to bring him back and ask him to fight your parents and people like Castor."

"I'll just be happy to pass the exam tomorrow, Ambria." My shoulder felt soaked, but Blue showed no signs of cutting off the flow of tears. "We barely know any magic, much less how to make the Alabaster Arches work again."

Ambria slumped. "Well, unless your parents are stopped, we'll all be looking for new packs."

Blue let go of me and looked up. "What are his parents doing?"

"His parents want to rule the world." Ambria said with a groan.

I didn't want Ambria talking about my parents to someone we didn't even know! I widened my eyes and shook my head.

Ambria caught my meaning and grimaced. "I'm sorry, but I can't talk about it."

Blue turned back to me. "Is this about your real last names being Rax and Edison?"

Ambria gasped. "How did you—"

The lycan girl touched a finger to her ear. "I have wolf hearing. I overheard you talking about it yesterday."

"Please, you can't tell anyone," I said. "Promise you'll keep it a secret."

"Oh, please do," Ambria said.

"What's so awful about your last names?" Blue's forehead pinched.

A sigh shuddered from my chest. "I'll tell you if you promise not to tell anyone."

"I owe you my life," Blue said. "I promise it will be our secret."

"My father, Victus Edison, was the Overlord."

It didn't take long for that to sink in, judging from Blue's horrified eyes. "You're the son of Victus and Delectra Edison?"

I hated the burden of guilt their names piled on me. "Yes."

"My father was Cyphanis Rax," Ambria said. "Thankfully, he's dead for good, unlike Conrad's parents."

"I've never heard of him," Blue said.

Ambria quirked an eyebrow. "He used to be the Arcanus Primus when Daelissa tried to rule the world."

Blue flattened her lips and shook her head. "Lycans don't care much about Arcane politics, but the Overlord affected everyone." Her forehead wrinkled. "Conrad, how can your parents be up to something? I thought they were dead."

Ambria laughed bitterly. "That's a long story."

I touched Blue's hand. "Just remember that whatever we tell you about our past has to be kept secret. Our parents were terrible people, but we're not."

The girl nodded slowly, eyes darting back and forth between me and Ambria. "I understand."

"It's why we're changing our last names," Ambria said. "We don't want to be judged by what our parents did."

"I promise I'll keep it all secret," Blue said.

I leaned back against a chair and decided on where to begin. "It all started in an orphanage."

The story took a while to tell, and by the time I was finished, it was past bedtime.

"This is unbelievable," Blue said. "And now your parents have broken through the barrier between this world and whatever is on the other side of the rift?"

"It seems so." I stood and stretched. "I'm going to get ready for bed. Goodnight, Ambria and Blue."

Blue kissed me on the cheek. "Thank you for the hug, Conrad. It was sweet."

My face suddenly felt very warm. "Um, okay."

Ambria looked at the other girl for a moment then came over and kissed my other cheek. "Yes, thanks, Conrad, for being a good person."

I almost rubbed the moisture from both my cheeks, but decided the girls might take it as an insult. I backed out of the room, then quickly headed upstairs and closed the bathroom door. I touched both of my cheeks and stared blankly at the mirror for a moment before shaking off the strange feeling the kisses had left in me. *Girls make me feel funny.*

You're almost a man, Vic said.

Della scoffed. *He won't survive that long.*

Chapter 6

Ambria and I woke up early the next morning and ate a quick breakfast. Blue came downstairs as we were getting our brooms.

"You're up early," Ambria noted.

Blue nodded. "I'm going to take the entrance exam too."

I blinked a few times. "You can do magic?"

She shook her head. "They have courses for shape-shifters like me." A hopeful smile lit her face. "Maybe I'll find other lycans there. If they like me, I can join their pack."

Ambria smiled at the other girl. "That's a wonderful idea, Blue." She looked around. "Unfortunately, we don't have another broom for you to use."

Blue stretched her arms over her head. "That's okay. I'll take the sky car."

"We'll see you there," I said.

Her face flushed. "See you there, Conrad."

Ambria and I flew across town to the small house near the western cliff where Max's uncle lived. Our friend was already waiting outside on his broom. He flew up to meet us and then we continued onward and upward toward the university on the towering cliff ahead.

"I can't wait to get this over with." Max dodged around a flock of geese and groaned. "I'm so nervous I could hardly eat breakfast."

Ambria laughed. "You know something is serious if it keeps Max from eating."

I grinned. "How much did you eat, Max?"

He shook his head. "I only managed four eggs, some pancakes, bacon, and toast."

"You call that hardly eating?" Ambria rolled her eyes. "You've probably eaten your poor uncle out of house and home."

"People who eat a lot are smarter," Max said. "It's a proven fact."

"In that case, you must be the smartest boy in the world," I said.

Ambria sniffed. "The only proven fact is that you'll eat anything and everything."

The sight of the university ended our conversation in a nervous silence. We landed just outside the main gate where guards in dark blue robes renewed our weekly security charms, and allowed us into the main entrance. People of all ages crowded the large hall. A teenaged boy stood with a group of his peers, laughing as they frightened small children with fireworks spells. A group of girls in bright pink robes looked Ambria up and down before sticking their noses in the air and giggling. Parents kept their young ones close to them, eyes watching an empty podium expectantly.

The roar of conversation and press of bodies was overwhelming, but I saw nowhere to seek relief.

"This is awful," Ambria shouted.

I nodded. "I didn't realize there were so many Arcane kids."

"This is way more than last year," Max said.

Ambria looked around. "I wonder if any of the children from Little Angel Orphanage are here."

After we'd rescued our fellow orphans from the Goodleighs, we'd soon discovered most of them had been abducted from their parents and were not orphans after all. In fact, they'd all been taken because their parents were skilled Arcanes. Apparently, children with good magical pedigrees could be sold for quite a profit.

I shrugged. "It's impossible to tell with so many people."

Something swished past my arm. I looked up and saw an old woman in a gray robe march past and up to the podium. The moment she stepped onto it, the hall went absolutely quiet.

"Welcome to Arcane University," she said in a mild Scottish accent. "I'm Professor Rhona Trask." She swept her eyes across the packed hallway. "Today marks the inception of another school year. Today, fates will be decided. Some of you will earn a place within these hallowed halls while other will fail." The professor's gaze seemed to catch on a few of the older children in the hall. "I wish you all good fortune, whatever the outcome."

She swung her arm to the left. "Neophytes report to Tiberius Hall for the early education entrance exam. If you haven't already, please place your registration forms in the box over there." She pointed out a large wooden crate in a corner.

The youngest children, herded by parents and other professors, did as instructed and moved in the indicated direction. Professor Trask waited until the last of them were gone. Ambria, Max, and I took the chance to drop our registration forms in the box. I'd kept the last name Edwards for my form. Ambria had chosen Smith, a common name she hoped would not draw questions.

I looked around and noted the crowd had thinned considerably.

Ambria nudged me. "Look, it's Stephan."

I spotted his tall frame in the hall opposite of us. Though he'd been grateful for us saving him from the Goodleighs, he'd never been nice to me before, and I didn't much care to say hello. "What about Alice or Catherine?"

"I haven't seen them." Ambria regarded me with a raised eyebrow. "I suppose all you care about are the girls."

Her strange comment brought a confused frown to my face. "Why would you say that?"

She didn't answer and nodded her head to the left. "And there's our neighbor and his friends."

Harris, Baxter, and Lily sat on a bench against the wall. Harris didn't look the least bit worried. I wondered if he placed too much faith in the prophecy about him. "They look bored," I said.

"Shh," Max said. "The professor is about to talk again."

I looked toward the podium and caught a hard look from the professor. She seemed to be waiting for us to be quiet. After a long uncomfortable moment of staring at us, she turned to the others and spoke. "Those of you who are here for the master's entrance exam will report to Colossus Stadium."

At this, the older children filtered away, leaving those who looked close to my age. Harris caught my eye and waved. I waved back. Baxter looked at his friend, then glared at me, as if I were a grave danger to their relationship.

Other children glanced from me to Harris, their eyes jealous. I suddenly realized how crowded it was near the other boy, as if he unconsciously attracted other people. I then noticed how other students tried to engage Harris in conversation, like fans trying to speak to celebrities they idolized. Harris seemed politely disinterested in whatever they said.

"That's Harris Ashmore," a nearby girl told her friends. "He is so cool."

"He's dreamy," said another girl. "Maybe if we stand next to him, he'll notice us."

Ambria groaned. "Well, we certainly know who the popular kid is."

A warm hand went over my eyes. "Guess who?" someone whispered in my ear.

"Blue, be quiet," Ambria hissed.

"Thanks for ruining it, Ambria."

The hand slipped away. I turned around to see Blue's sparkling eyes. "Did you just get here?"

She shook her head. "I couldn't find you in all these people."

"If you would kindly remain silent," the professor said.

I gulped and gave her a sheepish smile.

Max nudged me in the ribs and hid a grin behind his hand.

"You're cute when you're embarrassed," Blue whispered from directly behind me.

I stiffened and felt my face turn red hot.

Professor Trask kept her eyes trained on me and made the next announcement. "Those here for the changeling courses, please report to the Burrows."

"Where are those?" Blue asked the professor in a panicked voice.

"If you cannot find your way through the university, then you have already failed the exam," the professor replied in a calm voice.

I looked around and saw a group of children heading down a hall. "Quick, Blue, follow them."

She followed my gaze and smiled. "My hero." With that, she bounded after the others.

When I turned around, I found the steely gaze of Professor Trask bearing down on me. She silently reached into the sleeve of her robes and withdrew a tall stack of yellowed envelopes.

A young girl wearing black clothes and a short pointy hat raised her hand. "What about the entrance exam for witch's school?"

The similarly dressed boy next to her thrust his hand into the air. "And warlock school?"

"There is no separate exam for those minors," the professor replied.

"Minors?" The girl looked horrified. "I thought we could major in witchcraft here."

The boy's lips peeled into a sneer. "This blows."

The professor smiled pleasantly. "Well in that case, perhaps you'd like to leave." She pointed down the hall. "The doors are there."

The girl sniffed loudly and looked as if she wanted to cry. The boy threw his arm over her shoulder. She flinched and slipped away from him.

"Goodness, I hope they pass the exam," Ambria said softly. "They'll provide plenty of entertainment."

"Shush," Max hissed. "You don't want to get on Trask's bad side."

The professor waited for a moment, eyebrow raised expectantly at the hopeful witch, and finally returned her attention to the envelopes. "Malcolm, if you please."

Max glanced back with surprise as his uncle appeared pushing a levitating cart loaded with a large brass globe on a pedestal. The middle-aged man's lips curled back into what seemed like a permanent scowl, casting ugly wrinkles across his face. Frizzy white-blond hair shot in all directions from his balding head, and he walked with a discernable limp.

"Hey look, it's Cryberius's loser uncle," Baxter shouted.

Children burst into laughter. The scowl on Malcom's face deepened, but he looked at the ground and kept his silence.

Professor Trask's eyes hardened. "That is quite enough, Mr. Troy."

Max hid his face. Ambria put a hand on his back. "Don't listen to that loser, Max."

I glared at Baxter and wished the professor would punish him somehow.

Vic spoke in my mind. *Kill the worthless wretch.* His words sent a chill down my spine.

Our son is too weak, Della scoffed.

I tried to shake off the ill feeling those words planted in my stomach, but their voices seemed to be gaining strength in my head. When I'd been cursed, dark impulses seized me and foreign emotions invaded my mind. With the curse gone, my parents' souls were like having little horned devils on both shoulders. Thankfully, Cora was my angel. Memories of the love of my foster mother kept me strong.

The professor tapped her wand to the globe, and a round portal opened on the side. Malcolm placed the envelopes inside and the professor closed the hole. Max's uncle turned a handle on the pedestal. The globe spun. He released the handle and the contraption slowed to a halt. A bell rang and an envelope slid from a slit in the pedestal and hung halfway out.

Professor Trask pointed to the envelope. "The envelopes contain your exam instructions. You are not to discuss anything within the envelope with any other student. If you do so, you will be given a failing mark. If you decide to quit in the middle of an exercise, simply tap your wand against the top corner and say, 'I am a failure.'" Her lips flattened. "You may then drop your exam with me and leave." She pointed to the first envelope. "Now, which brave soul will take the first envelope?"

Harris Ashmore leapt to the fore.

"How appropriate." Trask smiled. "Good luck, Mr. Ashmore."

"Thank you, professor." He broke the wax seal on the envelope and withdrew a parchment. I found myself craning my neck along with the other students for a glimpse of what was on the paper, but from here, it looked blank.

"I'm going next," Max grumbled. He headed toward the globe, but Baxter beat him there and took the second envelope. Lily smiled at him as he reached for the third envelope. With a loud sigh, he motioned her ahead of him.

Lily curtsied. "Thank you, Max."

"Well, at least he was polite," Ambria said softly. She gripped my arm tightly. "I'm so nervous I want to throw up, Conrad."

I swallowed a hard knot in my throat. "Me too. I didn't think I'd feel like this."

Max finally got his envelope, opened it, and took out the letter. His face went pale. He looked at us and waved, before vanishing down one of the hallways.

Ambria's grip tightened. "He looked terrified."

I patted her hands, hoping she'd loosen the death grip on my arm. "You'll do fine."

"I can't bear waiting anymore. The suspense is awful!" Ambria rushed to the globe and took the next envelope just before Stephan reached it. He gave her a puzzled look as she ripped it open. Her mouth fell open as she read the contents.

I waved at her, but she seemed to enter a trance and stumbled down the opposite hall.

Now that I was alone, I felt rather eager to get started. Instead, I seemed unable to make myself move toward the globe. The crowd dwindled until I was the last person there.

"Well, I don't have all day, boy," Trask said.

I unlocked my limbs and headed for the final envelope. Anxiety wrapped its thorny tendrils around my chest. My heartbeat grew louder the closer I grew to the slip of paper containing my fate. *Why am I so nervous?* It made no sense at all, unless it had something to do with my parents. Then again, this was a milestone in my life. If I passed this hurdle, it would open me up to a world impossible to imagine just months ago.

Instead of being a nothing, I could become a fully functional member of society. Instead of relying on others for charity, I would forge my own path. *Assuming my parents don't take over the world in the meantime.* Thinking of that real and present danger melted the ice in my stomach, and killed the constricting dread in my chest. This exam was nothing compared to what I'd been through.

Pass or fail, I'll find a way to survive.

I snatched the envelope.

"I can tell you're a procrastinator," the professor said. "I doubt you'll pass with a lackadaisical attitude like that."

"Bloody good-for-nothing kids," Malcolm said.

A smiled tugged my lips. I looked at her and said, "Thanks, professor. I'll try to improve."

The rise of a single eyebrow expressed her doubt.

I walked a distance from the globe and broke the wax seal on the envelope. Heart racing, I peeled it open and withdrew the parchment. At first, the page looked blank. Suddenly, ink crawled across and just as quickly vanished. I was just about to turn around and ask the professor about it when a single sentence appeared.

Report to classroom XIII.

I had no idea where that was, so I walked down the hallway until I was out of sight of the professor. Digging in my pocket, I retrieved my arcphone and turned on the Arcane University map app. "Phone, where is room thirteen in Arcane University?"

"Please follow these directions," the phone said, and displayed a map of the interior. I followed a blue line on the map further along the hall, through a door, and down several flights of stairs. At least a dozen doors lined the sides of the corridor at the bottom. Though none had numbers on them, the phone seemed to know where to go. I stopped next to the door and opened it. Pitch black waited on the other side.

I stepped inside and fumbled on the wall for a light switch. The door creaked and slammed shut. Before I could cry out in alarm, a bright light blinded me. I staggered backward and felt cloth against my back. I grabbed at it, but it tore loose and I fell to the floor, the cloth falling over my head.

When I freed myself, I blinked in confusion. Beeps from heart monitors echoed around me. An old man in a rollaway hospital bed stared blankly at me. The cloth, I realized, was a privacy curtain.

I climbed to my feet and backed away. "Sorry, sir."

The old man didn't answer. A thin stream of drool hung from his open mouth. Though his eyes were open, he didn't seem to be conscious. I turned for the door and bumped into a man in a white coat.

"Ah, there you are," he said. "Follow me."

The man looked terribly familiar, but I couldn't place him. "Is this part of the test?" I asked.

He ignored me and continued down a hall, past rooms filled with patients. An eerie sense of déjà vu spread through me. *Have I been here before?* It wasn't possible, of course. I'd only barely seen parts of the university. The man stopped outside a door and pointed inside. "I'm afraid she doesn't have much time."

What I saw inside stole the breath from me.

Chapter 7

"Mummy?" I rushed to Cora's bedside.

She tried to lift a frail arm, but the effort was too much. Cancer had stolen her strength and the glow of vitality, leaving behind a shadow of the woman I'd known and loved as my only real mother. "My good boy is growing up." She smiled.

Tears blurred my vision. I buried my faced in the crook of her neck. "Please don't die, Mummy. Please don't leave me alone."

"There's nothing more we can do for her," the doctor said.

She's going to die. I stiffened. *Wait, I can use magic now. I can save her!* I stood and looked down at the phone. "Phone, is there a spell to cure cancer?"

The phone displayed a list of results and recited the top one. "A skilled healer is required to counteract serious diseases, including cancer."

"Where is the nearest healer?" I asked, thinking of the one I'd met in the healing ward.

The screen garbled and went blank. I tried turning it back on, but it wouldn't respond. *I have to find the exit and bring back a healer!* Before I could leave, Cora grasped my hand.

"There's nothing you can do, son," she said in a hoarse whisper. "Death makes us all powerless."

I pulled out my wand. "No, I refuse to be powerless." *Help me heal her,* I sent to my parents' soul fragments.

She is weak and worthless, Della said. *Let her die.*

Vic pshawed. *Only the strong survive.*

I hate you! I HATE YOU! Tears ran down my face. I wiped them away furiously and tried to come up with something to help Cora. I gripped her hand and kissed it. "Please hold on, Mummy. Give me some time."

"There is no more time." She smiled. "Sometimes, there is no answer and you have to accept the inevitable." She gripped the necklace she always wore and rubbed her lucky green pebble at the end. Its luck had run out.

Chest shaking with sobs, I pressed her hand to my heart. "You will never die as long as I'm alive, Mummy. I will always keep you alive here."

Tears trickled down her cheeks. "I know, sweet boy. Finding you was the best decision I ever made."

I wiped my eyes. "Finding me?"

She looked toward the nightstand next to her bed. I saw a picture of us at a carnival. "If you are ever lonely, think of me, and I'll be there, my dear Conrad." Her body slumped, and the light faded from her eyes.

"No," I whimpered. "Please, not again."

"It's time to go, boy," said a flat emotionless voice behind me. I spun and saw Mr. Goodleigh standing in the doorway. Rage burned through the sorrow. I held up my wand and snarled, "I'll never go with you!"

The room grew brighter and brighter until I had to squeeze my eyes shut against the glare. I staggered back, expecting to feel Cora's bed behind me. Instead, there was nothing. When I blinked away the spots in my vision, I stood in a dim room, empty except for a glowing blue sphere on a pedestal.

Using the hem of my shirt, I dried my eyes and looked at the room. There were no mirrors or alcoves for anyone to hide in, but I still shouted, "Who's here? What just happened to me?"

No one answered.

It occurred to my sorrow-stricken mind that this had been some sort of test. Whoever designed it was sick in the head.

A new message appeared on the instruction sheet. *Report to Gauntlet Room IV.*

My phone functioned once again, so I used it to navigate my way. It took me further down the hallway and up a flight of stairs to a wide circular room with arched open doorways. Several students stood in the middle looking at the numbers over each door. I spotted mine and went down the tunnel.

The gauntlet room at the end stretched nearly fifty yards wide, divided into sections by stone walls. Other children were already using most of the stations, so I got in a line and waited my turn. It was evident from the candles what I was supposed to do here. When my turn came the parchment told me to ignite and blow out the candle. I quickly did so and stepped away for the next in line to take their turn.

Go to the upper examination hall.

Following my phone's instructions, I wended through the passageways and arrived at a large room lined with desks. A tall thin man with black hair, matching robe, and a dour expression handed me a scroll. I recognized him at once. *Professor Gideon Grace.*

"Put your name at the top of the exam, complete it, and proceed to your next destination," he said in a bored tone. His eyes narrowed. "Haven't I seen you before?"

I'd seen him at Chicken Little, a restaurant in Queens Gate. He'd rescued a man attacked by Max's twin brothers, Rhys and Devon. I shook my head. "No, sir, I don't think so."

"Hmm." He turned and picked up another scroll for an incoming student, so I quickly made my way to a desk near the back before he remembered me.

Lily looked up from her test and smiled. I returned a half-hearted smile, nodded, and took a desk. The exam was simple enough, asking questions straight from the study guide my friends and I had used. I completed it within an hour and set it in a bin on the professor's desk. Professor Grace was busy handing out scrolls to more students, so I exited the room before he asked me again who I was.

The instruction parchment handed me the easiest task yet. *Go to the dinner hall and eat lunch.*

I went there and looked for my friends, but they weren't anywhere to be found. Someone touched my shoulder. I jumped to the side and saw a merry smile on Blue's face.

"Are you done?" she asked.

I shrugged. "I don't know. The instructions told me to come eat."

"Then let's eat." She sat at an empty table and I joined her.

"Did you have to take a test?" I asked her.

Blue nodded. "I had to change into a wolf." She shrugged. "It was easy." Her eyes widened. "There were two felycan kids who changed into big cats. I never met one of those before."

"Were they nice?" I leaned back as a golem placed covered plates in front of us.

She lifted the cover and licked her lips at the sight of the juicy pork cutlet beneath. "Oh, they were a little stand-offish, but I've heard felycans are like that."

I cut into the pork with a knife and savored the first bite. "Were there other lycans?"

"Oh, yes, a lot." She gnawed on a stalk of asparagus. "Groups of kids from different packs."

I considered my next question and hoped it wasn't impolite. "What exactly do they teach to lycans? You already know how to change, right? Is there more to it?"

Blue swallowed and nodded. "Sure. Most lycans are born that way, but older ones can turn people into one of us. There's also the possibility that some of us can learn to be free-changers."

"Free changers? You mean like different animal forms?"

"Yep." She jabbed a fork into the meat and bit off a chunk. "One of the professors here can do that."

I considered the possibilities. "Can he look like other humans?"

Blue stopped chewing for a moment. "I suppose so." She shrugged. "But why would you want to do that when you could shift into a bird?"

I'd change my face so my parents couldn't find me. "I still don't understand where all the extra mass goes when someone shape shifts. Matter is neither created nor destroyed, so where does it go?"

That drew a long silence and confused look from her.

"I'm sorry, I think that was something from my father's knowledge." It wasn't. I'd studied science nearly as much as magic.

"Magic doesn't always make sense," Blue finally said. "You just have to accept that it's not science and deal with it."

I smiled. "Sure."

"You're really smart, though," Blue said with a smile. "And you're strong." She touched my arm. "I'll bet there aren't any other kids who could beat a whole gang of vampires like you did."

Not many other kids carry around parts of their evil parents' souls either. "I'm not really that strong."

"I wish the lycan kids were as nice as you." She sighed and stabbed her fork in the asparagus. "Sometimes I wonder if I'll ever find a place to fit in."

"You fit in just fine with us," I assured her.

She put her head on my shoulder, unaware a piece of asparagus was stuck in her teeth. "Do you really mean that?"

My face grew warm. "Y-yes."

"Ahem!"

I looked up and saw Ambria standing across the table from us, arms akimbo. "I see you started lunch without me, Conrad."

"But you weren't here," I said. "I didn't know how long you'd be."

"Did you even wait a moment before sitting down?" She dropped into the chair to my left. "It doesn't matter. I suppose you have a new best friend now."

"You sound cranky," Blue said to her. "I think you're just hungry." She took a slice of bread. "Would you like me to put some jam on this for you?"

Ambria leaned forward and looked past me at Blue. "While you and the other shifters frolicked around, I was put through a distressing psychological test and a written exam."

"Um, I'm done eating," I said and pushed my chair back from the table, desperate to get out of there.

Ambria grabbed left hand. "Conrad, stay. I could use some company during lunch."

Blue stood and clasped my right hand. "Would you like to take a walk? It's lovely outside."

I froze and stared at the instruction sheet on the table, praying it would give me new instructions. When it didn't, I decided to change the subject entirely. "Have you seen Max?"

Ambria frowned. "Yes, I saw him enter the examination hall when I was leaving. He said he had to wait in a long line for the gauntlet room."

"Me too," I said, praying the girls didn't feel the sweat breaking out on the palms of my hands.

She frowned. "That awful Baxter boy came in behind him and started throwing insults at him, but Professor Grace didn't say a thing about it."

"Gideon Grace hates Max's family," I said. "He told me so."

"How about that walk?" Blue asked, squeezing my hand.

I struggled for something more to say, when I noticed the instruction paper finally changed.

Report to the Underground.

Repressing a cheer, I freed my hands and reached for the sheet. "Well, it looks like I have another test to take."

"The Underground?" Ambria's forehead wrinkled. "I don't recall reading about that."

"I can help you find it," Blue said.

"No, that's all right." I held up my phone. "This should take me there."

"Wish I had a phone," Ambria said. "I've had to use the paper maps."

"If only you had a good sense of smell," Blue told her.

Ambria smiled sweetly. "It's certainly strong enough to know when someone stinks."

I sidestepped from between them and made a hasty retreat into the hallway. My phone guided me up a winding staircase, which seemed the wrong direction for a place named Underground, but long ago someone had taken great pleasure in designing the university with misdirection in mind. It suddenly occurred to me that I was no longer going up, but descending, even though I hadn't detected a change in the staircase. I turned around and backtracked until I felt gravity shift ever so slightly.

Upon closer inspection, I saw the stairs ended at a gap. I got down on my knees and peered over the edge to see the bottom of the stairs. Harris Ashmore walked into view and I swayed with disorientation. He was walking upside down on the bottom of the stairs!

He saw my face and his mouth dropped open. "Where's the rest of your body?"

At this point, I didn't know which way was up. "I'm under the stairs I think."

Harris stopped at the gap and we looked up—or down?—at each other for a moment. He took another step forward and his body swept around to my side so we were both beneath the stairs.

"That was unexpected," he said.

"This place is so confusing." I stood up. "Are you headed to the Underground as well?"

He nodded and showed me a paper map with a moving black dot and an arrow. "Well, now I know I had to go up to go down."

"Or left to go right," I added with a smile. "A mischievous person built this place."

He started down the stairs. "Someday, I'll be Arcanus Primus, and I plan to have the university rebuilt so it's not so confusing."

I walked beside him. "That might make it boring."

Harris raised an eyebrow. "Order is not boring."

"Yes, but you need chaos sometimes to make you think differently," I said. "Otherwise, everything remains the same and you don't try new things."

"All chaos ever brought me was death and destruction," Harris said. "The Overlord was the master of chaos. When I come into power, I'll make rules so nothing like that happens again."

Rules hadn't kept my father from destroying the Overworld government, but I kept quiet about it. Harris didn't seem like the sort who listened to other people's ideas when they differed from his own.

Harris looked at me and smiled. "If you're loyal to me, I'll make sure you're part of the new order, Conrad." He punched me in the shoulder. "We'll eradicate evil in our time."

I stumbled sideways, caught off guard by the "friendly" punch. "That would be spectacular," I told him.

The staircase ended in a stone corridor with a red brick path that once again challenged my sense of direction by corkscrewing up the wall and to the ceiling where it straightened. Harris came to a halt, but I kept on following the path, eager to find the test so I could leave his company. Despite my expectation of falling off the wall, the press of gravity never left my shoulders, keeping me firmly attached to the brick path. I reached the ceiling and turned to look at Harris who watched me with a strange expression.

"Are you coming?" I asked.

His face a bit pale, Harris stepped forward. "I don't like this one bit," he said. "I don't even know where the ground is anymore."

I shrugged. "Someone recently told me that magic doesn't have to make scientific sense, you just have to deal with it."

He took tentative steps forward. When he reached the curve up the wall, his foot slipped off it. He tried to walk up the wall again, but it didn't work.

"I don't understand." He said. "I can't do it."

"Why don't you walk underneath me and I'll pull you up?" I said.

Harris walked beneath me and held up his hand, but our fingers were a few feet apart.

"We'll have to jump at the same time," I told him.

He nodded. "One, two, three."

We jumped. Our hands met and we held on tight. Instead of me pulling him to my floor, we hung in midair, suspended.

"It's not working," Harris said in a strained voice.

My fingers slipped. "I can't hold on anymore."

"Me either." He lost his grip and we dropped back to our respective floors.

Movement caught my peripheral vision. I looked down the corridor toward the stairs and recoiled at what I saw. Snakes, snakes, everywhere—so many it appeared the floor itself crawled. A cobra reared up and spread its hood, answering my next question—were the snakes poisonous? Clearly, yes.

Harris cried out and backed down the corridor, but the susurrus of slithering reptiles emanated from corridor beyond. Snakes in front, snakes behind.

He was trapped.

Chapter 8

I ran back down the path to him. As before, gravity shifted and held me to the path until I was on his ground.

"This doesn't make any sense!" Harris ran up the wall and slid back down over and over again like a hamster in a wheel. "Where did all these snakes come from?"

I thought back to our earlier conversation about order versus chaos. "Do you believe more in science or magic?"

He looked up at me. "My mother was a scientist and my father was an Arcane. I believe in both."

"Yes, but which did you feel more comfortable with?" I calculated the snakes would be here in less than a minute and desperately thought of a way to help him up the wall.

Harris's eyes narrowed. "What are you getting at?"

Heart thudding, I rushed my words. "You don't seem to trust magic much."

His lips curled into a snarl, and he seemed to forget the snakes. "Magic killed my parents."

"If you're to be the savior of the world, what will you use to fight evil?"

His lips tightened. "Magic, most likely.

I raised my eyebrows. "Even if you don't trust it?"

"Well…" he didn't finish his sentence.

Walking up the wall had to be part of the test. You had to trust magic enough to walk up a wall; otherwise, you didn't deserve to study at the university. But were the snakes part of the test, or had my parents seized another opportunity to attack me? Somehow, I had to make him believe that he could walk up the wall. I could only think of one way to motivate him.

The river of snakes was only seconds away from surrounding us.

"Your parents died in vain, Harris."

Anger simmered in his eyes. "What did you say?"

"I said your parents died in vain if you don't turn around and walk up that wall." I pushed him in the chest. "If you don't believe in your future, then you should let the snakes eat you for all I care."

"I will not die here," he shouted.

"You don't believe in the prophecy, do you?" I pushed him again. "Your parents died for nothing. The prophecy is false."

"Don't you say that about my parents!" He shoved me back. "I'm supposed to save the world. I can do anything!" With that, he turned and walked right up the wall and to the ceiling. Face red and breathing heavy, he looked down at me. "See?"

I ran up the wall to join him and watched as the snakes completely covered the floor where we'd been. "That was close."

Harris pressed his lips together and stared at me. The red faded from his cheeks, and his breathing calmed. "Thank you, Conrad. For a minute, I forgot who I am and how important I'll be to everyone."

That wasn't exactly the lesson I hoped he'd learn. "What's important is that you never give up."

"Look, they're gone," Harris said.

The corridor was empty once again. The snakes had been an illusion.

He grinned and patted my shoulder. "Let's find out what's at the end of this tunnel."

I was more than happy to move on. We reached another twist in the brick path that took us back to what I assumed was the actual floor. At the end stood a closed wooden door with a black iron handle. My instruction sheet offered no more direction, so I reached forward and opened the door. On the other side was a short but wide hall with a room at the end. In the center of the room stood a table with a plate bearing two slices of cake with red frosting.

A wooden sign hanging on the wall to our right gave us the next objective.

Enjoy a slice of cake.

The door creaked shut behind us. I tugged on it, but it wouldn't budge.

"Well, I guess we can't go back," Harris said.

I wasn't sure if he and I were supposed to do this together, but since there were two slices of cake, I assumed it was okay. "I suppose not."

"Hmm, I wonder if that cake will do something to us," Harris said.

I thought back to books I'd read. "Maybe it will shrink us so we can walk through a tiny doorway."

His forehead wrinkled. "I don't see a tiny door on the other side of the room." He motioned me on. "Let's go get the cake."

"Wait." I grabbed his arm. "It might be a trap."

"Like the snakes?" He snorted. "This time we'll know anything that comes at us is fake."

"I doubt they'll use the same trick twice." I knelt and examined the floor and the walls to make sure they weren't booby-trapped, but didn't see anything suspicious. Putting my eye level to the floor, I tried to see if any bricks rose higher than the others since I didn't want to step on a pressure plate. But after staring across the floor, nothing obvious stuck out.

Harris raised an eyebrow. "Well?"

"Everything looks normal—well, at least for this place."

He stepped forward. "Let's go."

I followed his lead. At first, nothing stood out of the ordinary until I realized it was taking us longer than expected to reach the end of the hall. "Is it my imagination, or are we not getting any closer to the cake?"

Harris broke into a run and I hurried to follow. The end of the hallway remained tantalizingly close, but we weren't closing the gap. I looked at the floor to see if we were on a conveyer belt, but the red brick path looked no different than before.

Panting, Harris stopped and I ran into him. We both sprawled on the floor, chests heaving.

"What's happening?" the other boy said breathlessly.

I sucked in a breath. "It's like a dream where you run as fast as you can, but don't go anywhere." Closing my eyes, I hoped for some insight from my parents, but their soul shards remained quiet. *Think, Conrad.* The goal was the cake, but walking toward it kept it out of reach. I propped on my elbows and looked behind us. The door remained twenty feet in one direction. I glanced toward the cake and estimated it seemed only slightly farther away.

"Maybe directly approaching the room is the issue." I stood up. "Let's walk away from it and see what happens."

Harris pushed himself up. "I'm willing to try anything at this point."

We walked to the door and tugged on it again. It remained locked.

"Any other bright ideas?" the other boy said.

I came up with one. "Let's walk backwards and not look at the cake."

"Backwards?" He groaned and threw up his hands. "Fine."

"How far does that look?" I asked.

"About fifty paces." Harris shrugged. "Let's count our steps."

I nodded and turned away from the room. "Remember, don't look back."

"I won't."

Keeping our eyes on the door, we walked backwards. "One, two, three," we counted, putting distance between us and the door.

"I think it's working!" Harris said.

I wasn't ready to congratulate myself just yet. Once we hit about twenty paces, the door remained the same distance. We took a hundred steps back but failed to enter the room and even worse, failed to get a piece of cake.

Harris blew out an angry breath and looked back. "It didn't work."

I paced back and forth, but couldn't figure out the puzzle.

"I just want to leave," Harris whined. "This is a stupid test. I'll bet the cake tastes bad anyway." He continued to gripe, and I let him, trying to sort this out in my head.

I looked down at the red brick path. It continued straight to the room. Earlier this test had forced us to stay on a marked route. But now it wasn't leading us where we needed to go. *What if we aren't supposed to stay on the path anymore?* "Step off the red bricks," I said and walked onto the bare stone to the side of the pathway.

"This is a waste of time." Harris rolled his eyes and stepped to the side with me.

We walked forward, but still remained stuck in place. I was about to join Harris's complaints with my own when I thought about the earlier part of the trial. I looked at the wall. *Maybe we have to go farther off the path.* I put a foot on the wall and stepped forward with my other one. I grinned as gravity shifted and let me stand on the wall.

Harris gasped. "But there's no path up there."

"I think that's the point." I pointed toward the door. "Back there, the test made us stay on the path, but sometimes, you have to leave it. Sometimes you have to take your own way."

"I am Harris Ashmore, son of prophecy," the other boy said, and stepped up the wall. He stood beside me and belted a laugh. "We're gonna get that cake."

We walked all the way up to the ceiling and continued toward the room at the end. This time, we reached it. I walked across the ceiling behind the cake and strode down the wall. Harris and I reached the floor and stood two steps from the goal.

He took a deep breath. "Here goes." Harris reached forward and touched the table.

"Yes!" I shouted. Hesitantly, I reached for a slice of cake and took it. It smelled heavenly and looked so moist.

Harris took his slice and held it up. "Here's to having our cake and eating it too."

"Cheers," I said with a grin. *I hope this cake doesn't do something terrible to us.* I took a bite and moaned with pleasure. "It's so sweet." Every bite melted in my mouth like strawberry ice cream. I finished it off regrettably fast.

Harris swallowed his last bit and brushed crumbs from his mouth. "I was wrong. The cake is really tasty."

A click and a creak echoed behind us. We turned and saw a door that hadn't been there before open into a brightly lit room. I retrieved my instruction sheet from my pocket.

Congratulations, you've completed the test. Proceed to the main hall and await your results.

Harris showed me the same message on his parchment. He pumped a fist. "We did it, Conrad! We won!"

We were finished with the test, but that didn't necessarily mean we'd passed. I kept that thought to myself. Harris and I stepped through the doorway and found ourselves back in the main hall near the front entrance to the university. Disoriented, I turned back around and saw only a small closet through the doorway.

Harris and I exchanged confused looks.

"Magic," Harris said with a shrug.

I nodded. "Magic."

Dozens of other students sat in the hall, some of them looking downcast while others laughed and talked excitedly with their friends. I didn't see Max or Ambria. Then again, they were probably only now taking the path trial.

Harris clapped me on the shoulder. "I was wrong, Conrad." He flashed his teeth. "I think we can be good friends."

Lily walked around the corner and saw us. "You're done!"

"Just now," Harris said. He nudged my arm. "Conrad here saved the day."

"Oh?" Her eyes grew curious. "Do tell."

"Well, you know, the path test," he said.

Her forehead pinched. "Path test?"

Harris nodded. "You know, where you have to walk on the ceiling, and the snakes come, but you get delicious cake at the end."

"I didn't take that test," she replied. "I had to carry a candle through a windy room without it going out."

"Hmm." Harris shrugged. "That sounds hard."

"Couldn't you just hold your hand over the candle?" I asked.

She giggled. "No, silly. The wind shifted in every direction at random."

I tried to imagine the situation. "Did you have anything to enclose the flame?"

"Nope." She bounced on her heels. "Guess again."

"Well, it's rather hard to do that without more information." I considered the path trial. "What happened on your way to that room? Were there other features of the room that might help you?"

"Conrad's brilliant," Harris said. "He came up with ideas I never would have considered."

"He's definitely a thinker," Lily said. She tapped a finger to her lips. "Well, I had to escape a maze of rotating tubes before I reached the windy room."

"Were the tubes movable?" I asked.

She tilted her head slightly. "Yes...how did you—"

"You moved the tubes from one room into the windy room and placed them in a row." This time, my father's knowledge filled in the gaps. "When the tubes rotated, they redirected the air using the Magnus effect."

"Wow." Lilly stared at me. "I'm speechless, Conrad. I studied everything before this exam, even Science Academy texts. That's how I figured out what to do."

"Well, the Magnus effect seems like magic, but it's actually science." I smiled. "I studied the Science Academy texts too."

"Amazing." Lily shook her head slowly. "I was going to use the tubes to make a wall, but there weren't enough of them to block both sides of the path. That was when I remembered how spinning cylinders or spheres affect airflow."

Harris put a hand on my shoulder. "I don't think we met on accident, Conrad. I think this is fate."

"I agree," Lily said. "I haven't met many people as smart as me."

While I appreciated the compliment, it seemed that Lily and Harris were a bit full of themselves. Lily was obviously smart, but it felt like she'd talked down to me with that comment.

"What's going on out here?" Baxter, red faced and dripping in slime stepped out of the closet Harris and I had exited. Behind him emerged a slimy, frustrated Ambria.

"Whoa, what was your final test?" Harris asked.

Ambria growled and glared at Baxter. "We had to defeat a giant frog. How I ended up in the same test as him, I'll never know."

"Defeat a frog?" I asked. "Did you have to kill it?"

"It was blocking the door," Baxter said. "We couldn't move it, and when we cast spells at the bleeding thing, it smacked us with its tongue."

Lily burst into giggles. "How did you beat it?"

"You crawled through it, didn't you?" I said. "That's why you're slimy."

Harris chortled. "Like I said, genius!"

Baxter narrowed his eyes. "Yes, you wanker, we had to crawl into its mouth and out its bum. The next thing I saw was your ugly mug when the door opened."

"We had delicious cake when we solved our puzzle," Harris said. "It was the best cake ever."

Ambria stomped her foot. "You got cake?" She held up her arms. "Look at me, Conrad! Just look at me! I'm covered in filth. If anyone deserves cake right now, it's me."

"You two stink," Harris said. "You deserve a bath."

Ambria scowled and stiffened her shoulders. "Maybe you deserve a hug."

"No." Harris held up his hands in surrender. "I don't want one."

"Well, you're going to get one." Ambria ran at him.

He dashed around the group, gripping Lily's arms and hiding behind her. "Stop!" He burst into laughter as Ambria dodged back and forth. "Stop it!"

Before long, we were all laughing at their antics. Ambria flicked her fingers and sprayed Lily and Harris with slime, then crossed her arms and glared at them. "Fine, I won't hug you."

That brought on another round of laughter.

I saw Max exit a door on the opposite side of the hall. He flinched when he noticed Harris and the others, but I motioned him over.

"Hey," he said in a meek voice. "Are you all finished?"

Baxter sneered. "What was your test, Cryberius?"

Ambria slapped the unpleasant ginger on the shoulder. "His name is Max, you rude boy."

"Well, I had to walk through a dark room filled with monsters," Max said.

Only then did I realize how pale his face looked. "How do you know there were monsters in there?" I asked.

"They grabbed me, and some of them bit me." He shrugged. "Every time I tried to illuminate using my wand, this scary white lizard would bite my ankle until I put it out."

"How awful," Ambria said. "Is your ankle okay?"

He nodded. "They didn't bite hard."

"I'll bet you cried and wet your pants," Baxter said.

Max stared at him. "I can tell you that after walking through a pitch black room of horrors, I'm not afraid to admit how scared I was." A wan smiled touched his lips. "When I reached the door on the other side, the lights came on and nothing was there."

"Not even the white lizard?" Ambria said.

He shrugged. "There were holes in the walls, so I guess all the monsters went in there." Max shivered. "I certainly wasn't going to look in those holes."

Rhona Trask appeared alongside Gideon Grace and began calling out names and handing out envelopes.

"Conrad Edwards," Grace said.

I walked over and took the envelope. "Thank you, sir."

He didn't reply and handed out more envelopes. Before long, most of us had an envelope. Lily tore hers open the instant she received it. Her eyes lit.

"I passed! I'm in!" She jumped up and clapped her hands.

"Me too," Harris said as if it couldn't have gone differently.

Baxter stared at his envelope and finally opened it. The resulting smirk told everyone he'd passed, but he still held up the card inside. *Passed.*

Ambria let out a long sigh and slumped. "I did it, Conrad." She wiped a tear from her eye. "I passed."

I looked long and hard at mine. *Surely if Harris passed, then so did I.*

"Tiberius," Gideon Grace called in a condescending tone.

Max gulped and went to retrieve his envelope. He walked back over, gripping it tight enough to make his knuckles go white.

"Well, aren't you going to open it?" Baxter said.

I broke the wax seal on mine and looked inside. It did not say *Passed*, nor did it say *Failed*. Instead it bore the word *Exemplary*.

Baxter snatched Max's envelope from him and held it out of reach. "What's the matter, Cryberius? Afraid to see if you made it?"

Ambria stomped Baxter's foot. "Give it back!"

Baxter yelped and jumped back. "You're so mean!"

"I'm mean?" Ambria sounded absolutely indignant. "You're the mean one, Baxter. Now give Max his envelope."

"Fine," Baxter sneered. He opened the envelope, took out the card, and tossed the envelope to Max. He looked at the card and howled with laughter. "Oh, this is brilliant!" Baxter turned the card for us to see. *Failed.*

Ambria's mouth dropped open. Max's eyes went dead. He turned and ran away without another word.

Chapter 9

"I wish I could turn you into a roach and squish you," Ambria said to Baxter in a low hiss.

"That was mean," Lily said and shook her head. "Boys are just awful sometimes."

"It was hilarious," Baxter said. "Besides, the Tiberiuses should be banished from the Overworld."

"They supported the Overlord," Harris said in a quiet voice. "I think they should all be jailed and executed."

"Max never did anything to anyone," Ambria said. "Come on, Conrad. Let's go."

"Conrad, why don't you come with us?" Harris put an arm on my shoulder. "We could use someone really smart as a friend."

My heart felt light with joy. These were the kids everyone wanted to be friends with, and now they wanted me to be part of their group. *I'm special!*

Ambria looked at me with disbelief. "Well, I guess you have new friends now." She ran after Max.

"Why would you two hang out with that loser?" Baxter said.

"Let's go get some more cake," Harris said. "I know a great place that always gives me free food."

"Lily frowned. "Baxter, I can't believe you did that to poor Max."

"Poor Max?" Baxter snorted. "Don't feel bad for that loser."

A part of me desperately wanted to go with them, but a gut feeling told me it would be a mistake. The path trial had told me a great deal about Harris Ashmore. For one thing, he gave up easily. Instead of passing the test on his own merits, he planned to use his connections to get a passing grade. Plus, his best friend, Baxter, was a mean-spirited bully. Lily seemed nice enough even if she liked to brag about her intelligence.

"Well, are you coming?" Harris said.

"Exemplary?" Baxter snatched my card from me. "What's this mean?"

Lily's eyes widened and she snatched it from Baxter. "The last person to receive an exemplary was—" she swallowed hard.

"Was who?" Harris said in a low voice.

Lily laughed nervously. "I thought I remembered, but I forgot."

"Is it something special?" Baxter asked.

"By its definition, exemplary is special," Lily replied, a hint of jealousy in her voice. Her eyes narrowed. "I'd be interested to see your written exam score, Conrad."

"Let's go, let's go," Harris said impatiently. "I want some more cake."

I took a step back. "Please go without me. I have to catch up with my friends."

Harris and the Baxter froze in place, eyes wide, mouths hanging open.

"We're your new friends," Harris said in a querulous voice.

"Maybe we can become friends," I said. "But Max and Ambria are my true friends, and if Baxter can't be nice, then I can't be friends with him."

"And to think I thought you were smart," Harris said. "Do you know how many people want to be our friends?"

"I want to be your friend." I looked at Baxter. "But Baxter is ruining it for you." Before they could reply, I turned and ran after Ambria and Max.

When I exited the building, I saw Ambria racing toward the forest near the cliff overlooking the valley and ran after her. When I finally caught up, she was already talking to Max.

"There you are," I said.

She flicked her head toward me. "I thought you were hanging out with your *new* friends."

I walked up to Ambria. "After all we've been through, what makes you think I'd abandon you just like that?"

Max grinned. "Well, hey, at least you get to be friends with a loser like me."

"You're not a loser, Max." I bit my lower lip and stared back at the university. "How do you think you did on the written exam?"

He shrugged. "I knew everything on there, or at least I thought I did." He shook his head. "I must've failed the psychological scenario, or done something wrong on the final trial."

"I assume you performed the candle test?" Ambria asked.

He nodded. "Took me two minutes."

"Something's not right." I motioned them to follow. "Let's ask to see your written test."

Blue stood outside the entrance. Her eyes brightened when she saw us and she loped over. "Hey, I was looking for you, Conrad."

I took a step back and gulped. "Oh? What about?"

She frowned. "I was looking around in the front hall for you when I heard that awful Baxter kid talking about Max."

Max looked down. "Yeah, he doesn't like me much."

"Oh, well it's worse than that." Her eyes darkened. "He said he switched your test for one he filled out with the wrong answers."

"He what?" Max shouted. "I'm going to beat the—"

"Maxwell Tiberius, you will not get into a fight," Ambria said. "Somehow we need to get your real test."

"That explains why he was following me so close when I went to turn in my test," Max said. "I heard him laughing when I left the room."

"Professor Grace didn't see him?" Ambria asked.

Max shook his head. "He was busy handing out tests to other students." A hiss escaped his clenched teeth. "I hate Baxter."

"Do you think he threw away the real test somewhere?" I asked Blue.

She quirked her lips. "Well, I didn't see him showing off anything to the others, so I'd bet he did."

"Oh no." Max's eyes widened. "We have to find the right rubbish bin before the golems empty it."

"Let's start at the classroom and look around," I said.

We dashed inside and found the first rubbish bin next to the examination room. I lifted off the lid and dug through the crumpled papers inside. We sorted through candy wrappers, soda bottles, and other odds and ends, but found no test papers inside.

Ambria looked up and down the hall. "Baxter probably went to eat next like the rest of us."

Max sighed. "Let's go."

The dining hall had two bins outside the door and none inside.

"I hope he didn't leave it on his dinner plate," Max said. "If he did, it's probably gone for good."

Blue sniffed around the containers. "I got Baxter's scent when I was close to him. I don't smell him on these containers."

"How can you tell his smell from the rest?" I said. "Dozens of students have been through here."

"He uses soap that smells like lilacs," she said.

Ambria wrinkled her nose. "Are you certain you didn't smell that on a girl? Boys don't use lilac-scented soap."

Blue nodded. "It's more than just the lavender smell I sense, but it's hard to explain to someone with an ordinary nose."

The other girl sniffed. "Well, I think my nose is just fine."

I heard rustling behind me and saw Max digging through one of the bins. "Nothing but bottles and this." He held up a crude doll with pins protruding from it. "An old voodoo doll."

"What an awful thing," Ambria said. She took it and examined it. "Do these actually work?"

Max nodded. "Sure, if you know what you're doing." His lips curled up. "I'd sure like to make a voodoo doll of Baxter and stick him with needles." He removed one from the doll and jammed in its backside. "How'd you like that, Baxter?"

I peered into the other rubbish container. "This one is almost empty." I shook my head. "No test."

"Told you," Blue said with a smirk. She lifted her nose and sniffed. "He went this way."

We followed our lycan friend down the hallway and through several turns before stopping near an arched doorway.

"This is where I found him before we went through our final test," Ambria said. "When he saw me, he gave me an awfully guilty look."

"Were you with him the rest of the time?" I asked.

She shook her head. "No, I gave him a dirty look and went into this door and up some stairs. A few minutes later I walked out of a door in another hallway and he came out of a room across from me."

"Odd," I said. "It's almost like the building made sure you two ended up taking the last test together."

"Kind of like you and Harris?" Ambria said.

I looked at our surroundings with increased suspicion. "What if this building is alive?"

Blue laughed, but Max nodded seriously. "I've heard some haunted houses are alive."

Ambria tentatively patted a wall. "Nice university."

I snorted. "Making friends?"

She sniffed. "Well, it certainly doesn't hurt. I don't want this building forcing me to see Baxter all the time."

Blue's nose twitched. She stalked down the hall to another arched doorway and peered inside. "There's a bin in here." She lifted the lid and poked around for a moment. "Aha!" She lifted a crumpled test with Max's name on it.

"My test!" Max took it and smoothed it out against the wall. His smile faded. "What if Professor Grace doesn't accept it?"

"He'll have to," I said. "Blue can be our witness."

Ambria clenched her fists. "That no-good little rat. Maybe we can get him expelled."

Max rolled up the test. "I'll just be happy to get a passing grade."

We returned to the main hall and found Gideon Grace still handing out envelopes. He looked down his nose at Max. "What are you doing here, boy? You failed."

Max held up his test. "No, I didn't. Baxter took an extra test and filled it out with wrong answers, then replaced mine with it."

Gideon snorted. "A likely story."

"We can prove it," I said. "Show us the failing test and compare it with Max's handwriting."

"Baxter Troy is a good lad, unlike Maxwell Tiberius," Grace said. "He would never do such a lowly thing."

"Then let us prove it," I said.

"Who do you think you are, talking to a professor that way?" Grace looked down his nose at me. "Despite your high mark, I could have you expelled before classes even begin."

"What's going on here?" Professor Trask stepped beside Grace. Her eyes flared when she saw me. "Ah, Mr. Edwards. Congratulations on your high mark. Quite an achievement, indeed."

"Young Tiberius claims another student switched his test with a fake," Grace scoffed.

"It's true, Professor Trask." Max held up his test. "Baxter Troy replaced this one with a fake and threw the real one away."

"A serious accusation," Trask said. She took Max's test and looked it over. "Come with me."

"This boy is desperate," Grace said. "The Tiberius family is well known for lying and scheming to get what they want."

"Yes, well, a simple handwriting examination should clear this right up," Trask said. She headed down the hallway.

Max hurried after her, and we followed. The professor took us inside an office with a wide oak desk. She sorted through a stack of tests on her desk and reached one with Max's name sloppily scrawled across the top. She laid Max's original test and the fake side-by-side then handed Max a quill.

"Write your name, please," she said and handed him a sheet of parchment.

Max obliged. His handwriting looked nothing like Baxter's forged version.

Professor Trask studied the two, then said, "Copy the answer to the first question."

Once again, my friend did as instructed.

The professor made a thoughtful sound. "Wait outside, please."

We stepped into the hallway.

"Do you think she believed me?" Max whispered.

Ambria nodded. "I hope you passed the test, Max, or I'm going to be vexed with you."

He held up his hands. "I'm sure I did."

Blue snickered. "It would be kind of funny if he failed again."

Max's eyes hardened. "No, it wouldn't."

"Maxwell, come inside," the professor commanded.

He gulped and stepped into the office. I peered around the corner as the professor studied a separate sheet of parchment. She looked up and stared at Max. "I've taught your brothers and your sisters, Mr. Tiberius. I certainly hope you're nothing like them."

He shook his head. "No, Professor. I don't like them much."

Professor Trask raised an eyebrow, then wrote something on a card and stuffed it into an envelope. Max watched as she sealed the envelope with wax and stamped it, then blew on it. She stood and handed him the envelope. "Good day, Maxwell."

Max stepped outside the door, holding the envelope in trembling hands.

"Well, are you going to open it?" Ambria said impatiently.

"I can't bear to look." He held it out to her. "You open it."

Ambria sighed and took the envelope. Blue snickered and watched with bright eyes. Max and I held our breaths as Ambria broke the seal and looked at the card inside. She frowned and gave Max a disappointed look. "How could you?"

Max's shoulders slumped. "I failed?" he asked in a miserable voice.

Ambria snorted and grinned then flipped the card toward us. *Passed*.

"I'm going to kill you, Ambria!" Instead of attacking, Max burst into laughter and jumped up and down. "I did it! I passed!"

"Quiet yourselves, children, and clear the hall," Professor Trask said in a stern voice.

Giggling, we dashed away and back to the front entrance.

"Do you think she'll take action against Baxter?" I asked.

Max stopped laughing and shook his head. "I doubt it."

"Just be glad you're in," Ambria said. "I'm sure Baxter will get what he deserves eventually."

"When do classes start?" I asked.

Ambria pointed to a large schedule posted on the wall. "We start in two weeks." She ran a finger down the calendar. "We have to come back tomorrow to get our school uniforms."

"Um, there's one thing I didn't think of," I said.

The others looked at me.

I felt a little dumb asking at this point, but I hadn't given it much thought. "How much does it cost to go to school here?"

Max laughed. "It's free."

Blue hugged me. "You're so cute when you're confused, Conrad."

Ambria gave her a sharp look. "Did you pass your entrance exam, Blue?"

"Of course I did." The lycan girl smirked. "It was easy."

"Well," Max said, "I don't know about you guys, but I'm hungry."

"I was invited to eat with another pack," Blue gave me a sad look. "I'll see you all later."

"Why do you look sad?" I asked. "Isn't the invitation a good thing?"

"Oh, yes," she said. "But it would be nice eating with you."

I shrugged. "I'm sure we'll have plenty of chances."

She leaned uncomfortably close and nudged my nose with hers, then giggled and sprinted away.

"She's a bit odd," Max said after she was gone. "I guess being alone without a pack must make a lycan mental."

"I suppose." I touched my nose and wondered if her nudge was a lycan thing, kind of like dogs sniffing each other's bums.

Ambria took my arm. "Let's go get some food so we don't have to listen to Max's belly grumble."

We retrieved our brooms and flew back into town. I felt light and happy. I was going to university!

The power will soon be yours, Vic declared.

His words darkened my mood and my thoughts turned to my parents' mysterious plot. School might not be a pleasant place if they succeeded in their quest.

Chapter 10

We went to the university the next day for the school uniform fitting and joined a long line wending around the corner of the hall. When I finally reached the room at the end, a woman with droopy eyes and a tired expression flicked her wand at me. I felt something invisible tighten around my waist, arms, and legs.

A moment later, she reached behind her and handed me a ribbon-wrapped parcel. "Good day," she said in a bored voice and turned her attention to Ambria behind me.

I stepped into the crowded hallway and waited for my friends.

Blue strolled up to me. "How does the uniform look?"

I shrugged. "I haven't looked at it yet. Don't you have to get one?"

She shook her head. "We don't need them for shifter studies." She glanced back at the fitting room. "What are you doing after this?"

"We hadn't really planned anything," I said.

Blue clapped her hands together. "Good. I'd like to show you something."

My curiosity tingled. "Oh? What's that?"

"It's a secret."

"The others should be out in a minute and we can go."

She shook her head. "This is just for you to see."

I couldn't imagine what it was, but I wanted to find out. "Okay. I'll tell Ambria."

"Tell me what?" Ambria said, emerging from the fitting room with her parcel.

"I'm going to borrow Conrad for a little while," Blue said and took my hand. "We'll be back." She pulled me away, leaving Ambria with a concerned look on her face.

"I'll meet you soon," I said as I lost her face in the crowd.

"I hope you like this," Blue said. She let go of my hand and skipped down the hallway and out of the back door.

I followed her down the paths leading through the Unicorn Garden and onto to a grassy field. Beyond, the Dark Forest spread into the distance. I slowed. "Where are we going?"

She walked behind a hedge. "Right here."

I couldn't imagine what hidden secrets lay on the other side of the hedge and hesitantly walked around it. Blue sat on a blanket with sandwiches and fruit spread out before her.

She grinned. "Surprise!"

I blinked. "This is the secret?"

Blue nodded. "I made a picnic for you."

"Oh."

Her bright eyes dimmed a little. "You don't like it?"

Where are my manners? "Yes, it's thoughtful, Blue." I sat cross-legged on the opposite side of the blanket and forced a smile. "Thank you for lunch."

The light returned to her eyes. "You're welcome, Conrad." She picked up a sandwich and handed it to me. "I hope you like ham."

"Yes, of course." I unwrapped the paper and took a bite. It tasted as pleasant as any ham sandwich I'd eaten. "It's tasty."

Blue giggled. "I hoped you'd like it." She took a sandwich and devoured it. "Roast beef is my favorite, but we only had ham at the house."

"I enjoy roast beef as well." I wasn't really sure what to talk about, so I moved to what I hoped was a safe topic. "How did your supper go with the other lycans?"

"It was great." Blue nibbled on another sandwich. "One boy is the son of the alpha, so he's real bossy." She shrugged. "I don't like him all that much, but the others are nice."

I imagined the expectations on the son of a pack leader could be stressful. "How do you become part of another pack?"

"If they like me, the alpha would officially adopt me." She seemed to forget the sandwich in her hand and stared into the distance. "But if Castor, the alpha of my old pack challenges the adoption, the other alpha might have to fight him to set me free."

I grimaced. "A fight to the death?"

Blue flinched, as if reliving an unpleasant memory. "Sometimes. The Overworld Conclave doesn't like that sort of thing, but can't outlaw it."

I'd read enough about the conclave to know the different factions had their own rules for internal conflicts. "Do you have to tell them Castor was your former pack leader?"

Her forehead creased. "If I lied, the alpha would find out and probably not adopt me."

"I certainly hope Castor doesn't challenge the adoption."

Blue's lips pressed tight. "A part of me hopes he does and the new alpha kills him." She remained silent for a long moment then flashed a grin. "Enough about that." She leaned forward. "I like spending time with you, Conrad."

I fumbled for the right response as my face grew warm. "I like seeing you as well, Blue."

Lithe as a cat, she hopped over the food and knelt next to me. "How much do you like seeing me?"

My throat tightened. "Um, a lot, I guess?" I couldn't help but notice how intently her lively eyes gazed at me, as if I were a rabbit hunted by a wolf. I didn't know if I should remain still, or get up and run.

Blue pecked a kiss on my nose and giggled.

Evadora leapt from behind the hedge, threw her arms in the air and declared, "Play time!"

Blue yelped, leapt straight up, and spun in one fluid motion. Teeth bared, she crouched and stared down the other girl. "Who are you?"

I stood and positioned myself between them. "Blue, I'd like you to meet Evadora."

"Play time," the odd girl whispered. "Time to play." She ran in place, toes plucking blades of grass.

"What do you want to play?" I asked.

"Tear maker." Evadora produced her glass bottle and tapped it with a sharp fingernail. "It is empty. I heard the voices of the little ones here. They make lots of tears."

Blue wrapped her arm around mine. "Is she mental?"

"No, silly." Evadora reached out a finger and touched Blue's hand. A warm peach hue flowed up her silvery skin, making her look

84

less alien, though her large eyes and pointed ears would still attract attention. A sense of familiarity tingled in the back of my mind as looked at the girl. *Have I seen her somewhere before?* Something about her face reminded me of someone.

Blue stared wide-eyed at the transformation and belatedly jerked her hand away. "What are you?"

"I am what I am," Evadora sang. "What I am, I am."

"What's this about tears?" I asked.

Instead of answering, she skipped toward the school. I chased her around the hedge and grabbed her arm before she could go further. "Evadora, I saw people going into the rift after you. Did they enter your land?"

Her eyes fixed on my hand then slowly drifted up to my face. "The people came, but they don't know what to do."

"What are they supposed to do?" Blue asked.

"They don't know, they don't know," Evadora sang. She pirouetted out of my grasp and continued toward the hedge sculpted in the shape of a rearing unicorn. The laughter of little children echoed from within the hedgerow. A delighted smile flashed across Evadora's face. She ducked around the corner.

Blue and I ran after her.

Two little boys chased each other around the unicorn while their parents sat on nearby benches and talked.

"Ron, slow down," his presumed father shouted.

"No!" the boy yelled back.

"Oh, let him be, Harry," the mother said.

"Boys do love to run," said the other father.

The first father scowled. "The shouting gives me a bleeding headache."

Evadora watched the kids intently. "Round and round they go. Where they stop"—she thumped her other hand with a finger and the first boy tripped, plowing headfirst into a thorny rosebush—"only I know."

Cries and screams of pain rose from within the bush. Evadora raced over, bottle at the ready, before the startled parents could react. She dragged the boy from the bush and held the bottle to his cheek. The harvested tears sent a bright red glow into the bottle.

"What happened?" the mother asked. She saw the bleeding wounds on the boy's face and burst into tears.

"He fell," Evadora said.

"I knew it!" the boy's father said. "It's all fun and games until someone falls into a rosebush."

"Oh, Ron, what did you do to your face?" the mother said.

Evadora pressed the bottle to the woman's cheek. "Cry for me, mother of Ron."

The woman jerked her head back as a tear shaded the bottle blue. "What are you doing, child?"

"This girl is beyond mental," Blue said in a low wavering voice. "She frightens me."

"I don't know what to make of her either," I said. "But I need her help if we're to stop my parents."

Shouts from Ron's father chased Evadora away from the scene. She raced past us and hid on the other side of the hedge. "Need more tears."

"So your people can feel again?" I asked.

She nodded.

"Did you make that boy trip?" Blue asked.

Evadora smiled. "I helped."

The lycan girl's forehead creased. "That was terribly cruel. He was bleeding!"

I could tell we didn't have much time before Evadora sprinted away, so I tried to bargain with her. "I will give you a lot of tears if you help me understand your people and why the man wants to free them."

Evadora's large eyes fixed on me. "All kinds of tears?"

"All colors of the rainbow," I assured her.

"Ooh," she said, her lips forming an O. "I will help if you help and we help each other get help."

Blue shook her head like a wet wolf shedding water. "What did you say?"

"She'll help," I said.

"For tears?" She backed away. "I won't cry for this strange little monster."

"Let's find the others," I said.

"But what about the picnic?" Blue said. "We didn't finish talking."

From what I remembered we hadn't been talking about anything important. "Do you need help cleaning up?"

Blue's expression went flat. "No, I'll clean it up." Her eyes narrowed at Evadora then she turned and stalked away.

"Aw, I thought she would make tears," the strange girl said. "It looked like she wanted to."

I felt guilty although Blue told me she didn't need my help cleaning up the picnic. Though I wanted to fake ignorance, I had a feeling Blue wanted more than friendship. I didn't need the inner voices of my parents to see what the purpose of the picnic had been. Blue was pretty and I enjoyed being around her, but I didn't know what else she expected of me.

"Let's find my friends," I told Evadora, and walked down the path to the main hall.

Evadora skipped along beside me, eyes bright. "What are friends?"

I stopped outside the door. "Friends are people you like to be around and they like to be around you."

She tilted her head to the side. "Strange. I do not have any of these friend people."

Perhaps it was a concept someone like her couldn't understand. I went inside and made sure she followed me. The long line for the school uniform fitting was considerably shorter, but the crowd had simply moved down the hall to the dining room. Other students cast curious looks at Evadora whose large eyes, green hair, and shimmering dress cast her apart from everyone else. Thankfully, her skin wasn't silver like the first time I met her.

Evadora noticed the attention and stared back at the onlookers.

"I could get a lot of tears here," she said.

"What kind of tears?" I asked, looking around for Ambria and Max.

"Mostly pain," Evadora replied. "I do not know how to make happy or sad tears."

"Does your bottle separate the tears?" I stepped into the dining room and spotted my friends near the back.

87

"Oh, yes. It makes them different." She took my hand. "So many people. So much noise."

"We'll leave here soon," I promised her.

Ambria flinched when she me and my guest. Max's eyes widened with concern.

"What in the world are you doing with her?" Ambria said. "Did Blue take you to see Evadora?"

I shook my head. "No, Blue took me on a picnic."

Ambria sniffed. "The nerve of that girl. She hardly even knows you, but acts like she's your best friend."

"I like picnics," Max said. "What kind of food did she bring?"

"Ham sandwiches." I waved off the topic before Max got his hopes set on ham. "Evadora came along after we finished eating. She wants more tears."

Max grinned. "Do I need to kick you in the knee, Conrad?"

"No, thankfully." I noticed curious looks from other students and felt uncomfortable remaining here. "If you're finished eating, let's go outside and talk about this."

"I sort of wanted dessert," Max said.

Ambria stood up. "Then sit here and gorge yourself. We'll be outside."

Max got up and grabbed his clothing parcel. "I didn't say I wasn't coming."

That reminded me I'd left my parcel with the picnic. *I hope Blue holds onto it for me.*

We went back outside to the Unicorn Garden and all the way to Colossus Stadium so we could be alone.

Ambria stopped when we reached our practice area. "So, what's this all about, Conrad?"

"I promised Evadora more tears if she helps us understand what's going on with my parents and her people." I looked at the odd girl. "Isn't that right?"

She nodded. "More tears for more help."

"Well, then," Ambria said. "Let's get started."

"Starting with what kind of supernatural you are," Max said.

Evadora clambered atop the large golem head, using the cracked crystal eye for a foothold. The rest of us followed until we all sat on top of it.

"I thought about your question. I asked what our people were called before the separation." Evadora traced a finger down a large crack in the head. "They called us Lyrolai."

Max frowned. "I've never heard of them."

"What's the name of your land?" I asked.

"It lost its name," she said sadly. "Once it was part of this world."

I scratched my head. "But this place is a pocket dimension."

"It is part of your world," Evadora said. "It touches our realm. This is what the queen told the people from Eden."

Ambria gave her a perplexed look. "The queen? What else did she tell them?"

"The man said he had read ancient texts about our world. He said he knew what the queen wanted the most." Evadora shook her head sadly. "He wants to help, but I do not think he can."

"I'm sure there's a price for his help," Max said. "What does the queen want the most?"

"To leave our world."

Ambria frowned. "What's keeping her there? You don't seem to have a problem crossing over."

"She will grow old and die in this world." Evadora closed her eyes and tilted her face to the sun. "I think it would be better to live this life and die than live forever in the Glimmer."

"The Glimmer?" Max and I said at the same time.

Evadora kept her face to the sun. "It is the after name, not the before name."

"Whatever that means," Ambria grumbled. "I take it the queen is immortal if she stays in the Glimmer?"

"Yes. She sent others to this world long ago, but they all died." Evadora looked away from the sun and blinked her eyes open. "One by one by one. She made them do things to see if they lived, but they died."

Max grimaced. "Of old age?"

Evadora stared at him. "Old age?"

"Yeah, when you get wrinkles on your skin." Max pinched his skin.

"Oh, yes." Evadora giggled. "Some people came back with all the wrinkles. They begged the queen to let them stay, but she sent them back, sent them back to die." She made a shooing motion with her hand then sang, "Go away and die, wrinkly man. Go away and die."

Ambria's mouth dropped open. "That's awful! She sent her own people back here to die?"

"Yes. All but my mummy." The girl's eyes went distant. "She lived the longest of them all. When she died, wrinkly old age did not take her."

"I'm so sorry to hear that, Evadora." I reluctantly put a hand on her shoulder. "How long did your mother live?"

"The queen called them centuries." Her hands rubbed frantically on her bottle. "Mummy came back after she had me. She left me with the queen, but I ran away. Mummy came back again when she was sick. The queen told her she could never come back." Lips trembling, Evadora twisted the cork. "No, no, no. Do not waste emotions. Do not waste them, silly girl." She tucked the bottle somewhere back in her dress.

"The queen sounds like a monster," Max said in a rough voice. He looked at me. "If your parents are working with her, this is even worse than we thought."

I thought back to the dire warning from the Lady of the Pond and wondered if it had anything to do with the Glimmer. "Evadora, someone told me the anchored world must not be freed. Do you know what that means?"

Evadora sucked on her hair. "The Glimmer holds the realms together." Her eyes perked. "It anchors them."

Ambria looked confused. "How does it do that?"

"It just does." Evadora leaned down and rubbed her nose on the boulder. "The Glimmer is cold and numb. It has no feelings like Eden."

"If she's telling the truth, we just solved one of the oldest mysteries in the Overworld!" Max jumped to his feet. "Everyone's always wondered where the pocket dimensions came from and where they're located." He jabbed a finger toward the crack in the world. "The answer is right over there somewhere."

"I'm certainly not going into that rift thing," Ambria said. "You go right ahead if you want the glory."

Max shook his head. "No, that's not what I'm saying. We should go tell someone right now—someone like Galfandor who can explore it. Once he confirms everything, we'll get the credit for the find."

I shook my head. "There's only one thing we should be worried about right now, and that's what my parents are up to with the queen."

"You are wrong, Max." Evadora spread her arms and turned in a circle. "This is Eden, not the Glimmer. This is where your world touches mine." She leapt off the golem head and grabbed a handful of pebbles from the ground. The strange girl cleared a patch of sand and packed the pebbles together while the rest of us climbed down after her.

"What are you doing?" Ambria asked.

"Showing you." Evadora touched the pebbles. "Once there was one land ruled by a mighty being."

"By a god?" Ambria asked.

"God?" Evadora tried out the word a few more times. "God, god, god."

Ambria huffed. "Yes, a supreme being with incredible powers."

"Mummy said this word once when telling me the story," the other girl said. "Kathazal and the others of its kind were like gods."

Max fumbled the name. "Uh, so Kathazal was the one in charge?"

"Yes, it was." Evadora ran her fingers through the sand and shivered. "Other beings like it wanted control. Their war shattered"—she smashed a fist into the pebbles and scattered them across the sand—"the land. The realms drifted apart, lost from one another."

I dropped cross-legged onto the sand. "All the other realms were once part of Eden?"

"Oh, yes. Mummy called it the Sundering." She moved the pebbles into a circle. "Many mortals died and the gods were cast apart. Some realms had no god while others had one or more."

"This is amazing." Max rubbed his hands together. "There's a theory that all the realms were once one and Evadora can prove it! We're gonna be famous."

Ambria regarded Evadora with suspicion plain in her eyes. "Are you sure you're not making this up? It sounds like a fairy tale to me."

"Ask the queen," Evadora said. "She will tell you."

Max's enthusiasm waned. "I'm not so sure about talking with your evil queen." He looked at me. "Maybe we should just tell Galfandor and leave it at that."

"The queen is not evil; the queen is not good," Evadora said. "The queen just is."

"What's that supposed to mean?" I said.

"I told the queen about you."

My heart nearly stopped beating. "What do you mean you told her about me?"

Evadora tilted her head. "She knows who you are, Conrad. She wants to meet you."

Chapter 11

I jumped up and backed away. "Why does the queen want to see me?"

"I did not ask why." Evadora approached me, huge eyes blinking innocently. "You have so many questions. Maybe it is a good idea."

"You don't trust her do you, Conrad?" Max stepped in between me and the girl. "She's mental."

Ever since Evadora changed her skin to a peach tone, I felt a sense of déjà vu whenever I looked at her face. I shook from my thoughts. "Oddly, I do trust her. Her tale about the realms seems too strange to make up."

Max blew out a breath. "You're crazy if you go with her."

"I hate to agree with Max," Ambria said, "but in this case, I think he's right."

Max frowned. "Thanks, I think."

Evadora grabbed my hand and tugged. "Come, Conrad, come!"

Ambria grabbed my other hand. "Stay, Conrad, stay!"

"Leave him alone." Max tried to pry Evadora's fingers off mine.

Evadora abruptly let go, and Ambria and I tumbled to the ground. The Lyrolai girl knelt next to us and whispered, "I promise I won't ever chew your bones, Conrad. I promise all the way to the top."

"Chew his bones?" Ambria shrieked. "You're a little monster."

"No," Evadora shook her head vehemently. "I am not a monster." She touched my knee. "I know you want to come, Conrad."

I desperately wanted to meet the queen, but Evadora's promise about chewing my bones unsettled me, to say the least. "I don't think I should."

Her eyes narrowed and air hissed between her teeth. "I see right through your skin, Conrad. Your words are lies."

I gulped and backed away. "Now I definitely don't want to come with you."

Evadora frowned and stood up. "If I make the way safe, will you come?"

"Even if there weren't creepy light guardians in the rift, I'd be scared to death of you," Max said.

"What if I know how to make you safe?" she asked.

Ambria shook her head. "At this point, I'm not sure anything you say would help."

Evadora looked at me. "Bring me the green pebble."

An image of Cora's lucky green pebble flickered into my mind. I sucked in a breath. "How do you know about that?"

"Bring it to me," she repeated. "I will meet you at the gate to the Fairy Garden tomorrow morning. I will show you the safe way." Evadora grabbed my hand and jerked me upright with ease. "Do not be afraid." She raced away in a flash.

"What's that about a green pebble?" Max asked.

"I've seen it," Ambria said. "You used to sit in the hall at the orphanage and rub it."

"It was Cora's lucky pebble. I kept it after she died." My vision grew blurry. "When Ambria and I came here, I put it in a closet with my other things at Levi Rax's house. I lost it after the house collapsed."

Ambria's eyes twitched at the mention of the brother she'd never known—the one who'd tried to murder me. My shovel to the back of his head had killed him instead.

Max scratched his head. "What's so special about a green pebble?"

I shrugged. "Cora, told me it was her lucky pebble." Images from the psychological test flashed through my head, sending a chill down my back.

Ambria put a hand on my arm. "She's the one you think of as your real mother, isn't she?"

I nodded and swallowed a knot in my throat. "Seeing her die was part of my test yesterday."

Max and Ambria grimaced.

"That's awful," Max said. "My brothers and sisters teased and beat me up in my psychological exam." He looked at Ambria. "What happened in yours?"

She glanced at me and her face flushed. "I'd rather not talk about it."

Max flashed a grin. "Let me guess—your hair was a mess and you had no brush."

Ambria put her hands on her hips. "Yes, Max, that's it precisely."

"I'm going to find the pebble," I told the others.

"That house is a wreck." Max tossed one of the pebbles against the golem head. "We'd have to dig through tons of rubble to find anything."

"Max is right," Ambria said. "How are we supposed to find something as small as a pebble in that mess?"

"I think I have an idea," I told them and headed back toward the university so I could get my broom.

"Well, I hope it's a good idea," Ambria said.

We left Colossus Stadium, walked back through the Unicorn Garden, and retrieved our brooms from the broom rack in the front hall of the university. After flying back to the house at the corner of Dowling and Bucket, I went upstairs to my room and rummaged in a bag of supplies Galfandor had previously given us. I found what I was looking for in the form of a black bottle.

"What is that?" Max asked.

"It's what destroyed Levi Rax's house," I said.

He stared with horror at the bottle. "You've been keeping that here all this time?"

"Conrad, where did you get that potion?" Ambria asked. "I thought Galfandor only gave us one rot potion."

"He gave us three bottles," I replied. "We only used one to destroy the Goodleigh's orphanage."

"I don't understand what you plan to do with it," Max said.

I went back downstairs and climbed on my broom. "Then I'll just have to show you."

We flew several blocks over and found the derelict house in the same condition we'd left it. While exploring a secret tunnel in the basement, we'd accidentally freed a massive frogre. The creature chased us into the basement and knocked over a shelf with a bottle of rot potion on it. The liquid had crumbled the wooden foundation and destroyed the house.

I landed next to the pile of rubble and estimated where my room had been. With a pop, the cork came out and I poured the rot potion liberally on the wood.

With a sound like a thousand termites gnawing, the rot potion smoked and turned the wood into brown sandy dust. We backed away and watched as the potion ate away at the rubble until only stone and piles of dust remained.

"Conrad, you're brilliant," Ambria said.

Max grunted. "Should have brought a sifter."

I hadn't thought of that, but at least we wouldn't have to worry about jagged wood and nails and could dig through sand instead.

"I'm surprised the city never cleared the lot," Max said. "Guess the government just doesn't care anymore."

"Most streets aren't lit at night, I never see Templars patrolling, and half the houses seem unoccupied." Ambria regarded a pile of rot ash. "I believe the government and everyone else stopped caring about this city a long time ago."

I dug my hands into the dust and scooped it between my legs like a dog digging for bones. "My belongings were in a white cloth sack. Hopefully it will be easy to find."

By the time the sunlight faded to dusk, we'd burrowed all the way to where the basement had been, but still no bag.

Max wiped his dirty face, leaving a trail of mud in the sweat. "This is hopeless, Conrad. We need shovels or spells."

"What if the rot spell ate it?" Ambria said.

Max shook his head. "It only works on wood." He frowned. "I think."

"It should have been here," I said. "I put the bag in my closet. It had clothes and some other knick-knacks inside."

Ambria jerked upright and gave us a worried look. "Oh, dear."

"What?" I walked over to her. "Are you okay?"

"For the moment." She walked several feet away and began excavating with her hands.

"Why are you digging there?" I asked. "That's where the bathroom was."

Ambria reached into the mound of dust and withdrew my travel sack. She held it out to me and smiled sheepishly. "I'm sorry, Conrad. I completely forgot I'd taken it into the bathroom."

"Why in the world did you take it to the bathroom?" Max asked.

She looked down. "I was snooping if you must know the absolute truth."

I didn't care one bit about her snooping, but felt rather irritated that we'd wasted so much time digging. I took the sack to the stone patio and dumped its contents. My old work clothes spilled out along with a toothbrush and a bent picture of me and Cora eating ice cream in the park. My mouth went dry and salt stung my eyes.

Cora sets the bird cage on the ground in front of a park bench and opens the door. The bird hops through the door and looks around.

"Go, little bird," Cora says with a smile. "Fly free."

The bird flutters its wings as if it hasn't used them in a long time. Finally, it soars into the air and flies away.

"Didn't you spend all your money on that bird?" I ask.

She nods.

"Why did you let it go?"

Cora squeezes my hand. "Would you find happiness in a cage?"

Though I'm not bright, I know the answer. "No. It would be boring."

She laughs. "Forever alone in a cage is no way to live. We should never want others to suffer like that, Conrad. It is better to die free." She rubs the green pebble dangling from a silver chain around her neck.

Cora is the most wonderful person in the world, I realize. "Will you be my mummy forever?"

"Forever." She kisses my forehead. "I'll protect you and keep you safe." She tucks the necklace under her shirt.

"Why is that your lucky pebble?" I ask.

Cora's eyes grow distant. "It saved me from a fate worse than death."

My eyes widen. "What's worse than death?"

Tears pool in her eyes. "Life without love. Existence without emotion." She presses my face against her chest. "I gave up eternity gladly."

The picture came back into focus and the memory blurred back to a dull ache in my heart.

Ambria leaned her head on my shoulder. "Oh, Conrad, I know you loved her very much."

"I still do," I said and pressed a hand to my chest, wishing I could loosen the knot.

"She's lovely," Max said. "I wish my mother was like Cora."

Ambria felt the sack. "I still don't see the pebble."

I dropped to my knees and shook out the old work clothes. The pebble clattered to the stone. The silver chain had been stolen by another set of foster parents but I hadn't cared, so long as I could keep the pebble. I picked it up and rubbed it. The surface felt smooth as glass, and when I peered into it, I saw my reflection looking back.

I wiped away my tears. "Let's go home."

The vampires were up and about when we went inside the house.

Sonia's lips peeled into a snarl. "What have you filthy little animals been doing?" She stepped into our path. "Take off your shoes or you'll track all over the place."

I wasn't in the mood to be yelled at by the unfriendly woman. "Get out of my way."

Her eyes glowed red and fangs protruded beneath her upper lip. "Or what, you little mouse?"

My wand was in my hand before I realized it. I flicked it up and opened my mouth.

"Sonia, leave them alone." Desmond grabbed his sister's arm and jerked her aside. "I'm sorry. She's been impossible lately."

"Impossible?" Sonia shrieked. "You let these vermin live with us, and then allow them to bring in a stray lycan! I'm sick of it."

"You hardly ever see us," Ambria said. "We're quiet and courteous, and we keep the house neat. What more do you want?"

"I want you gone," the vampire girl snarled.

Desmond clenched a fist. "If it's that bad, sister, then we'll move."

"No!" Sonia stomped her foot. "We were here first."

"We'll have to live on campus when school starts," Max said. "Then you'll almost never see us."

Sonia narrowed her eyes. "How much longer before you start school?"

"Two weeks," Ambria said. "Even the lycan will be attending."

The vampire's fangs retracted and the glow faded from her eyes. "I suggest you look for another permanent home to return to."

Desmond sighed. "Having people living here during the day protects us, Sonia."

"Protected by children?" She jerked from his grasp and went through the iron door the basement. "Rubbish!"

"Desmond, you're the nicest vampire we ever met," Ambria said. "If we need to move to make things better with your sister, we will."

He shook his head. "Her attitude keeps getting worse. I think she's just using you as an excuse to shout and throw tantrums."

"Why is she so upset all the time?" Max asked.

Desmond ran a hand through his thick hair and sighed. "It's the lifestyle. She hates not being able to enjoy the daytime anymore. She hates staying up all night pretending to be friends with other vampires."

"It's the same old thing over and over forever," I said in a quiet voice. "She wants real friends, not fake ones."

"Precisely," he replied. "She's bored out of her mind because she can't have real friends. She has to fake her emotions around them all the time."

"Can't you just leave and travel the world?" Ambria said. "Surely there's more you want to see than Queens Gate."

"There is, but we owe a debt to our master, and he won't let us leave." Desmond's eyes grew sad. "He could track us anywhere we went."

"How can you repay the debt?" Max asked.

The vampire shrugged. "He said he'll tell us when the time is right." Desmond turned for the basement door. "Maybe one day we can escape our fate. Until then, I'll try to keep Sonia under control."

"How sad," Ambria said. "To be trapped somewhere you don't want to be."

I'd known that feeling over and over again during the course of my life, from the moment I'd found myself at the orphanage, and with every foster parent except for Cora. Here in Queens Gate I felt free at last. If I could help free anyone else like I had Ambria and the others at the orphanage, I would.

Cora would be happy if I did that.

"Conrad?" Ambria stood in front of me. "Max asked you a question."

"Oh?" I glanced back and forth at her and Max.

She rolled her eyes. "It's about food, of course."

"We just spent the afternoon digging through the wreckage of a house," Max said. "Of course I'm hungry."

I wasn't terribly hungry. "You two go ahead. I'm going to eat something here and go to sleep early."

"Is something the matter?" Ambria asked.

"No, I'm just tired." I smiled to prove I was okay. "Plus, I really want a shower."

Ambria looked at her dirty hands. "Goodness, I think we all need to clean up."

"We can eat dirty," Max said. "Or get something to go."

The front door opened and Blue came inside. She looked at me and smiled. "I put your parcel in your room, Conrad."

"Thanks, Blue." I scuffed a shoe against the floor. "Thanks for the picnic."

The lycan girl looked at us with a confused expression. "Why are you so dirty?"

"Ugh," Max said. "We had to dig through the rubble of a destroyed house to get Conrad's stuff."

She didn't seem any less confused. "Where did your strange little friend go?"

"Probably back to her horrid home," Ambria said.

"I'm going upstairs to wash," I said, and shuffled away while the others answered Blue's questions.

After the shower, I came downstairs and noticed Ambria and Max were gone, probably to eat. I toasted some bread and cooked an egg, then sat at the kitchen table to eat. I felt a whisper of air on my ear.

"Boo," Blue said.

I leapt up and just as quickly tripped backwards over the chair. She burst into laughter.

"I'm sorry, Conrad. I shouldn't have scared you like that."

I righted the chair and sat back down, trying to maintain at least a shred of dignity. "It wasn't nice, especially while I'm eating."

Still giggling, she said, "I know."

I finished my egg and started on my toast. "What did you do for the rest of the day?"

Blue traced a fingernail along the tabletop. "The children of another pack invited me to play hide and go hunt in the Dark Forest."

I stopped chewing. "That forest is dangerous and full of monsters."

"That's what makes the game so fun," she said. "We stay near the outer area since most of the monsters live deep inside."

"Most of the creatures in there were created by my father," I said. "They were made for killing and nothing else."

Blue touched a hand to her chest. "Why, Conrad, are you concerned about my safety?"

"Of course I am." I finished the last bite of toast. "You're my friend."

She jumped up, ran over, and hugged me. "You do like me, don't you?"

My face burned. "Yes."

Blue kissed my cheek. "Would you like to go on a walk, or play a board game?"

"I'd love to, Blue, but I'm exhausted." I patted her hand and stood. "Perhaps tomorrow?"

She clapped her hands together. "That would be wonderful."

"Goodnight, Blue."

She pecked a kiss on my nose. "Goodnight, Conrad."

After brushing my teeth, I climbed into bed and touched my nose. Though the skin seemed no warmer to my hand, it still felt a bit hot where Blue had kissed me. Girls were so different from boys when it came to friendship. Boys liked to hit each other, but girls like to giggle and hug. The living curse had severely blunted my social skills. My time with Ambria and Max was all the experience I had with friendship.

I just hoped I'd live long enough to experience it more.

Chapter 12

True to her word, Evadora waited at the Fairy Garden gate early the next morning.

"You brought it?" she asked, jumping up and down. "Show me, show me."

"Hold on, Conrad," Max said. "Don't let her take it from you."

"I hadn't planned on it," I said.

Ambria looked up and down as she watched the energetic Evadora. "Calm yourself, girl."

I dug into my pocket and withdrew the pebble. Holding it between thumb and forefinger, I showed the girl my prize.

Evadora stilled and her eyes grew so wide I saw the stone reflected in them. "You have it," she whispered. "Now we can go."

"Go where?" Max asked. "I'm not walking another step until you tell us."

She pointed across the field. "To the pond."

"Whatever for?" Ambria asked.

I clenched the stone in my fist. "How did you know I had the pebble?"

"The queen knows," Evadora said. "She can tell you why."

"But—"

"Come, come, come!" Evadora skipped ahead.

The rest of us looked at each other with concern.

"I hope she doesn't plan to drown us," Ambria said.

I shook my head. "Yesterday she showed me how strong she is. I think if she wanted to hurt us, she would have already." My curiosity made it easier to convince myself to follow Evadora. Thankfully, the others followed.

She waited at the edge of the pond when we caught up to her. "What is it when something is over another thing?"

I set my broom down at the edge of the pond. Ambria set hers next to mine.

"When something is above something else?" Max said, dropping his broom carelessly on the ground.

"Ah, above." Evadora squished mud through her toes. "That is the word." She pointed to the water. "Conrad, rub the stone and say the words, 'As above, so below' then hold my hand and we will leap into the water."

Ambria gasped. "She does mean to drown you!"

"What game are you up to?" I asked.

Evadora tilted her head. "I will show you the safe way to the queen." She held out her hand. "Come, Conrad. Do what I ask."

"You promise this isn't a trick?" I said.

"Look inside my skin." Evadora pressed a hand to her chest. "Look deep, Conrad. Do you see a trick?"

I stared at her for a moment, completely unable to see through her skin and instead relied on the sincerity shining in her eyes. "I see no trick, Evadora." I held out my hand.

"No, Conrad!" Max grabbed my arm. "This is insane. Besides, that water looks poisoned."

"He won't get wet," Evadora said. "The bad water won't touch him."

I pulled my arm free from Max. "I *must* find out why the queen wants to see me, and how she knows about this pebble."

Ambria jabbed a finger at Evadora. "Ask her, then."

"Cannot tell," Evadora replied. "Only the queen can."

"Fine." Ambria grabbed my wrist. "I'm coming too."

"You're all mental," Max complained. "Do I have to hold Conrad's hand?"

Evadora held out her other hand. "No, but we must all touch."

Staring at the water, I didn't know what to expect when we jumped in. Would the pebble allow us to breathe underwater? Would it keep us dry? Would it allow us to walk on water? My body trembled with excitement and apprehension while the moisture evaporated from my mouth. The water reflected a worried expression on my face.

Evadora squeezed my hand. "Rub the stone, Conrad. Say the words."

I rubbed the pebble with my thumb. "As above, so below."

"Jump!" Evadora cried.

We leapt into the water. There was no splash, no rush of wetness into my clothes, or the rumble of water against my ears. I felt a sickening wrench in my guts that passed as quickly as it had come. We flew out of the pond and tumbled ungracefully on the ground. Evadora pulled me upright while Max and Ambria climbed to their feet.

"Hurry," Evadora said. "Our others will feel us here if we stay too long."

"Stay where?" Max said, brushing dirt off his trousers. "We're right where we started!"

Ambria stared at the water. "I don't understand. Did the pebble make the water bounce us back out? Why did I feel as if my body turned inside out?"

"We are in the reflection," Evadora said. She pointed to forest of stumps.

The entire scene rippled as though a watery reflection and my jaw fell open.

The wide-eyed look on Max's face told me he'd just figured out what the girl meant. "We're in a reflection of the real world?"

"Yes, a reflected world," Evadora said. "Come, fast! We do not want our reflections feeling us here."

Judging from the urgency in her voice, I decided now was not the time to argue. We raced through the path between the stumps all the way to the crack in the wall. Evadora dropped to her knees and crawled inside. I followed close behind, mind racing as fast as my heart.

"What about the guardians?" I asked.

Evadora didn't answer.

"That's a good question," Ambria said breathlessly behind me.

We reached the end and stood in the starry rift between worlds. Evadora waved a finger around at the emptiness. "The guardians do not have reflections." She was right—there were no floating orbs of light.

"Why don't they reflect?" I asked.

She shrugged. "Some things cannot be reflected."

"You never answered my question last time," Ambria said. "It looks like we're in space, but we can walk as if we're on land."

Evadora blinked. "I wish I knew, but I do not." She motioned us on. "Hurry. We must reach the looking pool soon." She dashed across the void.

I stepped out and found firm footing then chased after her, my friends close behind.

"What happens if our reflections find us here?" Max asked.

"Bad things," was the only answer Evadora gave us.

We reached a tunnel on the other side, this one tall enough to walk through, and ran inside. We emerged in a grassy glade surrounded by tall, bleak-looking trees. A small pond of black water rippled, and the world around us rippled with it.

"Join hands, everyone." Evadora said. "Rub the stone Conrad, but reverse the words. So below, as above."

I rubbed the stone and said, "So below, as above."

We leapt.

Once again came the gut-wrenching yank, a flicker of the deepest black, and we hurtled from a pond on the other side and back to our world. I landed hard and rolled onto the ground. A greenly glowing moon hung among a starlit tapestry, the shadow of a mountain with a crooked peak lurking beneath. I sat in a glade of purple grass surrounded by twisted trees with spiky bark.

We weren't back in our world.

We're in the Glimmer.

Max stood up and looked around. "Where are we? Why is the moon so huge and green?"

"We're in Evadora's land," Ambria said. She huddled next to me. "It's night but the moon is so bright it's nearly like daytime."

Despite its unusual brilliance, the moon didn't mute light from the dense clusters of stars.

"Eternal twilight," Evadora said in a whisper. "We do not have daytime or nighttime." She shivered. "Just time."

"No wonder you're mental," Max said. He ran a hand over the grass and jerked it back. "Feels more like snake scales than grass."

I gave Ambria's hand a squeeze, and climbed to my feet. As I regarded the impressive sight, I realized the moon itself had satellites—each one a mere fraction of the size, except most had white clouds and blue skies.

"Are those planets around the moon?" I desperately wished for a telescope.

Evadora pointed a finger at one moon and spun on her heel. "Not planets, Conrad. Those are realms."

Max gasped. "Realms like Seraphina?"

Though the cloud cover blocked a good view of the surface, I noticed at least two of the worlds had nearly identical continents to Europe. One looked nice and green, while the other was the beige of desert sand.

Evadora pointed them out. "Eden, Seraphina, and Sturg." She whirled a finger. "Aquilis and Draxadis are on the other side."

"What about that white one there?" Max said.

She shook her head. "Some are dead."

"That's not all of them," Max said. "What about all the others?"

"Some are dead," she replied. "Some we do not know what they are called."

"What in the world is that—a black hole?" Ambria pointed to a swirling darkness directly above the moon.

"The Abyss," Evadora replied in a hushed tone. "The old gods are trapped inside."

I felt as though the longer I stared at it, the more something within stared back out at me, as if the prisoners could see the tiny speck I called a body.

"Can you go to the other realms from here?" Max held up a hand as if he could touch the moon. "It looks like you could climb to the top of that mountain and touch the moon."

Evadora giggled. "From the mountaintop, you can see all the realms hanging in place, but you cannot reach any of them." She plucked a blade of the purple grass. It struggled in her hand like a snake, much to her amusement.

Ambria shrieked and hid behind Max. "I don't like this place one little bit."

I stared at the mountain, fascinated with the nameless realms slowly orbiting the great green moon. Had people once lived in all of them, or were they born lifeless when the gods sundered the world? It made me feel even smaller in the grand scheme.

"Where did the tunnel between our worlds come from?" Max asked.

"The old man cracked the world," Evadora said.

I looked away from the moon. "My father did this?"

She shook her head. "No. Your father made the hole bigger. The old man cracked the world so he could find help here. Help against the Seraphim."

"Justin Slade?" Ambria said.

Max grunted. "Justin Slade isn't that old."

I sucked in a quick breath as another name came to me. "Was it Galfandor who made the hole?"

Evadora's forehead pinched. "His name was Moses."

"Whoa." Max looked back at the crack. "He must have done it during the First Seraphim War."

Ambria shrunk away from the long grass. "Can we please leave this awful meadow and go to the queen?"

"Yep!" Evadora pointed toward the crooked mountain. "She lives up there." Without another word, she skipped through the grass toward the dense forest. At the last minute, two trees uprooted and stepped away from each other.

Ambria jerked to a halt. "Those trees just walked!"

Max didn't look too surprised. "Just like the ones in the Fairy Garden used to."

"Walking trees?" Ambria regarded the forest suspiciously. "Can they grab us with their branches?"

Evadora petted one of the trees like a cat. "They move for us. They will not hurt you."

Why are my friends so frightened? By now, Evadora had plenty of chances to hurt us. I walked over to the tree and touched it. The bark felt strange—like chitin on a bug, but jagged. "The trees won't hurt us. Let's go."

Max took Ambria's hand and led her forward. I turned back to our guide. "We're ready."

Evadora clapped her hands. "This way." Past the glade, a curving path, lit by what looked like large pulsating mushrooms, wound through the dense forest. Unsettling chittering and clacking noises emanated from the darkness, and shadowy shapes skittered across the way.

Ambria screamed and grabbed her hair. "Something touched me."

"Stay on the path, the path, the path," Evadora sang, seemingly unconcerned about the creatures hiding in the forest.

Max and Ambria huddled together and walked slowly. I couldn't stop thinking about the queen and how Evadora knew about Cora's green pebble. The desire for answers burned in my stomach and subdued my fear. I had to know more.

The quest for knowledge is the quest for power, Vic said.

Della added her own thoughts. *The weak fear treading the path to glory. Perhaps this boy is worth saving after all.*

Perhaps, my father replied. *We shall see.*

I'm in here too, you know, I said to the voices in my head. *Just because you were parts of my parents' souls doesn't mean you have to be like them. You could be better.*

They didn't answer.

I wondered how much knowledge those soul fragments held. Did they still have a link to my parents, or were they limited to me? Could my parents still sense them?

"Oh, this is the lovely part." Evadora bounced on her toes and pointed to a light at the end of the forest tunnel. "You will like this so much."

"Thank goodness," Ambria said. "I can't wait to get out of this unbearable place."

Max stepped up the pace, guiding her with him. "Me either."

"Come!" Evadora loped down the path.

I ran after her, the others close on my heels and skidded to a halt at a precipitous ledge. My stomach felt as though it had dropped into a bottomless pit. Staring back at me was a chasm of nothing but space and stars. A giant tree arched over the infinite drop and met another tree in the middle, where they twined together and rose into a majestic umbrella of crimson leaves.

Ambria's lips peeled back in a silent cry of terror. Max got down on his hands and knees and peered over the cliff. "There's no bottom," he whimpered. "What happens if you fall?"

Evadora looked down. "Why would you fall?" She pointed to the tree trunk. "There is a bridge."

The tree had a gradual incline so as to be almost flat except where it curved directly up in the middle with the other tree. The trunk looked wide enough to accommodate a car. I looked toward the mountain. *The answers are there.* Without waiting for Evadora, I stepped onto the tree bridge, my vertigo rinsed away by impatience.

She jogged up beside me. "You are not afraid, Conrad."

"Why would I be?" I asked. "You promised not to chew on my bones."

Evadora nodded vigorously. "Yes. I will keep your bones safe." She pointed up at the tree tops in the middle of the bridge. "From there you can see everything."

"How far are we from the queen?" I pointed toward the crooked mountain.

"Not far." We reached the top of the bridge.

I looked out, filled with wonder at the sight spreading out below. The land looked as though it had been shattered into islands and set to drift in outer space. As with this island and the next, giant trees bound the broken shards together.

Evadora looked back and laughed. "Your friends are so frightened."

I glanced at Max and Ambria. Though their faces were pale as ghosts, they hurried to catch up with us.

"Conrad, please wait," Ambria said, voice trembling.

Max looked from side to side, eyes blinking with disbelief. "This world is broken." He pointed to other floating islands with tree bridges in the distance. "It's not shaped like a planet at all."

"The anchored world was crushed by the other realms," Evadora said. "It was broken to keep the others whole." She resumed walking.

"How many people live here?" I asked, trying to make conversation so the others wouldn't think about the endless void beneath us.

"Many," Evadora said. "But not so many as Eden." She sighed wistfully. "The people are in the unbroken land on the other side of the mountain, but I never see them."

"What does the queen think about you running off to Eden?" Ambria asked.

"She does not care." Her huge eyes filled with pain. "The queen looks so alive." She touched my arm. "She feels warm to the touch like you." Her fingers traced my lips. "She feels soft." Her gaze found mine. "Do not be fooled. She is dead inside."

109

Ambria shivered. "Is she really so cold and emotionless?"

The other girl nodded. "Yes. Everyone who lives here is like that." She proceeded to the middle of the bridge where the two trees met and walked along a thick branch that curved around to the other side. Though the branch was wide, it was only half as wide as the rest of the bridge and even I felt the pull of vertigo on my senses.

In the distance, a dark cloud of birds swirled into the air and funneled in our general direction us, the flock changing directions seemingly at random.

"You have emotions," I said.

Evadora skipped along the branch, completely unconcerned, or perhaps supremely confident in her ability to stay balanced. "Because I go to Eden. I gather tears in my bottle."

I followed slowly, glad there was no wind to threaten us. The birds whooshed by overhead with a cacophony of warbling shrieks. Several of them gathered in the branches and stared at us curiously. With furry webbed wings and feline heads, I realized these were more like bats than birds. They took off nearly as quickly as they'd landed, vanishing into a forest of spiky trees.

Ambria watched the last one take flight. "What were those things?"

"More importantly," Max said, "do they eat people?"

Evadora laughed. "Mewlies eat anything. I saw them swarm a pony and strip it to bones in no time."

"Oh my." Ambria's knees wobbled. "I'm glad they didn't attack us."

"They usually don't eat people because the queen keeps them away." Evadora hopped to the wider section of the tree bridge.

"The queen controls them?" Max asked.

The girl nodded. "She can if she wants."

That ability reminded me uncomfortably of Levi Rax mind-controlling a flock of sheep and ordering them to stomp me to death, so I pushed away such thoughts.

We reached the other side of the bridge and walked down it toward the next island. Below, wind traced patterns in wide fields of grass. Herds of miniature ponies galloped across the land, pursued by sand-colored elephants only a little larger than their prey.

"They're so cute," Ambria said. "Look at the tiny horses and elephants." For the first time since entering the Glimmer, she smiled.

One of the ponies turned on the elephants and opened its mouth to reveal rows of jagged teeth. It bit into the other creature and a fierce fight ensued. The elephant's trunk coiled around the horse like a snake, fangs burying themselves in the pony's hide. Black blood sprayed across the grass and the equine whinnied horribly, going silent and limp.

Ambria shrieked and looked away.

Max gasped. "This place is filled with little monsters."

"Monsters are good," Evadora said and continued walking. She led us around the field and to another tree bridge. The crooked mountain sat on the other side, lights glittering at the top. "The queen is there," she announced.

We walked across the chasm and reached the base of a steep cliff on the other side. Evadora walked right up to the shiny black rock and pointed at her feet. "Stand next to me."

We did as instructed.

"Is there a door in the cliff?" Max asked.

Evadora ran a finger on the rock face and we suddenly hurtled straight up with nothing below us. Ambria gripped me frantically and buried her face in my chest. Max shouted and squeezed his eyes shut. Wind whipped our hair about our faces and made my eyes water.

I met Evadora's calm unblinking gaze. She grinned. "Before the tears, I never knew how much fun this is."

It took everything I had to keep my knees from turning to jelly. Despite my earlier bravado, flying straight up a cliff without any visible means of support terrified me. I held onto Ambria and drew as much comfort from her as she seemed to from me.

Seconds later, we drew level with a wide stone terrace. I quickly stepped onto visible rock and just as quickly stopped, stunned by the mesmerizing view. The entire Glimmer spread out before me. Huge portions of unbroken land spread out to one side of the mountain, while the area we'd come from looked like an unfinished puzzle held together by bridges of living trees.

Herds of unidentifiable animals swept across a barren plain in the distance. A flock of birds erupted from the trees of a dense forest. Something that resembled a large blue whale lumbered peacefully in the sky above a crystal sea. The huge moon hovered directly overhead. I looked up at the peak of the mountaintop and wondered if I could climb one and touch the big glowing sphere.

Ambria looked around with wide eyes. "It's the most beautiful place I've ever seen."

"I wouldn't say that," Max replied. "It's the oddest place I've ever seen."

The realms hovered overhead like sparkling jewels around the moon. Again I wished for a telescope to see if I could actually view the inhabitants of the different realms of Earth. "Are we at the center of the Glimmer?" I asked.

Evadora nodded. "The middle of *everything*."

"You have brought him," said a cold feminine voice.

"Yes, Queen," said Evadora.

I turned around. My heart stopped and my mind went blank.

One word squeaked from my mouth. "Mum?"

Chapter 13

The queen's flaming orange hair framed her fair face and journeyed down both shoulders all the way to her waist. Brilliant green eyes sparkled like gems as they gazed upon me, but the queen's expression remained flat. The hem of her silky black dress trailed several feet on the ground behind her.

My stomach felt as if someone had punched me. I took a tentative step toward her. "Cora?"

Her full lips curved ever so slightly up and fell back into a flat line, trembling as if she were trying to smile, but couldn't. "I am not the one you call Cora," she said in a flat monotone. "She was my sister. I am Naeve."

Evadora pranced over to her and held up her bottle. "I have many tears for you, Queen."

Naeve stared long and hard at the bottle then shook her head. "I will not taste those tears, little one. I will not tempt insanity for a fleeting moment of ecstasy."

"Do the tears drive you mad?" Ambria asked.

The queen turned her unsettling gaze to my friend. "Imagine a spark of heat after an eternity of cold void."

Ambria gulped. "Yes, I see your point."

I couldn't stop staring at the ghost of my beloved foster mother. She looked the same but lacked the warmth and love. Tears blurred the painful sight and sadness lodged in my throat. I wiped my face with a sleeve and took deep calming breaths. At last, I freed my voice from the pain. "Why did you want to see me?"

"Cora came to see me shortly before she"—Naeve stared blankly for a long moment, then spoke again as if she had never stopped—"and told me about you. I wished to see if she had succeeded."

113

My stomach clenched at the unspoken word. *She died.* I recovered and asked another question. "Succeeded at what?"

"If she nudged your course from fate." Naeve stepped closer and touched my face. "You are alive and healthy." Her eyes betrayed no hint of happiness. "She succeeded or at least delayed the inevitable."

"That's really the only reason you wanted to see me?" I said.

Naeve walked to the edge of the terrace, her long black dress trailing behind, and waved a hand at the realms. "Your parents are ambitious, Conrad Edison. They wish to answer our ancient dilemma and release me from this tomb." She gazed at the moon. "I once thought I had the answer, but it slipped from my grasp."

Max meekly spoke. "You mean immortality in Eden?"

"Precisely." The queen turned back to us. "Even now an Abyssal god walks Eden. I told your parents it may have the answers I seek."

"An Abyssal demon?" Max stumbled back a step. "How did he escape?"

"With the help of the only one powerful enough to completely draw him through," Naeve replied. "Justin Slade used him as an ally. The Abyssal fed on many souls that day and has wandered Eden ever since."

"I'm surprised he hasn't tried to take over the world," Max said.

"After millennia in the Abyss, I am certain a few centuries would not be much delay for him," Naeve replied. "It is likely he hunts for those who imprisoned him, so they cannot put him back."

I had so many questions about Justin Slade and this Abyssal god. Unfortunately, story time would have to wait. "My parents think they can give you immortality outside the Glimmer?"

"That is their belief, yes." She touched a finger to her cheek. "Cora thought she had the answer. She searched the void and found a fragment of the anchor stone."

I pulled the pebble from my pocket. "This?"

Naeve stepped closer but made no move to touch the stone. "Yes. She used it to escape. The last time she visited me, she was emotional." Light flickered in her eyes, and her lips parted. "Eden gave her the gift of life in full bloom. She told me how wonderful food tasted, of the sickening depths of sadness, and the soaring heights of love." The void of expression on her face told us she had no understanding of what Cora had told her.

"What did she think would solve the problem?" I asked.

"The stone you hold in your hand," Naeve replied. "Obviously, it did not protect her."

I bit my lip to hide the pain her comment caused me.

"The Glimmer preserves," Evadora said. "Stay here, live forever." She gripped handfuls of her hair, squeezed her eyes tight, and screamed, "Why did you make Mummy leave? Why didn't you let her stay?"

My legs went weak and I stumbled backward. Max caught me before I fell.

"What's wrong?" he asked.

I stared at Evadora and realized why she looked so familiar. "You're Cora's daughter."

Evadora opened her tear-filled eyes and nodded. "Your curse killed Mummy."

My gorge rose and I gagged on remorse. *I killed her.* Salt stung my eyes. I wanted to throw myself off the terrace and let the void swallow me whole. The curse of an orphan boy had taken Cora from her true daughter.

Someone hugged me. "Conrad, I'm here," Ambria said. "Everything will be okay."

Hot tears stung my eyes and flowed down my face.

I felt a bottle against my cheek and looked into Evadora's pain-filled eyes.

"Get that away from him!" Ambria shouted.

I held Evadora's wrist and pressed the bottle to my cheek. "These belong to you," I said.

Her eyes misted, and she nodded solemnly. "They are tears for our mother, Conrad. They are ours. You are my brother."

I squeezed her hand. "You are my sister." We weren't related by blood, but by a woman who had rescued one child when forced by this cold queen to abandon her own.

Naeve knelt close to me and stared at my face. Her pale hand reached toward my cheek. She jerked it away suddenly, stood and backed off. "Cora was weak," she said in a whisper. "She could not resist the lure and lost everything for it. That is why I banished her to Eden. Now her daughter is infected with emotion and will likely suffer the same fate."

115

"Will you banish Evadora also?" I asked.

Naeve shook her head. "There is no need."

Max patted my back. "You okay?"

The pain refused to fade, but I knew Cora wouldn't want me to mope. As for the queen, nothing I said or did would change the past. If I shouted every terrible thing I wanted at this woman with no heart, she might kill all of us.

I hear crying and open the bathroom door. Cora sits on the floor, face buried in her hands. When she looks up, I notice the bruises on her cheek and under her eye.

"Bill hit you again," I say in a dull voice.

She clears her throat and stands. "Yes, Conrad. He used to be so kind, but something has changed him."

"Why do you stay with him if he hurts you?" I ask.

Cora smiles. "I hope whatever is wrong with him will pass and the man I love will return."

I vaguely remembered how nice and friendly Bill had been when I first moved in with him and Cora. Over the course of time, he'd soured into a bitter man. I felt certain my curse had affected him as it had anyone I'd stayed with for long. But there were other questions the queen might answer. "How did Cora find me?" I found my feet. "Why me?"

The Glimmer Queen looked away from my wet cheeks. "When Evadora was born, Cora knew the girl could not remain in Eden. Her features were too strange for the mortals to comprehend." As if to demonstrate, she held up her bare hand and changed the hue of her skin from one color to another. "She wished to bring her mortal lover to live in the Glimmer."

Evadora's eyes brightened. "Daddy!"

Naeve ignored the outburst. "During Cora's last visit, she told me she dared not have another child of her own and decided to adopt. Cora never said how she found you, but did say she felt drawn to you from the moment she laid eyes on you." The queen looked me up and down. "Why that was, I am not sure."

"I don't know either," I admitted. The curse made me frail and weak—not the ideal child for anyone to adopt unless they wanted a handout from child welfare services.

"Cora told me something pulled her"—Naeve poked her fingers against her chest—"from inside. When she found you, she sensed your tortured soul and knew she had found you for a reason."

"Was this when you banished her?" I asked.

"No," Naeve replied. "She begged to bring you and her mortal lover to the Glimmer. I refused. It was not so much that I banished Cora from the Glimmer, but that she refused to return when I forbid her from returning with you and her man."

"Knowing she was mortal, that she could die, she stayed with me and Bill." I thought of how my curse had warped Bill into a wife beater. How Cora kept me safe and loved me even when Bill began to beat her. How she had finally killed Bill.

"Yes," Naeve replied. "Knowing that, she stayed. Staying, she died."

"Staying with me cost her everything." My lower lip trembled. "You're wrong, Naeve. Cora wasn't weak. She was strong. She found me and saved me. Without her to give me a conscience, I might be just like my parents. You are the weak one."

The queen's eyes glittered. "I am the Glimmer Queen, eternal ruler of the anchored world. I am not weak."

Her words, devoid of anger or pride, still carried an unspoken threat. The absence of emotion meant she could kill all of us without the least hint of remorse and I didn't want to test her.

"I have a rather silly question," Ambria said, a bit too quickly, as if to change the subject. "How do you speak our language so well when Evadora can't?"

"The girl lived wild when she was old enough to walk," Naeve replied. "I let her do as she willed since I am no mother."

"How did she survive?" Max asked.

"Here she cannot come to harm," she said.

"What if she fell into the stars below the trees?" Max asked.

Naeve paused. "How could she fall?"

It seemed no one here thought it was even a remote possibility. "Will you help my father?" I asked.

She nodded. "If he finds the answer to my problem."

"If you thought Cora was weak because she felt emotion, why would you want to be immortal in Eden?" I asked. "It doesn't make sense."

"I simply wish the freedom to leave here without fear of withering into an old woman," Naeve replied. "Unlike Cora, I will rule emotion, not the other way around."

The queen obviously had no idea how difficult that was, but I knew better than to argue with her.

The queen continued speaking. "If Victus helps me, I will help him secure his victory over Eden."

"You mustn't help him," I said. "He's evil."

"I must do what is best for my people," Naeve replied.

"Do you have an army?" Ambria asked.

"The world is my army," Naeve replied, a reminder of what Evadora had told us about the queen controlling the cat birds.

Max didn't seem to remember the comment. "How is the world your army?"

Starlight flared in Naeve's eyes. One of the vines clinging to the terrace whipped around Ambria and lifted her from the ground. A choked scream tore from her throat and her eyes flashed with terror. Just as abruptly as it had seized her, the vine lowered her to the ground and reattached itself to the stone.

Ambria shivered violently. "How did you do that?" she asked in a quavering voice.

Naeve tilted her head slightly. "I willed it so and the vine answered."

"Whoa." Max backed away from the queen. "You control plants?"

She motioned at the mountain palace and the natural stone terrace. "My people commune with nature in different ways. Some with animals, others with plants, and even a few with the earth beneath your feet."

Anyone who could make the world fight for them wouldn't need an army. "Did my father say how long it would take him to solve your problem?" I asked.

"Several months at least," Naeve replied. "A minute, a month, a year, is but a fleeting instant in our existence. To even hope or dream for his success is beyond my ability and yet I find the future holds more allure than it once did."

My parents were brilliant. If there was an answer to the Glimmer dilemma, they would find it eventually. The situation seemed hopeless. And yet, Naeve's reply to my earlier question led me to ask her something else. "If I find the solution first, will you help me instead of my father?"

The queen spread her hands. "Of course."

"You would help me defeat my parents?" I asked.

"If that was your desire," she replied.

Max glared at me as if he thought I was mental. "You barely even know magic, Conrad. How do you think you'll beat your parents to an answer?"

"Conrad can do it," Ambria said in tone that brooked no argument. "After all, he has me to help him."

Evadora clapped her hands and giggled. "Tears and smiles forever for everyone!" She danced around us chanting her words over and over.

Max pressed his hands to his ears and groaned.

With this ancient being before me, I decided this was a good chance to find out if Evadora's story about the realms was true. "Naeve, can you tell me the story of the Glimmer?" I asked.

The queen stared at the glittering sky. "Yes, but I will keep it brief since your existence is but a heartbeat in the continuum."

I tried not to let her words frighten me and nodded. "Thank you."

She began without prelude. "My people were once a part of Eden as were all the other races of the other realms. Then came the Apocryphan." Naeve's eyes glittered. "Some believed they were the progeny of the Seraphim and Sirens, while others theorized they were the descendants of the dragon folk." The queen shook her head. "Their origin is uncertain, but their powers were unmatched. One of them seized control of our kingdom while his kin claimed other kingdoms as their prizes."

"The world was divided into kingdoms?" Ambria asked.

Naeve nodded. "I use the term loosely. Our kingdom was the forest, the field, the mountain, while the Seraphim claimed the clouds and the Sirens ruled the sea."

"What about the demons?" Max asked.

119

"The demons did not exist as they do today," she said. "Centuries after the Apocryphan arrogated our world, they began to fight among themselves. War consumed the Earth, pitting once peaceful realms against each other." Naeve motioned to the vines on the terrace wall. Slithering like snakes, they wound around one another until they formed a verdant throne.

Max's mouth dropped open. I swallowed nervously and felt Ambria's hand tighten on mine.

The queen sat as if nothing out of the ordinary had happened and continued her story. "The incredible outpour of magic ruptured the world, breaking it apart and dividing the kingdoms into different realms. The split ripped the souls from some beings and cast them into a spiritual realm we call Haedaemos." Naeve narrowed her eyes. "My ancestors believed the Sundering was far too neat to be an accident. They believe Xanomiel, one of the Apocryphan who ruled no kingdom, was responsible for crafting the spell that fractured the world."

"Is this story true?" Ambria asked. "It sounds like a fairy tale."

"You are but a whisper of breath to a world far more ancient than you can imagine," Naeve said in her cold voice. "If your mind cannot comprehend the enormity of all that has gone on before, perhaps you should simply refrain from speaking."

Ambria squeaked. "I'm sorry."

"After the Sundering, our realms remained in contact but were drifting apart across the astral divide." Naeve looked up at the moon. "The Sirens discovered there were locations where the walls between the realms were thin enough to walk between the planes. They devised a plan to reunite the realms, but first wanted to imprison the Apocryphan so this would never happen again."

"They constructed the Abyss," I said.

Naeve nodded. "The Sirens are gifted builders and willingly served their master, Posthaneid. He was supposedly quite benevolent for an Apocryphan, and taught them a great deal. They used this knowledge to construct the Abyss and the anchor stone." Starlight blazed in her eyes and just as quickly vanished.

It was the closest thing to emotion I'd seen from her.

Naeve folded her hands into her lap. "Once all was constructed, they trapped the Apocryphan in the Abyss, and sang the anchor stone into existence out of the bedrock of a realm arbitrarily selected by the Sirens. Without our knowledge or permission, they chose the Glimmer. As you can see, the song tore our realm apart and built the anchor stone."

"So in all the thousands of years you've been here, you've never been able to solve your immortality problem?" I asked.

"Yes. In all our wisdom, we have accomplished nothing," she replied.

Her words gave me hope. If her people hadn't solved the problem of gaining emotion while keeping their immortality, it didn't seem likely my parents would figure it out in a matter of months or even years. Only one race might have the answers. "Have you ever asked the Sirens for help?"

Naeve looked up at a blue globe in the starry sky. "We have not seen one since the Anchoring, though I suspect they never leave Aquilis. I hear their realm suffered less than most."

"You never tried to find one of them?" I asked.

"As my sister and others before her proved, any who leave the Glimmer risk their immortality." She took her eyes from the realm and looked at me. "Have you seen a Siren?"

I shook my head. "No, but there's a lot I haven't seen." *How would my father approach this problem?* I listened for a hint from his soul fragment, but it didn't speak.

"I think it unlikely you or your parents will find the answer," Naeve said. "It is good I cannot hope, or feel the crush of despair when you have failed."

I put a hand in my pocket and rubbed the smooth pebble. "Where is the anchor stone?"

Naeve blinked at me. "Is it not obvious?" She looked up. "It is plain to see."

Max, Ambria, and I looked into the night sky and immediately saw what she meant. The anchor stone was none other than the giant moon rotating slowly in the night sky.

Naeve is right. We'll never find an answer for her people.

And that was a good thing.

Chapter 14

The Glimmer folk would never feel emotion and that made me happy. I wondered if that meant I was evil.

Naeve saw through me. "Your skin holds no secrets from me, young one. You hope for your parents to fail."

"They're bad people." I backed away a step, hoping she didn't tie me up with a vine. "I don't want you to help them conquer Eden."

"It is understandable," she replied.

A shock of fear jolted my nerves when I thought of my parents' next visit here. "Will you tell them I was here?"

Naeve shook her head. "Telling them would cause them to focus on you instead of the goal I wish them to achieve."

I wasn't sure if I should thank her or not.

A chime rang in the distance and the queen stood from her chair of vines. "Duty calls and I must away. You are welcome to stay in the Glimmer for as long as you wish." Naeve ran her unsettling gaze over me and my friends. "You should take care. Your frail mortal state may not take well to our shattered home."

The Glimmer Queen strode away into her mountain palace.

Evadora climbed into the vine chair and snuggled up as if to take a nap.

"I think we should return to Queens Gate," Ambria said, her eyes large and filled with uncertainty. "This entire place feels unnatural."

I looked up at the slowly spinning moon and at the Earth-shaped realms held within its orbit. "It makes me feel tiny."

"The queen makes my hairs stand on end," Max whispered. "No emotions—can you believe it? Killing us wouldn't make her sad even a little bit."

Ambria shivered and rubbed her arms. "Can we go home, please?"

"Let's go." I shook Evadora to wake her.

She leapt up, skin shading to match the rock around us, then blinked at us in confusion. Her flesh shaded back to a warm peach. "Why did you wake me?"

"We want to go home," I said. "Can you guide us back?"

"It is easy to leave." She pointed into the distance. "Go back that way."

"I'm not wandering around out there without a guide," Max said. "We need you, Evadora."

The girl flinched. "Need me?"

"We can't get back without you," Ambria explained. "We want you to come with us."

I touched her hand. "You're my sister, right?"

"I am!" A smile stretched across Evadora's face. She giggled and pressed her hands to her chest. "This makes me feel warm inside. Happy." Her eyes flashed. "Being needed is good."

"You've never felt this way before?" I asked.

She shook her head. "Nobody needs me here." Evadora skipped to the edge of the cliff and motioned us to follow.

Swallowing nervously, Max followed but refused to look over the edge. Ambria joined them and clasped Evadora's hand. I stepped up beside them and stared out at the land of twinkling stars and eternal twilight. We dropped over the cliff edge and plummeted earthward. Ambria shrieked. Max blanched and squeezed his eyes shut as the starry sky streaked past.

My body felt cold from the inside out. It seemed as if the warmth slowly drained from me every minute I remained in this strange world. What had stolen emotions from these people? Had they just become bored of living forever or was there something about the Glimmer that did it?

We reached the bottom of the mountain palace and Evadora skipped ahead of us singing, "They need me, they need me!"

I was happy to reach the small glade of purple snake grass and spiky trees. The black water of the looking pool seemed more inviting than this dreary world. "Grab hold," I said, and held the pebble in my hand.

Evadora stepped back and waved.

"You're not coming?" Ambria asked.

The girl shook her head. "You can find the way without me. I will see you soon."

"Um, maybe you should come with us just in case," Max said.

I hugged her. "Maybe one day you can come live with us for good in Eden."

Her head tilted to the side. "I think I would like that, brother."

It felt strange hearing this odd girl call me brother, but it also made me feel connected to someone else Cora had loved. I couldn't imagine my beloved mum abandoning a child, whatever the reason, and yet, she had. I didn't know why, but I felt obligated to help Evadora if I could. Staying in the emotionally bereft Glimmer seemed unhealthy. It was no wonder she acted so strange.

Evadora kissed my cheek. "Bye!" Without another word, she spun and skipped away.

"Lot of help she is," Ambria grumbled. "She wouldn't stop singing about how needed she felt, then leaves us to go through that frightening rift again."

"This is the easy part," I said. "We just have to get back to our pond fast."

"I hope you remember the way," Max said.

"It was a straight path," I replied. "We can do it." I rubbed the stone. "As above, so below."

We jumped into the water. My insides twisted backwards and forwards. We flew from the pond and landed heavily on the shore.

Max pushed up on his hands and knees and heaved. "I'll never be hungry again," he whined.

Ambria stood and tugged on his shirt. "Don't be a baby. Get up."

I climbed to my feet and brushed off my pants. The Glimmer made me feel uneasy, and its reflection only amplified the knot in my stomach. "Let's go before our reflections find us."

Max groaned and got up. "Do you really believe our own reflections would try to get us? I mean, they're part of us, right?"

Ambria shook her head as we began to jog down the path toward the crack in the world. "If Evadora was afraid, then I don't want to find out."

We reached the tall fracture in the rock and ran through the tunnel until we entered the rift. Though I knew what to expect, my stomach lurched with vertigo at the sight of the star-dusted blackness. I took a tentative step forward and breathed with relief as my foot found solid ground.

Max bent over and touched the invisible floor. "Are the stars an illusion, maybe?"

"I think it's a projection, like a movie theater," Ambria said.

I noted a faint but visible bar of light connecting the stars beneath us like dots. I got down on my knees and crawled to my left, reaching a hand out as I did. A few feet from my friends, I found emptiness and my chest tightened.

Max walked toward me. "What are you—"

"Stop!" I held up a hand, but it was too late. Max stepped over the invisible edge.

I leapt for him, hoping to knock him sideways before his momentum carried him over. He fell and rolled. Max shouted as his feet and body slid off and dangled in space. Somehow, his fingers gripped the side of the light bridge. I quickly fastened my hands around a wrist and pulled.

Ambria shrieked and ran to my side.

"Help me," I groaned, trying desperately to lift Max's weight.

She grabbed his other wrist. "I'm trying, but he's so heavy." She jerked on his arm to no effect. "Why do you have to eat so much, Max?"

Max's teeth chattered and his face went as green as the pebble in my pocket. "I'm going to fall into the stars and be lost forever."

"Try to pull yourself up," I told him. "I'll grab your belt and pull on it."

"I'm trying," Max said. "My fingers are slipping! Help!"

Ambria screamed and pulled harder. "He's so sweaty, Conrad. I can't hold him."

Desperation took hold and I could think of only one way to save his life. I took out my wand, pointed it at his hand and shouted, "*Affixiato!*" His right hand flattened against the bridge just as his left hand lost purchase and swung loose.

Max and Ambria screamed at the tops of their lungs.

But Max did not fall. I had magically glued his hand to the top of the bridge.

"Oh, god, I'm going to be sick," Max said.

Ambria slumped. "How are we supposed to get him up here?"

I had the answer. "We left our brooms at the edge of the pond." I gave Ambria the pebble. "Can you fetch one?"

"You're not coming with me?" she said in a high-pitched voice.

I shook my head. "I need to make sure Max doesn't fall." I jabbed a finger at the crack on the other side of the rift. "Hurry!"

Ambria clenched the pebble and ran.

I turned back to Max who now hung limply from his single hand. "I never realized how hard it is to pull yourself up over a ledge," he said in a calm voice. "It's so ruddy hard, Conrad."

I nodded. "Do you know of any other spells that might help me get you up here?"

He put his free hand to his chin. "Hmm, I don't know any levitation spells."

I shut my eyes and tried to think. I'd studied so much for the entrance exam, it seemed I might have learned something useful. I could light Max on fire, or send a breeze across his face. I only knew the affix spell because Max had once accidentally used it on me. I had no choice but to wait.

Minutes ticked past and I hoped Ambria had not become lost. I stood up and thought about going after her, but a scuffling noise caught my ear and Ambria crawled from the crack in the wall, a broom in hand.

"I'm back!" she called. Panting desperately, she held out Max's salvation.

I raced across the bridge and grabbed it from her, then turned and went back to Max. Praying that the broom worked in the reflected rift as it did in the real world, I activated it. The broom hovered and I breathed with relief. Since I'd have to fly the broom beneath Max with the levitation spell active, I turned it off. The spell wasn't strong enough to support the two of us.

I leaned over and handed the broom to Max. "Can you turn it on with one hand?"

"Yeah." He grasped it with his free hand and twisted with his hand. The broom leveled off just between his legs. Gritting his teeth,

126

he pulled up on the handle and the broom drifted upward until he rested comfortably in the seat. Max sighed with relief and leaned his forehead on the broomstick.

"We did it," Ambria said. "Thank goodness."

"What's the spell to unglue your hand?" I asked Max. I couldn't remember the word.

"Um…" He tried to move his right hand then remembered it was fixed to the bridge. "I think the word is *disruptus*. You have to flick the wand up, back down, and then point it at my hand." His forehead pinched. "Or is it the opposite?"

I followed his instructions. "*Disruptus*!"

His hand pulled free. Max winced and rubbed it. "Ow. It's a bit numb."

"From holding up your entire body," Ambria said. "You need to lose weight so you won't be so heavy next time we have to pull you up a cliff."

"Maybe you should exercise," Max shot back.

A strange tingle worked its way up my spine and I remembered Evadora's warning about our reflections. "We need to go, now!"

Max shot forward on the broom and headed toward the crack while Ambria and I ran to keep up.

"I'm—so—tired," Ambria said breathlessly. She stumbled.

I caught her and helped her back up. "I'll help you." I wished I could carry her, but even her small frame was too heavy for me.

Max whipped back around on the broom and hopped off. "Take the broom, silly."

Ambria looked as if she wanted to say something, but couldn't catch her breath. She climbed onboard and flew for the crack. Max and I ran after her.

"Leave the broom and I'll carry it through the tunnel," Max called.

Ambria got off the broom and left it there, then vanished inside the tunnel. I went ahead of Max and he came behind me with the broom, shuffling furiously on his knees. Once we reached the other side, Ambria climbed back onto the broom and flew toward the pond.

The tingling sensation along my back grew stronger and stronger. "We've got no time to waste," I told Max. "Run for your life!"

"It feels like something is crawling up my back!" Max shouted.

I motioned him forward. "It must be our reflections coming for us."

We ran past the destroyed mansion and toward the forest. The burn in my leg muscles burrowed deeper like paralyzing venom. My legs grew heavier with every step and sweat trickled down my face. Max wheezed with every step.

"Too"—he sucked in a breath—"far."

I tried to offer him encouragement, but it was all I could do to put one foot in front of the other. It hadn't seemed so far during the walk toward the crack. Running only seemed to make our goal impossibly far away. Our sprint turned into a ragged shuffle through the remainder of the stump forest, the pond on the other side growing closer. Finally, we staggered out of the stumps.

Two familiar figures raced through the iron gate at the edge of the Fairy Garden, their gait never faltering. My knees went weak when I saw their faces. Mine and Max's twins stared back at us.

"Your reflections!" Ambria cried.

"Land the bleeding broom," Max shouted.

Ambria still had the stone. I rallied a breath. "Get the pebble ready!"

The terrifying sight renewed my energy. Sucking ragged breaths, Max and I scampered for the pond. Our reflections never once slowed, their faces twisted into maniacal grins as they closed on their quarry. I had no idea what would happen if they caught us. My breaths sounded like sandpaper on rotten wood. My legs were nearly numb with burning agony. I embraced the pain. After Cora died, pain had been my only friend, the one thing that let me know I was alive.

Once again it was here, urging me on, and reminding me there were far worse things than pain in the world.

We reached the pond. Max stumbled, arms splayed, and slid face-first through the mud. Ambria tugged on his shirt, trying to help him up. He sputtered and leaned heavily on her to pull himself up to his feet.

I dared a look back at the reflections. Even from this distance, I could tell there was something terribly wrong with them. Their bodies rippled like water, and blackness seeped from their eyes. Ambria fumbled with the pebble and dropped it. I dove forward, and caught it right at the edge of the water.

Rising on wobbly knees, I said, "Grab hold!"

My reflection shouted something unintelligible and Max's chimed in.

"What did they say?" Max asked.

I didn't know what they'd said, but the analytical voice of my father spoke. *They're talking backwards.*

It was time to go. "As above, so below!" I bent my knees to jump.

Max jerked my arm. "No, no, say it in reverse."

I had forgotten and nearly cost us dearly. "So below, as above!"

Our reflections screeched. I felt something brush against my back.

We leapt.

The black water swallowed us. My insides wrenched inside out and suddenly the ground in the real world rushed toward me. I landed on useless legs and rolled. Ambria tumbled into a heap next to me and Max narrowly avoided squashing me. I sat up and basked in the warmth of the sun.

My legs were simply too tired to move so I lay back down. "I need a moment."

"It feels wonderful to be back," Ambria said. "Let's please never go to that awful place again."

Max groaned and stayed on the ground, hands folded behind his head. "You've got my vote."

I lay there for several minutes until the burn in my legs faded, and my breathing came easier. Rolling to my knees made standing a little easier. When I retrieved my broom from beside the pond, my reflection glared back at me, hollow eyes burning with rage. A yelp burst from my throat and I stumbled onto my backside.

Max stood over me, a puzzled expression on his face. "What's wrong?"

I pointed toward the pond. "M-my reflection."

He peered into the water and promptly fell over backwards next to me. "Evadora was right," he said in a hoarse whisper. "You don't want those reflections finding you."

"Why didn't mine come?" Ambria asked, sounding a bit hurt. "It doesn't make any sense."

"Sure it does," Max said. "You left the reflected world to get the broom. Your reflection probably lost the scent while you were here."

"Or maybe my reflection is dumber than yours." She frowned. "I hope my reflection isn't stupid."

I dared another peek into the water. My visage peered over the side, black smoke drifting from the blank eye sockets, its lips curled into a malicious smile. I waved a hand over the water and the reflection mirrored me as it normally would, but the face contorted with rage, a puppet who hated his master. "I hope this thing doesn't follow me into every mirror I look into."

Max's reflection appeared next to mine as he leaned over the water. He shuddered. "I already hate the way I look in the morning, but if this awful monster follows me around, I'm never looking into a mirror again."

Ambria looked at her normal reflection and sighed. "I can't believe I have a stupid reflection."

Max patted his stomach. "Let's go. I'm—"

"You can't be starving," Ambria said with disgust. "Not after all that."

He picked up his broom. "I was going to say I'm tired. I haven't run that hard since my brothers wanted to test a new transformation spell on me."

I wholeheartedly agreed with him, though my stomach rumbled since it was well past lunch. "I could use some food. I think I burned every ounce of energy in my body."

"If that were the case, you'd be dead," Ambria commented dryly.

Max wobbled his head side-to-side. "Well, now that you mention it, I could eat something too."

Ambria folded her arms across her chest. "It seems coming back to the real world has given me an appetite as well."

We boarded our brooms and headed away from the Fairy Garden and hopefully our frightening reflections. Though my parents might never find the answer to the Glimmer Queen's quest for emotions, I couldn't simply hope the issue sorted itself. Right after lunch, we had to pay a visit to Galfandor.

I just hoped the old headmaster would take action.

Chapter 15

"The headmaster is not in," said a short professor we met in the hallway while looking for Galfandor. He adjusted a pair of wire-rimmed glasses and peered down at us. "You understand he's quite a busy man. Who are your advisors and why are you so filthy?"

Ambria frowned and looked back and forth between Max and me. "Advisors? Nobody told us about that."

"You should have received the information in the post today." He twirled the end of his long black mustache. "You'll find the letter to be quite thorough. I suggest you go to your homes and read it before bothering the headmaster with concerns that are too trifling for him to worry about."

"Yes, sir." I just wanted the unhelpful professor to go away.

He brushed his hands together like a man finished with an unpleasant task. "Excellent."

Max stuck out his tongue as he watched the professor go. "Trifling concerns? I'd like to drop him into the reflected world and let his reflection find him."

Ambria snorted. "Maybe his mirror self is nicer."

Max brushed at the mud crusted on his pants. "Since we can't find Galfandor, I'm going home to clean up. Then I'll come over."

"We should go home to check the post," Ambria said to me. "It's probably important to know who our advisors are."

"Probably," I agreed. I still couldn't get the Glimmer Queen's face from my mind. The ache in my chest hurt a little more every time I thought of my beloved mum's twin. So many emotions piled up in my stomach, I couldn't think straight. "Why don't you go ahead and I'll catch up later?"

Ambria's forehead creased. "You were so quiet during lunch. Were you thinking about Cora?"

Pain pinched my throat tight. I nodded and swallowed hard so I could speak. "I need some time."

She flung her petite form against my chest and squeezed me hard. "Of course, Conrad."

Max put a hand on my shoulder. "I think you're lucky to have had her, Conrad." He backed away and looked down. "At least you had a mother who really loved you."

Ambria kissed my cheek. "I'll be at home if you want to talk." She cleared her throat and grabbed Max by the arm. "Stop being a nuisance, Max, and go clean those filthy clothes of yours."

He grinned. "See ya later."

After they climbed on their brooms and flew away, I stood staring at the sky for a long moment, wondering if a realm existed where Cora might still be alive. Was there an afterlife, or was her beautiful soul lost forever?

I imagined a wise old woman sitting in a rocking chair, knitting needles working furiously. After a time, she would hold up a shimmering new soul she'd just completed. "Oh, this one is the loveliest I've made in a while," she'd say. "It will be special."

Beautiful, special souls shouldn't be wasted on oblivion.

"Please still be out there, Mum." It felt like a prayer. I didn't believe in gods, but I believed in Cora. She had taken me, this lifeless lump of clay, and molded it into something better despite all the evils in my life that had tried to twist me into something bad. I would never want to disappoint her.

I dearly cared for my friends and valued their advice, but at times like this, I wished there was someone older and wiser I could turn to for advice. The only person who came close to fitting that role was Galfandor, only because he already knew all there was to know about me. There was one other place he might be if he wasn't at the school. I ran a hand down the polished wood handle of my broom until it found the grooves of the etched symbols enchanted with the flight spells.

The broom hovered in place with a simple twist. I climbed onboard and directed it up the hill toward Moore Manor where the headmaster lived. The shout and clang of people doing noisy work echoed from somewhere ahead. The road curved around a section of forest to my right that concealed the estate of Moore Manor. An unpleasant smell bit my nose just before a work crew came into sight.

Burly men beat the old worn road with sledgehammers, tearing loose cobblestones while another group stood around a large barrel filled with steaming pitch. I realized that was the source of the foul smell. No one paused in their work to watch me flit past and take a right down the gravel road toward the mansion.

A flutter of white caught the corner of my eye. I spotted people in white robes kneeling and chanting on earth blackened by demonic symbols once used in an attack on the mansion. Slowing to watch them, I wondered if they were healing the earth. Another group on the other side of the road tended to the large demon-summoning rune there as well.

I came to a stop in front of a marble statue of Ezzek Moore. The robed sculpture looked to the stars, his hand raised as if trying to pluck a heavenly body from its perch. A tablet at the bottom read:

Here lie the ashes of one man who lived many lives: Moses, father of the Arcanes, Ezzek Moore, founder of Arcane University, and Jeremiah Conroy protector of Eden. Despite the demon-ravaged earth, life once again sprouted here in the spot he died. May he be remembered so long as Eden lives.

A perfect circle of white lilies and grass grew around a small sapling that had grown considerably since the last time I'd seen it. I knew from studying that Ezzek Moore would be a large part of my history class. I looked forward to learning more about him.

"Hmm, yes," said a soft voice from my side.

I flinched and tumbled off my broom.

Galfandor looked down at me, amusement dancing in his bright blue eyes. "Apologies, young Edison." He reached down a hand and tugged me to my feet.

I finally recovered from the surprise. "I didn't know you were there."

"You stood here for quite some time." The headmaster stroked his beard. "Oh, there's no shame in it, of course. I find myself contemplating the man behind the statue."

"Did you know him?" I asked.

Galfandor made a thoughtful noise and changed the subject. "So, young man, what brings you out here?"

I looked around at the people in the woods. "Well, it's top secret."

"Come inside then." He headed toward the house. The large wooden door swung silently open at a touch, and closed just as quietly behind me.

It was no wonder the old man had been able to sneak up on me. I suspected he enjoyed it. Rather than lead me to his sitting room, Galfandor walked up the stairs just past the foyer and turned right at the top. The bubble of boiling liquid accompanied by the hiss of said liquid hitting fire reached my ears before I followed Galfandor into a room with a flickering orange glow. A large black iron kettle hung over a large stone hearth in the center of the room. The chimney in the ceiling funneled red smoke up and away, but it hadn't done anything to keep the foul odor from the room. It smelled like rotting broccoli and cow manure.

Despite the stink, I thought he might be preparing supper, but a quick look at the strange contents inside the kettle told me otherwise. "What is this?"

He chuckled. "An attempt at divination in the old ways." The headmaster took a large wooden spoon and stirred the concoction. "It's going rather poorly, I'm afraid."

Something shaped like a lizard bobbed to the top. I shuddered and backed away. "How is it supposed to work?"

Galfandor stared into the bubbling liquid. Water spattered over the edge and hissed angrily down the side of the kettle until it steamed away. "The ingredients that boil to the top are supposed to indicate something about the future, but I believe I misread them."

"What did they say?"

He picked up a piece of parchment from a nearby table and showed it to me. The neatly quilled ink said, *From starlight, danger.* "Unless the stars fall, I can't fathom what danger it means."

My stomach went tight with apprehension. "I think I know what it means."

Galfandor raised an eyebrow. "Another whisper from your parents' souls?"

"We went through the rift to the other world," I said quickly.

His eyes flashed surprise. With a flick of his wand, he snuffed the fire beneath the kettle and motioned me to follow him. We settled in the sitting room downstairs, a steaming pot of Earl Grey tea on the table between us. I took mine with a little milk and savored the strong flavor.

Galfandor dribbled milk into his tea. "I'm ready for your account, young Conrad."

I took a moment to rewind my memories back to the best starting place. Cora's face intruded when I closed my eyes, so I left them open and started with the green pebble. "Evadora wanted me to retrieve this pebble." I showed it to him.

The headmaster took it in his hand and rubbed it. "I sense great power and gravity in such a small package." He weighed the stone in his hand. "It's incredibly dense."

Letters and numbers from complex equations flashed through my mind. *Denser even than osmium*, my father said. I'd noticed the weight, but had been too preoccupied to analyze it. "Somehow, it enables me to travel through water into a place Evadora calls the reflected world."

At this, Galfandor nearly dropped his tea. With a trembling hand, he set his teacup back on the platter. "You have been there, I take it?"

I nodded. "Evadora told us to be careful so our reflections didn't catch us."

"There are places we were never meant to visit, Conrad." His voice was sterner than usual. "This stone bends the natural order. Using it in such a manner could completely break the foundation and invite chaos."

For a moment, fear tightened its grip on my heart when I considered he might not return Cora's legacy to me. Galfandor regarded it for a while longer, then set it in the center of the table.

I reached out and took it. "Does this mean you trust I won't break the world?"

He shrugged head. "I simply want you to be aware of the implications."

"What do you know about the reflected world?" I asked.

"Enough to know how dangerous it is." Galfandor flicked his hand to the side. "Continue your story, please."

I didn't want to continue. I wanted him to tell me what he knew about the world where my frightening reflection roamed free. For example, when I jumped into the water, why wasn't my reflection already there? How did it know I was there in the first place? But the firm resolve in Galfandor's eyes stopped me from peppering him with questions. I briefly considered trading him for information, but I was the one who'd come to him for advice and possibly comfort, not the other way around.

I shared the story with him. My chest constricted with pain when I told him the Glimmer Queen's relationship to Cora. Somehow, I managed to push through without crying. Half an hour later, I'd laid out everything for him, including how mine and Max's reflections had chased us. I felt it offered me some wiggle room to ask him about that strange place. "What would have happened if our reflections caught us?"

The headmaster picked up the teapot and poured himself another cup. He poured in a bit of milk, stirred, and took a sip. His blue eyes settled on me for what seemed like a long time, though it might have only been a second. I almost looked away, but it felt too much like the times I'd faced the old bull at the Goodleigh's farm. Sometimes, you had to stare down the beast or you'd get trampled.

I didn't want Galfandor trampling on my right to receive answers.

He set the cup on the platter. "The reflections have no souls, Conrad. They are, in a sense, not real at all."

"They seemed real when they were running at me," I said. "They looked evil."

"What you saw was their emptiness," the headmaster replied. "They lust after one thing, and that is to be real." He stood up abruptly and paced away from the table. "Unless you plan on giving up your soul, Conrad, do not let your reflection touch you."

I flinched at the suddenness of his departure. "Yes, sir."

Galfandor stopped in the doorway. "As for the Glimmer Queen and your parents, I believe you're right." He turned to face me. "If the Glimmer folk, in all these millennia, have been unable to cure their dispassion while retaining immortality, I doubt your parents will discover the solution."

His affirmation gave me more comfort than I wanted to admit. I was just a boy who barely knew magic. My parents were probably too powerful for even someone like Galfandor to fight. What hope would I have against them?

The old man smiled reassuringly. "Besides, I am quite confident your parents aren't truly looking for their help at all—at least not in the way they've led the queen to believe."

My face screwed up with confusion. "But I heard them talking to Serena about it."

"Yes, but what you overheard could be interpreted many ways." He leaned against the doorframe. "Turn it around in your head, Conrad."

"Turn what around?" I imagined an army of Glimmer people marching through the rift and invading Queens Gate. I reversed the process, picturing my parents leading an army to invade the Glimmer. It didn't make sense. Why would they want to conquer such a dreary world? "You think my parents want to rule the Glimmer?"

"The Glimmer Queen told you herself that her people were mortal before the Sirens anchored the realms." He folded his arms across his chest and waited.

I took his silence as another chance to solve this riddle. The Glimmer folk were mortal, then the Sirens gave them immortality as payment for shattering their world.

Gave them immortality.

I thought back to what Delectra had said. *They will pave the way to our eternal rule.*

Suddenly, I knew what my parents really wanted.

Chapter 16

I blurted the answer. "My parents don't want the Glimmer Queen's army. They want her immortality."

Galfandor's grin widened. "Precisely."

"But how?" I held up the stone. "Queen Naeve thought this piece of the anchor stone might be the answer, but Cora still died."

He held up a finger. "An excellent question." The old man stepped outside the sitting room. "I am curious how your parents found out about the Glimmer. Only one other person has ever written about it."

I followed him into the hallway. "Who?"

"Ezzek Moore, of course." Galfandor stroked his beard. "When Evadora said the old man put the crack in the world, I believe she referred to him." His eyes narrowed as if trying to see into the past.

"What did he write about the Glimmer?" I asked.

"In one of the letters Ezzek wrote to his close friend, Alexander Tiberius, Ezzek made a passing mention to the Glimmer—more of a clue, really." Galfandor walked away without another word, and I hurried to catch up. We entered a tall room that stretched several stories high. Bookshelves lined every square inch of wall. The scent of leather and paper mingled pleasantly with that of old wood.

He went directly to a free-standing shelf in the center of the room, hefted a thick black book from it, and laid it out on a sturdy oak table. The headmaster flipped open the book to reveal yellowed parchments covered in quilled ink. Thick red thread bound them together. Galfandor screwed up his lips. "Now which letter was that?" he murmured to himself. A few moments and several pages later, he proclaimed, "Aha," and pointed to a page. He flipped it around to me.

I tell you there is no other explanation but that the realms were once one. I have found the glimmering anchor holding them together and realized its secret must never be revealed. Only a madman would tempt fate with that sort of power.

The letter changed subjects completely in the next paragraph. "Ezzek found the Glimmer and decided it was dangerous for anyone else to know about." I frowned. "If it was supposed to be a secret, how did you get his letter?"

"The ruins of the first mansion held many secrets," Galfandor said. "Before I decided to rebuild, I took the time to search the remains and found this book of letters stored in an underground vault. Alexander Tiberius and other members of the original Arcane Council stored records here before they moved into their own abodes."

I puzzled over Ezzek's words. "I guess he thought the power of immortality was dangerous."

"I'm certain there's far more to it than that," Galfandor said. "For now, Conrad, I believe you can rest easy. There will be no invasion by the Glimmer Queen. If anything, your parents will be far too busy discovering the path to immortality to bother with us."

"But if they gain immortality, won't they be unstoppable?"

"There are two types of immortality, Conrad." Galfandor closed the book of letters and filed it back on the shelf. "The most common kind that vampires, Daemos, lycans, and so forth possess simply gives them a long life and lasting youth unless they are killed." He headed for the door, still speaking. "The rarest of the rare, means the subject is unable to be killed by any means."

"Even chopping them into little bits?" I asked.

Galfandor nodded.

I thought about the lycan, Brickle, who Ambria, Max, and I had inadvertently fed to a demon. "What about if a demon eats their soul?"

Galfandor paused in the hallway and pursed his lips. "What an interesting question. I suppose if I find someone truly immortal, I will ask them."

"So, the Glimmer Queen and her people can die if someone kills them?" I asked.

"Unless proven otherwise, I would say yes." Galfandor led me to the foyer. "Your parents may discover a fountain of youth and long life in the Glimmer, but that does not make them indestructible."

Thinking of my traitorous, evil parents sent a quiver of anger through my shoulders. "What's the most certain way to kill them?"

Galfandor regarded me, lips and eyes flat. "I certainly hope you don't intend to hunt your parents, Conrad." He put an arm on my shoulder. "I believe you should concentrate on your studies and let the adults handle this matter."

I wanted so badly to trust him, but what if he really didn't mean to do anything about my parents? Whatever held him back from helping with the Goodleighs might prevent him from helping now. It seemed best to agree with him for now and see what happened next.

"Yes, sir." I hesitated to burden him with another problem, but didn't know when I would next see him. I tapped my temple with a finger. "My parents' soul shards have been talking a lot more and it worries me."

The headmaster took out his wand and pointed it toward my head. "May I?"

I nodded. "Will it hurt?"

Galfandor chuckled. "Not at all." He twirled the wand and tapped it to my head. I felt a slight tingle and saw a bright flash broken by two dark silhouettes. Galfandor grunted thoughtfully.

I waited a moment for an explanation. When he said nothing, I asked outright. "Will I be okay?"

"I can't rightly say, Conrad." Galfandor tucked away his wand. "The reason you hear them speaking more often is because the soul shards are slowly melding with your soul."

I flinched. "Melding?"

"Yes." He folded his arms. "The process could take months or years. I can measure you again in a month's time and perhaps determine how long you have."

The last phrase sent a cold chill into my stomach. "Will it kill me?"

Galfandor hesitated before answering. "I believe it depends." He squeezed my shoulder. "The demon that preserved your living curse also separated the three souls inside your body, keeping them from merging over time. If that had happened, the dominant soul might

140

have overcome the others." He took back his hand and shrugged. "It is difficult to say. While I see no immediate threat to your well-being, it is possible that the soul shards could become dominant if not kept in check."

I felt sick to my stomach. "The shards could take over my soul?"

"Yes, Conrad." Galfandor sighed. "But the possibility is unlikely, so long as you nurture your soul with your own experiences and remain strong against the invaders."

"Can't you remove them?" I asked in a plaintive voice.

"Unfortunately, I know of only one way."

He didn't have to finish that thought. "Death."

Galfandor's eyes tightened. "Yes." He offered a smile. "Feed your soul with knowledge, with laughter, with friendship, Conrad, and I am confident you will emerge the victor."

I didn't share his confidence, but it gave me all the more reason to study hard and make my own life. I had to be the stronger soul. I swallowed the knot of fear in my throat and forced a smile. "Thank you, sir." It seemed there was nothing more to say, so I walked toward the door.

"Conrad," Galfandor called after me.

I turned around. "Yes?"

"I believe what Cora said about you." When I returned a puzzled look, he clarified. "She found your tortured soul for a reason."

Salt stung my eyes. I turned away, the door now a blur in my wet vision. "Goodnight, sir."

"Good night, Conrad," he replied.

I left the house. The pink rays of the late afternoon sun failed to warm me as I flew my broom for home. A deep cold anger hung heavy in my chest because my parents dominated my thoughts. Knowing they were alive and well hung over me like a black cloud filled with lightning that could strike at any time. They'd alredy tried to kill me twice and they would never stop until they got the rest of their souls back.

Why can't Galfandor do something about them?

It seemed so unfair they should be alive while the one person who'd loved and believed in me rotted in a grave. For now, I'd do what Galfandor suggested and concentrate on school. But I'd use my spare time to study what made the Glimmer people immortal and

141

what could make them mortal again. A deep ache worked into my jaw, and I realized I was grinding my teeth.

I hate my parents so much.

I arrived home to find Blue in the yard next door playing rocket darts with Harris, Lily, and Baxter. She hit a bull's-eye and burst into cheers.

"Conrad!" She dashed over and gave me a hug I found difficult to return with any enthusiasm. "This game is so much fun. Do you want to join us?"

My mood hung like a wet blanket around my shoulders. "Not now."

The others waved at me.

"Come on, Conrad," Harris said. "You look like you could use some fun."

"You should be celebrating that you passed the exam," Lily added, her face flushed with happiness.

I mustered a wave. "I'm tired," I mumbled, and went inside the house.

"Hang on," Blue said, and ran after me. Her forehead pinched with worry. "What's wrong?"

"Nothing." I didn't want to talk about it. Her annoyingly happy presence just made me angrier. I ran up the stairs and closed the door behind me.

"Conrad, why are you angry?" Her voice cracked with hurt. "Do you want to talk about it?"

I buried my face in the pillow and ignored her until she went away.

The next morning, I packed some food and flew back to the crack in the world to lay in wait for my parents. A second-story window in the ruined mansion provided me with a good view of the grove hiding the fissure. Only a battered leather chair remained in what might have been a bedroom during better days. It, the dusty marble floor, and rotting draperies were only sad reminders of the mansion's past glory.

Rather than stare idly out the window, I brought several basic magic textbooks with me and spent the time reading and practicing spells. If I wanted to have a chance against my parents, I needed to accelerate my learning. I needed to know what they were doing in their search for immortality. I wouldn't beat them by brute force, but by stealth and cunning.

I hoped I was up to the task.

"Where have you been all day?" Ambria asked the moment I returned home that evening.

"Practicing magic." The half lie slid easily from my mouth.

She frowned. "Without Max and me?" Her eyes widened. "Did you go back to the Glimmer?"

"No." I tried to go upstairs, but she grabbed my arm.

"Conrad, we should tell Galfandor what happened to us."

"I already did." Once again, I tried to leave.

"When?"

I told her about my conversation with him. "My parents want immortality, not help from Naeve."

"Well, it's certainly better than what we thought," she replied.

My fists tightened. "Those murderers are the last people who deserve immortality, Ambria. The curse they put on me killed Cora!" I yelped her name, like a dog struck by a car.

Ambria's forehead creased and her eyes misted. "I agree it's awfully unfair, but if your parents hadn't done what they did, you never would have met Cora."

The cause and effect didn't matter to me. Anger and pain filled me and the effort of bottling it up made me feel like I was going to explode.

"We never would have met, Conrad." Ambria pressed my hand between hers. "You wouldn't have saved all those other kids, and I would have been sold into slavery."

I looked out the window and saw several adults in the Ashmore's backyard. A tall man who vaguely resembled Harris hovered over a smoking grill. Another man kicked a black-and-white checkered football with Baxter and Harris while Lily spoke with two older women.

I thought his parents were dead.

Harris saw us through the window and motioned us over.

Ambria grabbed my arm and dragged me toward the front door. "Let's go have some fun."

The last thing I wanted to do was have fun.

Self-pity is for the weak, Della said.

143

I bit back a retort when I realized she was right. Feeling sorry for myself; wallowing in pity would be a waste of time. I had to push forward through the pain and be ready for the next time my parents tried to hurt me.

"Fine," I said, and followed Ambria outside.

"I'd like you to meet my Aunt Kara and Uncle Louis," Harris said when we arrived, and it suddenly made sense why Harris resembled the man.

"What a pleasure," Kara said. "Harris told us all about how you two solved the final puzzle for the entrance exam."

"He's lucky to have a friend like you." Louis patted my shoulder. "You're a good lad."

Harris clapped my shoulder. "Hey, let's go kick the football." We ran over to Baxter.

I expected the boy to say something rude, but he simply booted the ball our way, his face flushed with pleasure. I wasn't good at kicking, but managed to keep up with the other two boys. Blue showed up later and joined us instead of hanging out with Lily and Ambria.

"You're really good," Harris said to her.

She bounced the ball off her knees then punted it off her head at me. "It's because I'm a lycan."

Harris grinned. "Maybe you could turn me into one so I'll be a better player."

"Me too," Baxter said.

Blue flushed and looked at me. "Would you like to be a lycan, Conrad?" She grabbed my arm and pretended to bite it.

I jumped back and the others laughed.

Later, everyone sat around a large picnic table outside eating the sausages and vegetables Louis had grilled.

At some point, I realized my anger and sadness had faded away, replaced by a strange feeling I didn't quite recognize. Even though these adults and children weren't family, I felt like I'd temporarily found a home, a place I belonged.

"What focus will you choose, Conrad?" Louis's question snapped me from my thoughts.

I hadn't given it much thought since we didn't have to choose for two more years. "Umm, I don't know." I chewed my lower lip and thought. "Elemental, maybe?"

"Almost no one chooses potions anymore," Baxter's mother lamented. "There's a shortage of good apothecaries these days."

"I might go with healing," Lily said. "Supplementing it with potions would be ideal."

"You're such a smart lass," Kara said.

Lily's father smiled proudly. "Healing would be a wonderful choice." He hissed air between his tongue and teeth. "Most of the good healers vanished in that fool's quest to conquer Seraphina, and the Overlord killed those who didn't agree with him."

"Let's not talk about that now," Lily's mother said, directing a worried look at Harris.

But the mention of my father only seemed to fuel Harris. "I want to be a Magitsu master someday, so I'm going to focus elemental like Conrad."

Louis ruffled the boy's hair. "You'll do us proud, lad."

"What's Magitsu?" I asked.

"It's a magical martial art," Kara said. "It nearly died out after the Blue Cloaks were trapped in Seraphina along with the rest of Slade's army, but there are at least two masters left in Eden."

"I want Master Kanaan to teach me," Harris said. "Everyone says he's the best."

"How powerful is he?" I asked.

Harris's eyes widened. "He killed Seraphim with nothing but wands." He flicked his hands around as if fighting invisible monsters. "There's a story about him fighting a demon lord named Karak and winning."

"I thought he killed a demon overlord," Baxter said.

Lily sighed. "You two always make the stories sound better than they were. If you'd read the actual book you'd know that Kanaan fought Karak, but the great Banisher herself, Emily Glass, sent him back to Haedaemos."

Ambria met my eyes and I could tell she felt as out of place as I did for not knowing much of Overworld history. At least none of these people seemed to notice or care, and that made it okay by me.

"Does Kanaan live in Queens Gate?" I asked.

Harris shook his head. "No, but he comes to town once a year to recruit graduates from the university for the Blue Cloaks."

"He's got a long way to go before he rebuilds," Baxter's father said. "There's too much money in being a freelance battle mage these days."

Louis snorted. "With the Arcane Council nearly broke, that's no surprise. They can't afford to pay themselves, much less the military."

The conversation soon turned political and I stopped listening. It became clear to me what I had to become if I were to one day defeat my parents.

A Magitsu master.

It seemed strange, me sitting here thinking about ridding the world of my parents while Lily and Baxter sat happily next to theirs. Even Harris acted as if his aunt and uncle were his true parents. I looked at Ambria and saw the uncertainty on her face as she listened to the others swap family stories. She looked at me and a smile cleared away her troubled look.

Ambria and Max weren't my flesh and blood, but they were my family. I couldn't bear it if something happened to them. They were the reason I had to end my parents once and for all.

Chapter 17

I divided my time over the next week and a half between watching for my parents at the crack in the world, studying, and having fun with my friends if for no other reason than to pretend everything was normal.

On the day before school, I went back to the fissure leading into the rift. Despite all the time I'd spent watching the place, I hadn't seen my parents come past here once. When school began, I'd have even less time to watch the crack.

I reached inside my backpack and removed the *Basic Enchantments* textbook I'd taken from the closet beneath the stairs. I skipped to the last quarter of the book where I'd marked the page for simple wards. Following the instructions, I drew a chalk oval on the smooth stone at the base of the fissure opening so anyone entering the crack would have to cross it. I pressed a thumb to the chalk and repeated the words from the book.

"*Si fracti promptus ego.*" A tingle ran up my thumb and into my arm. I jerked back my hand in surprise, though it hadn't hurt. I stood and stepped on the line. Invisible fingers seemed to pinch my arm. I yelped and clapped a hand over the spot, but the pain quickly faded.

I didn't appreciate the alert method, but at least it worked. With the ward broken, I had to wipe away the chalk and redraw the oval. I armed it with the magic words once again and covered it with a light coating of sand so intruders wouldn't see it. Once satisfied, I retreated to my hiding spot in the dilapidated mansion.

A grin tugged my lips, and pride warmed my insides. It was a small accomplishment, but it felt like progress. *I'm going to be the best student ever.*

But now wasn't the time to bask in self-satisfaction. I took out my wand and pointed it at the battered leather divan in the middle of the room. I twisted the wand in a circle and flicked my wrist. "*Torsious*!"

The worn old chair remained where it was.

Blue sprang through the window. "Boo!"

My wand clattered to the floor. I yelped and stumbled backwards through a doorway to the adjoining room. My foot found emptiness since the floor had collapsed all the way down to the basement. "Gah!" I shouted, unable to form a coherent cry for help as I toppled over the edge.

Blue leapt forward and gripped my wrist. She pulled me back to safety and pecked a kiss on my cheek.

She grinned. "Am I your hero?"

Pathetic, Vic said. *Frightened by a child.*

Della's laughter rang in my head. *He will never defeat us.*

My face burned and my fists clenched. I was an idiot. One simple surprise from Blue and I'd nearly fallen to my death. What hope did I have of fighting my parents? "You almost killed me!" I shouted. I was furious with myself, but couldn't stop from taking it out on Blue.

Her eyes grew round and filled with hurt. "It was just a joke."

"Why are you stalking me?" I kicked the old divan and almost slipped on the marble floor. This added failure only made me angrier.

Tears pooled in her eyes. "I'm not stalking you, Conrad." Her lower lip quivered. "Can't you see I like you?"

My anger evaporated, replaced by leaden shame.

"Why don't you like me?" Her voice squeaked with despair. "Is it because I'm a lycan? An animal?"

I reached for her. "You're not—"

She jerked away. "No, Conrad! I see how you really feel." Blue kicked the chair and sent it skidding across the floor and slamming into the wall. She ground out the last words between clenched teeth. "I'll just leave you and your stupid friends alone."

Before I could shout at her, she bounded out of the window and vanished in a flash. My arm dropped to my side and I stared blankly for a time. *She likes me.* Or at least she had before this. I'd heard older kids in foster homes talking about how they liked someone. How they wanted to kiss them and be around them. One girl had run away to be with an older boy, though the police had soon tracked them down and brought her kicking and screaming back to the foster parent.

I knew as much about romantic love as I did about magic. Thankfully, Blue had taken out her frustrations on the chair instead of me. I hoped she'd calm down so I could talk to her later. I did like her, though I wasn't too sure about all the kissing stuff. I supposed we could hold hands a little bit, so long as Max and Ambria didn't make fun of me.

My knees went weak and my hands trembled. *Am I afraid of love?*

I didn't have time to contemplate it when my newly installed ward pinched my arm. I bit back a shout of surprise and scurried over to the window just in time to see Serena vanish inside the grove of trees around the fissure. I grabbed my wand and let a count of thirty seconds pass before climbing out of the window and clambering down the rubble to the trees. I peeked inside the tunnel and saw a glowing light source about halfway through to the rift.

Echoes of voices drifted out, but I couldn't understand what they were saying. I stared into the tunnel for over a minute, trying to decide what I should do. I assumed my parents were with Serena. Even if I followed them to the rift, then what? How would I follow them past the guardians? If they turned around and came back while I was still in the tunnel, I'd have to crawl backwards as fast as possible to escape them. The only value in following them would be gathering information because I certainly couldn't fight them.

I wanted to eavesdrop, to discover their plans or any advances they'd made in the quest for immortality, but fear rooted me to the spot. The longer I contemplated the dangers, the deeper those roots dug into the ground. Several minutes later, and with great relief, I decided trailing my parents would be too dangerous.

"What am I thinking?" I hissed. Only a few minutes ago, I'd nearly died due to Blue's simple prank. I was physically fragile and had nothing with which to fight my parents if they discovered me. I squeezed my eyes shut. All the anger in the world wouldn't help me— only patience and stealth. I hoped Galfandor would do something about my parents before they gained their immortality, because there was nothing I could do.

I opened my eyes and cleared the blurring water from my eyes. A few moments later, I retrieved my broom and flew home.

Ambria and Max jumped up from sitting on the front porch when I arrived at the house.

"Something was wrong with Blue," Ambria said. "She stormed inside, took her things, and left before Max or I even knew she was leaving."

"She left?" I looked up and down the street, as if she might still be in view.

Max nodded. "She went next door and talked with Harris and the others, then they all hopped in a horseless carriage and left."

I dropped onto the front steps and buried my face in my hands. "It's my fault."

Ambria dropped next to me. "What happened?"

Max sat on my opposite side, noisily chewing gum. "I can't wait to hear this."

"I was hiding in the mansion near the crack—"

"Why would you do something so foolish?" Ambria pushed my shoulder. "You're going to get yourself killed if your parents find you."

"You're mental," Max breathed. He leaned forward so he could crane his head and look me in the eye. "Did you see them?"

I didn't answer that question and continued with my original story. "While I was waiting, Blue surprised me and I nearly fell into a hole going from the second story all the way to the basement." They frowned at me, so I continued. "I was upset. I yelled at her and she ran away."

Ambria patted my hand. "Well, she pestered you all the time, so of course it's natural for you to get upset."

"Duh, she likes him." Max snorted. "My brothers talk about girls all the time now and it's a good thing, too. They're so busy chasing girls they don't have time to play tricks on me." A huge gum bubble grew from his mouth and exploded with a loud pop.

"Conrad doesn't need a girl like Blue," Ambria said.

Max's forehead wrinkled. "Why not? I kind of like her, and she's pretty." He began to blow another bubble.

She sniffed. "Well, for one thing, she's a lot stronger than Conrad, and nearly his height."

Max's bubble popped.

Ambria slapped him on the arm. "Will you stop that? It's annoying."

He smiled sheepishly. "I can't help it—it's Trouble Bubble."

"What?"

"It blows huge magical bubbles without even trying." He took out two pieces wrapped in bright yellow wax paper. "Want some?"

Ambria groaned and snatched a piece from him. I took the other piece and tucked it in my pocket.

Ambria stood up. "Anyway, it's a well-known fact women like their men stronger and taller than themselves so I don't understand why Blue would like Conrad."

"Women are just too picky." Max patted me on the shoulder. "Don't worry, Conrad. Girls get upset over stupid things all the time."

Ambria gasped. "No, we do not." She folded her arms. "Maxwell Tiberius, you don't know a thing about women." With that, she stomped away and into the house.

Max chuckled. "See?" He stood and stretched. "I'll bet Blue will come back in no time and you can apologize to her. In the meantime"—he rubbed his belly—"let's go get something to eat."

The next morning was the big day.

I woke up early and ate breakfast with Ambria.

She nibbled at a slice of toast. "I'm so nervous I can hardly eat."

For some reason, I felt completely calm. I'd fallen asleep quickly last night despite all my worries and woken up with the alarm I'd set on my phone. I finished chewing my sausage and swallowed. "You'll be starving before lunch if you don't eat something."

Ambria stared at the parchment with our class schedule. "I'm certainly not looking forward to Elementary Magic with Professor Grace."

I finished eating and put my dishes in the sink. "Which period do we have his class?"

"Third," she said, and compared her schedule with mine. "Looks like we have two classes with Harris, Lily, and Baxter."

"Shouldn't they be in more advanced classes?" I asked. "I thought they went to other magic schools before this."

She rolled up the parchment and shrugged. "I have no idea. You'll just have to ask them."

I really didn't care to know the answer. I grabbed my backpack, now filled with all my worldly possessions, and slung it over my shoulder then helped Ambria secure her small suitcase to the back of her broom. We flew our brooms over to pick up Max at his uncle's. He was already circling over the house on his broom when we arrived, and zipped over to meet us.

"Wow, the first day of university," he said breathlessly. "Can you believe it?"

Ambria put a hand on her chest. "I'm so nervous I can hardly think straight."

Max pulled even with me as we flew up the cliff. "How about you Conrad? Has is sunk in yet?"

"Yeah." The excitement of starting this new chapter in my life had dwindled away. I should have looked forward to a journey into the unknown. Instead, it seemed like a years-long slog through a marsh. My parents were decades ahead of me in knowledge and skill. Even if I survived to graduate, I'd still have years of studying ahead of me. By then, they might have discovered the secret to immortality and taken over the Overworld again.

"I think he's more nervous than me," Ambria said.

I replied with a wan smile. "Sure, that's it."

Scores of flying carpets flew up the cliff ahead of us, many of them coming from the direction of the main entrance to Queens Gate. The sky ferry, still in the shape of a pirate ship, glided up the cliff with a full load of students and their families. We glided past a massive flying carpet carrying furniture and luggage along with a girl and her parents.

Max waved at them as we passed, but they were too busy talking among themselves to notice.

"How rude," Ambria said.

An unpleasant view greeted us when we crested the trees at the top of the cliff. A mob of students and parents waited in line at the security gate.

"So many people!" Ambria said.

Max groaned. "Maybe we should have gotten here earlier."

"We were just here the other day," I said. "Shouldn't our security charms still work?"

"According to the note included with the class schedule, they change them on the first day of class," Ambria said.

Max threw up his arms. "This will take ages."

We landed our brooms and got in line.

Max took out his schedule and looked it over. "Do we have classes today?"

"Today is orientation," Ambria said, standing on tiptoes and craning her neck to look at the gate—a futile effort with so many people in front of us. "This line is even worse than the one on exam day."

"Yeah, because all the students are here," Max said, "and not just the ones taking the test."

Ambria shook her head. "I can't believe they'd reset security on starting day. This is ridiculous."

Something popped and a chorus of shouts rang out. Brilliant light flashed somewhere near the gate, and then a loud boom thundered through the air.

Before I could react, the herd of parents and students turned into a stampede. Bodies pressed against me, jostling me this way and that. Ambria shrieked. I grabbed her hand and pulled her close as panicked people sprang like deer from the explosions and static crackle of energy. A heavyset man, eyes wide and frenzied, slammed into me. Ambria and I tumbled into Max and we sprawled in the dirt.

When I got up, I saw two men exchanging crackling bolts of magic with three security guards. One of the guards screamed and flew backwards, smoke trailing from his chest. His body slammed into a low stone wall next to the gate and bounced off. The other two guards ducked behind the barrier, occasionally rising high enough to fire another shot with their wands.

The attackers wore slim-fitting black leather robes and used long staffs instead of wands. Every attack from the guards splashed harmlessly against an invisible shield in front of the men.

The taller of the two laughed. "This is security for the mighty Arcane University?"

The other man thrust his staff forward and jagged light exploded against the wall, blowing chunks of rubble in all directions.

I realized with a shock that I recognized the men—or at least the soul fragments of my parents recognized them. *Calvin Fain and Eolius Bane.* Fain, tall, blond and bearded, looked like a Nordic Viking. Bane stood much shorter and thinner. Images flashed through my mind—Bane incinerating a screaming man, Bane slicing through a pleading woman with a blade of white-hot energy. I squeezed my eyes shut, but that only made the images more vivid.

Fain might look large and imposing, but my parents' memories proved Bane was the deadlier of the two. Neither placed much value on any life except their own.

An alarm wailed in the distance. Bane whirled his staff. Brilliant energy discs hummed in all directions. I dropped to the ground as several sang past my head. Thankfully, the crowd of students had all but vanished by now, so the discs exploded against trees and the ground instead of people.

Fain grinned and destroyed another chunk of the stone barrier protecting the guards. Without a word, the attackers ran to the left and into the trees just as a dozen people in dark blue security robes arrived at the gate.

I pushed up to my knees and looked around. Max and Ambria lay prone next to me. People peeked cautiously from behind trees and boulders. The guard who'd been hit moaned.

They're terrified, Della whispered in my mind. *How delightful.*

I felt smug and realized it was my father's soul fragment reacting to her words. *And so it begins.*

Chapter 18

The extra guards quickly disabled the security wards near the gate and ushered the crowd inside just in case of another attack, but Fain and Bane didn't return.

"Why did they attack?" Max asked for the third time. "It doesn't make sense."

Ambria voiced a question I'd heard several times from the people around us. "Who were they?"

I knew the answer to Ambria's question, but solving Max's question might be far more important. The attack had been about something besides terrorizing everyone.

Ambria gripped my arm as we followed the crowd into the main entrance. "You know something, don't you?"

I nodded. "Those men worked for my parents," I whispered.

Max leaned close. "What did you say?"

Ambria whispered in his ear and his eyes bugged.

He opened his mouth. I shook my head. Max clamped his mouth shut and nodded. The guards herded everyone into the main dining hall. The three of us took a table on the far right to keep us out of earshot of anyone else for the moment.

"Ever heard of Calvin Fain and Eolius Bane?" I asked Max when we took our seats.

He frowned. "They were two of the Overlord's top battle mages."

"Their names certainly rhyme," Ambria added. "Did your parents tell you who they are?" She tapped her temple to indicate she meant the soul fragments.

I nodded. "Vic said 'And so it begins.'" I bit my lip and shook my head. "I don't know what he meant by that."

"Maybe your parents want to scare people away from the university," Ambria said.

"What good would that do?" Max pressed his lips together. "Maybe they were trying to break in. Not even battle mages can get past the shield around the university without a charm."

"Then how did Conrad's parents and Serena get past it?" Ambria said.

"The barrier doesn't go all the way to the Fairy Garden," Max replied. "They probably went around the edge."

"How far does the shield extend?" I asked.

"According to my uncle, it stops somewhere around Colossus Stadium." He traced a circle on the table as if illustrating it.

Ambria looked relieved. "Well, the battle mages didn't break into the school, so I guess they failed."

I wasn't so sure. "There's more to it, I think."

Max leaned forward. "What do you mean?"

"That's what I'm trying to figure out." Unfortunately, Vic and Della weren't giving me any clues.

Ambria looked around at the frightened faces of parents and children. "Well, whatever the reason, they certainly made a point these people won't forget."

"Neither will I." Max dropped his forehead on the table. "There must be a safer place to go to school."

"That may be true, but there's only one Arcane University," Ambria said. She patted him on the shoulder. "Now, now, don't be such a ninny, Max."

He sat upright and gave her a dirty look.

Harris and his friends entered the dining hall. Baxter jumped up on a table and looked around the room. His eyes flashed when he saw me. He pointed in my direction then hopped off the table.

"Oh, goodness, I really don't feel like dealing with Baxter today," Ambria said. She took a deep breath and plastered on a smile.

"Maybe you should frown instead," Max said. "That keeps everyone away."

She sniffed. "You're the one who keeps people away with your bad breath."

Harris strode toward us, face red, teeth and fists clenched.

"Goodness, the attack must have really wound him up," Ambria said.

Max grunted. "He does look a bit irritated."

I wished Harris and the others would sit elsewhere since I wanted to talk in private to Max and Ambria, but after the cookout, I'd actually grown to like him and Lily, though I could still only tolerate Baxter. I forced a smile, held up my hand, and waved.

Harris punched me in the face. My chair flipped backwards and crashed into the floor with a loud clatter. A metallic taste bit into my tongue and the world went hazy. With a roar, Harris leapt toward me. Max got up, but Baxter grabbed him from behind, trying to keep him in place. Lily's typical pleasant demeanor was gone, replaced by a scowl.

Harris's weight pressed against my chest. He swung his fists wildly at me and it was all I could do to deflect his blows with my arms.

"Stop it!" Ambria cried. "Have you gone mental?"

Lily slapped her. "Shut up, you dirty little liar!"

Ambria screamed with fury and leapt toward the other girl.

Harris's fist connected with my temple and everything went black for a split second. I heard shouts and the scuffing of chairs against the floor all around me. Tasted more blood in my mouth.

"What in the world is going on here?" someone roared.

The weight vanished from my chest. I blinked open my eyes and saw Gideon Grace standing over me.

"Get off the floor, boy." He turned his glare from me to Harris. "You'd better explain yourself."

Harris struggled in his grasp, face crimson, and eyes burning with hate. "It's him!" he yelled. "He shouldn't be here!"

I rolled out of the toppled chair and pulled myself up by the edge of the table. Rhona Trask held Lily and Ambria apart and Galfandor held Baxter firmly by the ear while Max nursed a bleeding nose.

"Calm yourself, boy," Gideon said in a low cold voice. "Or I'll calm you myself."

The fight went from Harris, doused like a fire, but it was obvious the cinders of his anger still smoldered. Gideon finally let him go.

The dining room fell silent. I felt all eyes on me and confirmed it by simply looking around. Everyone seemed to have moved on from the shock of the violence outside and was now entranced by the violence inside.

Harris jabbed a finger toward me. "That boy lied about his last name. It isn't Edwards." His body trembled and his hands tightened into fists. "His last name is Edison!"

His shout echoed across the dining hall.

For those who hadn't figured it out, Harris filled in the blank. "His father was Victus Edison, the Overlord!"

Gasps of disbelief and cries of outrage rang out in the room.

"Can't be true," I heard a woman say. "Their only child died."

Harris turned his finger on Ambria. "She lied about her last name too. She's the daughter of Cyphanis Rax."

"Now we know why they hung out with Cryberius," Baxter said. "Old man Tiberius was best buddies with the Overlord."

The rumblings around us grew in volume like a distant waterfall growing closer and closer.

Gideon's lip curled into a sneer. "Is this true, boy?"

I gulped. My insides went cold and my heart felt tight as a drum. I didn't know what to say, what to do. I met Ambria's frightened, tear-stained eyes and knew there was no way out of this.

"It's true," Galfandor said loudly.

Gideon and Trask looked at the headmaster with shocked expressions and even more gasps puffed from the crowd.

Galfandor stepped up onto a chair and waved for the crowd to sit down. When the room was once again silent, he spoke. "Conrad Edison and Ambria Rax were sent to an orphanage at young ages. Only recently did they find out who their parents were, or even discover the Overworld."

"It's a lie," Harris growled.

Galfandor arched an eyebrow. "Why, Mr. Ashmore, are you accusing me of lying?"

The boy blanched, suddenly realizing who he'd insulted. Son of prophecy or not, there were some people who wouldn't put up with his self-importance. "I'm sorry, sir. I mean Conrad is lying."

The headmaster simply looked at him until Harris lowered his head and shut his mouth. Then he continued. "Conrad and Ambria came to me, concerned their last names might start a witch hunt. I agreed that they could use different last names." Galfandor looked around. "I expect everyone here to treat them the same as any other student. Here at Arcane University, we don't judge a child by the sins of their parents."

I spotted several scowling, narrow-eyed people in the crowd around me who apparently didn't agree with that statement one bit.

"But, Headmaster, his parents murdered mine," Harris said in a plaintive voice. Tears pooled in his eyes. "He tricked me into thinking he was my friend."

Galfandor's eyes softened. "I'm sorry for what happened to your parents, Harris, but fighting with Conrad won't bring them back."

"No good will come of this," Grace said in a low voice. He frowned at me. "You'd better believe I'll have my eyes on you, Edison."

I had no doubt he wouldn't be the only one.

"Professor Grace, kindly escort young Ashmore and his companions to a table across the room," Galfandor said.

"Very well." Grace motioned for Lily, Baxter and Harris to move ahead of him.

Harris gave me one last glare and went with the professor. His status as future savior protected him and his friends from any punishment.

Galfandor sighed and gave me a wan smile. He leaned forward and whispered in my ear. "I'm afraid you'll have to be more careful from now on." Then he straightened and walked toward the podium in the front of the room. Rhona Trask, Gideon Grace, and a third professor I didn't recognize sat at a table to the left of the podium.

The fight was over, but I felt exposed and naked in front of these people and their judgmental eyes. A mother and father stole glances at me and whispered something to their child. One woman gave me a sympathetic smile, while the woman across the table from her stared daggers in my direction.

My face burned and my body prickled with cold. I wished the ground would swallow me up and drop me straight into its volcanic center. Burning up in an instant would be preferable to this. I righted my chair and sat down, doing my best not to tremble. Ambria rubbed her wet eyes and took the seat next to me. Max wiped at the trickle of blood under his nose and sat down next to Ambria.

I reached under the table and squeezed Ambria's hand. She whimpered and buried her face on my shoulder.

"How did he find out?" Max hissed. "I don't understand."

I shook my head. "Neither do I."

Galfandor stepped onto the podium and put his wand to his throat. When he spoke, his voice echoed clearly all the way to our table at the back of the room. "To say that this year has gotten off to an interesting start would be quite the understatement."

The room rumbled with uncomfortable laughter.

"This school has seen more than its fair share of troubles." He swung a finger to point to his right. "Colossus Stadium still bears witness to the violence that shattered the Overworld over six years ago, and yet, here we have today the largest group of students Arcane University has seen in years." Galfandor swung his solemn gaze across the crowd. "There will always be malignant forces eager to sow chaos and confusion in an orderly society. It is our responsibility as citizens to remain steadfast against such evils and to push for progress."

Murmurs of agreement broke the silence and drained some of the tension from the room, though I still felt the weight of a hundred crushing stares.

A short man with curly brown hair rose. "If we're to stand against evil, then why were you protecting the scions of Edison and Rax?" He jabbed a finger toward our table. "After what the Overlord did to us, they have no right to be here."

"Our tax money is paying for them to go to school!" A thin woman in a knit robe leapt up beside the man. "They should be banished."

Galfandor pursed his lips. "How many of you agree with these two?"

A scattering of hands shot up. Some people looked toward us uncertainly, but left their hands down.

The headmaster nodded. "Good. There aren't as many as I'd feared." His face darkened and his voice grew harsh. "For those of you who would banish children, and orphans, no less, you should be ashamed of yourselves." Galfandor's eyes hardened. "Charles and Eleanor Peeves, given your son's poor conduct rating from his previous school, I suggest you worry about things closer to home."

"Well, I never!" Eleanor huffed. She mustered a defiant glare that withered like a dandelion in a forest fire beneath Galfandor's steady gaze.

Charles scowled but sat back down.

The pressure in my chest loosened and the sick feeling in my stomach faded a little. I honestly hadn't expected Galfandor to rise to our defense, at least not in such a blunt way. He'd left us to do our own thing when fighting the Goodleighs and hadn't even committed to helping me against my parents. His words were unexpected, but welcome. Even Ambria stopped crying and looked up at the headmaster with surprise.

"Now, let us return to the business at hand," Galfandor said. "Security is paramount here at Arcane University. To ensure this, the security charms will be changed frequently, and the perimeter will be expanded to encompass the entire plateau all the way to the security gate near the sky car dock. I would encourage students not to leave the campus during the school year but to check out with security if they must go into town for some reason."

Nobody seemed surprised at this and I wondered if it had always been this way at the school.

A man a few tables over raised a hand and said in a loud voice, "How do these charms work?"

"The security barrier cannot be penetrated by anyone without a charm," Galfandor replied. "If a section is breached, the wards will alert our security staff."

The man didn't seem reassured. "Can just anyone get a charm at the gate?"

Galfandor shook his head. "The charms will penetrate any disguise and reveal any dangers."

"No wonder it made me tingle," a woman at the neighboring table said to her husband.

"That's awfully intrusive," someone across the room shouted.

The headmaster nodded and smiled. "It's intrusive, but it won't work without the full consent of the person being given the charm." His smiled vanished. "Would you rather the school be safe, or your personal liberties left intact?"

Murmurs filled the room and quickly faded.

The headmaster waited a moment. When no one else raised objections to the security measures, he continued. "Now that I have covered the unpleasant issues, I'll move on to more positive developments." He removed a parchment from his robe. "The Arcane Council, in cooperation with Science Academy, has announced new funding for repairs to Colossus Stadium."

A chorus of cheers and claps filled the room.

Galfandor smiled and nodded, waiting for the noise to die down before continuing. "By the end of the year, it's possible we'll once again host the first Grand Melee since the end of the Second Seraphim War."

More cheers erupted.

The headmaster held up a hand and the room grew quiet once more. "Kabash League games will start in two weeks. Science Academy is fielding three teams this year so competition will be tougher than ever."

The earlier cheers were replaced by boos.

"Science Academy shouldn't be in our league!" someone shouted.

A woman pumped her fist angrily. "Magic will always beat science!"

Galfandor smiled politely. "Yes, well, let's prove it on the field."

For the first time since being punched in the face, Max grinned. "I hope I can qualify to play."

"What's the Kabash League?" I asked.

"It's like fighting a war on broomsticks." He leaned in front of Ambria. "Your team has to destroy the enemy base with a flying disc."

It certainly sounded interesting, but I doubted I'd have time for fun and games.

"Last but not least, I'd like to introduce the new teachers who will be educating our fine students this year." Galfandor waved a hand to the table, indicating a lean man with a shaved head. "Professor Sideon hearkens from the land down under and will teach Enchantments in the place of Professor Cruikshank who is out due to illness in the family."

Sideon stood and bowed to the room then sat down.

Polite clapping filled the room.

"He will also be the ward of House Tiberius this year," Galfandor continued. "Next, is the lovely Esma Emoora, our new Magical Defense teacher."

A woman who looked barely old enough to be a teacher rose from her chair next to Sideon and waved to the crowd, cheeks dimpled with a brilliant smile and curly blond hair bouncing as if it had a life of its own.

"She looks young," Ambria said softly.

Galfandor continued down the table. "Eleanor Beetle will be the new history teacher."

Professor Beetle stood up, but she was so squat and plump, it hardly looked as if she were standing at all. Thick spectacles hung on the tip of her nose, and her brown hair rose from her head in the shape of a beehive. She said something, but her voice didn't reach the back of the room.

"Lastly, please welcome Asha Fellini." The headmaster smiled toward the end of the table. I couldn't see the new teacher until she stood thanks to the tall man at the table in front of me.

A lovely woman with rich black hair and fair skin rose. Though her nose was a bit longer, and her cheeks not as high, I at first mistook her for Delectra. A squeak emerged from my mouth, and the urge to run nearly had me bolting from my seat.

Ambria gave me an alarmed look, and Max met my eyes.

"Is it just me, or does she look like, um, you-know-who?" Max said.

"She looks much like her," Ambria confirmed.

I swallowed hard and forced myself to look at the woman as she waved regally at the room. *It's not her.* It couldn't be. Galfandor wouldn't be stupid enough to hire a criminal.

With the introduction done, the headmaster rolled up the parchments on the podium and tucked them into his robes. "Now for keep assignments."

The tension in the room thickened. Parents looked hopefully at their children while they, in turn, looked worriedly up at Galfandor.

I hardly paid attention. All I could think about was Asha Fellini, the woman who looked like my mother.

Chapter 19

"Keep assignments?" Ambria squeaked, tearing me from my dark thoughts. She glared at Max. "I thought you said they stopped dividing people into houses."

Max chuckled. "Keeps are just the dormitories students live in."

Ambria visibly relaxed, her shoulders dropping lower. "Oh, well I suppose that's okay." She frowned. "I wish we could go home every night."

Max shook his head. "Not until your third year." His eyes went distant. "I always fantasized about living away from home, especially at university. I hope it's as fun as I imagined it." He elbowed me. "If we're in the same keep, we can be roommates. Won't that be great?"

Until recently, I'd never even considered university and since I'd never lived continuously in one place longer than a year, moving again felt natural.

Ambria watched Galfandor as he shuffled through parchments. "Are you certain there's nothing special about which keep we're placed in?"

"Not that I've ever heard." Max put a finger to his lips. "He's about to start."

Galfandor's eyes brightened, as if he'd found the parchment he wanted. "This year it's more important than ever that the students live on campus. Even if you are eligible to live elsewhere, I beseech you to reconsider." He made eye contact with some of the older students. "With that said, keep assignments will now begin."

"First up is Graeven Keep." He circled a wand over his head. A spark flew across the crowd. Gasps, oohs, and ahs rose from people as it floated overhead.

The spark hovered over a girl who looked a bit younger than me.

164

"Abigail Bainbridge, please come forward," Galfandor said.

The wide-eyed girl stood, looked at her parents. The mother smiled proudly, while the father looked a bit grumpy. The mother motioned the girl to move, and Abigail walked to the front of the room where Galfandor pointed to an area next to the podium.

The spark continued around the room, summoning people seemingly at random and the headmaster would call them forward. One moment it settled over someone on the far right corner, then zipped over to the opposite side. Not even the students' names were in alphabetical order. At one point, the spark zipped toward us. Max stiffened and held his breath, but it passed us by and chose another boy.

The next name Galfandor called caused my stomach to clench. "Blue Blackburn, please come to the front."

Blue popped up from the other side of the room and walked to the front. She glanced in my direction but quickly turned away when she saw me looking. I felt terrible about hurting her feelings and resolved to apologize the moment I had a chance.

After several more minutes of flying around the room, the spark faded away. The selection was apparently complete.

Rhona Trask rose from the front table next to Galfandor. "I am the advisor for Graeven Keep. If you need advice or support, you will come to me. Is that understood, children?"

Those gathered at the front nodded.

"Excellent." She motioned them to the right of the podium.

"Next is Moore Keep," Galfandor said.

Once again, the spark flitted around the room, gathering children for the keep. It streaked for us and hovered over Max's head.

His face fell when the spark danced back across the room without choosing me or Ambria. "I hope we all get in the same keep," Max whispered. "I don't want to be alone."

Ambria patted his hand. "We'll think about visiting you sometime."

His shoulders slumped. "Great, thanks."

"Maxwell Tiberius, please come to the front," Galfandor said.

Our friend pushed himself up and trudged to the waiting crowd of students bound for Moore.

"Well, it looks like we'll be in the same keep at least," Ambria said to me. As if it had heard her, the spark zipped across the room and selected her. Eyes wide, she covered her mouth with her hands. "Oh no. Please choose Conrad next, spark!"

But it faded away, signaling the end of the selection.

So much for being Max's roommate.

My heart drooped. I'd hoped to have at least one of my close friends in the dorm with me. Ambria's lip quivered as she stood and waved goodbye. I caught a horrified look from Max where he stood with the others bound for Moore Keep.

Gideon Grace rose from the table and walked to the group. "As the warden of Moore Keep, you will follow my every command, children." He strode up and down before them like a general leading them to war. "I expect nothing but the best behavior from each of you, or you will find yourselves living in the basement." He stiffened and shouted, "Is that understood?"

"Yes, sir!" the children shouted back, voices filled with fear and uncertainty.

Max and Ambria looked horrified.

Galfandor smiled. "Very good, then. I think you'll find Professor Grace to be strict, but fair." His words didn't seem to lessen the fear in the eyes of Grace's wards.

The headmaster summoned another spark. It seemed a bit strange to do so since there was only one keep left. Shouldn't everyone else know which building they'd live in by default? I suddenly realized that all of the older students were still seated. Only children my age and younger were in the groups at the front. The spark only chose the new students since the older ones were already assigned keeps.

"And now for Tiberius Keep," Galfandor said. The spark settled over someone I couldn't see. "Harris Ashmore, please come to the front."

The name was like a slap to the face. A few selections later, Baxter was directed to join those bound for Tiberius Keep, and Lily was chosen not long after. Two teens with white-blond hair slinked between the tables and slid into the empty chairs where Max and Ambria had been sitting.

The boys looked identical. Only a freckle told me who was who.

"Hello, Rhys," I said to the boy with a freckle on his right cheek. I remained calm and nodded at the other. "Devon."

Their eyes widened and delighted grins spread across their faces. They glanced at each other across me, and in that moment I felt as though one of them had escaped from the reflected world and now haunted the other. Unfortunately, I knew Max's older brothers were up to no good.

"How did you tell us apart?" Rhys asked. He waved away the question before I could answer. "Never mind. I really don't care, but it's touching that you cared enough to make the effort."

"Always address someone by their name when greeting them." Devon tapped a finger to his chest. "It shows respect."

I couldn't decide if they were being serious or sarcastic, so I remained still and phrased my question carefully. "How may I help you?"

"It appears you'll be in our keep," Rhys said.

"Along with Harris Ashmore and his little play friends." Devon snickered. "Looks like the infamous Edison boy will need protection from his haters."

His brother snorted. "And we're here to help."

I didn't like the sound of that one little bit. "I think I can take care of myself." Judging from Max's horror stories about these two, I'd be in just as much danger from them as I would from Harris and the others.

Devon put a hand on one shoulder, and Rhys put a hand on the other. They leaned in and whispered at the same time, "You'd do well to let us help, little boy." It sounded like a nightmare in stereo.

Puny boy, Vic said derisively. *Your weakness sickens me.*

Rise up and destroy them, Della said. *You have my blood in your veins and my magic in your blood.*

Heat prickled down my scalp and flushed my face. I felt my fists clench tight enough to hurt. I was so angry, I wanted to punch Rhys and Devon until they bled. I also wanted to punch my parents' soul fragments until they burned away like black smoke. I was furious, but I wasn't stupid. There would be no rising up and destroying anyone from me. Physically and magically, I was no match for these two. I'd seen them throw an old man off a balcony and then wrap the railing around his leg with a spell.

A big man with a rainbow mohawk slams his bearded opponent onto the fighting ring tarp and the crowd roars with approval. Cora winces and looks away. Bill grabs her hair and forces her head up.

"Don't look away, you bleeding twit." He jerks her head sideways. "I paid good money to come here."

A tear trickles down Cora's face, but she says nothing. She puts an arm on my shoulder.

The mohawk man seems victorious. But another figure runs from outside the ring and kicks him in the face. The bearded man works his way free and flips to his feet. The mohawk man's partner rushes into the ring, but is no match for the other two fighters. They take turns punching him until he goes down in a pool of blood.

"Whoo!" Bill shouts. "That's what I like to see!" He finishes off his sixth or seventh beer and holds up a crumpled piece of paper. "You're looking at a winner, folks."

Cora smiles uneasily and rubs her fingers on the green pebble—a piece of the anchor stone—hanging from the chain around her neck. "That's wonderful. How much?"

Bill does some counting on his fingers. "Fifty quid at least."

Another greater roar rises from the crowd. I look back at the ring and watch the mohawk man beat the bearded man and his partner senseless with a metal chair. Staggering, but still upright, he holds up his fist in victory.

Bill screams and tears up the paper.

Cora's eyes darken and she looks at me while her fingers work furiously at the polished pebble. I know that look well. It means Bill will probably beat her tonight. But tonight will be different, my future self knows. Tonight, Cora will push Bill down the stairs. Tonight, he'll be the victim.

The present roared back into focus.

Devon snapped fingers in front of my face. "You awake, Edison?"

If I hoped to win a fight against these two, I'd have to follow the mohawk man's example and cheat. Even then it might not be enough. I'd soon be trapped in a dorm with people who hated me so much, they might even kill me. Harris saw himself as a son of prophecy. I wanted to kick myself for encouraging him to believe that, because now it meant he could justify doing anything to me simply because of my last name.

Thanks to my parents, the world was a more dangerous place for me.

"I'm awake." At that moment I wondered if it would be better to simply go to sleep forever. No more parents. No more threats. No more worries. But that would mean Max and Ambria would be left alone to face whatever terrible future my parents wanted. I would be leaving Cora's only other child torn between two worlds. She was now my family. I owed Mum that much.

The selection spark streaked in my direction and I knew it was coming for me.

"If you don't say yes before that spark reaches you, you're on your own." Rhys bared his teeth.

"Alone against the world." Devon waved his arm at the room to underscore the point.

The spark zipped over my head and selected a boy behind me. Its job done, the spark faded. The crowd burst into applause.

Rhys and Devon exchanged almost comically confused looks. "What?" they said simultaneously.

"It's even worse than we thought." Devon's face shone with delight.

Rhys shook with laughter. "The boy with no home. How sad."

"Sad, sad, sad!" Devon doubled over with glee.

I was at a loss. Did this mean I had no keep to live in, or had Galfandor suddenly decided to revoke my admission?

Professor Sideon pushed back his chair and rose from the table. He walked to the group chosen for Tiberius Keep. "I am Professor Sideon. It will be an honor to guide the children of Tiberius Keep through this school year."

"That concludes orientation," Galfandor said. "New students, please follow your advisors to your respective keeps for room assignments."

With a great rumbling of chairs being pushed back and the low murmur of conversations, everyone stood and began moving from the room.

Devon patted me on the back. "Poor Edison boy. It's a shame you rejected our offer of protection."

169

"I'm certain you'll come squirming to us in time." Rhys stood and the brothers wandered over to a group of boys their age.

Within a few minutes, the room was nearly empty except for Galfandor and some of the other teachers. I slumped as Max and Ambria's group left the room. Ambria gave me one last worried look before vanishing into the hallway.

Chapter 20

I wasn't sure what to do, so I gathered my backpack and broom and walked to the front of the room where Galfandor gathered his sheaf of parchments. He noticed me and gave me an apologetic smile.

"It appears there was a glitch in the selecting spell," he said. "I'm sorry you were left out."

"I don't have a keep?" My voice sounded sad.

"We can't have you sleeping in the park, now can we?" He patted my shoulder. "Perhaps you should just choose a keep."

My sadness vanished. "Really? But, why didn't the spark choose me?"

He tucked the parchments under an arm. "Let's not worry about that. Where would you like to stay?"

"With my friends," I said at once. "Moore Keep."

"Well, what do we have here?" said a bright voice.

I turned and saw Esma Emoora looking quizzically at me.

"One of our new students wasn't selected by the spark," Galfandor explained. "Would you be a dear and escort him to Moore Keep?"

Her eyes flashed. "I'd be delighted. What is your name, child?" She spoke with a proper accent that belied her young appearance.

"Conrad." I left it at that.

"Last name?"

I really didn't want to say it, but it wasn't like everyone didn't already know. "Edison, Miss."

She didn't even flinch at the evil name. "Come along." She nodded to Galfandor and walked toward the exit. She said nothing until we reached the hall where parents mingled and spoke in low tones. "Where is your family?"

Apparently she hadn't heard Harris's loud accusations earlier. "I'm an orphan," I lied.

She stopped in place and gave me a strange look. "An orphan?" A frown. "How awful for you."

I nearly told her it would be a relief to be an orphan, considering who my parents were, but shrugged instead.

Esma sniffed. "Well, is it awful or not?"

"Being an orphan?" I didn't like the way she asked the question. It was as if she wanted me to feel terrible. "I think it's better for everyone else that I'm an orphan."

She raised an eyebrow. "Interesting." With that, she resumed walking.

I hurried to catch up. The silence between us felt uncomfortable, and I wished Galfandor had simply let me walk alone to the dormitory. I tried to bring up polite conversation. "Where did you teach before this?"

She gave me a sideways glance. "At a private Arcane school in America."

"Oh? Which city?"

"Atlanta." Her reply sounded bored, like someone who's already repeated the same story dozens of times. Esma's eyes brightened. "What do you plan to study, Conrad?"

"Elemental magic." *Whatever makes me strong.*

"Excellent choice." We left the main building and walked down the sidewalk to the imposing dormitories. Graeven Keep towered to the right, a rectangular building with a high-pitched roof and square towers each corner. Wide balconies with ornate black iron railing protruded from nearly every window.

I heard laughter from far above and saw a crowd of older students looking over the parapets of one of the towers. One of them pointed my way and fresh laughter rained down on me. The circular walkway curved in front of each of the keeps. In the middle was a large pool of clear water with brickwork around the edges. Coins of all shapes and sizes glittered beneath the surface.

Esma stopped and looked over the edge. "Do you have any wishes for the wishing pool, Conrad?"

I had plenty of wishes, but tossing a coin into water wouldn't grant any of them. "Not really."

"Hmm."

We walked around the wishing pool and came to Moore Keep. Though I'd passed by it before, I hadn't given much thought to how different it looked from the other dorms.

Two round towers flanked a short square building with a wide oak door. Turrets with spiked roofs protruded seemingly at random along the height of each tower, while a third round tower rose from the roof of the square building. It looked as if a child with miniature building blocks had simply thrown it together.

"It's rather different, isn't it?" Esma said in a quiet voice. "They say Ezzek Moore designed it himself to prove that order can be found in chaos."

The only orderly thing about it was the square building in the middle. "Maybe he just wanted it to look strange." I looked toward Tiberius Keep. A long four-story rectangular building with a red brick façade and evenly spaced gables, it resembled a Victorian manor that might also serve as an insane asylum.

"Rather plain, isn't it?" Esma said. "I heard Tiberius never was much for creativity."

It looked more frightening than boring, while Moore Keep made my mind run in circles. "I think Graeven Keep looks the best."

"I suppose it is a bit posh." She raised an eyebrow. "Well, perhaps you'll learn better in time." The professor motioned me toward the door. "Go on inside, young Edison. I'll see you in class tomorrow."

I should have been relieved that I would soon see my friends, but instead felt a sickening dread in my stomach. What if Max and I couldn't share a room and I ended up with someone who despised me because of my last name? *If I stand out here any longer, Max might have a roommate before I find him.* I swallowed hard and turned to thank Professor Emoora, but she had already walked away.

The front door swung inward on well-oiled hinges, opening into a great hallway with dark wood flooring and gray walls. Glass chandeliers hung from the vaulted ceiling, their candlelight flickering, but somehow keeping the room brightly lit. Haphazardly hung portraits adorned the walls. Not a one of them was lined up evenly with the next, and most hung slightly crooked.

The first image was of a robed man raising his hands in a V shape before two great walls of water. Another showed a group of men sitting around a table, bored expressions on their faces as they presumably waited patiently for the painter to finish. I walked down the hall, trying to be quick about it, but instead allowing the art to distract me. There was a painting of a beautiful blonde angel, blazing wings spread wide, and a frightening scowl on her face, unleashing a spear of white light toward an old man on his knees. I thought back to the memorial at Moore Manor and wondered if the angel was Daelissa and the man was Jeremiah Conroy, the last incarnation of Ezzek Moore.

On the other wall hung the painting of a fantastical landscape with floating islands of land hanging above a brilliant vortex of energy. The next one, of a pretty blonde woman and a girl about my age, caught my eye. I looked at the bottom and found a small notation: *Alysea and Ivy*. The girl had to be Ivy Slade. I wondered where she had gone after defeating my parents. I could really use her help right about now.

The next image caught my attention because it was so plain compared to the others. It was the painting of a stone door with a curved triangle engraved in the center. Only the initials S.M. gave any indication of the artist. S.M. certainly had a love for doors, judging from the fine lines and attention to detail. The closer I looked at the patterns on the door, the more they resembled a maze.

I backed away and glanced down the row of paintings, suddenly aware I'd been taking far too long to go inside and find Max. I hurried down the long hall to the end and nearly tripped over my own feet when I saw the last portrait.

A huge green moon hung in a starry sky above a craggy mountain peak and before it, broken islands of land hanging in a sea of stars. *It's the Glimmer.* The initials at the bottom were the same as the one for the door painting. I wondered who this S.M. was and how he'd painted the Glimmer. It was doubtful he still lived, but he might have left behind journals about his travel into that strange land. It was definitely something I wanted to look into, but first, I had to find Max and the others.

I sprinted up the curving stairs and heard voices emanating through a door on the third floor. Peering around the corner, I saw

Gideon Grace in a long rectangular room, a fire crackling in a huge hearth behind him. The boys were lined up on my left and the girls on the right. With the fire flickering behind him, he looked like a demon lord overseeing his minions.

Two curved couches hugged either wall. Small round tables surrounded by plush leather divans and lamps looked like good places to study or gather with friends.

"This great room is for common use," Grace said. "Females shall not go up the stairs to the male rooms and vice versa." He walked down the line of boys, eyes boring into them. "Do I make myself clear?"

"Yes, sir!" the boys shouted.

I spotted Max on the far end of the line, his eyes wide and nervous. Ambria stood in the middle of the girls, her mouth turned down in a frown.

Grace spun on his heel and marched to the girls. "Very well, then. Go claim your rooms."

The sighs of relief were audible across the room. The boys vanished up the stairs on the left and the girls went up their stairway.

Swallowing nervously, I stepped into the great room and walked toward the professor. A quick glance out of the window on the right gave me a view of the large round turret protruding from the side of the tower where the girls' rooms were.

Grace spotted me coming. "What are you doing here, *Edison*?" He spoke my name as if it were poison.

"Galfandor told me to," I explained. "He said the selection spark glitched by not choosing me."

The professor's upper lip curled with distaste. "How unfortunate for us."

"Does Max Tiberius have a roommate yet?" I asked.

"I have no idea, boy." He jabbed a finger to the stairs. "Why don't you go find out?"

His harsh attitude hurt, but it also made me angry. What had I ever done to him? I didn't think defying the professor would help matters, so I simply nodded and went upstairs. A round room with wood paneled walls and another lively fireplace lay through the door at the top. A curved leather couch in front of the hearth looked like a cozy place to read a book while wooden tables and chairs offered more practical places to study. It looked like a smaller version of the common room below.

A group of older boys sat on the couch laughing and talking while the younger kids huddled nervously in other parts of the room. I didn't see Max anywhere, so I walked through the room while carefully looking for him. A lanky boy with curly black hair made eye contact with me and did a double-take.

He said something to his friends and stepped in front of me. "Look what we found here. It's Conrad Edison himself."

"Yeah, Rory, it sure is," said a short tubby boy. "What're you doing in our keep, Edison?"

I tried to step around Rory, but his wide friend stepped in the way.

"Gregory asked you a question," Rory said. "You're in our keep and I know you didn't get selected for it."

"He didn't get selected at all," said another boy with thick glasses and a mop of brown hair hanging over his pimply face. "I saw him crying all by himself when we left."

The boys burst into laughter as if it was the funniest joke they'd ever heard.

My hands clenched and a tremble ran up my body. "I'm looking for my friend, Max."

"Oh, that's right!" Rory grinned. "His best friends are Cryberius and that Rax girl."

"They're like a tri—a tri—uh trilogy of evil." Gregory smirked.

I couldn't help correcting him. "Did you mean trifecta?" I hated having parts of my parents in my head, but at least it helped my vocabulary.

He snapped his fingers and grinned. "Yeah, thanks!" Gregory suddenly realized he'd thanked the person he was insulting and squinted with confusion.

"Edison thinks he's smart," Rory said, and bumped his chest against mine.

Caught off balance, I stumbled backwards, much to the amusement of the others.

Gregory chortled. "Maybe we should bag him up and take him to Harris Ashmore."

Rory's eyes brightened. "Yeah. That's a good idea."

The curly-haired boy gave me a wondering look. "Maybe we can hang out with Harris and his friends then."

I remembered how popular Harris was thanks to his big deal status. I reached into my pocket for my wand. *They're not taking me without a fight.*

Someone else shoved Rory so hard he plowed into Gregory and the pair tumbled against a table.

"If you know what's good for you, you'll leave Conrad alone." Stephan, one of the boys my friends I had saved from the Goodleighs, stepped in between me and the other boys.

I was so surprised, I could hardly stop staring at this unexpected ally.

Rory bared a fist, but looked at Stephan's stocky frame and reconsidered. All the time on the orphanage farm had put some muscle on Stephan.

Gregory recovered and didn't think twice about lunging at Stephan. The other boy stepped out of the way and kicked Gregory in the seat of his pants, sending him sprawling to the floor with a loud clatter of chairs.

A cry of "Ooh!" went up around the room, while others broke into laughter.

Rory got the point and backed away, his hands up in surrender. "You must be crazy, siding with Edison."

Stephan looked a little unsure of himself, but shrugged. "He saved my life once, so I'm just returning the favor."

"Huh?" Rory looked at the other boy as if he'd sprouted an extra head. "Saved your life?"

"Max is upstairs," Stephan said, and pointed to another staircase on the curved wall at the end of the room.

"Thanks, Stephan." I felt as though there were no words to express how grateful I was that someone who wasn't Max or Ambria had stood up for me. I hadn't even realized Stephan was in this keep, but it made me feel better knowing so.

He nodded. "I owe you." Gone was the boy who'd relentlessly made fun of me at the orphanage. In his place was someone who'd survived a nightmare and maybe matured a little bit because of it. Stephan gave me an apologetic shrug and spoke in a hushed voice. "Just don't expect us to be best friends, okay?"

I managed a wan smile. "Wouldn't dream of it." I made my way past a simmering Rory and went to the staircase. The next level up offered several rooms, none of which held Max. I went up another level and another, finally locating him in a large round room at the top, staring forlornly out of an open window.

"Already daydreaming?" I asked.

He jerked and spun around, eyes wide. "Conrad?" Max's face fell. "Did you talk to Galfandor about where you're supposed to live?"

"Yeah." I put on a sad face. "I have to live on a cot in the basement where the university janitorial staff keeps their equipment."

His mouth fell open. "What? Why would Galfandor do that to you?"

"He said it would only be for a few months." I couldn't hold back a snort at his horrified face.

Max's eyes narrowed. "Are you kidding me?"

I nodded. "He told me it was a glitch in the selection spell and then told me to choose whichever keep I wanted to stay in."

"Brilliant!" He clapped me on the shoulder. "We're going to be roommates."

"Well, I actually chose Graeven Keep, but I wanted to come tell you the news."

"I'll throw you out this window if you're telling the truth." He grinned and I reflected it back.

It felt good to be back with my friend. "Did you talk with Ambria?"

He nodded. "I'm supposed to meet her in the common room in twenty minutes."

"Good. What else is on the schedule today?"

Max leaned against the window sill. "Once we get settled in, we're supposed to meet back in the dining hall for lunch. Then we go pick up our textbooks."

I noticed Max's suitcase sitting on the bed next to the window and tossed my backpack on the bed next to his. "This building sure is strange." I looked out the window for a marvelous view of Graeven Keep and the former Greek Row where Moore Manor resided. Colossus Stadium rose in the distance, and to its left, I could make out the mansion ruins near the crack in the world.

Looking at it only reminded me that my parents were still up to something. I wanted to feel safe and protected now that the entire plateau all the way up to the security gate was protected by a magical barrier. Instead, I had a feeling that was a false hope.

Chapter 21

Max unpacked his suitcase and put folded clothes in the trunk at the foot of the bed. "Yeah, I heard this place is filled with secret tunnels in the walls and all sorts of cool stuff."

Pushing unpleasant thoughts of my parents away, I looked up at the tallest spire of the keep far above. "Hey, want to go exploring?"

Max stood beside me and looked up. "Definitely, but we don't have time before lunch."

I heard Grace barking orders downstairs and grimaced. "Sounds like we're already being summoned."

"I can't believe we got him for our advisor," Max groaned.

I blew out a breath. "He's not an advisor, he's our warden, remember?" I grabbed the piece of Trouble Bubble gum Max had given me the other day and put it in my pocket, thinking I might annoy Professor Grace with it.

"Yeah, everyone else gets a friendly advisor while we get an army sergeant."

We tucked our brooms under our beds and went downstairs to the great room. Gideon Grace was nowhere to be seen, but the other boys were sullenly filing out of the room and down the stairs to the common room. Max and I followed the crowd below and saw Grace ordering the girls to line up across from us.

The professor marched down the line raking his gaze from side to side. "I want a volunteer liaison from each group. You will be in charge of keeping order among your peers and reporting any deficiencies to me."

Rory immediately stepped forward. "I'd be honored, Professor Grace."

"Not him," Max hissed. "I hope someone else volunteers."

"Marisol Culpepper reporting for duty," said a short girl with wavy brown hair and a bright smile on her face.

Ambria stood next to the girl, a scowl on her face. She glanced to the over and spotted me. "Conrad!" She clamped her hands over her mouth.

Grace stormed over to her. "You have something to say, Miss Rax?"

Ambria looked down. "No, sir."

"Look at me when I'm talking to you." Grace tapped his foot until my friend raised her eyes.

"I don't have anything to say," Ambria said, an edge in her voice.

"Very well." Grace motioned Rory and Marisol to step to the head of the lines. "Unless and until they prove they are unworthy, Rory and Marisol Culpepper are the resident keepers for the novice group."

"They're related?" Max whispered through clenched teeth.

Rory and Marisol grabbed each other's hands and thrust them into the air in a victory pose.

Ambria palmed her face.

"We expect the best behavior out of each and every one of you," Marisol said, addressing the boys and girls.

"We will tolerate nothing that breaks Professor Grace's rules," Rory added.

Grace's lips curled up slightly. Apparently, he was quite pleased with his new keepers. "Very well." He took out an old pocket watch and looked at it. "Lunch begins in twenty minutes. Afterward, you will report to the library for your textbooks." He marched away and didn't look back.

Ambria rushed over to us and gave me a firm hug. "Did Galfandor let you stay here?"

I nodded and told her what he'd said.

"This is wonderful!" She clasped her hands together and grinned. "Shall we go eat?"

Max put a hand to his stomach and opened his mouth.

"Yes, yes, we already know you're starving," Ambria said.

Max and I laughed.

It felt so good knowing I'd be in the same keep with my friends.

We went to the dining hall and had lunch. Thankfully, Harris and his friends stayed away from us and we didn't have problems with anyone else. I watched the door carefully in case Blue came in so I could invite her to sit with us, but she never came.

"I still can't figure how Harris found out our real names," Ambria said. She looked toward the head table where Galfandor and the other professors sat. "Do you think the headmaster told them?"

I screwed up my lips and looked around the room. "What if it's someone from the orphanage?"

"Stephan is in our keep," Max said.

"I know, but I don't think it's him." I told them how he'd come to my aid against Rory.

"Alice, Beth, and Catherine are here as well." Ambria pointed to a table where the three girls sat, wearing matching blue and silver scarves. "Looks like they're already wearing the colors of Graeven Keep."

"Colors?" I asked.

"Every keep has its own crest and colors," Max said. "Once we get our uniforms, we'll have to wear something identifying our keep so any trouble can be reported to our advisor."

"Spectacular," I said. "What are our colors?"

He held up the end of Ambria's scarf and showed it to me. "Black and white."

"Tiberius is purple and red," Ambria said. "Rred for strength and purple for royalty."

"My family isn't stuck up or anything," Max said with a wry grin.

"I thought you said it didn't matter which keep you lived in." I now noticed more people wearing their keep colors. "But it seems some people take it seriously."

"You have to remember the keeps and crests have been around for centuries," Max replied.

"Well, it's a good thing they got rid of the Greek system," Ambria said sarcastically. "Soon we'll need to learn gang signs."

After lunch, we picked up our textbooks and took them back to the keep then decided to do some exploring around Moore Keep. I showed them the painting of the Glimmer in the main hallway.

"Professor Grace brought us through in such a hurry, I didn't even notice," Ambria said. "It looks like the lair of an evil witch in a fairy tale."

"What's this door painting about?" Max asked.

I shrugged. "I wondered that myself."

Ambria peered at it. "I've seen that symbol somewhere before." She backed away, eyes narrowed in concentration. "I can't remember where."

"I want to find out who made these paintings." I pointed out the initials S.M. at the bottom. "They must have been to the Glimmer to paint it. Maybe they left behind journals or something."

"It's worth looking into," Ambria said.

Max wandered off the hall and into a room. "Oh, cool."

I followed him in and saw glass cases displaying swords, suits of armor, various articles of clothing, and more. Placards described the contents.

"Wow, this is the staff and wand of Giuseppe Garibaldi," Max said, pointing at a case with a crooked black staff inscribed with symbols from top to bottom, and a twisted wand with a splintered end. "Garibaldi tried to stop Moore from founding the Arcane Council."

Ambria read the placard at the bottom. "I assume Moore won the fight."

Max grunted. "Obviously."

The first floor was a museum filled with artifacts collected throughout Ezzek Moore's long life, some dating all the way back to the fall of the Roman Empire.

Max nudged me. "Is it weird knowing this guy was your great-great-great-great-a bunch more greats-grandfather?

His comment struck me like a bolt of lightning. "I never even thought about it."

"Well, you only just found out who your parents are," Ambria said. "You haven't had a lot of time to get used to it."

"It was in my pedigree information the Goodleighs had." I still had a copy of the information on my phone, but I hadn't looked at it since fleeing the orphanage.

Ambria wandered down the aisle of displays. "I think I found our mystery painter, Conrad."

I jogged down to a case displaying several worn paintbrushes and the portrait of a man with a mischievous smirk on his narrow face.

"Serpus Mandracorn was an Arcane, a painter, and a founding member of the Arcane Council," Ambria read. "All of his paintbrushes were actually wands with different kinds of animal hairs affixed to the ends. As a result, his paintings were ultra-realistic. Some people claimed if you looked long enough, you could see the images in the paintings actually move."

"That's rubbish," Max said. "I think I'd notice if the people in the paintings moved."

"Oh, shush." Ambria gave Max a playful push and caught him off balance. He flailed and made a mad grab for the display behind him to stop his fall. Unfortunately, his hand grabbed a sword on display with a suit of medieval armor.

Max yelped, let go, and fell on the floor. He looked at the blood pooling in his hand and gave Ambria an accusing look. "I cut myself."

"Oh, Max, I'm so sorry." She knelt and looked at the wound. "We should get you to the healer right away." She took off her black-and-white checkered knit scarf and wrapped it tightly around Max's hand.

He rose with a grunt. "I hope this blood comes out of your scarf otherwise it'll have Tiberius red on it."

She shrugged. "I can always get another."

We left the keep and went through the front entrance in the university and down the hall to the healing ward. No one was in the lobby, so we walked into the main ward and saw Percival mixing a potion on a table. He did a double-take when he saw us.

"Ah, you're the children who brought Mirjana to me." A smile replaced the confusion. "Have you come to check on her progress?"

"Actually, we're here because this silly boy cut his hand," Ambria said as if it were completely Max's fault.

The healer's smile stretched into a pleased grin. "Ah, my first wounded student." He unwrapped the scarf and looked at the deep cut. "Wonderful, just wonderful."

Max's mouth dropped open, aghast. "There's nothing wonderful about slicing open my hand."

"Just so happens I have a new potion I've wanted to test." Percival reached onto a shelf filled with vials and removed one with sparkling red liquid.

Max held his hand protectively. "I'm not going to be your lab rat."

"It's not precisely an experiment," Percival said. "I used it to heal a cut on my finger, and it worked marvelously."

My friend narrowed his eyes at the healer. "Really?"

"Absolutely," the healer replied. "Just hold out your hand."

Movement in the back of the room caught my attention. I felt my jaw go slack when I realized the Lady of the Pond was sitting up in her bed looking at us.

"This might sting just a little," the healer said.

Max's screams jerked my attention back to him. He ran in circles holding his hand, all the while crying out as if he was being murdered in the most painful way possible.

Percival nodded sagely. "Unfortunately, extreme pain is a negative side effect. But that's the price for a proper healing."

Ambria backed away from Max, her teeth clenched in an empathetic grimace. "Good lord, what have you done to him?"

A moment later, Max slumped against a nearby bed, breathing heavily and sweating. A stupid grin spread across his face.

"Now enters the euphoria," Percival said.

"Is that part of the medicine as well?" Ambria asked.

He shook his head. "No, that's a natural reaction of the body after experiencing so much agony."

The cut on Max's hand had faded to a thin line. "Well, it certainly heals quickly," I said.

"It's worth the pain," Percival assured us.

Max groaned. "I don't know about that."

While Max recovered, I walked to the back of the room. Mirjana watched my every step, but said nothing until I reached her.

"I must thank you," she said in a hushed tone. "You saved me." A tear trickled down her cheek. "I fear I am the only one who survived the massacre in the Fairy Garden."

"What happened?" I asked. "Who killed all the trees?"

"Victus Edison," she said in a voice rough with anger. "He and two men I did not recognize."

I squeezed the railing on her bed and clenched my teeth. A gentle touch on my cheek brought my eyes up to meet Mirjana's.

"What your father did is not your fault, young man." She smiled.

185

"How did you know he's my father?" I asked.

"Galfandor informed me." She nodded toward the door. "He was here last night when I first woke from my coma."

"Why did he do that? Did it have something to do with the Glimmer?"

Mirjana nodded. "The juxtapositions the mortals refer to as pocket dimensions are, in fact, the places where Eden is rooted to the Glimmer."

"Juxta-what?" I asked.

"Where Eden intersects the Glimmer." She looked behind me.

I turned and saw Max and Ambria had joined me.

"Remind me to never trust that healer," Max said.

"How are you feeling?" Ambria asked Mirjana.

"I'm fine, child." She nodded at me. "I was just explaining something to your friend."

"Please continue," I said.

Mirjana folded her arms across her stomach. "Though Eden touches the Glimmer in many places, the wall is the thinnest here in this place you call Queens Gate. Many centuries ago, the one you called Ezzek Moore divined this location and broke the seal." A troubled look flickered across her face. "He later told me he was merely searching for the creators of the pocket dimensions."

"In other words, we're not really in another realm, are we?" I answered my question without waiting. "Queens Gate is still a part of Eden."

She pursed her lips. "In a way, it is part of Eden and a part of the Glimmer that was preserved even after the Anchoring."

"Are you from the Glimmer?" Max asked.

"No." Mirjana didn't elaborate and went back to her story. "Once Ezzek discovered the Glimmer and realized the danger, he sent his people to all corners of the earth looking for one of us."

It was then that I knew what Mirjana was. The answers had been there before me already, but I hadn't given it much thought. She lived underwater, for goodness sake. Why hadn't I put the pieces together already? "You're a Siren."

She offered me a faint smile. "Yes."

The next question left my mouth before I even thought to ask it. "Did you help create the anchor stone?"

She laughed. "No, I am not that old, nor am I that powerful. My parents were but peons in our society, left here in this realm to keep an eye on its inhabitants. I was born during the First Seraphim War. My parents died in the war, fighting to help the mortals since Aquilis decided to take no part in the battle."

"Seems stupid they'd let the Seraphim take over Eden," Max said.

Mirjana blinked, conjuring tears that trickled down her cheeks. "I met a mortal man several centuries after the war and gave him the gift of the sea so he could live with me in the water. It was around that time when one of Ezzek's people found me." She wiped the tears away. "Though Ezzek tried to seal the passage, I thought it best to remain guardian over this place. Some creatures still managed to leave the Glimmer. I bound them to the Fairy Garden where they remained happily until their foul murders."

"The trees and dryads," Max said, a deep ache in his voice. "Victus tried to kill you because you were guarding the crack in the world?"

She nodded. "I fear my beloved Klave is also dead."

Ambria's eyes welled with tears. "Is he the mortal you fell in love with?"

"Yes." Mirjana tried to sit up straight, but fell back with a groan. "I must go to the pond and find his body. Only then can I feel peace."

I felt awful about the massacre, but one part of Mirjana's story stuck in my head. "If Klave was mortal, how did he live all these centuries? Did you make him immortal?"

The Siren shook her head. "I am not powerful enough to grant such a gift. I used what the builders created to keep him alive."

In that moment, I knew Cora had been right about how to keep her immortality outside the Glimmer.

Chapter 22

My heart pounded in my chest. The anchor stone fragment should have kept Cora alive forever, but like Galfandor explained, it didn't make her impervious to death. My curse had overpowered its effect and killed her.

Ambria touched my arm. "You look a bit pale, Conrad."

I swallowed hard and looked at Mirjana. "The anchor stone fragments give immortality, don't they?"

"Yes," she replied. "Keeping a piece of it nearby will grant you long life."

Her confirmation filled my heart with such pain I could hardly bear it. Cora had lived for centuries in Eden and should have lived centuries more. My presence had killed her!

"Conrad, what's wrong?" Ambria cried.

I killed Cora.

I blinked away the tears and saw a look of concern on Mirjana's face.

"What is wrong, child?"

"My parents possessed me with a demon so they could preserve their souls and fake their deaths." I wiped at my blurry vision. "My foster mother, Cora, she was from the Glimmer. She had a piece of the anchor stone to keep her immortal, but my living curse gave her cancer and killed her."

Mirjana brushed my cheek with the back of her hand. "I am sorry for your loss."

It hurt to breathe. Pain inflated my chest until it felt ready to burst.

A lovely voice filled the air with song. It was like no music I'd ever heard, but it warmed deep into my bones, melting the icy sorrow, loosening the tightness in my chest. The tears dried, leaving a clear view of Mirjana softly singing.

She stopped and smiled.

"Was that a magic song?" I asked.

"It was a song of hope and love." Her hand squeezed mine. "No matter the terrible things life brings, one can always find something else to hope for, and someone else to love."

I thought of her recent loss and steely resolve filled me. "I'll go look for Klave. I'll let you know if he's…okay."

Her dark eyes flashed. "It would be a gift, child."

I nodded, suddenly unable to push words past the knot of gratitude in my throat. Her song had helped more than she could know.

The Siren motioned me closer, so I leaned in. Her hand gently touched my throat. "I will give you the gift of the sea. It will only last a few hours, so do not linger too long in the depths."

I didn't imagine it would take long at all to explore the small pond, but nodded. "Okay."

Once again, she sang, this time a different song with eerie tones and discordant melodies that seemed impossible for one throat to make. Obviously, the Sirens had the ultimate gift of song.

Percival walked to the other side of her bed and watched with awe. When she finished singing, he stared at me. "Do you feel any different?"

I felt my throat. "No. Do I have gills?"

Musical laughter tinkled from Mirjana. Suddenly she yawned. "I must sleep, child. Find my love and bring me his body if you are able."

I squeezed her hand. "I will."

Percival ushered us away from the slumbering Siren, then knelt and examined my throat, pressing his fingers under my chin as if checking for swollen tonsils. "I am extremely curious to know if you can actually breathe underwater." He dug beneath a table and pulled out a bedpan. "One moment while I fill this with water."

I held up my hands and backed away. "I'm not putting my face in that."

"It's quite clean, I assure you."

Max grabbed my arm and backed us away. "How about we tell you later, okay?"

The healer looked ready to cry. "Oh, if only I could come with you." He sighed. "Unfortunately, I can't leave this place unattended on the first day students are back." He nodded at Max. "You're proof of that."

Max cringed. "Yeah, nothing like horrific pain."

"But you're healed, yes?" Percival nodded toward Max's hand.

My friend looked at the thin line left where the sword had cut him. "Well, I suppose there's that."

"We're wasting time," Ambria said. "Let's go."

Something occurred to me. "Wait a minute. The pond is still poisoned. Even if I can breathe underwater, I don't want to poison myself."

"I analyzed the pollutants in the water," Percival said, "and brewed a potion to cleanse it from Mirjana's blood. Perhaps it will also cleanse the pond."

Ambria clapped her hands. "That would be wonderful."

He held up a finger. "One moment, please." He went to another table covered with glassware and lab equipment, then picked up a large bottle with a narrow neck and swollen round bottom. Clear blue liquid sloshed in the lower half.

Humming to himself, Percival dug around on a shelf and finally withdrew a tall glass flask, poured the concoction inside, and sealed it with a cork. "Pour this into the water, and wait for the poison to clear."

I gratefully took the flask. "Thank you so much."

He grinned. "Happy, as always, to help."

"Should we get our brooms?" Max asked as we hurried down the hall to the exit.

I judged the distance in my head and figured it would take us less time to walk to the pond, or about the same time as it would to go to the keep and get our brooms. "Let's walk."

When we finally reached the murky pond, I uncorked the flask and looked into the water. The liquid was so black, it looked like tar. Thankfully, the mirror image looking back at me didn't have empty eyes or an evil smirk. The pond was larger than I remembered, and I hoped there was enough potion to clear it. I poured the blue liquid into the pond and waited. The minutes ticked past, but the inky pitch remained the same. I set down the flask and stared.

"I'll have to figure out another way." Maybe I could wear a rubber suit.

Ambria tugged my arm. "Conrad, look!"

The water where I'd poured the potion turned light blue. The effect slowly spread across the pond, until nearly two-thirds of the surface looked clear. The rest of the pond remained filthy and murky, but the water on our side was so clear, I could see where the taint clouded deep beneath the water on the unclean side. I didn't see any sign of a body. Unless Klave's body floated in the filthy water on the other side, he must be deeper below.

Though the water was clear, it grew darker dozens of feet down and I couldn't see the bottom. I stripped off my shirt and shoes, but left on my pants.

"It'll be hard to swim in pants," Ambria said. "If it'll make you feel better, I can close my eyes."

I grinned. "I'll keep them on, thanks." I handed Max my wand. "Wish me luck."

He looked from me to the water. "Good luck, Conrad."

Looking over the edge, I noticed there was no gradual slope down into the deep water, but a steep drop-off. I automatically held my breath, and jumped in feet first. I just as suddenly realized what an awful mistake I'd made. The water was absolutely freezing. A reflexive gasp sucked down a mouthful of cold water. My body thrashed with panic.

I flail blindly in the water until I'm rescued by gentle hands. Cora holds me up and kisses my forehead. "Don't fight the water, Conrad. You'll lose every time."

Coughing up water, I grip her tight. "Please don't let go again."

"Let the water caress you, dear." She pushes me to the side of the pool so I can grab the edge, then reclines in the water and floats. "If you don't fight the water, it will support you." She stands up. "You try."

I don't trust the water, but I trust Cora. If she tells me something will work, then it will. My chest tightens with anxiety, but I let go of the side of the pool with one hand and lean back. A little water splashes on my face. I fight back the panic that I'm about to sink and force my body to relax. Suddenly, I'm floating.

Cora takes my other hand from the side of the pool and releases it. "You're floating, Conrad." She giggles. "You're floating!"

Let go.

I forced myself to stop fighting and floated just beneath the surface of the water, still holding my breath. The urge to breathe became unbearable, but I couldn't make myself do it underwater. My body's survival instinct screamed that it was suicide.

Let go, Conrad. I pictured Cora's smiling face when she taught me how to swim.

Learning to breathe underwater shouldn't be any different. Fighting my instincts, I opened my mouth and sucked in a lungful of water.

My body thrashed and jerked, but instead of drowning me, the water filling my lungs felt no different than air, just a bit heavier. I rose to the surface and blew out a lungful of water.

"I can breathe water!" I gurgled. I ducked underwater and sucked down another lungful, then came up and spoke. Though my voice sounded strange, talking was no different other than a stream of water trickling from my mouth.

Ambria and Max grimaced.

"It looks and sounds awful, Conrad." Ambria knelt next to the pond and patted my head. "You should stop wasting time and find Klave."

My excitement had nearly overwhelmed my sense of duty. "I'll be back soon." I dove back underwater, kicking my legs and moving my arms in a froglike movement. Breathing the water became easier and easier as my body's reflexes stopped resisting. Clear vision was another effect of the Siren's song. Even though the surface light faded, my eyes adjusted to the darkness.

The only place my vision couldn't penetrate was the inky murk on the other side of the pond. I realized that its oily tendrils reached deeper than I'd thought from the surface. Looking back up, I also realized something else—it was slowly spreading back over the pond. I didn't have much time to find Klave.

I swam deeper and deeper, realizing with every stroke that though this body of water looked like a pond from up above, it was far more than that beneath the surface. The sides of the hole resembled colorful coral, and the water was salty, not fresh. The pond widened the further I descended until I couldn't see from one side to the other in the darkening water.

Even with my underwater dark vision, I could only see about thirty feet in any direction, so I swam side-to-side, searching for a body. I suddenly broke through a veil of darkness and into a realm of gently glowing coral. Schools of brightly colored fish swam past. Something huge rushed behind me. I spun and shouted with fright as a monstrous shark zipped past in pursuit of the smaller fish. It was as if I'd suddenly been transported to the ocean, or else the bottom of the pond was vaster than I could imagine.

Then I spotted something even more amazing—a giant curved seashell easily three stories tall. *Large enough to live in.* Somehow I knew that was where Mirjana and Klave lived. Lying on the floor of sand in front of the shell, I saw who I was looking for.

Klave's long black hair clouded around his face like ink, moving with the ebb and flow of the water. Dark veins mottled his pale skin, and he looked still as death. He wore only a seaweed loincloth and a choker necklace made of tiny green pebbles—bits of the anchor stone—that looked like smaller versions of the one I'd inherited from Cora. I put a hand to his chest. It felt as though it was moving, if only barely. I looked up toward the surface, but the veil hiding this underwater realm blocked my view. I didn't need to see the pollution above to know I didn't have much time before it covered the pond again.

Then I realized another problem. How was I supposed to carry this man with me? Klave was lean and muscular, and at least two feet taller than me. I tugged on him and he floated easily off the seabed.

You're underwater, you moron, Vic said. *The body will cause extra drag, but even someone weak as you can carry it.*

He won't make it to the top, Della said. *He can't possibly swim that fast.*

I knew she was right, but I had to try. Grabbing Klave's wrist, I tugged on him and swam upward. Even though the water assisted me, I had to push myself twice as hard until I was gasping water. It took several minutes for me to reach the veil and several more to swim far enough to glimpse sunlight on the surface far overhead. The poison had already crept across most of the pond, leaving only the last third clear.

The last of the clean water was quickly vanishing, and I knew there was no way to swim there in time. While the poison didn't seem to kill immediately, it had struck both Klave and Mirjana unconscious before they could climb out of the pond. If I didn't reach the surface, the poison might knock me out. Max and Ambria wouldn't even see me through the pollution.

I redoubled my efforts, but the sunlight was vanishing quickly.

Surrender to death, Vic said. *It is inevitable.*

Chapter 23

I wished I'd thought this through a little more. If only I'd brought some sort of flotation device, or a rope—my eyes flashed wide and I dug in my pocket. I found the packaged lump of Trouble Bubble, took it out and unwrapped it with one hand. Chewing furiously, I prayed the magic bubble gum worked as well underwater as it did above. I felt the gum expanding in my mouth and pressed it against the inside of my lips.

A big pink bubble ballooned from my mouth and the gum nearly jerked itself free as the air tugged upward. Clamping down with my teeth, and using both hands to keep my hold on Klave, I let the bubble pull us up like an underwater air balloon. The bubble grew larger and larger, and I hoped we'd reach the top before it burst.

I couldn't see the taint on the surface as the pink gum blocked my view. Suddenly the upward momentum stopped, and I felt the bubble bobbing on the surface.

"I see him!" Ambria cried, words muffled from the water

"Help me pull him closer," Max shouted.

I reached out blindly with a hand and found grasping fingers. They pulled me to the side of the pond. With a loud pop, the bubble gum burst. Max shouted in surprise, but his grip remained firm.

"Get Klave," I wheezed, still out of breath from my earlier exertions.

Max got on his stomach and fished in the water until he gripped Klave. I released the man and grabbed the shore. Ambria tugged on the waist of my pants to help me out.

"Hurry, Conrad!" Fear contorted her face. "The poison is almost here."

I looked back and saw the poison only feet away from me. My body sent a shock of adrenalin coursing through my veins and I scrambled up and out. It still wasn't time to rest. I knelt next to Max and grabbed Klave's arm. We tugged and jerked him up and onto the shore just as the poison claimed the last of the surface.

I fell onto my back and lay gasping for air.

Ambria knelt over me. "We thought you were never coming back."

I tried to talk, but was too out of breath.

"That was pretty smart using the Trouble Bubble," Max said with a grin. "I just wish we'd thought to bring a flying carpet with us to get this man back to the healer."

I groaned and finally managed to speak. "I guess we're not good at planning things."

Ambria sniffed. "That's because you didn't let a female do it." She sighed. "The three of us can carry him."

Rolling over and pushing up, I managed to climb to my wobbly feet. I was almost too tired to move.

Max grabbed Klave beneath the arms. "Get his legs Conrad."

I was happy to take the lighter side.

"I suppose I'll carry the middle." Ambria's nose wrinkled when she looked at the loincloth. "I'm not going to enjoy this."

None of us enjoyed the trek back to the university.

"Can we please plan things out better in the future?" Ambria griped as we finally neared the entrance. "We could have run back for a carpet in half the time it took us to carry the man."

Max blinked away the sweat trickling over his eyes. "Almost there." He stumbled and recovered.

Ambria grimaced. "Oh, his skin is so clammy."

"Stop complaining," Max panted. "Just shut up and move."

A few minutes later, we finally entered the healing ward. Percival's eyes widened with delight. "You found him!" He pressed two fingers to Klave's neck. "I believe he's still alive. Hurry, get him to a table."

Max groaned like an angry but wounded animal. "You take him!"

The healer frowned, then perked up. "Ah, I'm sure you're exhausted from carrying him all this way. Next time, take a flying carpet with you to use as a gurney."

Murderous rage flared in Max's eyes, and Percival quickly relieved him of the load.

"Ick, ick, ick!" Ambria wiped her hands on her clothes, then dashed over to a sink and washed her hands.

"Can you save him?" I asked the healer.

Percival set the man on a bed and nodded. "Perhaps. I'll let you know." He took a vial of the blue antidote. Holding Klave's mouth open, he trickled it in, then held him upright to aid swallowing.

I walked back to Mirjana's bedside, but she was still asleep. I resisted the urge to wake her. So many questions remained. Her eyes suddenly flashed open and she gripped my wrist. I yelped and would have stumbled backwards if not for her grip.

"You found him?" she asked.

I nodded. "He was near your home at the bottom—alive."

She exhaled slowly. "I pray he survives."

"Is that pond in the ocean?" I asked. "It's huge."

Mirjana nodded. "It is the fragment of an ocean from the Glimmer that melded with Eden where the two touched." Her face grew sad. "Now all they have is an ocean of stars."

"May I ask you more questions?"

Her eyes settled on me. "I will answer what I can."

"Where can I find more fragments of the anchor stone?" I held up the green pebble given to me by Cora and the Siren's eyes widened.

"That is a large piece, indeed."

I held it in the palm of my hand. "It doesn't look that large."

"I found only fragments around the edges of the land where it meets the void," Mirjana said. "It took several to craft Klave's necklace. They likely kept him alive all this time."

I nodded. "Naeve told me Cora found this piece in the void between the islands in the Glimmer."

The Siren's eyes flashed. "Queen Naeve?"

"Yes."

"How did this Cora know the Queen?" she asked.

"Naeve said they were twin sisters."

Mirjana's mouth parted slightly. "Sisters, you say?"

I wondered why she sounded surprised. "Why?"

She shook her head. "I have not been in the Gimmer for centuries and only met Naeve once. She told me her family had died in the

Anchoring." Mirjana squeezed her eyes shut for a moment. "As you can imagine, the Glimmer folk do not like my kind. Though they lost emotion millennia ago, I am certain they still remember their hatred of us."

"My father destroyed the forest and tried to kill you on Queen Naeve's behalf," I said. "I think it was part of the price for him to do business with them."

The Siren's eyes flashed angrily. "Tell me what he wants from the queen."

"He told her he wants an army to conquer the Overworld, but Galfandor told me my parents really want immortality."

"They want pieces of the anchor stone," she said.

"Except they don't know that." I felt a smug smile creep across my face. "The Glimmer Queen suspected the anchor stone fragments were the answer to keeping her immortality outside the Glimmer since Cora lived so long. Naeve said Cora's death proved that theory wrong."

"When in fact, you believe it was your curse that killed her." Mirjana made a thoughtful sound.

"I'm sure she told my parents that the anchor stone fragment didn't work for Cora, so they'll probably look for other answers."

Musical laughter danced from Mirjana's throat. "The answer to their desires is plainly before them, but their own misdeeds hide the truth."

Thinking of Cora made my heart ache again. "Cora's daughter, Evadora, said she used an anchor stone fragment to escape the Glimmer, by travelling through the reflected world."

Mirjana bolted upright and immediately doubled over in pain. "I did not realize the anchor stone so thoroughly warped the boundaries of reality. You must be careful if you travel through the echo."

"The echo?" I asked.

"Our voices always cast echoes even if we do not always hear them. Is not a reflection but an echo of light?"

I hadn't really thought of it that way. "Is it true my reflection will steal my soul if it catches me?"

"Only but a part," she said. "But then it will no longer be a reflection, but a part of you."

I shuddered at losing such a vital part of me.

Mirjana looked longingly at Klave as the healer treated him.

"Is there a way to permanently seal off the Glimmer?" I asked.

She shook her head. "Even Ezzek Moore could not reseal what he had opened."

My heart grew heavier. "When you're better, can you help me fight my parents?"

The Siren turned her attention back to me. "If only I could, child. Unfortunately, I am not a warrior. Because you have rescued my beloved, I will answer any questions you may have, and will help you however I can. Unfortunately, that cannot include fighting." She looked toward Klave. "Neither is he a fighter, though he can divine the truth from any words uttered by man. I am certain he will help you if you ask, should he survive."

I tried to think of more questions, but I was exhausted and my mind refused to cooperate any longer. I saw Max and Ambria waiting across the room from me and knew it was time to go.

Mirjana kissed my cheek. "You bear a great darkness in your soul, child, but it is obvious someone lit a candle in that darkness and nurtured it into a flame." She squeezed my hand. "Cora's light burns on in you, Conrad Edison. It is up to you to make sure it never goes out."

My vision blurred as tears bit my eyes. "She was my sunshine." I leaned over and kissed Mirjana on the cheek. "Goodbye for now, and feel better."

Chapter 24

The next morning brought unwelcome aches and pains. Simply sitting up felt like a tiger had clawed my muscles all the way to the bone.

Max and I met Ambria for breakfast then went to our first class, Elementary Magic, taught by our warden, Gideon Grace. Like most classrooms, dark hardwood floors and gray wood-paneled walls made the large space look dim. Bookshelves lined the left wall and thirty wooden desks occupied the center of the room, leaving plenty of unused space.

People turned noisily in their desks and stared when we entered the room. Harris, Lily, and Baxter stopped talking and glared at us.

I stiffened to stop from trembling and made my way toward three empty desks across the room from my new archenemy. Rory and Gregory dashed in front of me and took two of the desks.

"Oh, I'm sorry, these are taken." Rory smirked.

Max groaned and turned toward other empty desks. "Let's take these—" before he could finish the sentence, a third boy tossed his coat over one desk and sat in the other.

"Taken." He grinned.

I caught a smug smile from Harris.

Ambria dropped quickly into a desk, but when I tried to take the one next to it, someone else hopped in my way.

My hands trembled with anger. "Get out of my way."

"Yeah, or what?" said the boy.

I noticed the boy had left his backpack next to his original desk in his haste to get in my way. I walked over to his backpack. "Oh, what do we have here?"

"Leave my stuff alone!" He ran over and grabbed his book bag, giving Max a chance to slide into the vacated seat.

Harris and Baxter strode across the room to me, chests puffed out, noses high, and stood between me and the boy with the backpack.

"Leave him alone or I'll report you," Harris said.

I was sick of these stupid games. "Who told you my last name?"

Baxter laughed. "He doesn't even know."

"Maybe you need better friends." Harris bared his teeth in a grin.

I glanced back at Ambria and Max. *It couldn't have been one of them.*

Harris shoved me and got in my face. My sore muscles protested and I nearly tripped over the desk behind me.

"I know what the prophecy means," he hissed. "It means I'm supposed to stop you." He leaned even closer. "Maybe I can't do anything now, but the minute you break the law, I will kill you."

Baxter smacked a fist into his palm. "Yeah, with magic."

I wasn't in the mood to argue, and Professor Grace would be here at any moment and take Harris's side. I backed off and shrugged as if I didn't care what he said, though it felt like he'd stabbed me in the stomach with a knife. "Do what you have to do, Harris."

He feinted toward my face with his fist. "Count on it."

I flinched and felt angry with myself for it. Did everyone expect me to follow the path of darkness taken by my parents? I was far too young to embark on world domination.

Max took his feet off a desk next to him and I finally sat down.

Professor Grace strode quickly into the room and to the front. "Take out your wands and make the tips glow."

His command caught everyone off guard, and there was a scramble through backpacks and pockets for wands. I took out mine, flicked it through the pattern, and said, "*Illumus.*"

Mine was the first wand to glow. Lily succeeded next, and most of the others followed quickly. Ambria, however, seemed flustered and couldn't get the pattern quite right. I leaned over to help, but Grace called out, "Time's up! Hold up your wands." His gaze locked on Ambria's unlit wand. "Fail." He pointed to another student without a glow on her wand. "Fail." He pointed out three more. "Fail, fail, fail."

Grace took a quill and scratched on a parchment while talked. "Next time, I expect you to be better prepared."

Ambria's eyes welled with tears. "Was that a test score?"

Grace glared at her. "Ask permission before you speak, girl."

Her lips trembled and her eyes widened with hurt. "May I—"

"No." Grace finished writing and stood. "Harris Ashmore, list every spell you can cast on command."

"*Illumus*, *ignitus*, *ventus*, *repellato*, and"—he paused for effect and looked around—"*hadouken*."

Students gasped, as if he'd just made a rather bold claim.

Max grabbed my arm. "There's no way he can perform *hadouken*."

I was still confused. "What does that mean?"

"It's a fireball spell used by Justin Slade." He formed a large ball with his hands. "It was super powerful."

"Impressive." Grace smiled proudly, as if Harris was his own son. "This is not the place, but I expect you to demonstrate *hadouken* for us in the near future."

"My pleasure, professor."

Grace looked around the room. "Does anyone else know any spells not mentioned by Ashmore?"

I almost raised my hand to mention *torsious*, but since I hadn't been able to reproduce it, kept my hand down.

"Hmm, I thought not." Grace went to the chalkboard and drew several diagrams on it. "Can anyone identify these wand patterns?"

I raised my hand. The professor looked right at me then turned and pointed to Lily. "Yes?"

She recited them without pause. "*Ventus*, *ignitus*, and *levator*."

"Can you perform *levator*?" he asked.

Lily shook her head. "Not yet, but I'm working on it."

Grace took out a wand and pointed it toward a piece of parchment on his desk. He flicked his wand. "*Levator*." The paper floated gently into the air. The professor looped his wand and the paper followed with a loop of its own, repeating whatever he did with the wand.

"Since you should have already mastered the spells from the entrance exam, we will work on levitation today." Grace tucked his wand behind his back and paced in front of the room. "First, I'll review the basics in case anyone has forgotten." He held up the wand. "What is this at its most basic level?"

Several students raised their hands.

"Yes?" Grace pointed to a girl.

"A wand."

The professor sighed. "No." every hand went back down except for mine. He stared at me for a moment and finally said, "Yes, Edison?"

"A focus," I replied. "Just like a staff is a focus."

His lip curled into a sneer. "Yes. Can anyone tell me why staffs are sometimes used instead of wands?"

Ambria raised her hand.

Grace ignored her and pointed to a boy with thick glasses in the front row. "Hutchinson."

"Staffs can focus more power," the boy replied.

"Correct. And as we well know, some people believe in nothing but power." His gaze hesitated on me for a second after making the comment and I wondered if it was supposed to be a statement about my parents.

I felt someone else watching me and caught Harris's glare from across the room. I thought back to his comment about needing better friends and suddenly I knew who'd told him my last name.

Blue.

The day of the argument, Ambria had seen her go next door to Harris's. She must have been so angry with me she told him everything. I expected to be furious with her, but felt disappointment instead. I'd yelled at Blue when she'd been nothing but nice to me. She still shouldn't have betrayed our trust, but then again, we hardly knew her. Maybe we shouldn't have trusted her in the first place.

A part of me was happy my secret was out. At least I didn't have to worry about hiding it anymore.

"Well, Edison?"

I blinked away my thoughts and saw Grace and the rest of the class looking at me. I tried to remember what the professor had been talking about, but couldn't recall a single thing he'd said for the past few minutes. "Sorry, what was the question again?"

"The runes," Max hissed. "Say it's the runes."

Before I could answer Grace strode across the room and leaned over my desk. "Report to the common room for cleaning duties after dinner tonight."

"Cleaning duties?"

Laughter echoed around the room. I glanced at Ambria and Max. They looked down at their desks. My face grew hot, but I forced my head to stay up. "Yes, sir."

"Paying attention in my class isn't optional, Edison." Grace straightened. "Who else knows the answer?"

Lily's hand shot up. "The runes."

Max palmed his face.

When the class finally ended, Max, Ambria and I quickly left the room and went down the hall to the Magical Defense classroom. Esma Emoora was already inside and smiled brightly at us. "Hello, Conrad."

"Hello, Professor." I tilted my head in greeting then walked toward the back of the room with my friends.

"Please sit in the front," Esma said. "Only dullards hide in the back row."

Ambria's mouth dropped open, but she turned around and we took the first three desks on the right side of the room. Harris and Baxter entered next, casting dirty looks at us when they walked past. Lily followed close behind and smiled at me briefly before flattening her lips and looking serious. I couldn't tell if her smile was genuine or sarcastic.

"Edison's got maid duties," Baxter taunted.

Harris sneered. "Yeah, better wear an apron."

I ignored them and pretended to talk to Max.

The professor looked from Harris to me, but said nothing. After the last students trailed inside, she stepped to the front of the classroom. "What is magical defense?"

Lily's hand went up. "The ability to protect yourself from harmful magic."

Esma flicked a wand from beneath her robes and aimed it at Lily. "Pop. You're dead."

The girl shrank back, her face pale. "I-I didn't know you were going to do that."

"Precisely, little one." The professor's smile suddenly seemed quite sinister. "The most common defense against spells is a shield." She spun on her heel and aimed the wand at Harris. Light burst from the tip of the wand and zapped him on the nose. "You're dead too."

Harris yelped and fell out of his desk, but seemed otherwise unharmed. Tension filled the room, and everyone had a slightly crazed look in their eyes, probably wondering if they'd be next.

Esma pivoted on her heel and spun our way. Before I knew what was happening, my wand was in my hand. I drew a complex pattern like a cursive S and with each flick of my wand shouted, "*Soros, quoros, eva equas*!" The air in front of me flickered. The professor's attack crackled past my shield and zapped poor Hutchinson who yelped like a hurt puppy.

"Excellent!" Professor Emoora clapped her hands and walked over to my shimmering shield. "This is how you defend yourselves."

"You stung me!" Harris rubbed the end of his nose. "You're not supposed to hurt students."

Esma's lips flattened. "Are you saying a tiny shock of static electricity hurt, little boy?"

Harris stiffened, suddenly aware that his manliness was being called into question. "No, Professor. But we haven't learned shields yet."

Without looking at me, her arm rotated to point at the shield. "Mr. Edison has."

Except I hadn't learned it. Like *torsious*, it was one of those spells I'd never studied.

Lily stared wide-eyed at the shimmer in the air and then at me. I couldn't tell if she thought it was wonderful or terrible. The shield spell finally burned through its aether charge and vanished with a ripple.

Harris's jaw tightened. "If Edison can learn it, so can I."

"We're not supposed to learn that spell until our third year of Magical Defense," Lily said. "It's a multi-cast spell because the shield is formed in layers."

Esma nodded approvingly. "Very observant, Miss Crown. What is the shield we'll learn?"

"*Soros*, the first layer of the Squee shield," she said, "named for the words used to evoke it."

"Precisely, and that is what we'll practice today." Esma frowned and looked around. "This layout will not do. Students, move your desks to form a circle."

There was a brief pause followed by a flurry of movement and the loud scrape of desk legs across the wooden floor. Students bumped into each other and snarled traffic as they all tried to move their desks to the side of the room with Harris Ashmore. My side of the circle consisted of Ambria, Max, Hutchinson, and me.

Esma stared blankly at the students trying to fit in on the overly crowded left side of the room. Finally, she stepped in front of them and waved her wand threateningly. "Other side of the room, please."

Eyes bugging for fear she'd zap them, the students quickly complied until the center of the room was clear and my side of the room was nearly as full as the other. Esma walked into the middle of the desks and smiled sweetly. "Miss Rax and Miss Crown, please come to the center."

Ambria gulped and did as instructed. Lily practically skipped forward.

"I will teach you both this rather simple electricity spell." She pointed her wand forward. "Up, down, quickly side-to-side thrice, and Zzt." A spark of static fizzled through the air. Several students leapt back even though they were in no danger of being hit. A smirk lit Esma's face. "Now, you try it."

Lily got the spell on her first try. It took Ambria three tries to finally summon the sparks.

"Now, you'll learn *soros*, the simplest shield spell." Esma traced a circle with the tip of her wand. "*Soros*." A shield several feet in diameter rippled in the air and vanished a few seconds later.

Ambria screwed up her face in concentration and followed the professor's lead. A sheet of translucent air the size of a dinner plate solidified in front of her. Lily made a slightly larger shield and smiled smugly at Ambria.

"Very good." Esma looked around at everyone. "For the rest of class, we'll take turns casting and shielding."

Nervous gulps echoed.

"Miss Rax, you will shield first." The professor backed away and held up her wand then swung it down in an arc. "Go."

Both girls shouted the words to their spells, but nothing happened. Ambria finally got a shield up on her third try, but it faded away by the time Lily finally zapped her with static. Esma seemed awfully amused. "Now switch."

Ambria shocked Lily on her first try, causing the other girl to drop her wand and shriek.

The professor called four more students and paired them off so two groups could go at a time. I practiced the simple shield while I watched. On the fourth round, Max and I were called out to face Harris and Baxter. I glanced at the professor and saw the tiniest smirk on her face. *She planned it this way.*

I took a deep breath to ward off my nerves and squared off against Harris. The other boy didn't look quite so confident against me as Baxter did against Max, probably because of my display of magic earlier. He didn't know that was something Vic or Della had managed, not me. Before the teacher gave us the word to go, Harris flicked his wand.

He's cheating!

I traced the shield and cast it just in time to intercept Harris's spell.

"Excellent, young Edison." Esma smiled almost proudly at me. "Winning a battle of spells is mostly about surprise and keeping your opponent off balance.

Max howled and jumped back as Baxter zapped him twice in a row and the professor's smile faded. "It seems some of you have a long way to go."

A bell gonged in the distance and students scrambled for their belongings.

Professor Emoora put away her wand. "Practice your spells tonight, children. Tomorrow we will practice this again."

From the angry look Harris gave me, I knew he'd be ready for me the next time.

Chapter 25

History with Eleanor Beetle was next. The plump little teacher sat on a stool in the front and recited the lesson directly from the history textbook. I barely managed to stay awake when she began to list the founders of the Arcane Council in a monotone voice.

Max rested his head on his hand, eyelids drooping. Ambria nodded off. A thud jerked everyone awake. Max sat up rubbing his forehead where it had hit the desk.

Professor Beetle didn't even look up from her reading.

Max yawned mightily when we sat down for lunch. "I'd rather get zapped in Professor Emoora's class than sit through another snore-fest like that."

"Me too," Ambria said without hesitation. She leaned on the table and looked at me. "Was your shield spell the work of Vic and Della?"

"Yes." My stomach growled noisily as I took the lid off my lunch plate. "If it's anything like the *torsious* spell, I probably won't be able to repeat it."

"Multi-casting is high level stuff," Max confirmed. "By the time you learn that spell you should be able to think the words in your head."

"Yes, thinking is normally done in your head," Ambria said dryly. "I can't believe Grace gave Conrad cleaning duty."

"I can," I mumbled. "He hates me but loves Harris."

Ambria sighed. "He's a rather unpleasant man to begin with."

On that we could all agree.

Max buttered a slice of toast. "There's something we haven't talked about yet." He took a crunchy bite and wiped crumbs from his lips.

Ambria raised an eyebrow. "Which is?"

"The anchor stone." He motioned toward me with his toast. "Mirjana told us how the Glimmer Queen can keep her immortality, so maybe we should tell the queen."

Her forehead pinched. "You think we should tell her?"

Max shrugged and looked at me. "If we tell Naeve, then we'll have solved her problem and she won't help Conrad's parents."

I shoveled down a hunk of brisket and nodded. "Unless the queen was lying."

"Why would she lie?" Max said. "I think we should get this over and done with."

"I agree," Ambria said. "We should also tell her that Conrad's parents didn't plan to help her in the first place. Maybe the queen will help us capture them."

One last spoonful of potatoes and my plate was clean. My stomach made an appreciative noise, but I still felt hungry.

Ambria waved a hand in front of my face. "Well, Conrad, what do you think?"

"I think it's a fine idea." I pointed to her toast. "Are you going to eat that?"

She sighed and handed it to me. "Boys are always hungry."

Max stopped one of the server golems as it took his empty plate. "Can I have seconds?"

The golem didn't seem capable of speaking and walked away.

I ate the toast and thought about telling Naeve the answer to her ancient problem. "I wonder how hard it is to find pieces of the anchor stone."

Max looked hopefully at Ambria's remaining potatoes. "From what Mirjana said, it's not easy."

Ambria huffed and pushed her plate over to Max. "Maybe we should ask Evadora to find a few pieces that we can give to Naeve. I wouldn't want the queen to steal Conrad's pebble."

The thought hadn't occurred to me. "That's a good idea. Maybe we can go to the Glimmer and look for her."

Ambria leaned back in her chair and shook her head rapidly. "I don't want to go through the reflected world or any of that again."

Max paused midway through lifting potatoes to his mouth. "Let's wait for Evadora to come to us. The Glimmer scares me."

I thought back to our mirror counterparts chasing us and wondered if mine still waited on the other side. My reflection looked normal yesterday when I rescued Klave, so maybe I could sneak through again if necessary.

After lunch, we went to Elementary Potions taught by Professor Trask. Her classroom resembled a lab with stations instead of desks for the students and a long table at the front covered in glassware of all shapes and sizes. It reminded me of Percival's table in the healing ward. Cabinets lined the front wall, their shelves laden with jars and bottles of ingredients. Pickled lizards and small brains floated in two of the largest jars.

Ambria stared at them. "Eww. I hope she doesn't expect us to handle tiny brains."

"You handle yours pretty well," Max said with a grin.

Ambria swatted him on the arm.

We were the first to the room so we chose the middle table on the second row from the front. I held my breath as students filed inside and finally let out a sigh of relief when Baxter and Harris didn't appear.

"Four to a table," Trask said.

Students looked around and found tables that needed more partners, but avoided ours until every table had four but ours.

Professor Trask raised an eyebrow and opened her mouth to speak when a straggler walked in. "Miss Crown, I expect you to be here on time."

Lily looked down. "Yes, Professor."

Trask pointed to our table. "Partner with them."

Lily's eyes bugged when she saw us. "But—"

"No buts, Miss Crown." Trask shooed the girl with her hands. "Go."

Keeping her eyes on the floor, Lily walked over to us and took a stool without saying a word.

"We don't bite," Ambria whispered.

"You lied to us," the other girl hissed back. "Besides, Harris is convinced he has to fight you to protect the world."

Max pshawed. "That prophecy is bollox."

Professor Trask's eyes locked onto him. "Mr. Tiberius, since you seem so eager to speak, perhaps you'll tell us the ingredients for a Juji potion."

Judging from the stunned look in Max's eyes, he didn't even know what a Juji potion was. During my studies in the ruined mansion, I'd read about the mixture and even made it once.

Max hemmed and hawed for a moment. "Um, water?"

Trask didn't appear amused.

Lily rolled her eyes and raised her hand. "Juji potion is an energy drink made of black nettles, a bee stinger, and crushed tube leaves."

"Excellent, Miss Crown." The professor narrowed her eyes at Max. "I suggest you read ahead in the textbook, Mr. Tiberius."

Max looked down at his hands. "Yes, Professor."

Trask turned back to the rest of the class. "The interesting thing about Juji potion is that none of the ingredients by themselves will give a person more energy." She turned to the shelf behind her, removing jars and setting them on her table while she spoke. "And yet, Juji potion will give a person a boost of energy with no negative side effects like caffeine or guarana." She set boiling flasks on the table next to the ingredients. "I want every table to send a representative up here to gather what they need to make a batch."

Lily jumped off her stool and went to the front before the rest of us had a chance to react. When she returned, she sorted the ingredients on the table and snatched the mortar and pestle.

"Do you plan to do it all by yourself?" Ambria asked.

The other girl looked up, brow pinched. "You can watch and learn."

"I learn better by doing." Ambria looked in the textbook and sprinkled the black nettles into the mortar. "Max, you crush them."

He took the pestle and pounded it on the nettles like a hammer.

Lily snatched the tool from him. "You're doing it wrong." She pressed the pestle on the nettles and twisted it. "Pound and twist."

Max groaned and held out his hand. "Fine, I'll do it your way."

The girl reluctantly handed it back to him.

After mixing the ingredients and boiling the concoction, we were left with a dark liquid with bits of leaves and nettles floating on top. Lily tried to strain it with a wire mesh, but couldn't get rid of the fine particles. I looked in the drawer on our table for something better, but

211

didn't notice anything except sponge cloth. The image of Victus straining amber liquid through the soft yellow material flickered in my mind.

I didn't know if Vic meant to help me, or if it had just been a random thought.

I tucked the cloth into the mouth of a jar and poured our potion onto it.

Lily looked aghast. "What are you doing?"

"Straining it," I replied. By then the liquid began to trickle through to the other side.

Ambria narrowed her eyes at Lily. "I guess you don't know everything after all."

By the end of class, we had a flask filled with black liquid that smelled slightly of cinnamon. Professor Trask walked around and inspected the results, grimacing at another table's batch that was thick as oil, and stopping in astonishment to stare at the toxic green liquid another table managed to produce.

"You took green nettles, not black ones," Trask said, looking at the jars on the table at the front. "I even set the proper ingredients on the table."

Hutchinson pushed up his thick glasses. "I'm sorry, I don't know how I picked up the wrong one."

Professor Trask picked up our flask and swirled the ingredients. "Excellent." She held it up for the other students to see. "A rich frothy liquid with virtually no impurities floating on the top." She held up the jar we'd used to filter the ingredients. "You used a sponge cloth. How interesting."

"It was Conrad's idea," Lily said.

"They're usually used for cleaning up spills, not filtering," Trask said.

"The strainer wasn't fine enough," I said.

The professor set the flask on the table. "Good work."

I couldn't stop the smile spreading on my face and noticed Max and Ambria grinning back at me.

Lily, however, looked troubled. "You're smart, Conrad. I just hope you're not as evil as Harris thinks."

I wanted to assure her I wasn't but didn't think it would do much good. Max, Ambria, and I went to our last class, Elementary

Enchantments. Rory and Gregory beat us to the classroom, but didn't try to block us from finding seats this time. The bell gonged shortly after we found desks, but Professor Sideon remained absent. As the minutes ticked by, the conversation in the room grew noisier.

Asha Fellini stepped into the classroom, her silky black hair tied back in a ponytail. "Tell me, where is Professor Sideon?" She spoke like a ruler to her subjects, a haughty edge to her voice. When no one could answer her question, she folded her arms. "Very well. Since I have no class this period, I will teach until he arrives."

Students groaned and just as quickly fell silent at a severe look from her.

Her gaze locked onto me. "What is an enchantment, Conrad Edison?"

An unpleasant chill shivered across my skin and my response froze in my throat. Her looks, her mannerisms, all reminded me of Delectra. It was as if my mother had disguised herself just enough that no one could guess her identity. Given that my parents were still officially considered dead, it wouldn't be hard to fool people.

An elbow nudged me. "Conrad?" Max whispered.

I flinched. "An enchantment is a spell placed on an object that temporarily or permanently changes its basic characteristics."

"Why are you looking at me that way?" the professor asked.

I shook my head to clear it. "Sorry, it's been a long day."

She walked over to my desk and looked down her nose at me. "An excuse will not save you in a magic duel."

That statement knocked me out of my stupor. "What does that have to do with enchantments?"

"Very little." Asha's robes swooshed as she spun around and went back to the front of the class. "What is the different between a charm and a curse?"

"A charm is a positive enchantment," Gregory said. "And a curse is a bad one."

Asha pursed her lips. "A simplistic explanation, but correct nonetheless."

Professor Sideon burst into the room, sweat glistening on his shaved head. "Thank you, Miss Fellini. I will take over from here."

"You would do well to notify another teacher when you're running late," Asha said in a no-nonsense tone.

Sideon bowed slightly. "Apologies, Professor Fellini. I am grateful you temporarily stepped in for me." If not for his trembling, high-pitched voice, he might have sounded more convincing.

Asha's forehead furrowed as if she didn't believe his sincerity, but nodded. "My pleasure." She looked directly at me on her way out of the classroom, some unknown emotion lurking behind her eyes. I shivered and looked away.

"Creepy," Max said in a low voice.

Ambria turned in her desk to face me. "If she's your mother, she's not hiding it well."

My next thought was asking Galfandor about this woman. "Don't they screen people before they hire them?"

"Of course they do," Max said. "There was a news story last year about a man who applied. He managed to fool the interviewer, but when they put the security charm on him, it melted away a disguise he was wearing and they found out he used to be one of Victus's henchmen."

"The security charm at the gate?" I asked.

"Yeah. They use the same charm on teachers." He glanced at the front of the room, but Professor Sideon had left the room again. "Uncle Malcolm said the charm they use at the gate allows people through the barrier, and makes sure people are who they say they are."

Ambria seemed convinced. "So there's no way Asha could be Delectra."

"Not that I know of," Max said.

His assurances made me feel slightly better. Besides, if Asha was my mother, why hadn't she tried to kill me yet?

Professor Sideon finally returned. "Read the first two chapters in your books, and I'll see you tomorrow." he said. "Class dismissed."

The early end of class prompted a minor celebration from several students. Ambria gave me a puzzled look. "This professor is so disorganized."

Max snorted. "Don't complain. Just enjoy the extra time."

The end of class gave me forty minutes before my cleaning duties back at the keep. "Let's get our brooms and look for Evadora."

"Good idea," Max said.

We returned to Moore Keep and put our backpacks in our rooms then met outside with our brooms.

"Let's look in the Fairy Garden first," Ambria said.

Max hopped on his broom. "I'll check out Colossus Stadium while you do that."

We headed out, flying low over the Unicorn Garden, keeping an eye out for a young girl stealing tears from kids, but the grounds were nearly empty. Max split away from us at the stadium while Ambria and I flew over the iron fence around the Fairy Garden and searched. Evadora was nowhere to be seen.

Max met us outside the stadium. "No luck," he said.

I sighed. "Let's head back. I don't want to get in more trouble with Professor Grace."

We were flying over the patchy field near the Dark Forest when Ambria pointed her finger at the ground. "Look there."

I spotted Evadora skipping out of the forest and angling toward the Fairy Garden. We swooped down and landed in front of her.

"Brother!" She launched herself at me, knocking me off my broom in a fierce hug and laughed at my shocked expression. "I was going to see you, but then I heard a loud roar from the forest, so I went to look."

"That was the tragon!" Max said. "Why would you even go in that dangerous forest? There are all sorts of monsters in there."

"Pretty, pretty monsters." Evadora climbed off me and sighed. "They're too slow to catch me."

I got to my feet and brushed dirt off my clothes. "Evadora, how hard is it to find pieces of the anchor stone?" I held up my pebble. "I need more chunks like this."

She shrugged. "Bits and pieces fell in the void but they are quite hard to reach."

"When you say the void, you mean the places between the broken land?" Ambria asked.

The other girl nodded. "Why do you want them? Do you all want to be able to go to the reflected world?"

I shook my head. "No." I nearly told her why, but asked a different question instead. "If I tell you a secret, will you keep it from the queen?"

Evadora nodded at once. "I will keep your secrets like I kept Mummy's secrets."

Max raised an eyebrow. "What secrets did your mum have?"

She toed the dirt. "I can't tell you."

"Can you tell me?" I asked. "I'm your brother, remember?"

She tapped a finger to her chin. "I don't think I should."

I decided not to press her, happy at least that I wouldn't have to worry about her telling Naeve anything if I asked her not to. "Okay, well, I have a secret reason for wanting pieces of the anchor stone."

A smile lit her face. "Your secret is safe."

I couldn't help but smile back at her. "The Lady of the Pond told me that the stones give immortality, so you can leave the Glimmer and get emotions, but also not die."

Evadora frowned. "No, Mummy thought so too, but she died." Her lips trembled. "She died."

"That was because of my curse." I explained how my parents preserved their souls and how the curse killed other people, namely my foster parents.

Her mouth dropped open. "You have bad parents."

"Evil," Ambria added.

I continued. "My parents told Naeve they want her help conquering the Overworld."

Evadora nodded. "Yes, but they need to—" her eyes widened. "If they find out about the anchor stone, they will tell her. Your bad parents will have their army."

"Yes, but what my parents really want is immortality for themselves." I squeezed her arm. "I want you to gather more pieces of the anchor stone for me so I can tell Naeve how she can come here but keep her immortality. Then she won't help my parents."

"I can tell her for you," Evadora said.

"I don't want her taking away my pebble," I replied. "I want to find pieces we can give to her when we tell her."

"Like a gift!" The strange girl jumped up and down, clapping her hands. "Yes, I will keep your secret and find you pieces." She hugged me. "Then I can stay here and be immortal too!"

"When you find the pieces, come find me in Moore Keep." I pointed to the distant building.

"I will, I will!" She giggled and danced in a circle.

Max and Ambria laughed with her.

"Do you really think the queen will help me if I solve her problem?" I asked.

Evadora nodded. "I'm sure of it."
I hoped she was right.

Chapter 26

Cleaning duty back at the keep was more humiliating than difficult. Grace made me dust the furniture and sweep the floors while the other students sat back and made fun of me.

"Missed a spot, Edison!" Rory shouted when I was cleaning the common room.

Gregory kicked some dirt off his shoes. "Hey, come get this, broom boy."

I wanted to shock them with Esma Emoora's static electricity spell. Instead, I finished my duties and stumbled off to bed, back and arms aching.

The days drifted by slowly. The week ended, and I still hadn't heard from Evadora.

"Finding those stones is probably a lot harder than she thought," Max told me Saturday morning over breakfast. "I'm sure she'll come through."

Later that morning we found the girl perched on the large golem head in Colossus Stadium. She looked up at me with sad eyes when we landed our brooms next to her and I knew she had bad news.

"No stones," she said mournfully. "I thought I found some but they were not from the anchor stone."

"It's okay." I sat down beside her and put an arm on her shoulder. "I'm sure they're somewhere out there."

Evadora pulled her knees up to her face and wrapped her arms around them. "I hope so." She frowned and looked over at me. "The queen has been acting rather strange lately."

Max snorted. "I think strange is normal when it comes to you people."

Ambria sat on the other side of Evadora. "How so?"

218

"Ever since the blonde woman started working there—"

"Wait," Max said. "Serena is still in the Glimmer?"

Evadora nodded. "The queen gave her a workshop in her castle on Moon Mountain. I spy on her all the time." Her huge eyes widened. "She's looking for parts of the anchor stone too."

Ambria, Max, and I looked at each other with alarm.

"Serena is a genius," Max said. "She might figure out the secret of the anchor stone before we find any pieces."

"Maybe we should tell the queen right away," Ambria said. "Maybe she'll kick Serena out of the Glimmer so she can't find any anchor stone pieces."

"Do you think Serena will find any stones?" I asked Evadora.

The girl nodded. "She is making something called a divining rod. I read her notes and she thinks she'll find some soon."

"Did she tell the queen she's looking for stones?" I asked.

Evadora shook her head. "No. I think she wants to keep it a secret."

Ambria's eyebrows pinched. "When you said the queen is acting strange, what did you mean?"

Evadora took out her bottle. "Serena found out how tears give us emotions. I think she gave some to the queen. Now she seems angry all the time."

Max threw up his hands. "Great, just what we need."

I stood up and walked across the giant golem head where its shattered crystal eye stared blindly up at the sky. "I'm going back to the Glimmer with Evadora to steal Serena's divining rod."

"You're mental, Conrad." Ambria grabbed my arm and looked at Evadora. "Can you steal the divining rod?"

The other girl frowned. "There is nothing to steal. Serena has not completed the rod." She tapped a finger on her chin. "I think she is missing something she needs."

"We have to know the instant she finishes the rod," I told Evadora. "We can't give her a chance to use it."

"At least it gives us more time," Max said. "Do you know what she's missing?"

Evadora shook her head. "Serena wanted a piece of anchor stone for testing."

A dangerous plan entered my mind. "I want her to finish it." I looked at their shocked faces. "Then we can steal it and use it."

Ambria shook her head. "Mental."

"How is she going to test it without a stone?" Max said. He flinched and his eyes flew wide. "Hang on, you don't plan to give her your stone, do you?"

I shook my head. "No. I'm going to ask Klave for one of his tiny pieces."

Evadora jumped up and grabbed my hands. "This will be fun, fun, fun!" She hopped up and down, giggling.

I squeezed her hands and tried to look serious. "This will be dangerous, but I need you to keep spying on Serena and let me know how close she is to finishing the divining rod."

She stopped jumping and pooched out her lips as if trying to appear serious. "And then I steal it."

"*We* steal it," I said. "Where is her workshop?"

"Inside the castle." Evadora spread her hands as if drawing a path. "I can lead you there."

I thought of another danger factor. "Have you seen my parents there?"

Evadora nodded. "They came yesterday."

Max eyes flared. "That's impossible. How did they get through the barrier around the school?"

Evadora tilted her head to the side. "Barrier?"

"Yes, there's a barrier around this entire plateau to keep dangerous people out," Ambria said.

"I do not know," Evadora replied. "I saw them during your nighttime."

Max ran a hand down his face. "Just wonderful. Your parents are inside the barrier with us."

Wolves among the lambs, Della said with glee.

"Maybe they never left the Glimmer," Ambria said. "Or maybe there's a crack at the edges of the barrier."

"I saw them leave the Glimmer," Evadora said. "They went back to the school."

My body went cold and my skin crawled with invisible spiders at the thought of my parents somewhere inside the university.

220

"I don't understand." Max paced back and forth. "The security measures should have kept them out."

Ambria groaned. "I know how they got in." She pointed toward the university. "The attack on the first day of school was a diversion."

"Oh no!" Max put a hand to his forehead. "Security pushed everyone through the gate without checking them. Conrad's parents probably hid in the middle of all the parents and then slipped away."

It seemed there was nowhere to hide from my devious parents. "If they're here, I wonder why they haven't killed me yet."

"Maybe they don't want to draw attention until they get what they want," Max said.

Ambria hugged me. "Oh, Conrad, I hope they don't try to kill you."

"If I see them again, I will follow them to their hiding spot," Evadora said.

"Be careful," I told her. "They're extremely dangerous." I squeezed Ambria and untangled myself from her embrace. "We'll have to be on the lookout all the time from now on."

Max blew out a breath. "We already are, especially with Harris Ashmore always looking for ways to hurt us."

Ambria huffed. "We're not popular people, are we?"

I couldn't help but chuckle. "Us against the world."

Max belted a laugh and put his hand in the middle of the group. "Us against the world."

Ambria put her hand on his and repeated his words.

Evadora's eyes shone with delight. "Yay! Us against the whole wide world."

I sighed and put my hand in the pot. "Yeah. Everyone against us." We threw our hands in the air, our call to battle sounding like a desperate cry for help. My nerves felt tight and the university suddenly seemed like one big obstacle course filled with hidden dangers.

We needed to find a piece of the anchor stone for Naeve so she wouldn't take mine when I told her the secret to keeping her immortality. Serena's divining rod seemed like the best way to do it, which meant I'd have to help her complete it before stealing it. The plan was crooked as a maze and dangerous as an angry frogre, but it was the only one we had.

"Evadora, keep looking for stones, but let me know when Serena is close to finishing her rod." I felt the pebble in my pocket, reassured that it was still there. "In the meantime, I'll ask Mirjana if I can have one of Klave's stones. Find a way to give it to Serena without her finding out that you know about her divining rod, okay?"

The girl nodded vigorously. "I will go look some more and watch Serena."

"Meet me here tomorrow," I told her. "I'll let you know about Klave's stone."

Evadora hopped lithely off the stone head and skipped away toward the Fairy Garden.

"I think we should tell the queen right now and ask for her protection from your parents," Ambria said.

Max folded his arms and nodded. "For once, I agree with Ambria."

She raised an eyebrow. "You agree with me all the time, Max." She elbowed him. "You just won't admit it."

"What if I tell her and she takes the stone Cora gave me?" I took out the pebble and rolled it in my fingers. "I don't want to lose it."

Max sighed. "I know you don't, but having it won't matter if you lose your life."

"Why do you want it anyway?" Ambria asked. "Is it because it was Cora's?"

I slid it back into my pocket. "Yes, and it also gives me a way to visit Evadora in the Glimmer."

Ambria shivered. "I'd rather her come here to visit you."

I hopped on my broom and hovered to the side of the golem head. "Let's go visit Mirjana and Klave."

Percival looked excited to see us when we walked into the healing ward. "Are you injured again?" He picked up his experimental healing potion. "I've got a new batch all ready for testing."

Max pushed me in front of him. "No, we're great, sir, I promise."

The healer's face fell. "Oh. I haven't had a chance to use it on any other patients yet."

"I'm sure you'll have plenty of opportunities," Ambria said curtly. "How are Mirjana and Klave?"

"Mirjana is up and about, but her husband is still weak." Percival looked wistfully at Max's healed hand. "I suspect he'll be able to leave in another week or so."

Ambria stepped past him. "Well, we're here to visit."

"Of course." The healer motioned us in. "I'm sure Mirjana would love it."

A lovely smile spread across Mirjana's lips when she saw us. "Children, it is so good to see you again."

Klave looked pale and terribly thin, but he had the strength to nod at us. "Thank you for saving my love and my life," he said in a faint voice.

Mirjana patted his arm. "Rest now, love."

I looked at the necklace of green stones on his neck. "The anchor stone pieces give immortality, but not supernatural healing?"

The Lady of the Pond blinked as if surprised by the sudden change in subject. "Larger pieces provide enhanced physical attributes, but only after keeping them close to your body over a period of time." She ran a finger up Klave's arm. "The magic seeps into the body."

"The stones on Klave's necklace aren't large enough?" I asked.

"They were enough to preserve his life when poisoned, but not to heal him once he drifted to the clean water at the bottom of the pond." She touched her husband's necklace. "I searched in vain for a piece large enough to simply keep in our abode, but finding even the smallest fragments was incredibly difficult."

Ambria's forehead pinched. "Keeping a really big piece in your house would give you immortality?"

"Yes, so long as you were near it several hours a day." Mirjana traced a finger up an arm. "The magic soaks into whoever is near."

"Naeve lives right underneath the moon," Max said. "I'll bet you couldn't kill her if you tried."

"How long does it take for the effects of the moon to wear off?" I asked.

"In the case of someone who has lived in the presence of the anchor stone, it could take months or even a year for the preserving magic to wear off." Mirjana shrugged. "Unfortunately, I have only anecdotal evidence."

"Soon it may be possible to find larger pieces more easily." I told the Siren about Serena's divining rod and my plan to steal it when completed. "For her to test the rod, she'll need a fragment of anchor stone. I can't give her mine because I need it to get in and out of the Glimmer."

Klave took a wheezing breath and pushed out an answer. "I say yes." He tried to move a hand to his necklace, but was too weak.

"A dangerous plan," Mirjana said. "But since you saved my love, I cannot say no."

"If we succeed, I'll find Klave a larger piece of the stone." I touched her hand, as if it might bind me even more to keep my word. "I promise."

"He speaks truth." Klave's voice was barely a hoarse whisper.

Without hesitation, Mirjana removed the necklace from her husband and unstrung the largest stone from it. Even so, the green fragment was smaller than the tip of my pinky finger. I hoped it was enough for Serena to test with her divining rod.

"I am feeling much better," the Siren said. "I will assist you so long as it does not involve fighting."

"Can you get us into the Glimmer without using the reflected world?" Max asked.

"Yes, but the song which grants passage past the rift guardians will alert the queen that a Siren approaches her kingdom." Mirjana spread her hands. "In this case, I believe stealth is in your favor. I suggest you use the echo world, but be quick about it."

Ambria stepped closer. "Does the stone work with anything that casts a reflection, like a mirror?"

"No, it is water magic," Mirjana replied. "It does not work on solid objects."

"Oh." Ambria puffed her cheeks. "I thought we could sneak through faster if we took a mirror with us."

"You need only a puddle of water large enough to fit through," the Siren replied.

Max snapped his fingers. "Yeah, we'll just bring a bucket of water and dig a hole."

"What if the puddle dries up before we come back?" Ambria asked.

Mirjana shrugged her shoulders. "Simply put, child, you will need to use another exit. Just know that wherever your echo being is in that world, it will know the instant you enter and come in a straight line for you. Do not let it catch you."

With those chilling words still ringing in my ears, we left the Siren and her husband in the healing ward.

The next day, we met Evadora in Colossus Stadium and gave her the stone from Mirjana.

"Is Serena any closer to finishing?" I asked.

Evadora shook her head. "And I have still found no stones."

"Well, don't leave any stone unturned," Max said with a grin.

"But not all stones are from the anchor stone," Evadora said, her eyes widening with concern. She turned to me. "Conrad, turning every stone would take forever! Is Max dumb?"

Ambria giggled. "He can be quite dense."

"It was a joke." Max threw up his hands. "If anything, it was a clever joke."

I managed a weak smile. "He has his moments."

Evadora rubbed the tiny piece of green stone between her thumb and forefinger. "I will give this to Serena when the time is right. Hopefully she will finish her rod soon." She twirled and looked straight up at the sky. "Then we will tell the queen the secret and all will be well."

I certainly hope so.

"Have my parents been back to the Glimmer?" I asked.

Evadora skipped away a few feet, then stopped and turned around. "Not yet, but I will say if I see." Then she skipped on her merry way.

Chapter 27

"Edison, are you asleep?" Professor Grace snapped his fingers and jerked me from the troubled thoughts swirling in my head.

"No, sir." I tried to recall what he'd been talking about.

"*Levator*," Max whispered behind me.

I repeated the word. "*Levator*."

Grace narrowed his eyes at me, but finally turned away. "Yes, *levator* is the spell we've been working on this week, and yet, none of you has been able to cast it."

Lily Crown raised her hand. "I did it last night, Professor."

Grace raised an eyebrow. "Then by all means demonstrate." He laid a sheet of parchment on his desk.

Lily confidently approached and took out her wand. With precise flicks, she guided the wand through the proper pattern and said, "*Levator*."

The parchment shuddered, but didn't rise. She tried it again and again, but failed to move it.

Max snickered then whispered to me, "She's such a know-it-all."

Grace's eyes locked onto the source of soft laughter and jabbed a finger at Max. "If you find it so funny, Tiberius, I suggest you come show the class how it's done."

Delighted grins split Harris and Baxter's faces. Lily gave Max a hurt look.

Looking down like a scolded dog, Max stood and trudged to the front of the class. He took out his wand and uneasily cleared his throat. "Um, it's a rather difficult spell."

"I don't care," Grace replied in clipped tones. "Do it now, or you're cleaning the common room tonight."

That straightened Max like a jolt of electricity. "But—"

Grace snapped his fingers. "Do it."

"Oh dear," Ambria said in a hushed voice. "I hope he remembers to flick left first this time."

Max flicked his wand to the right instead and failed to cast the spell. "Why didn't it work?" He looked at his wand and shook it as if it might be defective.

Ambria groaned.

Grace looked pleased. "Well, Tiberius, looks like you'll be cleaning tonight."

"Oh, wait, it's left," Max said. He flicked the wand through the pattern and pointed it at the paper. "*Levator*."

A paperweight next to the parchment rose instead. Max was so startled, he jerked his wand back and the glass weight flew through the air and smacked him in the forehead. Max fell over backwards and thudded to the floor.

Lily cried out and dropped next to him. "He's bleeding!"

Others in the class burst into laughter. Gideon Grace rolled his eyes with disgust.

Ambria and I ran to the front of the room and helped Max stagger to his feet. He looked blearily at Professor Grace. "I did it!"

The professor looked disappointed. "Yes, I suppose you did." The bell gonged. "Luckily for you, boy." He motioned us toward the door. "Well, get him to the healing ward."

Lily picked up Max's wand and handed it to me. "Well done, Max," she said in a quiet voice.

Struggling to hold up his head, he managed a grin. "You're smart."

She giggled.

Ambria and I grabbed our book bags and carried Max's while I helped our dizzy friend down the hall.

Percival clapped his hands together when he saw the trickle of blood on Max's forehead. "What do we have today, children?" He wiped away the blood with a cloth. "Oh, a concussion, how wonderful."

"It's not wonderful," Ambria said.

I helped Max sit down on a bench. "Do you plan to give him more of that painful healing potion?"

"Hmm." Percival cleaned the small cut. "No, I suppose this is too minor for that." He unscrewed a jar and smeared a tiny bit of smelly salve on the wound. "Just keep an eye on him and don't let him go to sleep for a few hours."

Max groaned and pressed fingers to his temples. "Oh, my aching head."

Percival handed him a small white pill. "Take this and let me know if it doesn't help."

Max looked at it suspiciously, then winced in pain. "What is this thing?"

"Something magical called ibuprofen." Percival taped a small bandage over the cut on Max's forehead.

"Never heard of it." Max swallowed it with some water anyway.

"Ibuprofen?" Ambria said with disbelief. "That's not magic."

"Sure it is," Percival said. "No matter where the ache is, it somehow knows what part of your body to relieve. That's magic in my book."

The bell gonged. "We're late," I said. "Can he go to class?"

Percival nodded. "Of course."

Esma Emoora didn't seem to even care that we were late as we slid into desks on our side of the circular formation. Though Max looked a bit silly with the bandage on his forehead, he seemed recovered from the blow he'd taken.

As usual, the professor kept everyone in the class on edge. She didn't hesitate to cast a shock of electricity to make sure some unlucky student remembered how to use the shield spell and other protective castings she taught us. I fended off two attacks, but she zapped me later on the third try because I flubbed the proper wand pattern.

The static shock hurt, but didn't injure anything except my confidence. *If my parents attack me, they'll do a lot more than shock me.* I had to be better prepared for that threat. When class ended, I told Ambria and Max to go ahead to history without me, and waited for the other students to leave before approaching the professor.

Esma regarded me with a warm smile. "Well, if it isn't my best student."

My face warmed at the compliment. "Thank you, Professor." I took a breath to settle my nerves. "I was wondering if you're available for tutoring after classes."

She raised an eyebrow. "If anyone needs tutoring, it certainly isn't you."

"I actually need it rather badly," I said. "I need to advance my skills much faster."

Esma's smile faded. "Is something the matter?"

"Well, it's a private matter—"

"Must be Harris Ashmore and Baxter Troy," she said with certainty. "Are they bullying you?"

"No, no, nothing like that." The last thing I wanted to do was get them in trouble and draw even more hatred on me. "It's just that, well—"

"Spit it out, child." She crossed her arms. "Tell me the truth and perhaps I'll help you."

How do I tell her about my parents? As far as I knew, Galfandor hadn't told anyone else my parents were still alive. But how could I explain the danger to the professor without telling her about them? I also didn't want to get other students in trouble. Finally, I decided to tell her a little of the truth.

"Will you promise not to tell anyone else?" I said. "This has to remain a secret for now."

She pursed her lips. "If your secret doesn't endanger anyone else, I will keep it."

My parents were a danger to everyone, but I desperately needed to get better faster. "My parents are still alive and want to kill me."

Esma's frown vanished and she stared at me for a moment. "Is that the secret?"

Somehow, I thought she'd have a stronger reaction, and then realized she probably didn't believe me. "It's the truth."

The professor nodded. "You want to strengthen your defenses considerably."

"Yes, please." I felt like a fool for not having come up with a convincing lie instead of the ridiculous truth.

Esma put a hand on my shoulder. "Don't worry, Conrad, I believe you. I don't think many of us ever believed your parents were ever truly dead, especially when their bodies disappeared. They are powerful Arcanes and not to be trifled with."

My relief flushed away the humiliation. "Really?"

"Yes, really." She put a hand to her chin. "I can fit you in right after supper twice a week. When would you like to start?"

"Today?" I said hopefully.

She smiled. "Today it is. Meet me in my office after supper."

I felt so relieved, it nearly brought tears to my eyes. "Thank you, Professor."

"Don't thank me yet, young man." Esma's lips curled into a smirk. "If you think I'm tough during class, you'll probably fear me even more during private lessons."

I probably should have been afraid. Instead, I suppressed a cheer. "I'll see you tonight." The class bell would gong at any moment, so I rushed down the hall and downstairs to the lower wing for history class. Just as I passed the restrooms, something caught my backpack and yanked me off my feet.

Before I could get up, a group of people wearing hoods and masks surrounded me. The first kick to my ribs ripped a scream from my throat. Another kick twisted me the other way. A flurry of blows met my midsection until I could hardly breathe.

"What's going on down there?" someone shouted from down the hall.

One of the attackers grabbed my shirt and got in my face. "That's for your parents killing our sisters, our brothers, our parents, and other loved ones." His voice was low and rough, but he sounded like a teenager. "Leave this school or next time we'll kill you." He dropped me back to the floor.

I groaned and clutched my sides as their footsteps faded. Another set of footsteps closed in on my position and a gentle hand brushed back my hair. "Who could do such a thing?" said a female voice I recognized. Asha Fellini knelt next to me, her hands touching my ribs. "Are you having trouble breathing?"

"Maybe," I groaned. "Everything hurts." This was the moment of truth. If she really was my mother, now would be the perfect time to kill me and blame someone else.

Instead, she sent someone to retrieve a healer. Percival showed up a few moments later with a flying carpet and rolled me onto it. "I have just the medicine for him," he told Asha, eagerly rubbing his hands together.

"I have reported the ruffians," she said to me. "You can be sure we will catch them, Conrad."

"Thanks," I wheezed. "Please tell Professor Beetle I'll be late to class."

"Of course," Asha said, and walked away.

Percival chuckled. "Late? You're going to miss that class, young man." He pushed the magic carpet ahead of him and started whistling. "I've never used my new elixir on such brutal wounds before." He looked down at me. "Or would you rather take the slower route to good health?"

I really had no choice if I was going to meet Esma for private lessons tonight. Besides, could the pain really be that much worse than what I'd endured in the hallway? "I'll take your elixir."

"That's a sport!" Percival pushed me into the healing ward and quickly retrieved the sparkling red potion. "Since you have so many internal injuries, you'll have to drink it." He smiled apologetically. "I'm afraid I haven't enhanced the taste much."

The man was a master of understatement. Drinking the small vial of potion was like downing a bottle of vinegar seasoned with pepper and rotten onions. If Percival hadn't practically forced it down my throat, I probably wouldn't have finished it. An instant later, every fiber of my body exploded with burning pain, as if I were being slow-roasted on a spit over an open fire. I screamed until I was hoarse and must have blacked out.

When I blinked open my eyes, Mirjana stood over me, her eyes wide and concerned. "Are you well, son?"

I felt absolutely wonderful. "Spectacular," I said. My body felt as if I were lounging on a cloud. I felt my ribs and my face. Crusted blood came off in my hand, but I didn't feel the least bit sore.

"Who did this to you?" the Siren asked.

"People who hate my parents," I replied.

"Those who punish children for the crimes of their parents are fools." She picked up a wet rag from a bowl on the nightstand and wiped at my face. "This world is a dangerous place for you, child. Perhaps you should consider leaving and finding somewhere to live in peace."

I closed my eyes and enjoyed her motherly touch.

Cora sings softly to me as she nurses the wounds on my knees where I'd skinned them. "I know of a lovely place we can go for a while to get out of the city."

"Where?" I ask.

"It is my homeland." She sighs. "People there once called me their queen."

I liked listening to Cora's fairy tales. They were even better than the ones I read in books.

I blinked back tears. Cora's stories hadn't been fairy tales. They'd been the truth.

"You went back to her, didn't you?" Mirjana said.

I nodded. "I can't help it." I took the Siren's hand. "Thank you for this."

She raised an eyebrow. "For what, child? I am simply cleaning your bloody face."

My vision blurred. "Your kindness." I wiped at my eyes. "It reminded me of Cora."

Mirjana dabbed at my face with the cloth. "You are a brave young man, Conrad. It is an honor to clean your blood." She squeezed my hand. "Perhaps when this is behind us, you would like to visit our home in the pond. We have a whale shark who loves to give rides."

I laughed and nodded. "I'd love to." Swinging my feet over the side of the bed, I winced in anticipation of pain that never came. I looked down at my clothes. It looked as though I'd rolled in dirt. "I'd better get to class." Hunger gnawed at my stomach. Apparently, the healing had given me an appetite.

"I'm afraid you missed the rest of your classes." Mirjana pointed to the clock. "It's supper time."

I jumped up with a shock and ran for the door. I nearly ran into Max and Ambria on my way out.

"There you are!" Max said. "We didn't know where you went."

I frowned. "Didn't Professor Fellini tell Professor Beetle where I was?"

"She came in the room and whispered something to her, but we didn't hear it." Ambria eyes grew round. "What happened to your clothes? Is that blood?"

Max's lips flattened. "Did Asha try to kill you?"

I shook my head. "No, it was a group of teenagers in masks." I told them how Asha had rescued me. My stomach grumbled loudly. "Can we go eat? I'm starving."

"Now you sound like Max." Ambria wiped a tear from her eye. "Oh, Conrad, why are people so mean?"

I shook my head. "They want to blame someone for their pain, and I'm an easy target." I hoped my training with Esma would change that.

After supper, I went to the dorm and changed, then told Max and Ambria I was going to study. I went to Esma Emoora's office, but the door was locked, and there was no light coming from beneath it. The clock on the wall told me I was a minute early, so I leaned against the wall and waited.

Five minutes ticked past then five more, and nothing. At twenty minutes, I finally decided to leave. With a heavy heart, I picked up my broom. Something rustled. I spun and saw a feminine figure in tight black robes, the face hidden beneath a cowl.

"Goodbye, son," said the cold cruel voice of my mother.

Chapter 28

Delectra raised a wand and flicked it. Chunks of stone burst from the wall. She flicked her wand again. My hand traced the air and the words, "*Soros, quoros, eva equas!*" burst from my mouth. The shield captured the impact of her attack. I flicked my wand again. "*Torsius!*"

My mother twisted her wand. "*Parrano!*"

Brilliant forces collided in mid-air as her attack parried mine.

My shield was slowly fading and I knew there was no way to survive a fight with Delectra, so I did the next best thing and hopped on my broom. The moment I did, she threw a broom in front of her, and leapt on it while it levitated in the air.

"This is awful," I muttered to myself. Max once told me my mother was a champion broom racer. I'd have to fly for my life if I hoped to escape her. I spun around and zipped down the long hallway. Bolts of electricity shot past me, exploding against the wall and shattering sconces. Leaning hard left, I veered the broom down another corridor then strafed hard right, flying sideways to guide the broom up a winding staircase.

I zipped past a group of startled students and took the next left. Someone shouted in alarm and a stack of parchments exploded into the air. A quick glance back told me what I'd feared. Delectra burst through the cloud of paper only a hundred feet behind me, her black robes fluttering in the wind, the black void beneath her cowl sending shivers down my back.

A desperate thought flashed into my mind. Had Delectra killed Esma and lain in wait for me to show up? My desire to protect myself might have cost the professor her life. One thing was certain—I had to find a safe place to go. The only place I could think of was Moore

Manor. Galfandor might be able to fight Delectra. But what if he wasn't there right now? Then I'd be out in the open and vulnerable.

First, I had to check Galfandor's office here, but reaching my phone in my pocket while flying like a madman through the hallways would be impossible. I thought back to the view from the headmaster's office and tried to imagine where it would be. Another crackle of energy exploded off the ceiling. I dodged around a cloud of dust and careened around the next corner. A chandelier appeared in front of me. I spun upside down and felt one of the crystals graze my foot.

The windows on the next spiraling staircase hung open to let in the cool night air. I skidded to a stop, twisted the broom sideways, and kicked off the inside wall to propel me out the third window. I looked up at the highest spires and realized Galfandor's office had to be there somewhere. Delectra flashed past on the stairwell, and for a heartbeat, I thought I'd fooled her.

Seconds later, she zipped through an open window above me and laughed.

Diving, I circled the tower, flitted between two turrets, and pulled back on the broom handle until I flew straight up the tower wall. When I reached the top, I angled for the tallest tower, praying that was Galfandor's office. Bolts of magical energy flew past, each one coming closer to striking me. I saw a light emanating from the window on the tower ahead.

Before I could reach it, something snared me around my shoulders. The sudden jolt caused my hand to twist the broom's throttle back to zero. Before I could recover, Delectra whooshed around me and spun to face me.

It was over.

I stiffened my back and glared into the dark depths of that hood. "Did you kill Esma? If you did, I promise I'll find a way to kill you before you kill me!"

She responded with laughter. It wasn't the cold maniacal laughter of a killer, but lighthearted enjoyment. My pursuer threw back the cowl to reveal Esma's amused face. "Oh my, Conrad! I haven't had that much fun in ages." She put away her wand and the noose around my shoulders vanished. "You're quite the broom rider."

All the terror and adrenaline burst into flames of anger. It took everything I had not to shout at her.

Esma didn't miss the rage in my eyes and her laughter faded. "You asked for my tutoring, young man. I told you it would be nothing like class."

A few deep breaths allowed my mind to clear and I realized what she'd done probably showed her exactly how I'd react in a dangerous situation. She'd studied me, and maybe that would help her teach me. I nodded. "I know."

Her lips pursed. "I have molded many champions, Conrad Edison, but I must say you are higher quality clay than most." She smirked. "I think this will be fun." Esma pointed toward the field in front of the Dark Forest far below. "Let's go there to practice."

I nodded and followed her.

Esma turned in her seat as we flew. "I'm touched that you offered to avenge me, by the way. Very thoughtful, Conrad."

The urge to zap her in the seat of her robes was nearly too strong to resist.

Once we landed, Esma got right to business. "This is the second time I've seen you reflexively use a multi-casted shield spell. In addition, you nearly landed an advanced telekinetic spell on me." She tapped her wand against her thigh. "Where did you learn those spells?"

If she had trouble believing my parents were still alive, this part would certainly blow her mind. "I have parts of my parents' souls inside me."

Her eyes flared. "Explain."

So I did.

"That was quite a tale," Esma said at the end of my shortened retelling of the living curse. "It appears the survival instincts of the trapped soul fragments—Vic and Della, as you call them—reflexively help you when threatened." She made a thoughtful grunt. "Well, I say it's time you learned how to cast those spells on your own."

"I'd be delighted to learn."

She smiled. "Then let's begin."

It was late when we finished, and I fell into bed the moment I returned to my room at the keep. Max was already asleep and lightly snoring, so I didn't wake him to tell him about the night's excitement.

The next day, I went through classes as usual, but kept a close eye on the restrooms when I passed them on the way to history class. No thugs leapt out to beat me. Professor Beetle droned through another lesson, putting nearly everyone into a drowsy stupor and then we went to Professor Trask's Potions class.

Lily greeted us brightly when we entered—a marked difference from the way she acted when Harris and Baxter were around.

"Some ruffians beat up Conrad in the hallway yesterday," Ambria said to the other girl in a low voice. She regarded her suspiciously. "I don't suppose you know anything about that, do you?"

Lily's eyes widened. "No." She looked away. "I will admit Baxter talked about doing it, but Harris said he didn't need to do anything, that the prophecy would sort things out."

Max snorted. "Must be nice having your life planned out for you like that."

"I think it's awful," Lily said with a grimace. "I'd rather be surprised."

Next up we went to Professor Sideon's Enchantment class. For once, the professor was on time and ready with a lesson. "Today we'll be making friendship charms." He dumped a pile of yarn on the table and set a bucket of beads next to it. "First, thread a bracelet or necklace, then follow the directions in the book for the charm." Sideon looked around the room. "Everyone understand?"

"Yes, Professor," was our uniform reply.

"Excellent." He strode from the room.

"What a lousy professor," Ambria said. "He's late most of the time, and then just leaves when he wants."

"Enchantments is one of those core freebie classes," Max said. "You don't see many people going into it as a specialty unless they want to be a flying carpet or broom maker."

"I could think of plenty of uses besides manufacturing," Ambria said. "What about enchanted swords like in the fairy tales?"

Max quirked an eyebrow. "The Templars used tons of enchantments for their armor and swords, but all their charmers went with them to Seraphina." He sighed. "I guess it's a dying art these days."

I went to the front of the room and gathered enough yarn and beads for three bracelets then returned to the table. We each took a length of yarn and began threading the beads.

Max took a blue bead. "So, where did you go last night, Conrad?"

I decided to go for a rainbow effect and chose a bead of every color. "Professor Emoora is tutoring me."

Ambria dropped a bead. It bounced across the table and fell on the floor. "Tutoring you?"

"I need to get better fast, so she said she'd help me." I leaned forward and whispered, "I told her about my parents."

Max sighed and shook his head. "I wouldn't trust anyone with that information."

"We still haven't told Galfandor your parents are on campus," Ambria said. "Do you suppose Esma will?"

"I didn't mention it to her." I'd forgotten to inform the headmaster, primarily because I hadn't seen him for a while. "Maybe I'll tell her tonight."

"Can we come?" Max asked. "I'd like to learn advanced spells."

"I don't think Professor Emoora would like that," I told him. "Sorry."

He rolled a bead between his fingers. "How often are you meeting her?"

"Twice a week right now." I fit another bead onto the yarn. "Hopefully she'll let me come more often."

"You're eating up her free time, Conrad." Ambria wet the yarn with her lips and twisted the tip to make it smaller. "You should be more considerate."

"Yeah," Max said. "More considerate."

Ambria gave him a cross look. "Max, finish your assignment."

He chuckled softly.

I finished threading the bracelet and tied it into a loop. When I put the enchantment on it, the beads glowed softly, but did nothing else.

Ambria sniffed. "What a waste of time."

"Lame." Max stared at his glowing bracelet. "Let's give our friendship bracelets to Harris and Baxter."

I snorted. "I'm sure they'd appreciate it."

That night, I once again met Esma for lessons. This time, she didn't frighten me half to death, instead, meeting me in her office.

"Survived another day?" she said dryly.

I sat in a chair across from her. "So far."

She smiled. "Well, with the barrier around the school, you should be safe until the end of the semester."

Though I'd told her about my parents, I hadn't revealed my suspicions about them being on campus. "Well, not entirely. You see, I think my parents are on campus right now."

Esma sat back in her chair. "What in the world gave you that idea?"

"When Calvin Fain and Eolius Bane attacked the front gate, security let everyone in without using the charm on them first." I felt a bit unnerved by her look of disbelief, but continued on. "They must be hiding somewhere. It's a large area, and I've heard there are plenty of secret passages."

She leaned forward. "You're rather smart and observant, Conrad. Whether you like it or not, it appears you've inherited good instincts from your parents."

I shuddered. "I wish I could be proud of it, Professor." A sigh deflated me. "If only they were good people."

Esma perked up. "Well, let's not squander any more time and get down to it." She picked up her wand. "You have notified security about your suspicions, haven't you?"

I shook my head. "No, I've been so tied up with classes and bodily injuries, I haven't had a chance."

"Well, I'll be sure to tell Galfandor." She ushered me into the hallway and locked the door behind her. "I'm certain he'll take care of matters."

The weight on my shoulders lightened. "Thank you, Professor."

The night's lesson consisted of shield practice. By the end of the two hours, I could summon a simple shield spell immediately.

"Excellent work, Conrad." Esma put away her wand. "Since you're so committed, and since it's possible your parents may be on this campus, I've decided we should practice more often. How about four times a week?"

I gasped at this marvelous surprise. "That would be wonderful, Professor."

She smiled, and mussed my hair. "You have a powerful spark inside you, young man. I intend to see it burst into flame."

I went home that night with a full, happy heart. It felt wonderful for someone to believe in me.

Chapter 29

Another week ended and I felt like my magic skills were getting better, though I still had a long way to go before I could defend myself from my parents. Max, Ambria, and I went to Colossus Stadium to wait for Evadora and an update on Serena.

The strange girl soon skipped into sight, twisting and twirling as though she hadn't a care in the world. With a leap, she grabbed the crystal eye of the golem head and pulled herself to the top.

"What's the good news?" I asked.

Evadora jabbed a thumb to her chest. "I am Serena's little helper."

Max scowled. "You're supposed to spy on her, not help her."

"Actually, it sounds like the perfect way to spy on her," Ambria said.

Evadora grinned. "She says it will be weeks before she finishes the rod. Maybe even months."

"That's great!" Max blew out a sigh of relief. "It gives us time to get ready."

"Still no anchor stone pieces," Evadora said. "Serena sends me looking for fragments so she can test the rod when it's ready."

"This is great news," I said. "Anything else to report?"

"Your parents have not been back," Evadora said, "and Serena keeps a journal of everything." She mimicked writing on a pad. "Always writing. I tried to read it to see if she wrote down where your parents are staying."

I sat up, suddenly alert. "And?"

"She almost never sets it down, but the day she does, I will get it." Evadora grinned brightly. "Does anyone want to go play in the forest?"

As if to answer for us, a loud trumpeting roar echoed in the distance.

"The tragon says no," Ambria said. "Why don't we go to town for ice cream?"

Max snorted. "Since Conrad's parents are somewhere on campus, it's probably safer for us in town."

"Ice cream?" Evadora danced on the balls of her toes. "Can I come, brother? Can I, can I?"

I smiled. "Of course."

"Can you fly a broom?" Max asked.

She shook her head.

"Let's get a flying carpet, then." Max pointed toward Moore Keep. "They have some loaners in there."

We flew into town and went directly to the ice cream shop. Evadora was so excited, she didn't know what to order. I got her a mixture of Wicked Witch Watermelon and Vampire Vanilla covered in sprinkles.

"Ooh, it's so good!" She shoveled down another mouthful. "So yummy!" Evadora followed every bite with an exclamation.

"We get the point!" Max said at last. He took a crunchy bite of cone and shook his head. "You'd think she never had ice cream before."

"Never ever," Evadora said seriously. She snuggled up next to me and kissed my cheek. "Thank you, brother."

I suddenly couldn't swallow my ice cream past the lump in my throat. "You're welcome, sister."

"Aww," Ambria said. "That's adorable."

Max ignored us and took a noisy bite of his cone. "The Kabash League tryouts are tomorrow," he said. "I was hoping we could get on the team for Moore Keep, but I doubt we'd stand a chance with Rory and Gregory standing in the way."

I'd forgotten all about it. "Is it a racing league?"

Max shook his head. "No, but you have to be really good with a broom. Why don't you try out with me?"

I hesitated to answer. *Do I really have time for something like that?*

Ambria seemed to sense my thoughts. "You need to enjoy yourself more, Conrad. Sitting around worrying about your parents won't help one little bit."

Max slapped me on the back. "All you do is study. Besides, I doubt we'll make the team since everyone hates us."

A wry laugh barked from my mouth. "You're probably right." I thought about it a moment. "I suppose you should tell me how to play the game first."

He grinned. "You got it. Let me hold your arcphone."

I handed him the phone. He set the phone on the table and projected the image of a large oval field. The sides of the stadium looked like castle walls with parapets along the tops, except these had rows of benches.

"Kabash is played on a tract—a field a hundred and fifty yards long and seventy yards wide." Max played the video forward. Two round towers sprang up from the ground, one on either side of a thick red line at the center of the field, and hovered about twenty feet in the air. Behind each opposing tower, a square keep rumbled skyward, followed at the ends of the field by a small castle.

"Each team has a tower, a keep, and a fortress to defend. The first team to destroy the enemy fortress wins the game."

Ambria peered at the paused image. "Destroy them how?"

"I'm getting to that," Max said. He resumed the video and we watched as two teams, one wearing yellow, the other in red, emerged from doors at either end of the stadium. They flew on brooms around the field, pumping their fists in the air while the crowd cheered them on.

Max zoomed in on one team. "Each team has three carries, two freezers, and three defenders." He sat back and cast a curious look at Evadora who danced in place while licking her ice cream. Shaking his head, he returned to the rules. "At the start of the game, a disc called the striker flies into the arena and circles around the middle. Each team races to get it first. Whoever gets it passes it off to a carry."

"Why are they called carries?" Ambria asked. "Because they carry the striker?"

He snorted. "No, it's because they're supposed to carry the team to victory. Make sense?"

Ambria nodded. "Yes, I suppose so."

Max took a sip of his milkshake. "Anyway, the carries throw the striker at the buildings. Four hits destroy a tower, six hits for a keep, and eight for a fortress."

"Both teams use the same striker?" I asked.

He nodded. "The defenders guard the carries and help with rebounds. The freezers carry freeze wands—or freeze rays if they're from Science Academy—and can disable anyone for ten seconds once every minute."

"Can the defenders and freezers attack the towers?" Ambria asked.

"Yeah, but their attacks only count for half damage." Max rotated the screen to the side so we could see the field in profile. "A team can shield their tower for five seconds once every five minutes, so if there aren't any defenders protecting the tower, they have a few seconds to get into position."

"Sounds simple enough," I said. "Are you allowed to make contact with the opposing team members?"

"Yes, you can push them by bumping them with your body, but you can't use your hands." Max made a grabbing motion. "If someone does, they're penalized and taken out of the game for three minutes."

I pictured using my body to divert another flier to the side. "Meaning, your team plays a person down."

"Exactly." He forwarded the video through some gameplay and froze it as the yellow team pressed an attack on the red tower. "Here's a classic tower attack."

Like the others on his team, the yellow pusher's uniform had small shoulder pads, elbow pads, and leather gloves, but no helmet, which seemed dangerous with a disc whizzing back and forth at high speeds. The only difference between his uniform and the others on his team was the hammer symbol on front of his shirt. One of the disablers, identified by the freeze stick in her hand, had a wand symbol on her uniform. I spotted a defender in the back with the image of a shield on his.

Ambria winced as the striker whizzed past a player's face, narrowly missing it. "Why aren't they wearing helmets? That disc looks like it could cut off your head."

Max stopped the video again. "The uniforms are charmed like armor to protect players from impacts to their bodies." Max pointed to a thick collar on a carry's uniform. "If the disc comes too close to your face, it activates a shield."

"What happens if you get knocked off your broom?" I asked.

"Players wear tethers, so even if they fall, they stay attached to their brooms." Max shrugged. "You can still get injured, but at least you won't lose your head."

Ambria shuddered. "I would scream if I saw that disc flying toward my face."

Max chuckled. "Maybe you shouldn't try out for the team."

"Wouldn't dream of it," she replied.

Max continued the video. A yellow carry flung the glowing disc at the tower. Two red defenders flew to intercept, but a yellow freezer froze one. A freeze attack missed the second defender who snagged the disc from the air. The dull glow of the striker brightened to an electric blue.

The defender relayed the disc to a carry who zipped between two yellow defenders while his fellow teammates cleared a hole by blocking opposing players.

Holding the edge of the disc between thumb and forefinger, the red pusher side-armed it toward the enemy tower. The striker smashed against the enemy building and two large cracks formed in the stone.

Max paused the playback again and turned to us. "When the opposing team intercepts an attack on their buildings, they have twenty seconds to attack the enemy tower for double damage." He traced a finger down the crack. "Every crack symbolizes a hit."

"Interesting," Ambria said. "I don't think I've ever heard of such an odd game."

"It's more fun than you can imagine," Max said. "My brothers play for Tiberius Keep. Some people say they might be good enough to go to the professional league."

I stared for a moment at the still image and agreed with Max that it looked like a lot of fun. Something in the holographic image caught my eye—a familiar face. I zoomed in on the red carry in the background and felt a sudden shock of electricity in my heart. The face was younger, the eyes full of genuine excitement, but there was no mistaking Delectra.

"Whoa." Max looked at something on the phone. "I just searched for one of the old professional matches. I didn't realize your mom was in it."

For some reason, I wasn't upset. "She looks so happy." *Delectra wasn't always evil.*

Max shook his head sadly. "I wonder what happened to turn her so bad."

I turned off the phone. "Let's try out for the team."

"Really?"

I nodded. "Looks like fun."

Max pumped a fist in the air. "Yes!"

We showed up for tryouts early the next morning behind the keep. Ambria came to cheer us on, but had no intention of trying out.

Rory sneered the moment he saw me. "What are you doing here, Edison?"

"Tryouts," Max sneered back.

"Go back to bed." Gregory jabbed a finger toward the keep, then burst into laughter as if he'd just said the funniest thing ever.

A tall teenaged boy with ebony skin and piercing blue eyes emerged from the back door of the keep and walked onto the field. A group of girls and boys close to his age followed close behind. I recognized some of them in passing, but didn't know their names.

Ambria sucked in a breath. "Goodness, what a handsome boy."

Max grimaced. "Gross. I'm sure the last thing he wants is to hear that from a little girl."

She slapped his arm. "Maxwell Tiberius, you're awful."

"Hello, candidates," the boy said. "I'm Elliott Cobain, the team leader for the Moore Skywraiths." His gaze seemed to pause on me before moving on. "I hope you're all familiar with the rules of Kabash. Otherwise"—he made a shooing motion with his hand—"move along and save my time."

Rory and Gregory laughed, elbowing their other friends until they uneasily joined in the laughter.

Elliott hopped on a broom with a dark polished handle and shiny silver stirrups. The orange bristles formed the shape of a candle flame. "The first test will be keeping up with us on the way to the stadium." He held his arm out to the side. "Candidates, form up."

Max and I quickly got on our brooms and lined up beside the others. Rory and Gregory shoved in between us and the others, rudely pushing us further out. Elliott's hand flashed down. The line rocketed forward. We zipped away from the keep and toward the iron gates guarding the campus. The barrier rippled slightly as our charms allowed us through it, and then Elliott dove low for the trees next to the edge of the plateau.

Max got in front of me, and we threaded our way through the trees. I heard grunts and thuds and saw three candidates tumble to the ground. The rest of us burst from the other side of the woods and dove after Elliott down the sheer cliff toward the valley below.

Movement in my peripheral vision alerted me, and I saw Rory angling to sideswipe Max. I drifted into Max's slipstream, lowered my head, and gained enough speed to slingshot myself past him just in time to intercept Rory. The other boy shouted in alarm as I bumped him away and flicked the tail of my broom, sending him into a flat spin.

He cried out in fear, but I saw from the way his broom spun that he was in no danger of crashing into the ground.

Max looked at me with wide eyes. "Thanks, Conrad."

I gave him a thumbs-up.

We soon reached the large oval stadium in the northeast corner of Queens Gate. It was nearly as imposing as Colossus Stadium, though it didn't rise quite as high and wasn't nearly as massive. We entered through an arched gateway at one end and flew onto the grass field.

Elliott spun around. "Today we're going to fly the obstacle course. First—"

Rory drifted inside the stadium and stopped next to Gregory. Elliott rose higher on his broom and pointed at him. "Why are you here?"

"To try out?" Rory said, his voice rising as if the statement were actually a question.

"No. I saw you spin out at the cliff." Elliott pointed to the exit. "Leave, or go sit on the sidelines and watch. Your tryout is over."

"But Edison—"

"Blocked you fair and square."

Two larger boys flew towards Rory. The other boy threw up his hands in surrender. "Fine!" He bared his teeth at me. "Next time I see you, Edison, you'd better run."

I didn't reply, and just stared as the red-faced Rory turned to go. He tugged on Gregory's arm, but his friend shook his head and remained.

"As I was saying, we're doing the obstacle course," Elliott said. He nodded to an older girl with close-cropped brown hair. "Jenna, hit it."

She swung over to a stone table inscribed with symbols and traced her fingers along several. Within minutes, the once peaceful field was a long gauntlet. Poles sprang from the ground, forming a dense treacherous forest to navigate. Next came a series of winding tubes interspersed with flaming rings, large swinging mallets designed to knock riders from their brooms, and jets of water shooting up or sideways.

I felt my mouth drop open. Tryouts were going to be more of a challenge than I'd thought.

Chapter 30

"I don't know if I can make it through that," Max whispered in a desperate tone.

"You have three tries to make it through the course," Elliott said. "We'll get started in a few minutes."

To the side of the course, I noticed a small crowd gathering. Gideon Grace stood next to Esma Emoora, Eleanor Beetle, and other adults I didn't recognize. Galfandor entered the stadium a moment later, seated on a flying carpet. He smiled and nodded at the crowd.

Percival followed soon after, his flying carpet loaded down with potions. His face lit up when he saw Max and me. Turning his carpet, he approached. "Well, I daresay my ward will soon be brimming with new patients." His eyes followed one of the swinging mallets. "Yes, several."

"You frighten me," Max said.

Percival was too wrapped up counting those present to hear him.

A tall muscular girl flew her broom into the stadium with a large group on her heels. She motioned them to stop and flew over to Elliott. The two talked for a moment and shared a laugh.

"That's Velma Shram from Graeven Keep," Max said in a low voice. "She's already gotten offers from two pro teams."

"Ladies and gents, we have arrived," boomed a familiar voice.

Heads turned as Devon and Rhys Tiberius led their keep's team and candidates into the stadium.

"Autographs will be given after the trials," Rhys said. He and his brother flew up to Elliott whose gaze darkened. "Well, shall we get this show on the road, people?"

Velma's expression turned sour. "Yes, let's."

"How does this work?" I asked Max. "Do we take turns?"

"Candidates to the line," Elliott shouted.

Max shook his head.

A deep crippling fear shivered through my bones. "We're all going at once?" I counted at least thirty contenders.

Max stared blankly at the gauntlet for a moment. "Yes." He trembled. "I watched tryouts from the sidelines every year I could. I never realized how frightening it is to do it myself."

Velma flew up next to Elliott. "There are ten checkpoints in the course. If you are knocked from your broom or miss a hoop or tunnel, you must start over from the previous checkpoint."

Devon drifted along beside her. "If you fall or miss three times you're out!"

"If you do not average high speed, you're out!" Rhys said.

"I'm going to be sick," Max groaned.

Elliott flew higher so everyone could see him and raised his wand. "Ready, set"—he twisted his wand and fireworks exploded from it—"go!"

With the roar of battle cries, the fleet of flying brooms jetted forward. Bodies bumped and jostled Max and me until I lost sight of my friend. I couldn't see over the bobbing bodies ahead of me, so I flew higher. A forest of poles came first. I didn't see any sense in trying to beat everyone else, so I slowed down to see better.

An older boy with a mop of black hair pulled up beside me. "Got a gift for you, Edison." He slapped the side of my broomstick and grinned wickedly. I didn't recognize the face, but his voice sounded like the tall attacker from the hallway. Before I could say a word, my broom jetted forward with a mind of its own.

I ran my fingers along the broomstick and found something stuck to the side. Frantically fumbling, I tried to pry it loose, but it wouldn't budge. I pulled the broom side-to-side. It responded to my directions, but the throttle wouldn't budge. Back and forth, I went, dodging slower fliers. I gave a moment's thought to pulling up and out of the fray, but then I'd likely disqualify myself from the tryouts.

I trembled with anger. *He thinks he can stop me?* "I'll show them."

Fly, boy, fly! Della shouted with glee.

I burst from the pack and entered the maze of poles. Like the forest on the cliff, I had little difficulty twisting my way through the first part of the course. I juked past two other fliers and hit a small clearing. A twisting tube lay ahead. I shot inside and nearly collided with another candidate. Della's reflexes twisted the broom to the side in a looping barrel roll, up and over the other flier. The tube narrowed and my shoulder bumped the side, pinging me back and forth, a hollow echo ringing in my ears.

Once again, I tried to slow my ride, but the throttle refused to budge. The dim tunnel ended in bright daylight. My eyes adjusted just in time for me to dive through a flaming loop. Though I passed through the flames, I felt no heat, and assumed they must be illusion. Up and down, side to side, I threaded my way through the hoops, nearly striking my head on the last one.

I followed a long twisting tunnel to its end. Three fliers appeared ahead. I caught up to them just as we entered a zone of swinging mallets and water jets. The first water jet unseated the first flier. The other two nimbly dodged it. One flier looked back and his eyes flared with anger.

I instantly recognized Harris Ashmore, and knew the red-headed flier in front of him was Baxter. Unfortunately, I would soon draw even with them. Baxter swooped right to dodge the first mallet, but the next one caught him and sent him spinning out of control and into a padded wall. Harris barely made it around the mallets and vanished behind them as they swung back to center. I counted the swings and positioned myself a little to the right. The first mallet hit its left apex while the second one hovered on the right. I punched through the hole and ducked low beneath a jet of water on the other side.

Harris increased his speed and cast a confused glance over his shoulder. The glance nearly cost him as a water jet narrowly missed him. He hit the next checkpoint, a large octagonal tunnel with a field of black poles shooting up and down from the ground. I tried to find a pattern but quickly realized the intervals were random. Even worse, a pole might take half a second to fully extend one time, or five seconds the next.

Harris swept left then right, but a pole caught the bristles on his broom, knocking him off course. A pole shot from the right and sent him spinning. He crashed into the wall. A section opened like a door and a rod with a hook at the end jerked him outside of the course.

I sensed another presence awakening and felt Vic analyzing the situation. I drew closer and closer to the tunnel and abruptly saw the pattern. The seemingly random thrusts were actually four separate patterns repeating every few seconds. I wished I could slow down and take it in one last time, but it was too late.

Pattern two erupted from all sides the moment I hit the gaping octagonal maw. I looped counterclockwise, always flying over a pole that was a split second from spearing from the floor or walls. When I hit the midsection of the beast, pattern three emerged, spiking the tunnel from all sides, leaving only a narrow gap. I charged through the opening and narrowly avoided the final group of poles as pattern four began. An instant later, I burst into clear air.

Before me lay only open field, and for a moment, I thought I'd finished. The cheer died on my lips when a flying disc rose from the ground and began circling erratically. Behind it, a tower exploded from the ground, and a squad of fliers flew from behind it.

Thanks to Max's instructions, I knew what to do. Lowering my head, I felt a grin stretch my face. Adrenaline burned through my veins like electricity. I watched the wobbling disc change directions several times, zigging and zagging, ducking and weaving, but always staying within a five-yard radius. I couldn't calculate where it would be when I reached it several seconds from now, so I aimed for the center.

I looked at the opposing fliers and realized they were Rhys, Devon, Velma, and Elliott.

You'll reach the disc one point five seconds ahead of them, Vic informed me.

Five, four, three, two—the disc shot sideways at the last second. Unable to slow, I veered hard and barely snagged it with my fingers. Despite the sullen orange glow, the striker felt cool and metallic in my hand.

Rhys and Devon angled right at me. I juked low then pulled up hard and shot right over them. Devon's shoulder caught me. I spun with the blow and Velma sped past, her shoulder narrowly missing. Still spinning, I held the striker under my hand like a discus. The tower came into range.

Now! Della cried out with joy.

I released the disc. It whirred straight and true, striking the tower. The rock grumbled and a long crack ran up the surface. Since I still couldn't stop my broom, I flew in a wide circle, anticipating a rebound from the disc. Instead, it stopped and hovered in place.

"Are you serious?" Devon shouted, face aghast.

Rhys glared at me with a mixture of disbelief and disgust. "This can't be real."

Velma motioned me to the side of the arena. "Get out of the way, Edison."

"You're done," Elliott said in a stern voice.

"Can't stop my broom," I shouted. "Someone hexed it."

"Then go fly in circles out of the way," Elliott said. "Go, now!"

I stopped circling and aimed for the sidelines, all the while prying at the thing stuck to my broomstick. I was flying too fast to simply jump off. I suddenly remembered a spell handy for such circumstances, and took out my wand. Flicking the wand up, down, and then directly at the object, I said, "*Disruptus*."

A small piece of metal the size of a coin dropped from my broomstick, and suddenly I was once again fully in control. Sagging with relief, I slowed down, circled back, and picked up the medallion. It would be my proof when I saw the other boy again.

A cheer went up from the Moore Keep crowd when I reached the sideline. Ambria raced over and hugged me.

"That was brilliant, Conrad!" She gave me a wondering look. "I can't believe you stayed on your broom. You were going so fast!"

Esma Emoora walked over, her pearly whites flashing in the sun. "Impressive, young man. You make me"—she broke off in midsentence and paused a second—"wonder how you managed such a thing."

"Yes, yes, impressive indeed," Galfandor said, from a few feet away. "I must say it was rather risky flying so fast."

"I couldn't help it." I held up the medallion. "Some other kid sabotaged my broom. I could steer, but I couldn't slow down."

"Troubling." The headmaster took the object and turned it over in his hands. "Percival also told me about the incident in the hallway."

"I think the boy who hexed my broom was one of them." I looked back toward the gauntlet as Harris Ashmore emerged from the tunnel of shooting rods and went wide-eyed at the new task before him.

253

Harris got to the striker and threw it, but missed wide when Elliott shouldered him from the side.

"Let us know if you see the culprit," Esma said. "We should put an end to this bullying straightaway, wouldn't you say, Galfandor?"

The headmaster nodded, his bright eyes looking at the group of washouts gathering on the sideline some distance away. "Let's go see if your ruffian is in this bunch, Conrad."

We hadn't walked two feet, when I saw the boy in question standing next to some other boys. He glared at me with open hatred, then hopped on his broom and tried to make his escape.

Galfandor's wand swept through the air, and the broom jerked from beneath the boy who plowed face-first into the ground. "Timothy Simmons, you and I need to have a talk." The headmaster patted my shoulder. "I will take care of this, young man. Congratulations on your spectacular run." He strolled to the boy and handed hi.m over to two Arcanes in blue security robes.

"Only one other person ever did what you managed today," Esma said in a low voice.

I flinched and turned around to see her and Ambria standing behind me. "What did I do?"

Esma laughed. "You made it through the course in one try, and in record time, young Edison. The only other person ever to do so was none other than your mother."

Chapter 31

For some reason, I wasn't the least bit surprised. Della burst into maniacal laughter in my head, obviously pleased.

Perhaps you are not a lost cause after all, she said.

Vic did not chime his agreement.

Within the hour, everyone who successfully completed the course lined up on the sidelines. Graeven had only four successful candidates. Just enough, Max informed me, to fill their roster. Harris, Baxter, and five other boys from Tiberius Keep made it through, while six candidates, myself and Max included, stood for Moore Keep.

Elliott Cobain walked up to our group and gave me a long hard look. "Looks like you got some of your mother's flying talents."

"But he's an Edison," Gregory, who had also made it, said angrily.

"Is his name Victus?" Elliott asked.

Gregory frowned. "No."

"Is it Delectra?"

"No, but—"

"Then stop your whining." Elliott glared at the boy. "You barely made the cut. I could kick you off the team and not lose a moment's sleep." He put a fist on my shoulder. "Conrad here proved he's the best flier I've seen since I was a kid and watched videos of his mum. Unless he starts killing everyone, he's on the team."

I felt my mouth drop open at this declaration of acceptance from the team captain. *Someone else wants me around?* I'd have to be careful, or I might start to feel happy.

The next day in classes, I overheard other students talking about Conrad Edison, the boy who'd broken his mother's obstacle course record. From the rumors swirling, some couldn't decide if that was good or bad. Unfortunately, the one thing I hadn't counted on was the after-school kabash practice for two hours each day.

Before supper, I reported to the practice field behind Moore Keep. It was only a half-sized field, but equipped with three practice buildings. Elliott ran us through blocking and relaying exercises with the striker, even going so far as to give us each a disc to sleep with at night.

"I want you to hold onto this striker until it feels like a part of your body," he ordered. "A good kabash player's reflexes will tell him exactly what to do before he even knows what to do."

After kabash practice, I ate a quick supper and met with Esma Emoora.

"My father took me to all the professional kabash games," she told me, as I practiced *parrano*, the spell she'd used to deflect my *torsious* spell on the first night. Esma sighed. "Those were the best days of my life."

"Is your father dead?" She looked far too young for her parents to have passed on.

Her eyes went distant, and time seemed to slip away from her as she relived something from the past. Esma shuddered and threw out her hands as if trying to stop something. She flinched and blinked as if waking from a nightmare. "I'm sorry, Conrad. What did you say?"

"Nothing," I replied, thinking it best I not ask if she was okay. Whatever happened to her father was none of my business.

The next day in the hall, Asha Fellini stopped me. "I am impressed with what I heard about you, young Edison."

I looked into that hauntingly familiar face and held back a shiver of fright. "Thank you." I so desperately wanted to ask if she was really Delectra, and if she intended to kill me at a convenient moment. My logical side argued she would have already done so. Then again, perhaps my mother liked to toy with her prey first.

"Is something wrong?" She placed a hand on my shoulder. "You seem troubled."

"I'm, um, late for class, Professor." I edged away. "Thank you for the compliment."

As the end of the week grew nearer, I became more and more excited. Our first game was on Saturday.

Friday, just after classes, Evadora sneaked up behind me in an empty hallway and nearly frightened me half to death. I jumped and spun around, nearly tripping over my own feet, visions of the punks who'd beaten me in the hallway, still fresh in my mind.

She giggled.

I breathed a sigh of relief and then realized this wasn't our normal day to meet. "Did something happen with Serena?"

She nodded. "Serena told me she has to go away for a while to gather important supplies for her divining rod."

That piqued my curiosity. "What sort of supplies?"

"She said the wood she has is *unsuitable*." Evadora mimicked Serena's voice almost perfectly.

"How long will she be gone?"

"Weeks or maybe a month." Once again, she mimicked Serena's voice. "What I need is extremely rare. You've waited all this time, surely you can wait another month or so."

"She was telling that to my parents?" I asked.

A lock of brown hair slowly shaded strawberry blonde as Evadora twirled it in her fingers. "Yes, and they were unhappy."

My senses perked. "Did you find out where they've been hiding?"

Evadora puffed out her cheeks. "No. They are sneaky people, Conrad."

"What did they say to Serena?"

"What sort of wood is so special?" she said in a voice eerily similar to my father's. "You're making excuses!" This time, she sounded like Delectra.

"Can you just say it in your voice?" I asked. "I don't like hearing their voices."

Evadora tilted her head and shrugged. "Your mother spoke of you, Conrad."

My heart beat a little faster. "What did she say?"

"She was impressed with your kabash tryout and wonders how you'll do in your first game. She sounded proud." A sad frown preceded her next sentence. "Then your father said they should just kill you and be done with it, that kabash was a foolish waste of time."

My emotions didn't know which way to go—up or down. "I wonder why they haven't done it yet."

"Delectra said they can't kill you because it would draw too much attention. They have to wait on Serena to finish her work." Evadora turned her frown upside down. "This is a good thing, I think."

It didn't feel that great to know my father was eager to end my life, and I didn't know what to think about what my mother said.

Evadora gripped my hand. "Be brave, Conrad. I will tell you if anything changes."

I returned the squeeze. "You've changed since we first met. It's like you're growing up really fast."

She sighed. "I know. I do not like this growing up. Sometimes I would like to run back into the wild and play, but now I have friends." Her shoulders slumped. "It is a great responsibility."

I chuckled. "Tell me about it."

That evening after practice, Elliott lined us up to announce assignments. Yuri Evans bumped hard into me on his way to line up with the veteran players, and gave me a venomous look in passing.

"What's up with him?" Max asked.

I'd never spoken with the boy, and wondered if negative feelings about my parentage were poisoning the goodwill I'd earned from the kabash tryout.

"Starting lineup tomorrow," Elliott said, "Defenders are Yuri, Phillip, and Julie. Peter and Ryan, you're our freezers."

Ryan, a new player like us, blew out a sigh of relief. Yuri's jaw tightened and his eyes smoldered.

Elliott folded his arms and gave a sideways look at the pouting Yuri. "Starting carries are Jenna, me, and"—he paused for a split second—"Conrad."

All the other newbies looked at me with envy and disbelief. Max pounded my back and whooped. "A starting carry, Conrad! That's amazing!"

Yuri bared his teeth. "You'd better do well, Edison. I was going to go carry this year."

"You're one of the best defenders I've seen," Elliott told Yuri. "You could go pro if you want. Anyway, you'll defend unless I need an emergency carry to step in."

Julie rolled her eyes at Yuri. "Everybody wants to be a carry."

"Because they get all the glory," Gregory said, looking at me enviously.

Elliott handed out the second string positions, listing Max as a freezer and Gregory as a defender.

Looking at the anger on Yuri's face, and thinking about the responsibilities of a carry, I wasn't sure if I should be happy or not.

Elliott took me to the side after he dismissed the others. "You look a little frightened."

I took a breath to quell my rapidly beating heart. "I wasn't expecting a starting position."

"Look, you're a great flier, and you've got an eye for angles. The only thing lacking is strength." He squeezed my small bicep and grunted. "Throw the disc as hard as you can." He held out the striker and let it go. It hovered in place, spinning with a quiet whirring noise.

I held it overhanded like a discus, but Elliott quickly corrected me. "No, flick it or backhand it."

I pinched the edge with thumb and forefinger and flicked it across the field in a sidearm fashion as hard as I could. The disc traveled fifteen yards before slowing, and drifted to a halt about thirty yards away. "I'm sorry my arm isn't strong. I can work out."

Elliott nodded. "You'll need to." He whistled and the practice kabash zipped back to him. "Try throwing it backhanded."

Gripping the edge in my hand, I crossed my arm over my body then swung it out as hard as I could. The striker flew slightly further. "Are you sure I should start as carry?"

"We just need to make sure we're close to the towers if you're striking." He retrieved the disc again and flicked sideways it. It whirled more than fifty yards before coming to a stop between the tower and the keep targets. "Go relax, Conrad. You're gonna need all your strength against Tiberius Keep tomorrow."

I met Max and Ambria inside the keep and we went to dinner. I felt the weight of stares on me as we found an empty table and waited for a golem to serve us. I'd grown used to people looking at me, the offspring of evil, but this time it felt different. I spotted Harris and Baxter looking our way and talking with Rhys and Devon. Max's brothers wore their customary smirks, and even winked at me when they saw me looking.

I dreaded playing them tomorrow.

"My brothers are sneaky kabash players," Max said.

Ambria sniffed. "Not to mention unpleasant."

"That, too." He shrugged. "Anyway, you'll need to be careful against them, Conrad. They're always coming up with weird plays to throw off the other team, and if they get a chance to hurt you, believe me, they will."

I was still new to the sport, so it was hard for me to imagine anything outside of what I'd learned. The food finally arrived and I was so hungry, I dug in and temporarily forgot my worries.

"That little boy is a carry, brother?"

I looked up and saw Rhys, Devon, Harris, and Baxter standing next to our table.

Devon looked at Rhys and sighed. "It's desperation, pure and simple."

"Leave us alone," Max said. "Can't you see we're eating?"

Rhys ignored him. "A shame our little brother won't be playing tomorrow."

"I'd love to see if he could even stay on his broom," Devon said.

Baxter snickered. "You boys are gonna get smacked tomorrow."

"Just to show that we're good sports," Devon said, "we'll have young Harris start as a freezer tomorrow."

Rhys winked at me. "Maybe he'll freeze you right when the kabash is flying at your face."

Harris smirked. "That sounds fun."

"How sad." Ambria sniffed. "I suppose Harris isn't good enough to be a carry."

"I'm plenty good!" Harris said.

Baxter smacked a fist into his palm. "I'll carry Edison's face right into the ground."

"I was certainly right about you, Baxter," Ambria said in an offhanded tone. "You're just an unpleasant little boy."

Baxter's face turned crimson. "I'll show you—"

"Now, now," Rhys said, gripping Baxter's shoulder. "Let's get you some warm milk and calm you down."

Devon snickered. "Perhaps he needs to sit in the timeout corner."

I forced myself to look back down at my plate and ate more potatoes, and the boys finally went away. If they noticed the tremble in my hands, they didn't say anything about it.

On our way back to the keep, we met Esma Emoora in the hallway.

She smiled. "Good luck tomorrow, Conrad. I'll be rooting for you."

"I hope I'm up to the challenge," I replied.

Esma pursed her lips. "I have no doubts about your abilities whatsoever." She nodded and continued on her way to the dining hall.

"Wish I felt as confident as her," Max said. "Truth is, I'm scared half to death for you, Conrad."

Ambria's eyes flared. "He's going to get smashed to bits, isn't he?"

"Probably," Max said.

I groaned and shoved Max. "Stop it. I'm nervous enough as it is."

That night in bed, I tossed and turned for what felt like hours, my mind churning through kabash scenarios. I imagined the plays Elliott taught us and the formations we used for defending our buildings and attacking the opposition.

The best laid plans end in chaos, Vic said in a smug voice. *Chaos leads to victory.*

True, Della confirmed. *Be unpredictable. Keep them off balance. Make them react to you.*

It was quite strange getting such sound advice from the voices in my head. *Thanks, I'll do my best.*

You are an Edison. Della's calm reply took away some of the fear and anxiety, and suddenly sleep pulled me into its depths.

Chapter 32

Game time arrived at noon the next day. Crisp fall air mingled with the faint scent of cooking sausages and the dull roar of a crowd eager to see the first game of the year.

I flexed my hands in the stiff leather gloves and made sure my uniform was snug. The black leather jacket and pants resembled something a motorcyclist might wear. The thick collar at the top bore enchantments to screen our eyes from the wind as a pair of goggles might, and in the case of an accident, to shield our head like a helmet.

I ran a hand down the large white symbol of a hammer on my chest.

"These uniforms are brilliant," Max said, admiring the white wand emblem on his jacket.

"I thought black and white would look drab," I admitted, "but it actually looks somewhat menacing."

Max grinned. "Hopefully menacing enough to make Tiberius quake in their boots."

"Broom up," Elliott commanded.

"Welcome to the first kabash game of the season," an announcer boomed from within the stadium. "For today's game, we have the Moore Skywraiths versus the Tiberius Titans."

Cheers and the pounding of feet vibrated the stadium itself.

"How many people are here?" I asked Max.

He shrugged. "Maybe a thousand or more."

My stomach lurched at the thought of so many people watching.

The announcer continued. "Next week's game will be Graeven versus Frankenstone, and the week after that, Tesla versus Edison."

"There's an Edison Keep?" I asked.

"Edison Lab," Max replied. "Science Academy doesn't have keeps."

"Labs instead of keeps." I shook my head. "I suppose it makes sense."

"After the Overlord died, some people tried to change Edison Lab to another famous bloodline, but nobody could agree to anything, so they ended up keeping it." He looked toward the gates into the stadium as they began rumbling open, chains clinking in the mechanisms. Max gulped. "Here we go."

Elliot held up a fist and then threw it forward. We flew inside the stadium and toward the center of the field while team Tiberius in their red leather uniforms with purple emblems approached from the other side. The announcer shouted something else, but it was lost in the rumbling roar of the crowd. I could hardly concentrate with so much noise, my nerves winding tighter and tighter.

The teams met in the center above the yellow scrum circle. Rhys and Devon exchanged nods with Elliott while officials in turquoise outfits hovered around the teams. Max's brothers reserved a glance and a smirk for me, making my insides squirm.

Mind games, Della said.

I know. But knowing didn't help my nerves.

The lead referee blew a whistle, and the teams went toward their end zones.

"Starters with me," Elliott said. "Second strings, go to the sidelines."

Max lightly punched my shoulder. "Good luck, Conrad."

I swallowed hard and nodded. "Thanks." My voice sounded feeble and frightened.

"Keep it together, Edison." Yuri scowled at me, hands clenching his broom handle. He turned to Elliott. "You sure this boy is up to it? It's not too late to change me to carry."

The team captain turned his cold blue eyes on the other boy. "Yuri, are you going to do your best, or should I replace you?"

Yuri stiffened. "Of course, but—"

"Then shut it, and keep to the plan." Elliott twirled a finger in the air and we formed a circle. "Moore Keep has been down these past few seasons, but this year is ours." He gazed calmly around at the others. "Keep a sharp eye for typical Tiberius tricks, and protect your teammates." He pointed to Jenna. "Don't forget to keep checking your left side. I don't want you getting blindsided like last year."

She nodded. "I'll remember."

"Then let's do this." Elliot put his fist in the middle of the circle and the rest of us pressed our fists together. "One, two, three."

"Skywraiths, form up!" everyone shouted at once.

A gong boomed and the towers burst from the ground on either side of the centerline, each painted with team colors. The keeps erupted upward next, followed by the castle-shaped fortresses in the end zones.

The gong rang once again.

We lined up in front of our fortress, carries in the center, defenders and freezers to the sides. The official threw the striker into the scrum circle and we shot forward.

Elliot reached the kabash first, but before he could grab it, Harris flicked his freeze wand forward. A bolt of ice shot from the end, striking Elliott in the side. The team captain froze in place, broom and all, leaving space for Rhys to scoop up the disc.

I skidded sideways and bumped into Rhys. He shoved back with his shoulder, and I bounced into Devon on my right. The pair sandwiched me and dragged me toward our tower. Jenna came in for the rescue, but two defenders blocked her path, and the other Tiberius freezer disabled Yuri.

"What a lovely day for a ride," Devon said.

Rhys chortled. "Here's your stop, Edison."

Using the tails of their brooms, they catapulted me forward right at the tower. I heard a whirring noise and rolled upside down just as the striker flashed past where my head would have been and slammed into our tower, leaving a crack. Devon grabbed the rebound and flicked the disc back at the tower. I regained control of my broom at the last second and shot upward to block the throw.

A bolt of ice hit me in the stomach. I couldn't move a muscle and watched helplessly as the disc rammed our tower again. Elliott sideswiped Rhys and intercepted the striker. He relayed it to Yuri who flung it to Julie. A bolt of ice from Peter stopped Harris from disabling Julie. Peter fired at Rhys and missed.

My body unfroze and I zipped back into the action. Elliott took a shot at the other tower, but a Tiberius defender intercepted the shot and flicked the disc to Rhys. The striker went from a muted glow to azure blue, indicating the double damage bonus.

Rhys threw the disc overhanded. The brightly glowing disc whizzed sideways, flashed between two of our defenders, and struck our tower for double damage. The final crack destroyed the tower and sent it crumbling to the ground.

The Tiberius seating section went wild.

I grabbed the rebound. Elliot swirled his finger and we grouped up into a protective formation. "We're down an entire tower, and no hits on theirs," he growled. "Peter, Ryan, I need you to focus Devon and Rhys." He jabbed a finger at Yuri. "Keep their freezers off me, okay?"

Yuri scowled. "Got it."

We zipped in for an attack, but Tiberius defenders formed a wedge and split us down the middle, and our offensive attack failed, giving Tiberius possession of the striker once again.

Our teams went back and forth, nobody scoring a strike. Peter and Ryan finally nailed freezes on Devon and Rhys, and the Tiberius formation fell apart. Elliott scored two strikes on the Tiberius tower before the twin brothers thawed and drove us off.

"Pay attention, you morons!" Rhys shouted, his careless façade broken.

The game raged on. I felt useless as the bigger players rammed me aside, and Harris Ashmore took every opportunity to freeze me, though I posed no real threat. As the other team formed up for another attack, I realized something. Even though we were flying, most teams stuck to a horizontal attack pattern and rarely flew higher than the towers unless trying to escape a freeze bolt.

I didn't know what good that information would do me, but tucked it away for the future. Other than that, Devon and Rhys liked to hog the glory for themselves. Their third carry, Allison Charms, rarely took a shot and looked cross every time the brothers forced her to relay it to one of them. Taking out Max's brothers weakened team Tiberius considerably, but the boys now had defenders blocking the freeze spells whenever possible.

Suddenly, I realized how my earlier revelation might help.

We took a defensive formation twenty yards in front of our keep as Tiberius circled for another attack. They'd scored five hits on it already, and only needed one more to destroy our second building.

"Elliott, have Peter and Ryan fly high and low to take out Rhys and Devon." I swooped my hand through the air. "They won't expect vertical attacks."

He frowned, then motioned toward the freezers. "Fly straight at them like normal, then Peter angle up, Ryan angle down, and hit them from both directions." Elliott slashed his hand forward. "Move out."

We jetted forward. Devon and Rhys flew at the center of a circle formation with defenders at the front and freezers somewhere in the back. The roar of the crowd grew louder and louder as our two formations streaked for a collision course. At the last minute, our freezers aimed their wands. The Tiberius defenders tensed to intercept the blow, but Peter and Ryan zipped above and below them. Freeze bolts speared for their targets.

Rhys and Devon cursed in unison just before the freeze spells silenced them. Our defenders drove a wedge into the opposing team, sending Tiberius players spinning away on their brooms. Elliott collided sideways into Allison and knocked the striker from her hand. He flung it to Jenna, and we left the enemy team floundering.

Jenna took a shot at the purple and red tower, but the air around it shimmered and the disc bounced off without leaving a crack.

"They fortified!" Elliott shouted as he caught the rebound. He waited a count of two before throwing the kabash. The shield vanished just before the disc struck home. Before Tiberius recovered, we took out their tower and scored two hits on their keep.

Their next possession, the Tiberius freezers tried our own tactics on us and caught Elliott off guard. Devon threw the striker just as Peter froze him. I streaked for the intercept, but missed, and the sixth hit landed on our keep, and the building crashed to earth.

Tiberius only needed eight more strikes to win. We needed twelve.

I caught the rebound and hung back for my team to circle up. Elliott took the striker from me. "We've got to keep the fight in their territory. Our only advantage now is that our last building is all the way at the end of the field."

My mind worked furiously on strategies as we flew downfield, but I came up with nothing. We earned two more blows on their keep before Devon plucked a rebound and raced ahead of everyone down the field and struck our fortress. After a long skirmish, we captured the disc and finally finished off their keep. Moore fans burst into applause as the purple and red building turned into a pile of rubble.

But we were still in trouble. Tiberius needed only four more hits to finish us off. We managed two strikes on their fortress, but Devon came back and slipped in two more blows on ours.

On our next possession, Elliott tricked the other team with a reverse relay, allowing Jenna to slip behind enemy lines. She flung the striker for a hit. I came up from the other side, recovered the rebound just before Harris got it, and threw it for one more strike.

Rhys rammed into Elliott and grabbed the rebound. Peter aimed a freeze bolt at Rhys, but missed and hit Elliott instead. Laughing, Rhys relayed the striker to Devon. Harris froze Yuri, and a bolt from their other freezer hit Jenna. The rest of my team raced after Devon, but he scored another strike before we could stop them.

A Tiberius victory was only one hit away.

Peter looked absolutely miserable when he rejoined us.

"Shake it off," Elliott told him. "Everyone misses."

"We're going to lose and it's all my fault," Peter said.

Elliott glared at him, then held up a fist.

"Time out called by Moore," the announcer said.

"Go to the sidelines and get Max out here," Elliott said.

Peter nodded sadly and flew away. I could see the whites of Max's eyes halfway across the field when Peter motioned him in. Max zipped over to us, the freeze wand held in a trembling hand.

"You ready for this, Max?" Elliott said.

Max nodded. "Y-yeah! You can count on me." He gulped.

"Keep calm and freeze one of your brothers," Jenna said.

"Just don't hit one of us," Yuri said.

Elliott threw up a fist. "Skywraiths, form up!"

We fought back downfield, the striker trading sides several times, but the skirmish never moved from center field. Everything became a blur as I tried to keep track of the disc and avoid freeze bolts and defenders. I realized I no longer felt nervous. Instead, I felt like this one long battle was my entire life. The broom was my ship, and the fight was a bucking ocean.

Max managed a crucial freeze on Devon and Elliott slipped past, throwing a twenty-yard attempt for a true strike on the Tiberius fortress.

We needed two more hits and it was over.

But Devon intercepted the rebound from Jenna's outstretched hand. A freeze bolt caught Elliott, and another snagged Yuri. Before our freezers could react, Tiberius defenders smacked into them. Ryan's freeze wand flew from his hand. He shouted and dove after it. Max recovered and fired at Devon, but missed entirely.

Suddenly, team Tiberius had the run of the field.

Our team straggled in pursuit. I flew directly behind Harris, using his slipstream to stay on target. A gong rang out, signifying the last two minutes of the game. I couldn't believe it had nearly been ninety minutes. I ducked and used Harris's airflow to slingshot even with him. He tried to freeze me, but since he'd just used his wand, it still had at least forty seconds to recharge.

Seeing that his wand was useless for the time being, he veered toward me. I looped beneath him, shot up, and waggled my broom in his airstream as I'd done to Max weeks ago. He lost speed, and dropped behind. Devon was still ahead of me by at least fifteen yards with Rhys right by his side, and the rest of his team hot on my tail.

Rhys looked back. "Say goodbye to your fortress, Edison!"

The two boys burst into laughter.

I pressed my body to the broomstick for the least wind resistance, and inched closer and closer. Finally, I reached their twin slipstreams. The reduced air resistance shot me forward, but they were in range of the fortress. Devon cocked back his arm and let the striker fly. He was so confident that he circled out of the way and pumped his fist in the air. I zipped past him in desperate pursuit of the disc, but had no chance of catching it.

Our shield rippled on at the last instant.

"Fortified!" Rhys shrieked to his brother.

I was going too fast, and the disc rebounded off the shield, skipping out of my grasp before I could reach it. Devon spun around and snagged the rebound. Baring his teeth in a smug grin, he flicked the disc hard right, opposite of the way I was flying. I veered back around, stretched, and gripped the disc by my fingertips just before it struck our keep.

"Yes!" Elliott whooped.

But we had less than a minute to go before the game was over, and Tiberius would win by default.

The kabash burst into azure blue. I had twenty seconds of double damage. I whirled around and darted toward the enemy keep. Two defenders blocked me. I ducked beneath them, then rolled sideways to avoid a freeze ray to my face. Yuri intercepted Devon with a vicious shoulder, and Jenna collided with another defender. I hit top speed, the time counting down in my head. Fifteen seconds of double damage left.

"Edison!" Harris swooped down from overhead and tried to ram me. I dodged sideways. He shouted and flung a freeze spell, but it flew wide.

I crossed the centerline, past the destroyed tower and toward the keep.

"Got you, Edison!" Rhys called from the side.

I looked left in time to see him veering at me, with no time to get out of the way.

A freeze ray zapped Rhys.

"No!" he shouted as his broom screeched to a halt.

"Go, Conrad, go!" Max shouted, holding up his wand.

"Ten seconds of game time left," the announcer said excitedly.

I'd never get in range of their fortress, especially with my weak arm.

Centrifugal force, Vic said. *Use it, you fool.*

Spin! Della shouted.

Still flying full speed forward, I jerked hard left on the broom and went into a flat spin. The world blurred around me. I ducked and went even faster. Holding the kabash underhanded like a discus, I timed the next spin and released it.

The disc whirred, an azure streak leaving my hand.

I stopped my broom's spin and wobbled dizzily. My eyes focused on the disc as it shot across the field. *Will it make it in time?* The countdown continued in my head.

Three, two, one—with a loud crack, the disc struck the opposing fortress for double damage, taking the last two strikes in one hit. The miniature castle exploded in a lightshow of fireworks and crumbled to pieces.

The crowd went wild.

"The Skywraiths win!" boomed the announcer. "Unbelievable comeback by the young Conrad Edison!"

I stared with disbelief. *It actually worked?*

Of course it worked, Vic replied smugly. *It's science.*

Something struck me from behind. Before I could turn around, I was smothered by my teammates, all clapping me on the back and whooping like mad. Max appeared in the mix, face red and excited.

"Greatest play ever, Conrad!" He held up his arm and laughed. "You should have seen the looks on my brothers' faces!"

Elliott shook his head slowly. "I've never seen anyone take a shot like that." He ruffled my hair. "But don't think it excuses you from working out those wimpy arms." He looked at Max. "Nice freeze on your brother too, Tiberius."

Max looked happy enough to faint.

"Edison."

I turned to see Yuri's face pinched into a scowl. It loosened to a grin. "I was wrong. You're going to make an amazing carry some day."

It was the best day of my life.

Chapter 33

The weeks flew by.

If I thought my victory on the field would bring acceptance from Harris and the others, I was sadly mistaken. Instead, our victory against Tiberius only seemed to make him hate me more.

Each day after classes, I went to practice, ate dinner, and four days a week, practiced my spells with Esma Emoora. I settled into a routine that wasn't quite comfortable, but at least made me feel productive.

Mirjana and Klave regained their health, but decided to live in Queens Gate for fear returning to the pond would only leave them open to another attack. I promised to tell her the moment the matter with my parents and Naeve was resolved.

In mid-December, Evadora found us with disturbing news.

"Serena is back," she told me and my friends. "She finished the divining rod."

Ambria groaned. "I hoped she'd given up."

"Did you give her the stone fragment?" I asked.

Evadora nodded. "She tested it, and it works."

I paced on top of our meeting place, the golem head in Colossus Stadium, and thought about what we should do. "Do you think you could get the rod and search for anchor stone fragments?"

"Oh, yes." She nodded enthusiastically. "The rod finds the nearest stone, so the one I gave her is interfering with it." Evadora giggled. "She's quite frustrated about that."

"Have you seen my parents?" I asked.

"They visited her, and she showed them how the rod works." A shrug. "Victus ordered her to let them know the second she finds anything."

Max posed a question. "Do they know you're helping Serena?"

Evadora scraped at the stone with a fingernail. "Probably. But they think I'm just a harmless girl."

"What's the range on the rod?" I asked.

"Hundreds of feet." She held out her arm as if holding a rod. "It tugs on the end when you're close."

I felt the pebble in my pocket. "When would be a good time to borrow it?"

Excitement flashed on Evadora's face. "Any night will do. Serena leaves the Glimmer at night and stays in the city."

"How's she getting in and out of the barrier around the university?" Max asked.

"Conrad's parents have the security charms," she said. "They seem to know when they're changed."

Ambria grimaced. "A lot of good the school's security does."

It was disturbing to know that my parents somehow had access to that information. "I wonder how they do it." Esma told me that she'd informed Galfandor about my parents' presence, so surely, he was taking precautions.

Max blew out a breath. "Probably have someone on the inside."

I thought about our options and finally reached a decision. "Let's do it tomorrow night."

"Wait, a minute," Max said. "You're going back into the Glimmer?"

"Yeah." I looked at my friends. "It's probably best if you stay here."

Ambria shook her head. "No, you can't go back. Surely, Evadora can do it herself."

I put a hand on her shoulder. "It's now or never. I'm going to find a piece of the anchor stone and give it to Naeve before my parents have the chance. We can't wait any longer."

Max ran a hand through his hair. "I hate to admit it, but you're probably right. We don't know if your parents will tell the queen about the stones."

Ambria pressed her lips into a tight line. "I don't like this one bit, but we can't risk letting your parents help Naeve. I don't want the school to be invaded by the Glimmer folk."

I turned to Evadora. "Meet me at the pond in the Fairy Garden tomorrow around eight." I tapped a finger against my chin. "What time does Serena usually leave?"

"Supper time," she replied. "She will be gone by then."

"Good." I stood up and stretched.

"I hope you don't get yourself killed, or worse," Ambria told me. "I'm worried about your reflection catching you."

"I'll take my broom," I said. "I can be in and out of the reflected world in no time."

"We'll wait at the pond for you," Max said. "Just in case."

The tightness in my stomach loosened a little. "I'd like that."

After Evadora left, the three of us made our way back to Moore Keep and went to the common room. Other students were already packing their bags in preparation for the holidays since tomorrow was the last day of classes until the winter semester. Ambria and I planned to go back to the house at the corner of Dowling and Bucket since we had no relatives to go home to. I wondered if Desmond and Sonia would still let us stay there.

There wasn't much work to do in classes the next day since the teachers seemed just as eager to let out for the holidays as the rest of us. Professor Grace didn't bother to sneer at me once, and Professor Sideon completely failed to appear for lessons. Eleanor Beetle showed us a history movie instead of reading from the textbook, and Esma showed us how to make harmless sparkles erupt from our wands just for fun.

The other students seemed excited to be going home to loved ones. Some talked about what gifts they might receive, while others discussed which holiday traditions they enjoyed the most.

Max, Ambria, and I listened wistfully to the hubbub of conversations. It didn't take a mind reader to see my friends wished for normal family lives as much as I did.

With a great cheering roar, students ran into the halls as the final class bell tolled. We flew our brooms to the top of Moore Keep and watched the crowds dwindle as parents picked up their loved ones and went merrily on their way.

"Must be nice," Max said with a sigh. "My parents don't believe in holiday traditions."

"At least you have parents," Ambria said. "I'm curious to meet them and see if they're really all that bad."

Max snorted. "Don't press your luck. I might actually invite you over for supper."

"At least they're not bent on world domination," I said.

He looked at me seriously. "For all we know your parents have already contacted mine. I'm sure my father will be happy to help them."

The dining hall was still open, so we left our brooms in the keep and went for a bite. Aside from a smattering of students, the place looked nearly empty. I spotted Galfandor eating at the head table.

"I'm going to talk to the headmaster and let him know what we're doing tonight," I told the others.

Ambria looked relieved. "I think that would be smart. Perhaps he can help."

"Sure would be nice having someone powerful on our side." Max glanced nervously toward the head table. "Um, we'll wait here."

I got up and walked over to the head table.

Galfandor greeted me with a smile. "Hello, Conrad."

"Hello, sir."

"You look troubled." He dabbed at his face with a napkin and set his empty plate aside for a serving golem to take.

I cut straight to the point. "It's my parents."

"Ah, yes. Professor Emoora told me you had concerns about their presence here on campus." Galfandor motioned me closer. "If they are, they've certainly done nothing to arouse suspicions."

"Evadora says they have the security charms, even when they're changed."

"Yes, I assumed as much." He leaned forward. "Despite outward appearances, I have tightened security, even going so far as to employ outside contractors. If they show themselves, we'll be ready."

The knot of stress building steadily in my chest over the past few months relaxed ever so slightly. I'd feared Galfandor was content to sit back and see what happened before acting. At times it seemed as though he didn't believe my parents were alive and well, but if he was telling the truth, I wasn't as alone as I'd feared.

I managed a smile. "Thank you, sir."

"Of course, Conrad." His eyes narrowed. "I sense there is more you want to tell me."

"It's about the immorality my parents want." I stepped around the table so I wouldn't have to speak across it and showed him the stone. "Mirjana, the Lady of the Pond, told me all they need is a piece of the anchor stone."

Galfandor regarded the stone for a long moment, his eyes betraying a sense of uncertainty. "Have they found any pieces?"

I shook my head. "Serena made a divining rod to help them locate stones, but I'm going to the Glimmer with Evadora tonight to make sure they don't."

He stroked his beard. "Is this not the stone Cora had?" His eyes softened. "She died, Conrad."

"My curse killed her." I pocketed the pebble. "Mirjana said you can still die even with a piece of the anchor stone, but that larger pieces might make someone harder or even impossible to kill."

Galfandor sat back. "In that case, *we* must prevent them from finding pieces of the stone. When are you going to the Glimmer?"

My heart went light as a feather. "You'll help us?"

He nodded.

"We're meeting Evadora at the pond at eight."

"I will meet you there." He looked around the room. "I think it better if you tell me everything else later." Galfandor smiled and patted my shoulder. "I will see you then."

It took all my willpower not to skip back to the table. I sat down with the others and finally allowed myself to grin. "He's going to help us!" I held out my hand to stop my friends from cheering. "Let's go get ready."

The moment we were out in the hall, Ambria hugged me and jumped up and down. "We're saved!"

Max clapped me on the back. "I don't know what you said to him, but I think we might just pull this off."

I could hardly believe Galfandor was going to directly help us. I didn't expect him to come to the Glimmer, but with him standing watch with my friends, I knew he could keep us safe.

The last rays of the sun painted the stumps of the dead forest red when we arrived at the pond in the Fairy Garden. Galfandor waited there already, dressed in dark robes and a stocking cap that kept his long white hair under control. Leaning on the ivory-colored handle of a broom, he looked up and waved as we approached.

"I can't tell you how grateful we are for your help," Ambria said when we landed.

He smiled and nodded at her. "I spoke with Mirjana and she confirmed what Conrad told me." The headmaster looked at the dark water. "She is eager for this to end so she can safely return home."

"Believe me, we're just as excited to end this, too," Ambria said.

Galfandor turned to me. "Tell me anything else I should know, Conrad."

I told him what had happened since my last visit to his house, which really wasn't all that much, since Serena had been gone for two months in search of whatever special ingredients she needed for the divining rod. "Our fear is that my parents will tell Naeve that the anchor stone pieces will give her immortality even outside the Glimmer. The queen promised she wouldn't help my parents if I helped her first."

"You propose to tell Naeve about the stones," Galfandor said. "Perhaps we should bind her with an oath to do no harm to Eden before we impart this information, and also ask her to forbid your parents from returning to the Glimmer."

"I sure am glad you're helping us," Max said. "I never would've thought of that."

Galfandor's statement hit me like an electric shock. Asking the queen for an oath had never occurred to me. I'd simply accepted that she wouldn't help my parents. But that wouldn't stop her from attacking Eden herself. After all, her price for allowing Victus and Delectra to even help her had been to murder Mirjana, Klave, and the other guardians in the Fairy Garden.

"How can we be certain she'll keep her oath?" I asked.

"It will be a magical oath. If she breaks it, the backlash will kill her." Galfandor shook his head slowly. "It is a good thing you informed me of this."

"Does that mean you're coming with me?" I asked.

"Yes, I believe it would be best."

My shoulders sagged with relief. I looked at the time on my phone. "Evadora is running late." Then again, she rarely showed up right on time and often came a little earlier or later than expected.

"Will she come from the reflected world?" Galfandor asked.

I shook my head. "She doesn't have a stone, so she runs through the rift past the guardians."

His bushy eyebrows lifted. "I see. She must be quick on her feet."

"She's a bit mental, but she knows how to trick them." Ambria twirled a finger around her ear. "One look at those frightening creatures convinced me to never go back if they're around."

Another ten minutes ticked past while I shifted anxiously from foot to foot. "Maybe we can go meet her on the other side." I took out the pebble. "It'll save time."

"Agreed." Galfandor took my hand. "Ready when you are, Conrad."

I said the magic words and we leapt into the pond. When we burst from the water on the other side, Galfandor landed easily on his feet and pulled on my hand to keep me from tumbling to the ground. We hurriedly boarded our brooms and flew to the crack in the world. I wondered if right now in the real world Evadora might be walking past this spot. I hoped we caught her before she entered the rift.

We reached the tunnel and got off our brooms so we could crawl through. When we finally reached the starry rift, we used our brooms once again.

Galfandor gazed at the infinite expanse of stars all around. "Rather unsettling, isn't it?"

"We're on an invisible bridge," I explained. "Max nearly fell off the side."

He grunted thoughtfully, but said nothing more. Despite our speedy travel through the reflected world, my back crawled as though something evil stalked me. I looked back often, but didn't see my reflection racing behind. Wherever it was, I knew right this moment it had homed in on me like a divining rod and was running straight at me.

Creepy as it was, I wondered what the thing did in its spare time when I wasn't looking into something reflective. For that matter, where were all the other reflections? Did they even exist when we weren't looking at our mirror image?

Galfandor as usual seemed to know what I was thinking. "There are some things that bend and twist logic so completely, understanding them means you must become as bent and twisted as they are."

I looked behind me again. "Sometimes I feel as though I'm already there."

He chuckled. "Indeed, lad, I know what you mean."

When we reached the pond in the reflected version of the Glimmer, I took us back through the water to the other side. We landed in the glade of purple grass. The gooseflesh on my back finally relaxed. I was in another world every bit as strange as the mirror world, but at least something wasn't chasing me.

As before—as it had always been since the anchoring—the huge moon hung above crooked Moon Mountain far in the distance while the realms rotated slowly all around it. The stars glimmered above and below, a blanket of endless space in a realm long forgotten.

We were back in the Glimmer, but Evadora was nowhere to be seen.

Chapter 34

I glanced at the crack into the rift. "Maybe I should go to the end and see if Evadora is inside."

Galfandor frowned. "Let's give her ten minutes. If she's already gone through, I'm sure she'll be back quickly once your friends tell her where we are." He motioned toward Moon Mountain. "Naeve's castle is up there?"

"Yes." I climbed on my broom and went higher for a better view above the spiky trees until I could see the edge of this island hovering over the magnificent and terrifying view of the galaxy. "I wonder if we can fly straight for the mountain, or if we need to follow the bridges."

Galfandor joined me. "An excellent question." He plucked a large twig from the top of a tree and cast a series of spells on it. When he finally released it, the twig hung in the air, both tips blinking red like airplane lights. "I've given it a simple version of a flying broom enchantment. Let's see what happens." He flicked his wand, and the twig flew off on its merry way.

It continued out from the island and across open space until it reached the next island over.

"How intriguing." He looked out at the stars. "I've seen many wonders, but this realm breaks every rule."

"The Sirens tore it apart but it still survived." I stared at the moon. "How much power do you think it took to create the anchor stone?"

"More than I can comprehend," Galfandor replied. He withdrew a pocket watch from his robes and checked it. "I believe we've waited long enough. Since we can fly straight for the mountain, perhaps we should take the most direct route."

"Maybe we should fly along the route Evadora took us." I pointed to the nearest tree bridge. "It might take us a little longer, but at least we'll see her if she passes by."

He nodded. "Yes, I suppose we'll need her help finding the divining rod."

We continued along, following the zig-zag path from island to bridge to island, flying across purple meadows, through dim tunnels formed by spiky tree branches, all the while keeping a sharp eye out for Evadora. I began to worry that we'd just missed her back at the tunnel and even now she was running to catch up with us.

Galfandor commented on the strange beasts we saw, pausing for a moment when we passed by a herd of the carnivorous miniature ponies. "Goodness, I didn't know equinothropes still existed. I thought they went extinct centuries ago."

"Those things existed in Eden?" I shuddered as one of the tiny horses ripped into the flesh of one of the snake elephants.

"Indeed. I imagine this realm holds a bevy of beasts that used to exist in Eden." He pursed his lips and stared. "Surely—no." He shook his head.

"No to what?"

"This place would provide your father with the capability to create mutants beyond his wildest dreams." Galfandor shivered. "Another reason we must deny your parents access to this realm."

If my father had created the frogres from harmless creatures, I couldn't imagine what he might create with equinothropes.

Galfandor continued onward. "Where do the people live? I see no signs of houses, no smoke rising from chimneys, or people out and about doing their daily business."

I looked down as a herd of kangaroo-like creatures with antlers hopped across the field below. "The queen told us most of them live on the other side of the mountain where the land isn't as broken."

He peered into the distance. "I would be most curious to meet them."

We finally reached the base of the mountain. "It's probably faster to take the invisible lift."

Galfandor looked up the sheer cliff face and nodded slowly. "I'll take your word for it."

I went to the place Evadora had taken us the last time and motioned the headmaster next to me. It took a few tries, but I finally flicked the correct place on the stone to activate the lift and we shot up at frightening speed. Galfandor's long beard whipped wildly in the wind, but he seemed not to notice, instead looking at the unbroken land beyond the mountain.

"Tell me if you see any houses, Conrad." He took a brass spyglass from a pouch and handed it to me.

I scanned the land and finally noticed what looked like a small town beyond a thick forest. "Over there." I handed him the spyglass.

He peered through the scope. "It is indeed a town, but I see no activity."

"Why are you so curious about it?" I asked.

Galfandor folded up the spyglass and tucked it away. "I'd simply like to know more about this place, especially if the queen has an army."

"I don't remember seeing anyone but the queen and Evadora," I said just as the lift reached the top.

Wands in hand, we stepped off the invisible platform and onto the terrace. The vine chair the queen had grown during my last visit was flowering into large round bulbs. I stepped closer to inspect one when the petals burst open and spat. I hardly even had a chance to think before flicking my wand and casting *soros*. Thick green liquid splatted against the invisible shield.

Galfandor looked surprised. "Impressive. I see you've learned well your first semester."

I gulped at the close call. "Professor Emoora has been tutoring me."

My shield dissipated and the green liquid dripped to the ground. "What is that stuff?"

The headmaster produced a vial from his pouch and scooped a sample inside. "I don't know, but it's certainly quite curious."

"Should we use a spell to hide us from the queen?" I asked. "I don't know what she would do if she finds us here."

"I'll tell her we've come across a possible solution for her problem, and ask her to take the oath," Galfandor said. "I don't believe Serena would have told her about the anchor stone fragments."

His plan sounded good so I nodded and followed him toward the entrance to the palace.

We kept a safe distance from the vines as we made our way along the terrace and went through an archway into the mountain. This first room made our jaws drop in wonder. Stretching in a dome far overhead, the ceiling glittered with diamonds, rubies, and other precious stones. The floor and walls were natural stone polished to a sheen, all its natural hues swirling around us like clouds in a nebula.

A ramp of polished jade led up to a throne of thorny black vines.

"Interesting," Galfandor said. "Quite a throne room."

I looked around and realized it there was no other furniture. The light seemed to come from the jewels in the ceiling. I noticed an opening in the wall to the right. "There's a door over there."

"Indeed." He headed toward the archway.

I followed behind, wary of this strange place, hoping the vines didn't come to life and snake toward us. *Evadora, where are you?* I desperately wished she was here to guide us.

A long corridor led to a large room with a single staircase winding along the curved wall to the next level, and then continuing up on the other side to the next level, and so on until I lost count of the floors. What furniture was there looked dusty and unused—a marble table covered in gray webs, a leather chair cracked and worn, bare and rotting rugs. A faded painting of Naeve surrounded by people dressed in rich attire hung on the far wall.

"This entire place seems to have fallen into disuse," Galfandor said. He looked down and pointed to footprints in the dust leading toward a small door beneath the large staircase. "I believe that is the way to go."

We took the stairs down to a long corridor lined with doors. The first room on the right looked like it had once been a bedroom, though the bedding had rotted away to almost nothing. Across the hall, the room had been converted into a small workshop. A crooked branch of silvery wood sat atop a workbench.

Galfandor gasped. "Is that silverwood?" He reached a finger toward it then jerked it back. "I have not seen a specimen of this in ages. It is no wonder it took Serena so long to procure what she needed." He turned to a polished rod sitting next to the branch. "The divining rod, I presume."

I reached out to touch it, but he gripped my wrist. "Not so fast, Conrad." Galfandor opened his pouch and withdrew a pinch of gray dust. Holding his hand over the workbench, he slowly sprinkled it from one end to the other. As the dust fell it revealed shimmering lines in the air around the table.

"Warded, of course." He took my shoulder and stepped back. "Shield your eyes, Conrad."

I did as told, but peeked just a little, curious to see what he did. A brilliant flash temporarily blinded me. I squeezed my eyes shut and blinked a few times.

Galfandor chuckled. "I told you to shield your eyes." He picked up the divining rod. The moment he did, it pointed toward me. "Ah, yes. Your pebble is interfering." He set down the rod, removed a shiny packet from within his pouch, and opened it. "This diamond fiber should block the pebble from the divining rod's detection spell."

I took the packet from him. "Why won't it be able to detect it?"

"Diamond fiber repels magic." Galfandor took the remaining branch of silverwood and strapped it across his back. "Unfortunately, neutralizing Serena's ward most likely alerted her to our presence."

I put the pebble into the diamond fiber packet and tucked it in my pocket. "Without the silverwood, she won't be able to make another rod, though, right?"

"Provided this is all of it," he said, and picked up the rod. It tugged his hand up. "Interesting. It has already detected another fragment of the anchor stone."

I frowned. "Maybe it's the piece I gave to Evadora."

"We'll need to put hers in the diamond fiber pouch with yours so it doesn't interfere with our hunt for bigger game," Galfandor said. "I believe our search will go faster with her help."

Back up the stairs, the divining rod led us up the snaking staircase instead of back toward the terrace. We followed its pull, winding our way up nearly twenty staircases.

Panting from the exertion of climbing so many stairs, I said, "I wonder what Evadora is doing up here."

"I'm not certain." Galfandor leaned over the balustrade and looked up. "We're nearly to the top." He climbed on his broom. "Perhaps it would be better to fly."

He got no argument from me. I climbed on my broom and went out over the railing. The divining rod pointed nearly straight up, so we drifted in that direction until it leveled out, pointing to the only door on the top floor. We got off our brooms on the landing. Galfandor set his broom and rod against the wall and peeked into the entrance.

He stiffened at whatever he saw.

"Come," said an emotionless voice.

The headmaster straightened and entered. "Greetings, Queen Naeve."

"Come, boy," she said. "I know you are out there."

Taking a deep breath, I followed the headmaster inside. Shaped like a large pinecone, the walls of the room sloped inward, ending at a wide hole at the top. Spiky black vines ran across nearly every inch of the walls, across the floor and thrusting upward into a throne nearly ten feet high. A beam of moonlight shined down through the opening and onto the lone occupant of that high seat: The Glimmer Queen.

I knew she wasn't Cora, but it was still like seeing a ghost.

The headmaster bowed and flourished his cap. "I am Galfandor, headmaster of Arcane University. It is an honor to meet you, Queen Naeve."

Naeve looked down at us with unblinking eyes for a moment. Finally, she spoke. "What brings you to my private chambers?"

"Conrad informed me of his agreement with you about your wish for immortality outside the Glimmer." Galfandor folded his arms across his chest. "I thought I would help him in his quest."

The throne sank slowly toward the floor, the vines receding along the floor and walls with the crack and scrape of rough, thorny wood.

The queen stood. "What is the price for your help, Headmaster Galfandor?"

"That you swear a magical oath to never attack Eden, and you ban Victus and Delectra Edison and any of their associates from the Glimmer."

"This is because they seek immortality," Naeve said. "They never intended to seek my help invading Eden, but to use my accommodations to ease their search."

My breath quickened and a ball of ice formed in my stomach.

Galfandor's eye twitched, but he simply nodded. "I'm afraid so. We, however, will help you, so long as you take the oath."

Naeve blinked. "Is that so?" She turned and walked toward the back wall. "This is one situation where emotions would benefit me."

"Emotions can be helpful, or harmful," Galfandor said. "I imagine after a seeming eternity of void, it will take some getting used to. I believe it would be easiest to ease into the experience so it doesn't overwhelm you."

"Perhaps." Naeve flicked a finger and the vines on the far wall parted, revealing a small girl bound to the stone. Eyes wide and full of terror, she wriggled, but the vines held her fast and covered her mouth. Another section of vines parted, revealing Serena. The woman blinked as if awakening and instantly looked just as frightened as Evadora, but was also prevented from speaking by vines.

"Evadora!" I cried. "What have you done to her?"

Galfandor took a step back. "What is the meaning of this, Naeve?"

The queen stared blankly at us. "Since I cannot fully appreciate this moment without emotions, I believe my long wait has ended." She plucked the bottle of tears from Evadora's waist and uncorked it.

"Please, no," Evadora cried out. "Not my tears!"

"Why did you tie up Evadora?" I asked. "What did she do?" I didn't bother asking about Serena, but the queen had probably interrogated them both. That was how she knew what my parents wanted.

"The girl finally told me the truth," the queen said. Another flick of her finger and a mound of vines pulled away from a rough green rock the size of my head—an anchor stone fragment. "You withheld the truth about the anchor stone, child. Like your parents, you sought advantage over me."

"No, it wasn't like that," I said in a pleading tone. "We couldn't find any anchor stone fragments. I wanted her to find one for you before we said anything."

"Where do you think your fragment of anchor stone came from?" Naeve said. "This is only a fragment of a larger deposit Cora discovered long ago." She waved a hand and the vine around Serena's mouth came free. "Tell me, witch, by your calculations, how much anchor stone is needed for true immortality?"

"Queen Naeve, I assure you I had every intention of coming to you with my findings," Serena said. "I—" She made an awful choking sound as a vine wrapped tight around her throat.

"I see through your skin, witch." Naeve's cold gaze remained upon us. "Do not make me chew your bones."

Serena's eyes widened. The vine pulled away, and this time she didn't try pleading with the queen. "By my calculations, you have enough anchor stone to be invulnerable so long as you spend at least six hours a day within close proximity of it."

Galfandor raised an eyebrow. "Are you saying anyone who spent that much time near it would be indestructible?"

"Yes, but it would take some months for anyone not already exposed to reach that level." Serena's eyes grew pleading. "I would dearly love to explore—"

The vine covered her mouth once again.

"It seems everyone except for me knew the truth of the anchor stone," Naeve said in a deadly quiet voice. "The truth was hidden from me by Cora's death, but now I know she died because her small fragment was not enough to make her invulnerable."

"We didn't know for sure," I said. "Please let Evadora go."

Naeve ignored my plea. "I am curious what emotions I should be feeling right now." She looked at Evadora's bottle. "I believe it is time to find out." Naeve put the bottle to her lips and drank deeply. The bottle shifted from red to blue and through a dozen other hues as she gulped greedily.

I had no doubts what the queen would feel first.

Rage.

Chapter 35

The ice in my stomach ran through my veins. "I don't think we're going to like what she feels, sir."

Galfandor shook his head. "I believe you're right." He stared at the anchor stone across the room and said in a low voice, "The advantage is hers, Conrad. Be prepared to flee."

I looked down at the vines beneath my feet. "What if she traps us?"

He held his wand by his side. "I will do what I can."

"What about Evadora?"

Galfandor shook his head slowly. "I don't know."

Serena and Evadora writhed against the vines, all to no avail.

Naeve dropped the bottle. It clattered against the floor. Shivers ran through her body, growing more violent with each second.

"Conrad, go now." Galfandor flicked his wand toward Evadora. The vines around her wrists and legs splintered and she tumbled to the floor. "Run, child!" He glanced at Serena, but didn't free her.

Evadora sprinted to the anchor stone and managed to lift it.

"Forget the stone," I said. "Run!"

She dropped it and raced toward us as Naeve fell to the floor gibbering and shaking. Serena's eyes bulged. Galfandor sighed and blasted the vines around Serena's arms and legs, then stared at the queen. "Forgive me, but I cannot let Naeve live."

"The emotions will make her crazy," Evadora said.

"You can't kill her, you imbecile!" Serena shouted. She dug a broom from beneath a pile of vines and hopped onto it. "Flee while you can!" With that, she soared out of the hole in the top of the room.

The headmaster didn't listen. Galfandor whirled his wand, gathering a nebula of white energy above it, then flung it toward the queen.

Naeve screamed and threw up her hand. The killing blow seared her skin, turning it bright red. Before I could blink, the blistered skin healed. Vines pulled Naeve to her feet like strings on a puppet. "You dare to strike down the immortal Glimmer Queen?" She reared back her head and laughed. "You cannot kill me here, wizard. Here beneath the moon, I am eternal."

"I prefer the term Arcane," Galfandor said, backing toward the door and motioning me out. "In any case, I do hope you enjoy your emotions." He thrust his wand at the floor beneath his feet. The vines there withered to ash. Galfandor pushed me through the door and into the hallway. "Get your broom, Conrad."

Naeve screeched at the top of her lungs. "You cannot escape me in my realm, wizard."

Galfandor waved his wand at Evadora. "I put a weight reduction spell on the girl so you can both fly on your broom."

I moved forward in the seat. "Get on!" I told her.

She leapt up behind me and wrapped her arms around my torso. "Go, go, go!"

Vines burst from the doorway like tentacles on an enraged octopus just as Galfandor and I dove our brooms off the ledge and toward the floor far below. At the last minute, I pulled out of the dive, flying straight and true through the archway. We swept through the throne room and out onto the terrace a split second before swarming vines blocked the exit.

Shrieks echoed from far above. I looked up and saw Naeve riding a wave of vines down the peak of the mountain. A huge bird swept in beneath the queen. She perched on its back and speared a finger toward us.

My heart nearly stopped.

"Keep going, boy!" Galfandor shouted as he flung spells toward the pursuing queen.

We flew straight for the closest empty expanse between islands. From here it was difficult to know which island had the pond we'd used to get into the Glimmer. I hoped Galfandor knew.

As we raced across the next island, the mewling of an enraged feline echoed through the land.

"The queen is calling the mewlers," Evadora said. "Watch out!"

Before I had time to process what she'd said, a black cloud rose from the trees in front of us and swarmed our way. I remembered Evadora's story of the bat-like cats devouring one of the small ponies and imagined them rending us down to bones before we even hit the ground.

"Behind me, Conrad!" Galfandor shouted.

I did as instructed and readied my wand, though I had no idea what spell to cast.

The headmaster cried out and the tip of his wand glowed brilliant white. The light pulsed brighter and brighter into a crackling sphere. Just as the dark vortex of mewlers funneled at him, he unleashed a cascading wave of blinding energy. With a great chorus of screeches, the cloud parted before us and we flew through a narrow tunnel of claws and fangs, scratching and biting at my arms and head. I ducked lower to avoid losing my eyes to the feral creatures.

Evadora shrieked and I felt her bury her face in my back. Finally, we burst into clear air. I looked back and saw the swarm twisting our way. A tree branch suddenly snapped up, grasping at my leg. I pulled up, narrowly avoiding it.

"She's got everything after us," I shouted above the din of creaking wood and snapping limbs in the now living and moving forest below.

"Over there," Galfandor shouted above the noise.

I saw the island with the pond and headed for it.

"Ready the pebble, Conrad," Galfandor shouted over his shoulder.

I couldn't dig in my pocket easily from my seated position while maintaining control of the broom. "Can you get it from my right pocket, Evadora?"

She furrowed her hand inside and I straightened my leg the best I could to help her. "Got it!"

We swooped into the glade and hopped off our brooms. Already, the trees here began to creak and come to life, branches thrashing, roots tearing from the ground. I snatched the diamond fiber pouch from Evadora and took out the pebble.

Galfandor grabbed my hand, and stretched out the other to Evadora. She took it as I fumbled to hold my broom under one arm. A tree swiped at us and thundered forward.

"As above, so below!" I shouted. We leapt. Another limb whooshed over my head the instant we hit the surface of the pond.

We sprang from the other side into the reflected world.

"Hurry," Galfandor said, releasing our hands and heading into the crack to the rift.

"Did the queen have a piece of that huge stone?" I asked Evadora.

She frowned. "I don't know. Everything happened so fast."

"Let's assume she does and make haste," Galfandor said, boarding his broom and flying across the starry rift to the other side.

Evadora and I followed on my broom then hopped off to follow the headmaster into the tunnel on the other side. After quickly crawling through the tunnel and emerging from the trees next to the ruined mansion, we once again flew to the pond.

Galfandor cocked an ear as we prepared to make the next leap. "I don't hear anything, so hopefully we're in the clear."

The moment he said it, a keening wail echoed eerily across the land. "Betrayal!" Naeve screamed. "Never have I felt such delicious pain!"

Evadora's eyes flared. "She's gone insane with emotions."

"Is she crawling through the tunnel?" I asked.

"She'd have no choice," Galfandor said. He reached out his hands. "Quickly, through the water, Conrad."

I gripped his hand, said the words in reverse, and we leapt through.

Max and Ambria yelled and leapt back in surprise when we flew from the pond and onto land.

"You scared me half to death." Max wiped his forehead. "How did it go?"

Ambria noticed the fear on my face. "Oh dear, what happened?"

"Fly, children, fly!" Galfandor said. "The Glimmer Queen is on our heels!"

"What?" Ambria leapt on her broom.

"Where do we go?" I asked.

"To Moore Manor." The headmaster mounted his broom. "Perhaps my wards there will stop her."

Once again, we flew for our lives.

Galfandor slowed as we neared the manor and pointed to the woods around it. "I don't know if Naeve has power over the trees here, but the manor may not be the safest place after all." He pointed to the peaks of Moore Keep down the rise from us. "Come!"

We hadn't gone far when the shriek of metal and crash of wood jerked my attention behind us. A wave of vines burst over the iron fences of the Fairy Garden and swept our way.

Max nearly fell off his broom. "She's chasing us with plants?"

Galfandor didn't answer, but angled his broom up to a high window in the central tower of the keep. We followed him inside, landing on the spiral staircase, then looked outside for the queen. Seconds later, the wave of vines reached the base of the keep. The queen stepped from the vines and stood on the walkway next to the wishing pool.

"What if she sends the vines inside?" I asked.

Galfandor took out a short but thick rod and snapped it out into a full-length staff. "I will fight her to the best of my abilities."

"Do not expect your buildings to protect you," Naeve shouted. "What good is stone against the power of nature?" She thrust her hands into the air, and suddenly trees from the nearby forest uprooted themselves and lumbered over to the keep. Thick branches pounded against the doors.

A group of children walking down the path from the university toward the keeps abruptly burst into screams and shouts when they saw the trees. Naeve turned toward them, and my heart stopped with fear. The rage contorting her face ripped away her resemblance to my dear Cora. This woman was bent by madness and evil. I had to stop her.

The headmaster hopped on his broom and dove toward the queen, a bright blast of light already leaving his staff.

"I've got to help," I said, jumping on my broom and flying out the window before the others could stop me. I took out my wand and aimed it at the queen. The only offensive spell I could easily cast was also not a powerful one, but I had to do what I could.

Galfandor's first strike splintered a twisting mass of vines as they snaked toward the other children. I used the diversion to hit the queen with a spell.

"*Ignitus*!" Fire flickered at the tip of Naeve's hair.

She screeched and quickly doused the flame before it could do more than singe her. A vine whipped from the side. I rolled left and looped. The creeper tied itself in a knot trying to catch me. Another coil attacked. I dodged it, but ran right into the grasp of another. Before I could react, it plucked me out of the air and whipped me toward the queen.

Though my arms were pinned, I kept my legs wrapped tightly around the broom. I looked to Galfandor for help, but he was busy fending off two large spruce trees whipping their branches at the other children.

The vine brought me face-to-face with the queen's leering face. Insanity shone in her eyes, and her lips trembled with unbridled emotions. Around her neck she wore a chain with a large green anchor stone fragment.

"I have waited too long," she hissed. "Finally, I am *alive*!"

"I promise I wasn't trying to trick you." I tried to wriggle free, but the vine wrapped painfully tight around my arms. "I had to find a piece of the anchor stone first."

Naeve giggled like a little girl, then clenched her teeth in a spasm of anger. She pressed a hand to her chest. "The other part of my soul still loves you, child—still wants you to live." Her eyes flared. "But me, the part that counts, knows you should die. This place will become mine. Then I will decide where to go next." She looked away. "Do I kill the Sirens? Yes, that would be wise and oh, so fulfilling." She burst into deep-throated laughter, then abruptly rambled incoherently for a moment. As if suddenly realizing I was still there, she blinked in surprise. "Why are you still alive?"

"What about the part of you that loves me?" I shouted, not understanding how any part of her could love me since she'd never had emotions before.

Naeve bit her lower lip hard. Blood trickled down her chin. "Cora is in me now." She burst into a fit of laughter and suddenly began to cry.

"Your sister is in you?" I didn't understand. "You love me because of her?"

"Sister?" the queen's lips curled up, then down, as if they didn't know which way to go. "I have no sister."

I heard shouts and saw Galfandor shielding the other students as a tall pine toppled toward them. I forced my attention back to Naeve, realizing I would have to keep her talking to stay alive long enough for the headmaster to come to my aid.

"Because she's dead," I said. "Your sister is dead."

Naeve shook her head. "Cora wanted to leave the Glimmer. She discovered how the anchor stone could take her into the reflected world. From there she safely crossed the rift." Her eyes grew unfocused. "On her third time through, I caught her." A manic smile lit the queen's face. "I caught Queen Naeve."

My mind whirled and tumbled as I realized the terrible truth.

Chapter 36

"Cora is actually Naeve," I said in a harsh whisper. "You were her reflection."

The queen waved her arm and three more trees uprooted themselves and charged Galfandor as he and the other students retreated. She turned back to me. "Yes. I caught her and took part of her soul. When she tried to escape, she took me back with her to the Glimmer."

I suddenly understood what she meant about part of her loving me. "When Cora died, did the rest of her soul come to you?"

"For a time, I felt everything she had, but the Glimmer drained it from me." The queen's eyes widened. "Cora had to keep her travels to Eden a secret. She convinced me to stand in for her while she was gone so her people wouldn't know."

"What people?" I asked. "I never saw anyone else there but you and Evadora."

"They sleep," the queen replied. "I found them unnecessary and burdensome." The insanity faded from her voice, though a twitch in her eye hinted at madness beneath the surface.

"Why did you let Evadora stay awake?" I asked.

"The girl did not bother me." Her unsettling eyes regarded me. "Before I put the people to sleep, before I realized my powers, I posed as the queen and took people into Eden using a piece of the anchor stone. I left them there and visited to see if they remained unchanged, or died."

"But only Cora lived on since she had a piece of the stone," I said.

"Indeed." Naeve's eyes twitched, but the attacks from her tree minions against Galfandor did not relent.

"I soon realized my true powers and no longer needed Cora. I banished her from the Glimmer and put the Glimmer folk to sleep. For centuries, Cora lived in Eden with her fragment of the anchor stone, and I thought it was the answer to immortality. Only once did I let Cora return, and that was for her to leave Evadora with me. Her long time away from the Glimmer had weakened her powers significantly."

Keep her talking. "Who was Evadora's father?"

"A worthless mortal." The queen's lips curled in disgust. "Not long after, Cora found you and died. Though I was pleased to have an entire soul to myself, the new flood of emotions made me realize how terribly sad I was that the anchor stone fragments did not grant immortality."

"It was my curse that killed her," I said. "If she'd had a larger piece of the anchor stone, she might have survived." I looked toward Galfandor and saw the two spruces were down—only a large pine, badly burnt and smoking, remained standing.

"You killed Queen Naeve with your curse. Now I am Queen Naeve. Now I am real." The queen smiled. "And now, I will kill you."

The vines squeezed tighter and tighter until I could hardly breathe. I tried to speak, but the world began to fade away.

Without warning, the vine went slack. I tumbled to the ground and landed next to my broom. I shook my head, trying to register what had happened and saw Esma Emoora twisting her wand and firing bolts of sizzling electricity at the queen.

Naeve shrieked and hurled a wave of snaking vines toward the professor. Esma chanted and a shimmering shield absorbed the attack.

"Run, Conrad!" Esma shouted. "I can't hold her off forever!"

I tried to run, but a vine wrapped around my ankle and jerked me off my feet. I flailed with my wand and shouted, "*Torsius!*"

The spell slammed the queen and knocked her to the ground.

"Die, you worthless betrayer!" Naeve flung her arm toward me and a swarm of spiky black vines rushed for my face.

For a heartbeat, I imagined them rending me to ground meat, but a blue bolt of ice hit Naeve in the chest and froze her in place. The vines fell lifelessly to the ground and I thudded next to them.

Max zipped past on his broom. "I used a freeze wand on her!" He waved two blue wands—the ones we used in Kabash. "Get out of there, I only have one charge left!"

Still dizzy from the fall, I stumbled upright just as the queen thawed.

"Stop standing there!" Max shouted. He flicked the other blue wand and froze the queen before she could block the spell. "You've got ten seconds, Conrad! Run!"

Esma wriggled free of the vines that had fallen all around her and shouted, "There is nowhere to run, Conrad. Sometimes you have to face your enemies and finish them."

The queen was completely helpless for several more seconds, but what could I do to her? I didn't know any spells that would disable or kill her.

The anchor stone fragment on the fine chain around her neck caught my eye, and behind her, the sparkling waters of the wishing pool. Suddenly, I knew what to do. I ran to the queen, gripped the stone at her neck, and jerked hard. The necklace snapped free. I backed up several feet, gripping the stone and shouting, "As above, so below!" Then I raced at the queen and slammed into her. We fell toward the rippling water.

An instant later, we flew from the pool on the other side and landed hard on the cobblestones in the reflected world. I rolled off the queen just as she thawed.

"Give me the stone, boy!" She lunged for me.

I ran around the pool, the queen chasing me in a deadly game of keep away.

"As below, so above," I panted.

"No!" the queen screamed. "Give me the stone!"

She lunged toward me, running through the shallow pool. I leapt into the water as she dove the final feet toward me, red-faced and screaming. Her fingers missed me by inches. I flew from the other side, back in the normal world and tumbled to the cobblestones. For once, I welcomed the pain. It meant I was still alive to feel it. I pushed up and looked into the pool. My normal reflection stared back. Staring up at me from the middle of the pool, the fake Queen Naeve knelt on all fours, her mouth open in a silent scream, fists pounding the water.

The glimpse into the reflected world faded away and the queen with it.

Esma looked at me from across the pool. "I believe the queen would have preferred death to such a fate." She tilted her head slightly and looked at me. "You are young and inexperienced, but you have potential, child."

"Thank you, professor," I told her. "You saved my life."

She nodded. "Perhaps one day you will save mine." Esma glanced back toward the university. "I should go check on the other students to make sure they escaped unharmed." She tucked her wand into a holster at her side and walked away.

Max landed his broom next to me. Evadora and Ambria ran from the keep doors a moment later.

"Whoa, did you trap her in the reflected world?" Max leaned over the edge and stared into the water.

I sat down as the weight of what had happened dropped onto my shoulders. "If you hadn't frozen her when you did, I'd be mincemeat."

"Are you just going to leave her in there?" Ambria shuddered. "What if her reflection gets her?"

Galfandor flew back into view and looked at the piles of lifeless vines and fallen trees. He spotted us and approached. "Esma said you handled things." His eyes wandered the ground as if looking for a body. "What happened?"

I still hardly believed what Naeve told me. No matter the truth, Cora would always be Cora to me, and Naeve, the queen with a heart of ice.

Max put a hand on my shoulder. "I saw her talking to you when she had you earlier, Conrad. What was she saying?"

"Cora had no sister." I squeezed shut my eyes and tried to untangle the lies. "Cora was the real Naeve. She went through the reflected world to Eden, but her reflection caught her and took a piece of her soul." The thought sent shivers through me.

"The queen was a reflection?" Evadora stared at me. "She looked so real, Conrad. But I told you she was dead inside."

Ambria looked at Galfandor. "Did the piece of Cora's soul make her real?"

The headmaster looked up from the waters, his eyes pensive. "What makes any of us real, Miss Rax?" He shook his head slowly.

297

"All I can say with certainty is that I must go back into the Glimmer and secure the other anchor stone fragments in the palace, and hide the silverwood so Serena cannot build another divining rod."

"What about the Glimmer folk?" I asked. "Naeve said she put them to sleep."

"She put up a wall of vines to keep me from going to the lands north of the mountain," Evadora said. "They are probably there."

"Maybe her spell will wear off now that she's gone." Ambria knelt and touched one of the vines. "I wonder how long they've been asleep."

"Centuries," I said. "Naeve said Cora lived in Eden for hundreds of years until she met me and died." At least now I understood why Cora avoided mirrors. Was she afraid she had no more reflection, or was it a reminder of what she'd unleashed on her people?

Galfandor stroked his beard. "I know you don't want to hear this, Conrad, but Cora's death protected Eden. Naeve remained in the Glimmer because she thought the anchor stone didn't grant immortality." He waved a hand at the heaps of dead vegetation all around. "What we witnessed today was only a sample of what Naeve might have done if fully unleashed upon the world."

My heart tightened, but what he said was true. "Even after death, Cora protected me."

"True," Galfandor said. "Had the queen not imbibed Evadora's bottle of tears and gone mad, she probably would have killed us all." He motioned toward the Dark Forest. "The queen demonstrated an ability to control nature itself. If her mind had been unclouded, she might have unleashed the monsters lurking in the forest upon us."

Ambria looked up at the old man. "Are you trying to say everything worked out for the best?"

Galfandor locked eyes with me for an instant. "I believe everything happens for a reason. I believe Cora loved Conrad, but also knew she would die if she stayed with him. Why she let that happen, I cannot say."

"She let herself die." The words threatened to choke me and tears blurred my vision.

"Perhaps." Galfandor put a hand on my back. "I must go attend to important details."

I gave him the stone I'd taken from around Naeve's neck. "You might need this."

He smiled kindly. "Thank you, Conrad."

"Wait, isn't it risky going back into the reflected world with the queen there?" Ambria said.

"The queen is most likely in this very spot on the other side," the headmaster replied. "I will return to the Fairy Garden and use the water there. That should grant me some distance from her." He climbed back on his broom and flew toward the Fairy Garden.

"Where will I go now?" Evadora said plaintively. "I have no home."

"Stay with us," Ambria said. "We have a home in the city you might like."

"Really?" The girl jumped up and down and hugged Ambria. "Happy times!"

Max kicked a bundle of vines. "I don't know about you, but I'm ready to go back to Queens Gate. I'll bet if we stay, Galfandor will have us cleaning up this mess."

I glanced into the wishing pool and wondered if Naeve was still just on the other side. If she had truly gotten the rest of Cora's soul, why wasn't she my mum? Why was she cruel and evil? Galfandor had said that some things simply didn't make logical sense, but I planned to find out all I could about reflections and souls.

Ambria squeezed my hand. "Let's go pack, Conrad."

I tore my eyes from the water and nodded. "Let's go home."

"Oh my god, they're back!" Sonia threw up her hands when we walked into the door that night. "Why can't I have peace and quiet?" She glared at Evadora. "And is that a new little brat?"

Desmond smiled. "How's school treating you?"

"You wouldn't believe what we've been through." Max took a step back from Sonia as she stomped upstairs to get ready for a night out.

"Love to hear," Desmond said. He checked the time. "I've got a few minutes."

"You want to tell him, Conrad?" Max asked.

I shook my head. "You go ahead." I took my suitcases upstairs and into my room. When I got there, I found a note on my bed. I opened it and read it.

Conrad, I'm sorry for telling Harris your secret. I liked you way too much and it made me do something mean when I thought you didn't like me. I don't expect you to forgive me, but I just wanted you to know that I feel awful and I'm terribly sorry.

-Blue

I crumpled up the note. With a flick of my wand, I set it on fire and watched it burn to black ash. What Blue had done seemed so minor now. She'd proven herself untrustworthy. While I might act friendly with her again, she would never be a true friend I could trust.

I went to the bathroom to brush my teeth and found myself staring into the mirror, wondering if it looked into the reflected world. I felt immensely sad thinking about Cora's soul bound up in the fake queen and wondered if killing the reflection would free her.

For now, the threat to Queens Gate was contained. My parents wouldn't have access to the anchor stone fragments, and Naeve was trapped in another world. Maybe Victus and Delectra would go away and leave me alone for a while.

It was probably too much to hope for.

Chapter 37

The holidays lingered for a while and then we returned to school. The remains of the fight with the Glimmer Queen had been cleared away and when I finally tracked down Galfandor and spoke with him, he assured me my parents would not have any reasons to return to the Glimmer.

Evadora did not stay with us long and vanished. When she reappeared a few months later, she told us she'd been in the Glimmer.

"The vines are still there and the people are still asleep," she told us as we walked toward the Fairy Garden.

"Can you do anything about it?" Ambria asked.

"I don't want to." Evadora giggled. "I don't like people. Your vampire friend helped me realize that."

"Sonia?" Max said. "She's an awful person who doesn't like anyone."

Ambria looked at me. "Maybe we should find a way to help the Glimmer people, Conrad."

I shook my head. "I wouldn't even know how to begin." I smiled at Evadora. "If you're happy, I'm happy."

"You are my friends," she said. "I will live in the Glimmer and come visit you."

Max frowned. "Well, if you don't care about your people, I guess there's nothing we can do about it."

We entered the Fairy Garden and went to the pond. The water was once again clean and pure, thanks to Percival's efforts.

Mirjana leapt from the water like a dolphin and landed next to us. She gave each of us a wet hug. "Thank you for restoring my home." She took my hand. "Thank you for saving my Klave."

Ambria looked sadly at the forest of tree stumps. "I wish we could do something about that."

"They are not totally dead," Evadora said. She put her ear to one of the stumps. "Maybe I will get my mother's powers. Perhaps I can revive them one day."

"I would dearly love to have them back," Mirjana said. "Perhaps it will come to be."

"Do you think we could get the gift of the sea like you gave to Conrad?" Max asked. "I'd love to see your home."

"We were just about to eat lunch," said the Lady of the Pond. "Perhaps you would all like to join us?"

Evadora giggled and jumped up and down. "Yes, yes, yes!"

"Oh, please," Ambria said.

I smiled. "I think that's a yes."

The school year continued and before I knew it, the last day of classes arrived. Max, Ambria, and I watched proud parents pick up their children and ferry them away to their homes. Once again, we would be returning to the house at the corner of Dowling and Bucket.

Max sighed. "You know what? I don't even feel sad watching all these normal kids go to their normal homes."

"I do," Ambria said.

"Why aren't you sad?" I asked Max.

He shrugged. "Because I have you two." He put his arms around our shoulders. "My parents' house doesn't feel like home. It's only when I'm with my best friends that I feel like I'm where I belong."

Ambria's eyes watered. "Why, Max, that's the sweetest thing you've ever said."

"Home is where the heart is," I said. I remembered Cora telling me that. Even though she was dead, a part of my home would always be with her.

Ambria giggled. "Max's heart is his stomach."

"Well in that case, let's go home," Max said. "I'm starving."

I hope you enjoyed reading this book. Reviews are very important in helping other readers decide what to read next. Would you please take a few seconds to rate this book?

For the latest on new releases, free ebooks, and more, join John Corwin's Newsletter at www.johncorwin.net!

Meet the Author

John Corwin is the bestselling author of the Overworld Chronicles. He enjoys long walks on the beach and is a firm believer in puppies and kittens.

After years of getting into trouble thanks to his overactive imagination, John abandoned his male modeling career to write books.

He resides in Atlanta.

Connect with John Corwin online:
Facebook: http://www.facebook.com/johnhcorwinauthor
Website: http://www.johncorwin.net
Twitter: http://twitter.com/#!/John_Corwin

www.ingramcontent.com/pod-product-compliance
Lightning Source LLC
Chambersburg PA
CBHW020227260626
47156CB00002B/574